Murders on Safari

Murders on Safari

LOWELL C. DOUGLAS

To order additional copies of this book, contact:
Xlibris Corporation
1-888-795-4274
www.Xlibris.com
Orders@Xlibris.com
28282

Contents

1: A Lion Kill 7

2: Long-distance and Local Calls 21

3: The First Contract 29

4: Recruiting a New Client 40

5: Creative Financing 61

6: Travels and Spas for the Last Client 76

7: London, Dreams, and the "Big Four" 100

8: Marking Time 118

9: The Killing Begins–Botswana 123

10: Keeping Up with the Joneses 138

11: The Burlesque Lion 161

12: Relocations and Disbursements 181

13: Investigating–Getting Even 197

14: Jennifer Prepares 222

15: The Last Safari 229

16: Tying It All Together 251

17: The Gift 258

1

A Lion Kill

The lion spoor indicated the cat was a large male; in all probability, a record-book specimen. To be in the "book," it would be more than five hundred pounds and over ten and a half feet between the pegs. Its muscles would have eighteen times the strength of a human's.

If it decides to charge, it will come at a speed of 3.4 seconds for a hundred meters. Its charge will come in a simulated crouch with its head rigid and its eyes immovably transfixed on its target. At all times it will use what is available for cover – a bush or tree trunk – to hide its approach until it roars into view only a few yards away. No mortal man can escape if the charge commences within forty meters of its target, unless it is brought down by a perfectly placed shot, powerful enough in foot pounds of energy to stop it in its tracks or kill it dead on its feet with vital placement in its brain. Whether it is madly provoked, with discernible rage in its eyes, or whether its expression mimics a day at the office where it is merely trying to secure a meal – the speed and the ferocity in its intent to kill are the same. Simply put, once a charge commences, you either have to kill the beast or it will likely kill you.

All decent hunters try to secure an animal without inflicting unnecessary pain and without provoking a charge, and the surest way to start this procedure is to get as close to the animal as possible for the first shot. In hunting dangerous game – particularly lion, buffalo, and elephant – closeness is extremely important.

This is when your trusted professional hunter and tracker earn their dough, and this is the time when the novice hunter of dangerous game gets the adrenaline rush of his or her life. Once the hunter has been guided into position at close range, the shot should be taken with deliberation and surety. As to lion, if the shot doesn't put the animal down immediately, only one question remains: can both the professional hunter and the client keep their cool and block out the inevitable oncoming roar, the glistening glare of snarling teeth, and the yellow eyes that seem to burn a hole into the chest of the chosen target?

Up to a point, the closer the lion comes to the end of the barrel, the better chance there is of felling this terrific beast of courage. But only a few can hold their fire to point-

blank range. The preferred aiming area for close work with a lion is right in the mouth or high on the chest; no other spots will stop this vision of flashing teeth and unblinking eyes. A common mistake for novice hunters is to aim between and just above the eyes to a make-believe brain – but it isn't there. The lion's eyes are only a half an inch below the top of its skull, so trying to get a killing shot into the brain from above the eyes is next to impossible. Unlike a quarterback leading his intended receiver, when trying to stop a lion, one must take the "lead" out of the equation. The hunter must squat or kneel to get the rifle on level with the target, then the hunter must hold his fire until the last possible split second to ensure the bullet placement.

All legit hunters value their sport for three reasons: First and foremost, they are taking an animal on license that will benefit the species being hunted, this adds revenue to the game department to continue conservation practices that ensure the survivability of all game animals as well as habitat continuance. The second reason is the detective syndrome of the hunt; that is, to study the quarry, know its habits, know its past, know its future, and like a detective, plan a strategy for a successful, and as painless as possible, kill. The third reason is purely physical, the hunter is dedicated to put forth whatever physical effort is necessary to accomplish a "fair-chase" kill, preferably on an older member of the species that is out of the breeding cycle and is an animal that is "in the book." There are several publications of Records of Big Game that are compiled for each continent. These records list the top hundred or so animals of a given species based on size or horn length of the animal. Any hunter worth his salt should always hunt for the largest specimen of the species in the area – never taking the easiest to acquire but the seasoned veteran that is a proven master of concealment and cunning. And finally, the last component of the physical reason to hunt is the adrenalin rush that must be controlled to bring an end to a successful hunt.

*   *   *

Dressed in the traditional hunting garb of dirty tennis shoes with no socks, khaki shorts, and short-sleeved khaki shirts, Brian the professional hunter, BF the client, and Ringo the head tracker, held high hopes of finding the lion that belonged to the overgrown footprints they were tracking. His roar had rudely awakened them prior to sunrise, and that had only been a couple of hours earlier. The hunting party of three departed camp almost half an hour after they heard the last morning roar, and they began heading toward that chilling sound of an obviously fat and sassy male lion. The weather had warmed to near seventy degrees Fahrenheit – up from the cool fifty at sunrise. The sky was a traditional clear blue with remnants of a typical colorful sunrise just above the horizon. The smell of the air was washed with the slight dew that remained attached to every molecule of oxygen that entered the lungs. Stillness gripped every portion of the landscape. The rest of the animal wildlife that inhabited the veldt was quiet, hoping against hope that their own position would not be given away to the killer in the area.

After parking the Land Cruiser at the bottom of a small hill, Ringo led Brian and BF down a partially concealed game path toward a familiar water hole. Ringo had a hunch the big cat was probably heading that way to quench his thirst after celebrating the consumption of about thirty-five pounds of meat from the earlier night's recently felled carcass. As the party neared an opening to view the water hole, Ringo stopped and stumped his right sockless black tennis shoe into the dirt to read the disturbed dust. The wind was moderate quartering from and to the right of the lion's expected location. Walking in a semicrouch, one person behind the other, holding their guns level and low to the ground, the three slid quietly around a fifty-foot circle of thick bush. Sure enough, Ringo's sixth sense had come through again – the lion was standing perfectly still, unalarmed, with his eyes in a daze and his nose lifted slightly above his eyes to savor the fresh cool air that rose off the water's edge. He was less than a hundred yards away, and he had just topped off his belly with semimuddy water. According to the read of the wind as indicated by the stumped dust, if the lion continued his stay at the waterhole, the party would have to deviate to the left to stay underneath the wind in order to make an undetected stalk for a less-than-forty-yard shot.

Even when the tracker and professional stack all of the climatic variables of wind and light in their favor, stalks end with disappointment more often than with success. In the world of hunting, the wind is the most important ingredient to consider because it carries scent and noise; sunlight is second in importance because of glare from the riflescope, watches, etc.

Managing all of the natural variables as best he could, six different times Brian got BF into proper range for a shot, but each time something was not quite right. Once, the lion had been facing away with no possible chance of getting a bullet through the "boiler room" – the area of the heart, lungs, and vital arteries. Once, the lion's head had been the only part of its body that was visible, and no one shoots a lion in the head for the first shot; there is no margin for error. Once, there was a small heard of alerted zebras several hundred yards directly in back of the lion, and the risk of a shot at that time and place would have put the zebras in harm's way. Once, the lion had been a perfect broadside with its left shoulder perfectly exposed, but when BF shouldered his rifle, the sun's glare prohibited him from even finding the lion in the scope. Once, the lion had been on the move and walking too fast; BF would have had to lead it too much – a chancy shot at best for the first trigger squeeze on a dangerous animal. And once, the lion had been lying down and a small thornbush was right in the path of the intended bullet direction – a deflected bullet is about the last thing a hunter wants when he is at close range and about to fire his first shot on dangerous game.

It was now nearing eleven o'clock, and the sun was bearing down its midday heat, about eighty degrees. Brian and BF had been stalking this lion for well over three hours. Finally the break that they had been hoping for came; the lion changed its course of travel and began walking through sparse five-foot-tall thornbush almost straight at them. At this time, the lion was one hundred and fifty yards away. Ringo quickly but silently pushed aside some brush and ground clutter to construct a blind out of the scrub-brush that was immediately adjacent to them. The lion kept coming toward them in a swarthy slow and sassy walk – obviously looking for a shade tree that would be suitable for a midday nap. There was a big tree to the left of the hidden hunters, and the tracker suspected the lion had its eyes on that tree. About forty yards away, in the direction the lion was strolling, was a small ten-foot clearing. If the lion trudged across that open space, it would make for a perfect shot. Brian motioned to BF to get ready as the lion approached the clearing. As the lion stepped into the open area, BF did not wait for instructions from Brian – he fired. Too early; he could have gotten a much better shot had he waited just a few moments more! However, it looked as if the shot was a good one; the lion jumped eight feet in the air with his back arched and his tail stretched upward. The shot had the earmarks of a lion reacting as if its heart had been blown apart.

But looks are deceiving. As the lion hit the ground it spun madly, biting at its shoulder where the hot steel had entered its body. Three times or more it madly circled itself in this biting motion; then it darted away toward the nearest cover. The roars were deafening, and the pain that had just begun forced the lion to seek cover to compose its thoughts for revenge.

Now was the time to be "cool." The hunting party tried to relax. They must wait at least ten minutes or so to let the lion either die in peace or stiffen up a bit to slow an impending charge. The quietness was overwhelming – not even a chirp from a bird could be heard. The peace and serenity of this semidry desert jungle had been irrevocably disturbed, and every creature was waiting to see what was going to happen next.

After the prescribed waiting period had ended, Brian signaled to Ringo to reassume his crouched walking position and began his stalk. BF followed Ringo as if he was a shadow, and Brian was nearly a shadow to BF. The idea was to present only one silhouette to the eyes of the pursued. The party stopped some ten yards before entering the thick bush where the wounded lion had sought its final ambush site. It was time to enact the plan that had been devised during their waiting period – after the lion had first been hit.

Ringo led with his unsheathed *assegi* (machete) held white knuckled in his black right hand. BF flanked him on Ringo's right side with his rifle at the ready, safety off! Brian trailed the two in front of him but only slightly. His eyes and rifle were aimed toward the left of Ringo, looking for any sign of movement. If the lion was spotted before a charge, Ringo would drop to his knee; Brian would move up alongside BF, and Brian would instruct BF when and where to shoot. If the lion surprised the trio, everyone was on his own. Ringo was likely to flee and climb the nearest tree. The other two were programmed to pump as much lead as possible into the charging fury.

The old and wise lion had circled to the right in selecting his ambush point of revenge. As the three stalkers rounded the densest area of scrub, the lion made his move. From only ten feet away, BF had no chance. Ringo instinctively turned away from the oncoming roar to run dead into Brian as Brian was raising his rifle to fire. But it would not have mattered. BF was standing between Brian and the charging lion. After BF tried a quick and wild shot in the direction of the lion's head, the lion knocked BF down and seized his skull between his gigantic teeth in less than two seconds. As fast as he could position himself for a shot, Brian fired down between the lion's shoulder blades about a second after that, but he was three seconds too late.

The lifeless lion fell right on top of the dead BF. Brian angled another round into the back of the lion's brain for surety's sake. Unfortunately, it was a double coup de grâce.

Dateline Maun, *Botswana, July 16, 2004, Associated Press Reporting: On Tuesday, July 15, 2004, B. F. Clark of San Antonio, Texas, USA, was severely mauled and killed by a lion that he had wounded while on safari with Hunters, Ltd., a local professional hunting organization. Mr. Clark's remains will be flown back to the States for burial within the week. Hunters, Ltd., states that this is their first fatal accident to a client in their twenty-two years of business. The accident occurred in the southeast corner of the Okavango Delta, approximately 150 kilometers northeast of Maun.*

A few days after this worldwide report, several professional hunters from different outfitters were lounging in the shaded confines of the waiting-room bar at Lanseria Airport just outside of Johannesburg, South Africa. Jo'burg is the traditional jumping off place for most safaris that take place in Botswana. Clients secure a short chartered flight from Lanseria Airport to Maun, Botswana, clear customs, and then board a smaller plane that ferries them directly into their respective camps. In less than five hours, they are transformed into true "hunter gatherers" from soon before "city slickers."

The professionals, dressed in their Hollywood safari casuals, either precede their clients at the departure airport and gather in clusters under the rotating ceiling fans to discuss their own past and future safaris and the respective clients that they are waiting to meet, or they remain for professional conversation after their safari clients have departed for home. On this day, Martin Smith, the field manager for Hunters, Ltd., sat at a table with two of his subordinate young professionals Jon-Keith Haley and Rob Manson and a couple of other more well-known professional hunters from the prestigious company Afrikana Safaris. Doug Hansen, who only last year was severely mauled by a lion and whose wounds were so grotesque that the story made every U.S. hunting magazine, and the famous East African professional hunter Harold Simon filled out the fivesome.

Unusual for this day, all had just seen their clients off after successfully completing twenty-one-day safaris in the Delta, and all welcomed the chance to unwind a bit before heading home for chores that were to be either self-assigned or wife dictated. As always, the chores were going to have to be rushed because each of them only had one or two days before their next clients would arrive.

Oddly, all five of the professionals had spent their childhood growing up in Kenya. Although they were separated by rather big differences in age, they had a similar boyhood in common. There had been other frequent meetings like this in the past and the conversation of the day would normally go quickly to reminiscences of their previous lives in Kenya – but not this day.

Doug couldn't wait to ask Martin about the article in the morning's Jo'burg newspaper concerning his last client's death. Martin was understandably a little sheepish about a detailed discussion because he had not had time to visit the site and reconstruct exactly what actually happened. But he knew that he couldn't dodge the questions of his cohorts.

"It appears that BF – you all remember old BF, don't you? They call him old 'Butt Face,' for his initials, up in San Antonio. Anyway, he's had almost every animal over here, but he was queer for another big lion – bigger than his last one he got in Tanzania. This time, he brought his real wife, his third one. I'm telling you, I saw her last year at the Game Trackers Convention in San Antonio, and she is a real looker. I have never understood why he has always brought some young thing along when he had that available. One day, I asked him about it. You know what he said? 'No matter how good lookin' they are, someone is tired of fuck'n' 'em.'"

"I'll remember that one," said Rob Manson as he pumped his fist in the air.

"Anyway, Brian Robison was the professional hunter, and for some ungodly reason, he agreed before the hunt that when and if they encountered a lion, he would hold his fire until BF was either out of ammo or was defenseless. Butt Face was determined to take the lion all by himself. Brian knew BF had nerves of steel and was a good shot, but he also knew that it was taboo to not immediately back up his client after the first shot was fired. Nevertheless, Brian acquiesced to BF's wishes. Evidently, the two hunters plus Ringo – Brian's head tracker – had followed this lion a pretty long way, and they had faced it several times without getting a chance for a decent shot. Finally they both felt comfortable with the circumstances that gave them the opportunity they were looking for. Brian had BF in a good position to shoot, but BF rushed the shot. Even then, Brian thought the shot was fatal – 'Right through the boiler room,' he said. The shot was taken from about sixty yards; maybe a bit far for being so sure just where the bullet hit – particularly in knee-high grass. But Brian said that the lion arched his back and sprang at least ten feet up in the air at impact – classic for a pure heart shot. Brian said that he knew the lion was 'bloody dead,' even though it ran into nearby thicket.

"Thoughtfully, they sat down and smoked a cigarette to let the big cat bleed a little more to lose energy, and hopefully, to stiffen up in case it wasn't dead. Then they followed the clear spoor into a dense patch of palm bushes. Ringo had already circled the patch where the lion went in, and there was no 'sign' that the lion had come out. So they had no choice but to follow the blood spoor in. After only a few steps, Brian said he became uneasy; he felt something 'fishy.' But after pausing for a minute or two, he dismissed the feeling. At this point, he stopped the follow-up to reconsider the first shot and warn BF and Ringo that he thought the shot must have been high and too far back – not a heart shot as he first suspected. The blood was at the top of the grass, very red, no bubbles, and not as much in volume as would normally be with a heart or lung shot. They then tried to determine if the lion was dragging a foot, which would tell them whether the lion's charge might be impeded, but things were so thick that they couldn't be sure. Here, they should have backed off, but Brian elected to go forward rather than turn their back on a possible wounded animal. Ringo continued to lead with BF just to his right; Brian said he was on Ringo's left but just a notch behind. They hadn't gone twenty yards when they stepped into about a five-square-yard clearing. Brian said the lion never hesitated; he just blew out of a bush to Ringo's right. He said the roar was deafening. Later at camp, Jeff James, the professional hunter in the adjoining concession came by to say that he had unmistakenly heard the lion roar in its charge – and he was nearly ten miles away.

"No way Brian could shoot because both his client and Ringo were in the way. At this point, Ringo evidently dove back behind a bush to allow a clear line of fire for BF, but it obviously didn't matter. The lion had a huge mane, and BF typically shot high trying to stop the charge with an amateurish brain shot. Brian said that BF held his fire until the lion was nearly on him, but the mane threw him off. The lion was on BF in three bounds. I told his widow how easy it is to aim above the eyes on a charging lion, and of course there is nothing there but hair. I told her that cats have no skull above the eyes when they charge – some consolation, huh?

"Brian said this cat must have weighed nearly six hundred pounds. When they got back to camp, they weighed it and it scaled at five hundred forty pounds – after it had lost quite a bit of blood and with the two back legs being held off the ground because the scale couldn't go any higher up on the damn tree. It might very well have been a six-hundred-pound bugger. If ever there was an eleven-foot-long lion, this one should have been it; but Ringo measured it just under eleven feet.

"When BF missed his only opportunity on the charge, he was dead. The lion hit him full bore, flat out. BF's neck appeared to be broken in three places from the blow – a hell of a whiplash! I'm sure he died instantly. All the bite to the head was good for was to give Brian time to finish off the brute. At least the doctors in postmortem thought that was the way it was. Imagine six hundred pounds of solid muscle and bone hitting you running at 3.4 seconds for every hundred meters, and that doesn't even count the explosion of his last spring right into your chest. God, Brian says he still hears the bones in old BF's neck breaking every time he tries to go to sleep.

"The lion died right on top of BF. Brian said that he shot the lion right through the right shoulder blade and then gave him another for final measurement. He was in a heap right on top of BF. Brian shouted for Ringo to help pull the bugger off his client, but it was a full five minutes before Ringo had the courage to come out of hiding. In the meantime, Brian rolled the thing off BF somehow but without the help of his trusty tracker. It's amazing how those guys can get out of the way so quick and then disappear into thin air when there's trouble.

"Brian radioed the base station for help immediately on reaching the vehicle, but Judy at the main camp could tell by Brian's tone of voice that BF was already dead. Brian and Ringo loaded both bodies into the rover and headed back to camp – a good ten to twelve miles. I really do feel for Brian – he's a solid chap. And now he will be penalized for the rest of his life for letting that damn client have his wish to go it alone. I guess we'll all learn from that one."

It took a few seconds for all of the listeners to change from a strictly listening mode to a two-way conversation one. The tension was thick during the oration because Brian was a friend of all, and it was the first details anyone had from someone that could fill in most of the blanks. "Okay, tell us about the wife – rumor has it that she was deliriously happy after the accident; she ran around camp screaming and shouting that she was *free*, really *free*! Could this be true?" Harold Simon asked with obvious consternation etched in his face.

"You're close," said Martin, "damn close. I don't really know whether or not she ran around camp like that or not, but I'll damn sure guarantee you that she hasn't shed a tear about what happened. And she hasn't got anything going with Brian either. From what I've heard, and from what I can surmise from what I've experienced with old Butt Face, I just think she was so misused back in the States that she has dreamed of this day for a long time but never really thought it could happen. It wouldn't have surprised me if she had killed the old son of a bitch a long time ago. She's a pretty dangerous feline herself if you ask me."

"What's she doing now?"

"Well, I don't know, but I'm scheduled to meet with her in London for a couple of days after the season; at least she says that she will be there the same time I'm scheduled to be there. She holds no ill feelings toward us or Brian; she's just a happy little rich forty-two-year-old lass. If she were just a little more my type, I'd have a go at her. Any of you interested in a new rich bitch for a new bride?" There was no answer. Two of the guys were already married, and the other two wouldn't get tied down for any amount of money.

Doug and Harold had a few errands to run before their next safari, so they politely excused themselves, picked up their tab, and left. Martin looked at Rob Manson and Jon-Keith Haley and suggested a smaller table over by the window in the corner. They flagged the waitress, and she gladly refilled their drinks and brought them over to their new hideout.

Martin had not run down yet, and he was first to open the new conversation. "With all due respect, I'm glad Doug and Harold had to go; I've got a business proposition that I want to talk to you about."

Rob and Jon-Keith sat back, took a sip of Lion Lager, and gave Martin their undivided attention. And Martin hesitated his proposition long enough to ensure that attention.

"You know, a lot of unhappy hunters' wives are out there waiting for someone to rescue them. I even know another one. Keep in mind BF's wife and her recent reaction after BF's accident as I go through this. I just got a call from Barbara Jones from Houston. I know you remember Clifford Jones who's been out with us several times. No doubt Barbara knows that Cliff usually brought a 'toy' with him when he came on safari, whether it was with us or somebody else. I'm sure that he practiced the same lifestyle at home, and in fact, Barbara said on the telephone that she has the goods on him there. She heard about BF's accident, and she was quite consoling in her conversation. She said that everyone knew there was a lot of danger on safari, and sooner or later, the odds were going to creep up on every safari outfit. I was so glad to hear from her. I respect her a lot for what she's had to go through with that two-timing husband of hers. You know money isn't everything, and she's living proof that having it sometimes isn't worth it. Anyway, as the conversation went on, I could tell she was holding something back. She hesitated a time or two, and then it happened. She had been so nice, and then you could tell the obvious hidden anger in her voice. She had the balls to ask me if we could arrange the same thing to happen to Cliff. I told her sure because I thought she was just kiddin' – I spoke too soon. Well, she's not kidding, and she wants to make plans.

"African hunting isn't going to last forever with all the 'antis' on the warpath at every step. Look, the three of us go way back – we can trust each other. I never thought I could be a part of a killing for hire, but the happiness that old BF's wife is enjoying has made me rethink. What's the difference between helping a girl that's about to be raped and freeing a woman that you know is getting that same treatment every day but can't do anything about it by herself? I'm not trying to be God, but being a part of documented injustice isn't my cup of tea either.

"To translate that picture to us – just imagine, if we took three no-good clients 'out' for their wives by simply setting the stage where they had to sink or swim on their own in very difficult circumstances, I don't think it would be murder. We would be honoring the forgotten wives! And besides, look how happy we'd make them."

"Since when did you start to give a damn about a woman?" Rob asked.

"When the money got right and when the chance of being accused went to zero. The investigation of BF's accident by the authorities is a joke! The police director even asked me to head the investigation. When I declined, he simply got an off-duty bicycle peddler to head it. I'm telling you, it's a joke! Sure there's paperwork that I'll have to fill out but only because the police don't want to fill it out themselves. I tell you, it is a cinch on this side of the pond.

"Over in the States, we have to be a little more careful. We've got to make sure that each client has plenty of life insurance and that it has been in force for over two years – a precaution to remove the enactment of the incontestability clause in case the insurance company thinks the accident might have been suicidal. We don't want an insurance investigator on our ass. It would cost the insurance company almost as much to handle an investigation over here as it would to pay the claim – and besides, they would know that coming over here would lend them little information. We are a relatively small business group over here, and we certainly wouldn't want to harm our future business by helping to confirm something detrimental to that business. They would also know that cooperation over here from the very people that depend on depicting safety as a selling point to their livelihood would be hard to come by.

"At this juncture I'm going to be a little presumptuous. If we got into this fantasy, for peace of mind, it would be nice to have some blackmail material on both the husband and the wife that we'd be dealing with. That would probably be easy to obtain with the right local private eye in their hometown and relatively inexpensive when you consider how much we are going to make. I would never want to expose any of the blackmail material on the wife for sure, but in all probability, we'd have to let the wife know some of our secrets on her husband just to get her to go along with us. Ideally, we'd require a minimum of $100,000 down to enact the plot. And listen closely to this. We'd never have any details in writing. That way there would never be any incriminating visible evidence for anyone to find. Everything would look like naturally booked safaris. If our little lady tried to back out early on, from our perspective, there'd be no evidence that we were going to do anything unusual. Only a money trail, and I've got an answer for that. The money that we'd receive as a down payment would be what's normal for a big safari. As usual, we'd have to black out some dates to make our calendar look right. We can always explain that we got paid early – not terribly unusual. If an inquisition occurs after the accident or if she refused to give us the rest of our promised share, then we would bring out the incriminating evidence on her. We'd be covered no matter what."

Rob and Jon-Keith were paying close attention, but they were both consciously uncomfortable with the early details of Martin's proposal. Their eyes were constantly surveying their immediate area, and they both swiveled their heads as if they were a part of some forbidden ethnic joke.

"We would insist that the involved wife would move to Europe and terminate her daily life in the States, just like BF's widow plans to do. Another safety precaution. If we pick carefully, each wife would get an enormous insurance settlement, plus the house, and business. How could you ever allege a death in the bush as intentional or nonaccidental? I know I'd hate to prove intent on anybody – particularly beyond a shadow of a doubt. As I said before, we'd be extremely selective of our applicants. Barbara Jones would be a natural because we all know so much about her and her husband. But the other two would really have to be researched. It would be nice if we could get a couple of other clients that have been with us before, but it's not necessary. What do you think so far?"

"First of all, are you really serious? You certainly put some thought into this thing and that indicates a measure of seriousness," Rob said with a frown. "I can't find fault with anything you've said. It looks as if you've done your due diligence, but there has to be something wrong with your plan or someone would have done it before."

"Be serious," whispered Martin, "who's to say the plan hasn't been done very successfully in the past, and everything went just like clockwork. We would have never known. There have been approximately seventy hunter-client deaths in the last twenty years that I know of – maybe even more. It's to everyone's advantage to keep this sort of thing quiet for business' sake. The outfitter, the country, the sport, the family – all benefit by calling the happening an accidental or health-induced death."

"How many net dollars are we talking about?" It was heretofore-silent Jon-Keith. "Let's cut to the chase and start counting money."

"I figure a year or so of high living and a million dollars in a Swiss bank for each of us. That is if we have three clients; maybe only two if they're really rich. I've even got the bank transfers after the accident worked out. The widow goes to Europe and directs money transfers from there. No transfers from the U.S. Our accounts will be the typical numbered accounts in Switzerland. After all the dust settles, we can then go our separate ways, or we can joint venture a hunting outfit in Australia or Alaska. Our days are numbered here in Africa, and none of us have the rand to go anywhere else."

"We're all over fifty, and we don't have much gambling time left, so, Martin, you can count ol' Jon-Keith in, as usual, on anything. But I do think we need a lot more planning in theory and execution – maybe I shouldn't use that word "execution"? How about you, Rob?"

"I'm sure that I'm in, but I want to sleep on it a night or so. When would we get into action? In order for me to really want to get a mad-on for the son of a bitch that I've got to see die, I'm going to have to see some pretty mean stuff that he has done to his wife. If I get over that hurdle, then I believe I can carry out my assignment without remorse. I'm assuming that each one of us would take one case each."

"Well put, Rob, and you're right about one case each. That way, no single professional would have multiple-client deaths hanging over their heads for future business. We've all got only one more safari this year. I suggest that we jump on Barbara Jones as soon as she can get everything together; hopefully, in time for the first safari next season. That would be the best time for elephant and Cliff always has a hankering for another big tusker. Oh, I almost forgot the bad news. So that we don't saturate this country with too many client deaths in one country in one season, one of you is going to have to carry out your business in Zimbabwe, and the other has to go back to Tanzania. I'll make sure you're named as the preferred professional in each case. It'll only be for a few months, and it will damn well be worth your time. When you think about it, it's insurance that we wouldn't be as likely to be investigated if our missions are spread out to different locals. No way would anyone tie all three of us together when these accidents happen far away from each other. Okay?"

After a brief pause, Rob tersely suggested, "Neither of us can stand Tanzania and the tsetse flies anymore, Martin. Why don't you go there, and we'll stay south?"

"I would if I could, Rob, but it is best that I work under the cover of Hunters, Ltd., in Botswana. They'll pay for my trips abroad and for much of our research. When I book your two hunts, I'll set them up at our cooperative camps in Zimbabwe and Tanzania. Hunters, Ltd., will still make good money on them – especially if we provide our own professional hunters. Trust me, I've thought it all out. Let's all sleep on it a couple of nights just to be sure, then I'll come out to camp in three days to meet you for more detailed discussions. You're both going to the southeast camp, aren't you?"

"We've both got clients that want sable, so I guess the camp choice is clear," replied Jon-Keith.

"Drink up, boys, we each have some thinking to do. I'll see you in the bush," Martin said as he flipped out a few rand on the table and waved good-bye.

"Rob, I guess he's serious; we could be rich next year – I won't know how to act."

"You don't know how to act now, so what's going to change?" They both laughed.

"You'll see, Rob, you'll see."

The two departed in separate Land Rovers to mull over their new venture. Excited but skeptical, each had committed to Martin. And for over twenty years of relying on each other as dependable friends and business partners, neither had ever broken a commitment to their leader. Martin had rescued them from lesser affiliations and had brought them here to prosper with a big name outfit – they were indebted. And they were fast becoming greedy for the rich, good life – just like the one their fabled clients had.

Barbara Jones's travel agency was more for fun than needed income. It kept her busy, and it kept her from thinking about the bastard that she was married to. The day was a typically hot August day in Houston, but today it was worse. The air-conditioning in her upstairs thousand-square-foot office had been acting up for weeks, and now it had finally cratered. It was at least ninety-eight degrees inside her stuffy little office, and she had to get out. She signaled to her part-time secretary while she was on the phone that she had a few ticket deliveries to make and that she would be back shortly after lunch. She lied. She was to meet her hired private detective for lunch and go over some new information that he had drummed up.

Captain Bullock, named for his old-time position with the Houston Police Department but now heading up his own prestigious private detective agency, was always on time; and he always had a few more bits of information than he let on during his contact call. As soon as they were seated in the Houston outskirt cafe, the captain placed an envelope of pictures on the table. The waiter had not approached their table, but the bus boy poured them ice water. With his hand pressed down on the envelope, he said, "You don't have to look at them if you don't want to. In fact, I recommend that you don't. I'll fill you in on my surveillance, and you can decide later if you even want the pictures."

"Why don't you just catch him at something illegal and shoot him for me?"

"Listen, Barbara, I better never ever hear anything like that come from your lips again; otherwise, I'm off the case and all my work goes with me, you understand? My license is the most valuable thing I own, except my reputation, and I won't fool around with anyone that might jeopardize either."

Barbara nodded in approval. "Just kidding."

"Being an ex-captain with the police force, I can sympathize with your feelings, but I also face reality. You're not in love with that guy, never have been. When you married him, you knew you would enjoy his status and his wealth or you wouldn't have picked an older gentleman that had been married twice before. You knew you weren't getting any saint. Besides, there are people actually starving all over the world, and you ain't one of them, so let's not get too heavy, and let's not ever talk about anything illegal – I have too much to lose! Let's order lunch before I ruin both our appetites."

Barbara sat back and looked "put-out" at the captain's remarks. "Hey, Captain, don't you understand – kidding? You must have had a bad day."

"Sorry, Barbara. You're very perceptive. Last night I had a very close call with a subject's girlfriend, and I nearly got us exposed. I didn't sleep much last night, and I guess my weariness shows. I apologize. Let's eat, and I will try to be a little more civil. I understand why we are here, and I want to be of all the help I can for you."

"Forget it, Captain. We all have bad days. Let's make the rest of your day a better one." The waiter materialized and cut short the conversation.

Barbara ordered a small chicken salad with almonds, and the captain ordered a steak sandwich, well done. Barbara thought about his no-class well-done steak order but hesitated from poking fun.

"Business is good, Barbara. I have three other clients in your same boat."

"You don't know enough about me to compare me with another woman, Captain."

The captain decided to take on a more southern speech pattern. "You mus'in be too sure, ma'am. I know just about all there is to know about my clients, but all that information is perfectly safe with me. It goes in here and here, but it don't come out here" – he gestured as he spoke to his eyes, his ears, and then his mouth. "This job is going to cost you a good thirty thousand before we've got an air-tight case. Then you're going to have to pay your lawyer double that to win. It is going to be a fighting divorce if you are going to manage to get anything out of it. I'm talking from experience. It'll take two years of depositions and courthouses before you finally get your settlement, so get used to heartache and people trying to screw you. I'd say the same to him. You've got the best with me, and he doesn't, so you have some advantage."

Fuck the advantage, Barbara thought. "I'm calling Martin Smith again as soon as I get back to the office."

The luncheon meeting lasted until 3:30 p.m. and Barbara had to hustle to get back to the office before her secretary had to leave for her night classes downtown. She barely made it.

As soon as the secretary walked out the door, Barbara skimmed through her Rolodex and placed a person-to-person call for Martin Smith in Maun, Botswana. It is abnormal for a past or future client to locate a professional hunter at his workplace; they are rightfully insulated by a booking agent that takes care of all of a client's wishes – true to the old Jewish business custom, "you never get both decision makers in the same conversation; otherwise, you have to state a position. You lose wiggle room." But the main booking agent for Hunters, Ltd., was located in Houston, and because of the many safaris that the Joneses had booked with them, they were much obliged to give Barbara any telephone number for Martin that she wanted.

Cliff Jones owned a local beer distributorship in Houston, and his chief duties consisted of hassling his secretary upon arrival at about 9:30 a.m., then checking the computer printout of the previous day's business, and finally checking with his manager about any special promotions for the day. After running the balances in the main checkbooks, he would either meet some good-looking woman for lunch or he would head for the country club for lunch, gin rummy, and/or golf. When he was in town and not out on a hunting trip, his daily routine hardly varied. His evenings were always spent in a late gin game or with another "honey" he just happened to meet. Cliff had three children by his previous two marriages. One son was a full-time student working on his second PhD in history at SMU. A second son was on a lifelong tour of Europe, and the only time the rest of the family heard from him was when he needed money – which, oddly enough, wasn't that often. There was a suspicion that he was into drugs, and that was probably correct.

Cliff's only daughter was a lawyer and married to a fellow lawyer living in California, and both were wrapped up in trying to save the world from pollution and helping save spotted owls. So Cliff was virtually all alone with his working wife whom he hardly ever saw except on formal occasions, and his men friends and girlfriends that daily extracted his money like newborns gouging a teat for milk. As far as Barbara thought, Cliff was worthless as a human being, with absolutely no redeeming values – he needed to be dead, and the whole world would be better for it.

Although Cliff and Barbara shared a beautiful eight-bedroom house in the lovely prestigious neighborhood of River Oaks, not far from downtown Houston, they had very little in common inside that house. Barbara lived her life upstairs with her own private everything, including her own private telephone line. Cliff lived downstairs where the butler always opened the kitchen door for him when he came home after midnight – usually too drunk to walk. If cohabitation was not a prerequisite, it was a great marriage, and no one kept it a secret.

After tossing and turning all night in anticipation of hearing from Martin Smith, Barbara was up early the next morning, and she raced to her office in hopes of receiving that return long-distance transatlantic telephone call. The call came in as expected. Plans were made for Martin to visit Houston for the next Houston Gun and Camera Club meeting in September. Barbara and Martin would then talk, and hopefully for both, Martin would sell a prime elephant hunt to Mr. Jones – with an added amenity.

Until then, Barbara would endure the daily and nightly abuses of her legal husband. More than twice she walked into restaurants where she caught him hanging all over some easily sold woman dining with him. In each case, she just turned and left without a scene. On each occasion it was obvious that he had not seen her, and his accompanying "pleasure-puss" was so wrapped up in what she was about to get that she was immune from any intruder. On another occasion, a friend called to tell her that she had just spotted Cliff in a bear hug with some gal in his car in the parking lot of Neiman Marcus in broad daylight. It was becoming old hat to hear from her friends regarding all types of "sorties" her husband was pulling on her. All her friends were begging her to get out of her strange predicament!

For the first few times, Barbara confronted Cliff with her accusations of mistrust and adultery, but he just became more abusive than normal with his shouting and cursing. He always had an excuse, or he just downright denied any involvement at all. Soon, Barbara discovered that it wasn't worth the humiliation and the disgrace that she felt for herself by confronting him – she just let things go. She couldn't help but remember the last time that she challenged him, though; that was when she threatened to divorce him the next day after one of his escapades. Drunk as he was when she confronted him, he stumbled into his trophy room, grabbed the pistol that he kept on top of his desk, and fired it through the ceiling, all the while shouting that he would kill her if she tried to divorce him. She thought about filing anyway, but she decided that he really might kill her – he didn't have anything else to live for, and he didn't have any friends to rely on to discuss the situation. The more she thought about it, the more she thought that he would indeed kill her. There was no one that either of them could turn to except each other, and that was out of the question! She was in a mess, partly of her own making, but regardless, a mess that she couldn't stand to tolerate any longer. She desperately needed Martin Smith and his newfound magic.

2

Long-distance and Local Calls

Martin Smith was genuinely enthused about his plan from his recent telephone conversation with Barbara Jones. Barbara's second call gave him more assurances, and anyone could tell she meant business. She even told Martin that she had hired her own private eye with her own nickel to get the ball rolling. Martin thought she must be reading his mind. She didn't mention that she was making a better business deal than a normal divorce. The divorce was likely to cost her many millions, a long and drawn-out legal battle, and a chance that she might not live to enjoy the spoils. Her business acumen in the travel business had made her a smart business lady.

To keep from arousing any suspicions from Barbara's first urgent call to him in Botswana, Martin placed a call to his home office in Houston to explain Barbara's call as one of condolence for the recent BF accident. And he was very appreciative. Martin was immediately passed on to the company president, Frank Black, who was always anxious to hear about the conditions in the bush. "Hi, Martin. How are you and how are all the camps? I'm still so concerned about our people's mental attitude since the accident. Do you think it is necessary for me to talk to each of them before next safari season – to show our concern and our feelings for them?"

"No, Frank, these people face death every day in one form or the other. You of all people know that; you lived over there for more than a decade."

"I know, Martin, but we have always made camp life so enjoyable for our clients, and I don't want to take any chances that it might change. I've had a call from every single future booking, and all of them are more eager than ever to go. I don't get it – seems like the more we publicize danger, whether real or pretended, our clients' interests heighten. I guess that we should just continue on as if nothing has happened, and we will be all right. But for me, I can't help worrying about what our clients think. As soon as we get another couple of safaris under our belt, I will feel a lot better. How are you holding up?"

"Fine, Frank. You know me, I stay in good shape, and I try not to worry about things that I cannot control." More cordialities were exchanged, and soon more pressing business objectives became center stage.

"Martin, have you finished your rough outline of your visits to the various hunting clubs in the States this winter?"

"Well, Frank, that is exactly why I called. It seems that Barbara Jones wants to surprise her husband Cliff with a gift of an elephant hunt next spring. She wants him to have the first hunt of the season, and believe it or not, she wants to accompany him as an observer, with no other guests in camp! She wants me to come to Houston for the Houston Gun and Camera Club meeting in September to book it. I'll have to rearrange some of my other appointments, especially Detroit, to make it, but you know I can't turn down a hot prospect. She has already called me overseas twice to talk about it."

"Great, Martin, that puts us off to a good start for the new year. You know you can count on all the cooperation you need out of this office for your travel arrangements."

"I plan to be on the phone nonstop when I get to London to firm up our best prospects. I'll spend about a week there, if it's all right with you, then I'll be heading for the Big 'H.' I assume you got the new photos and trophy measurement updates for the new brochure from last year's clients.

Hey! What's the printing calendar look like? When do I get to see my main selling tool?"

"I'll have all the new brochures and other publications you're asking for when you step off the plane here in a couple of weeks.

"Listen, Martin, you know how much I've preached to you about buttoning up the camps for the closed season. Have you hired proper watchdogs? You know I expect no troubling news while we're both over here trying to sign up new clients. Expect the worst in weather and attempted pilferage, and prepare for it! I don't even care if you leave an Uzi submachine gun with whomever you have left in charge to ward the bastards off. But make damn sure that you leave someone in charge of it that knows how to use it, maybe even an Israeli if you could find one. Ha! Ha! The world would probably be better off without a few thieves anyway." Pleasant good-byes closed the conversation, and Martin rested well that night with the belief that he had quelled any possible ulterior motive for Barbara's calls.

Frank Black was easy to read; he simply always told what was on his mind. Because of his penchant for details, he had to be that way. Martin couldn't remember the last time he had thought of a necessary detail before Frank. At times, all of Frank's employees felt like Frank was a bit anal, but they gladly put up with this idiosyncrasy to be a part of Frank's guarantee of success. He has had more executive experience in the safari business than all of his competition put together, and he had a sterling reputation of delivering exactly what he promised.

Frank Black was slightly under six feet tall and weighed twenty-some pounds more than he had in his married days. He still had a full head of thick black hair, and his ruddy complexion was a rough handsome. His build was typical for a man over middle age, and when he wore a suit, he was still a man with obvious charm. Frank had been married to a beautiful young woman from Norway. They had met in Nairobi when Frank and his brother were stationed there as part of a conglomerate oil operation that was owned by several big oil companies from the States. Frank's brother was a petroleum engineer, and Frank was the African operation boss. Janet was the daughter of the chief of protocol of Norway, and her family was a frequent visitor to the safari lands of East

Africa. Frank and Janet met under the thorn tree at the Thorn Tree Lounge adjacent to the Nairobi Hilton Hotel. As often happened in that quaint place of rendezvous, singles and couples were seated next to absolute strangers to conserve tables. It was on one of these occasions when Frank had been seated next to the girl that he would eventually marry.

The conversation had little mutual references until it got around to safaris. Janet and her accompanying girlfriend had just returned from a short trip to the Abedares to view a bongo, but they met with no luck. They had stayed two nights at the famous Treetops Lodge where the occupants are awakened during the night if a rare and special animal such as a bongo is sighted coming to the artificial salt lick located at the base of the overhanging veranda. It is publicized as the finest place in all of Africa to have a reasonable chance to see a live bongo. It was also the place where Queen Elizabeth and Prince Phillip spent their first night on their honeymoon some fifty years ago. That glorious night had came to an abrupt end when a messenger pulled down the rope ladder to the prince and princess's bedroom to give them the horrible news. The princess's father had passed away, and now she was queen! That love story is as good as it gets as a selling point to attract paying safari goers. But Frank was not surprised that Janet's quest to see a bongo was met with failure.

Well, Frank lent his expertise to the situation and suggested that the girls try a new operation in the same area – the Ark.

The Ark is built in the shape of Noah's ark with bedrooms facing a natural salt lick and adjacent watering hole. The recent success stories coming from their PR guy virtually assured seeing bongo.

Frank and Janet exchanged hotel telephone numbers, and the beginning of a beautiful romance had begun. Janet's father, who was accompanying the two girls, was a pain in the ass to make plans around, but Frank persevered and reservations at the Ark were soon completed, with Frank making it a threesome. The three had the time of their lives, and since Janet's companion had a steady boyfriend back in Norway, Janet and Frank had all the opportunity needed to seed a relationship – plus, they saw plenty of bongo.

Janet returned to her homeland, and she and Frank corresponded regularly via mail. Telephone calls were also somewhat regular, but the phone system in Kenya left much to be desired. When Frank was out of town on assignment, there was little chance of voice contact, so the written word became their main line of communication.

In two years, the two were married in Norway in the most spectacular and formal wedding any of Frank's friends in attendance had ever imagined. Frank and Janet bought into a photographic safari operation, which soon was expanded to the more profitable hunting operation. Their life was picturesque and busy. Their company employed twenty-five full-time native personnel and three European professional hunters. Janet ran the office, while Frank took care of all the permits, camps and camp supplies, guns and ammunition, and vehicle maintenance. When a special request came in for the two of them to lead a safari, the two would turn the office chores over to one of the professionals' wives and head to the bush. Of course, that was when they were in heaven.

Such escapades proved fatal for Janet, however. She contracted a terrible case of malaria that was complicated by a rare viral disease. By the time she was fully diagnosed, she was beyond help, and she died in her sleep at the Nairobi City hospital. It happened so quickly that her family in Norway had no chance to see her before she died.

Frank continued the Nairobi-based operations for five more years before moving the booking offices to Houston, Texas. By that time, Kenya had closed hunting to allow the poachers that worked for the president and his wife to continue their massacres unabated. Frank could not stomach such atrocities, so he moved all of his operational divisions out of Kenya to the new frontier lands of safari in Botswana and the rest of Southern Africa.

Despite his continued business success in safaris, Frank's life was lonely. He had experienced marriage to a truly romantic lady who shared all of his values and zest for the out of doors. All of that happened in one of the most beautiful places in the world, and that combination could never be recreated, in Frank's opinion. So Frank just worked hard and longed to hopefully share his wonderful experiences with others.

Everyone who booked a safari with Frank eventually met him, and all were as impressed with him personally as they had been over the telephone. He absolutely glowed at the mention of African safari life. He was the sine qua non of African adventure.

A week after his call to Frank Black from London, Martin built his plan of attack for visiting as many gun and camera clubs as possible in the United States. He had to take precautions for inconveniencing his potential clients in the six-to-eight-hour time differences from the American time zones from that of London's. From 2:00 p.m. to midnight every day he began calling the different secretaries of the gun and camera clubs in Pittsburgh, Los Angeles, San Francisco, New York, St. Louis, Atlanta, Milwaukee, Chicago, Dallas, Detroit, Seattle, Denver, etc. He needed to know the meeting dates and the programs scheduled for September, October, November, December, and the following year's January. Hopefully, there would be an African topic on the agenda in each club that would explain his presence when he wanted to be there. He had given up long ago trying to coordinate his visits to save on air fares, so he visualized his nightmarish crisscrossing of the entire United States to attend the twenty meetings that he knew were necessary for his bookings. After his initial telephone contacts with the various secretaries of each club, he had received positive responses in all but the Chicago chapter. And although Chicago was a very big city, his company never fared very well in bookings there anyway.

Martin racked his brain before every call to try and remember any previous observations or audiences that might have revealed any circumstances that would suggest that a member of that particular chapter might be having wife troubles or vice versa. For the life of him, he could not muster up any clues. He asked every secretary for the latest gossip, but he succeeded there about the same as he had from his own memory. Martin was now wearing two hats: one to book safaris and the other to support his animal-client elimination plan.

As customary, Martin laid it on a little thick to secretaries most of the time. He was a confident middle-aged bachelor, and he needed favors from them from time to time – for his own personal use and for the company's. He usually asked the secretaries to book his hotel for him for several reasons – they knew which hotel was the most convenient, and Martin wanted them to know exactly where he was staying.

From his London hotel room on the mezzanine, Martin enjoyed viewing the great swimsuit shapes by the pool. He had to force himself back to business. As two o'clock approached, Martin managed to clear his eyes and return to the telephone to start calling his East Coast contacts and then his favorite, the West Coast cities. Sacramento, Los Angeles, Las Vegas, Portland, and Denver were his target cities in the west, and he loved to haul in every one of them. All were eager to see him – at least that was what the telephone secretaries told him. He even had a token amount of success in remembering two potential clients that might be right for his accidental elimination scheme. Last year while he was in Denver, he spent one night out with the boys; included in that group was a lawyer that everyone seemed to dislike. Whenever he would get up to go to the men's room, there was always some snide remark about his wife, his ethics, or his ancestors. Martin's inquiries to the secretary proved fruitful – the guy was still a member, he and his wife were still never seen together, but they were still married. With a little work, he just might have struck pay dirt.

In Las Vegas, where the annual Gun and Camera Club Convention was usually held, the chapter secretary commented about a doctor who was a hunting fanatic but who had nonendearing qualities that might make him a candidate. He had hunted all of the North American game, and now he had announced that he was going to be the first doctor to hunt and bag all of the dangerous animals of Africa on one safari. Martin read into that statement that the ol' doc didn't spend much time at home or with his wife. That alone made him a candidate for the hit list. Further investigating was a necessity.

By 10:00 p.m. on the evening before his London departure date, Martin's schedule was all but complete. While he was reviewing it, he tried to remember some of the more important faces he would again come in contact with. *Boom!* Dallas! How could he forget? The prime client of all clients was a shrewd businessman that owned, "silently," the biggest "titty bar" in Texas. Everyone in the safari business knew of Lou Maxie's reputation, and included in that reputation was the reputed fact that he was the world's biggest womanizer and that he didn't particularly care who knew it. His wife hated him, and everybody knew that as well – but would she like to see him dead? Martin hurriedly looked up his Dallas Safari Club contact number again and dialed.

Good-lookin' Betty answered on the second ring, just like all good administrative assistants are supposed to do. "Betty, this is Martin Smith again. I hope that I'm not being a bother. I know that it's about quitting time there, but if I could steal a few more minutes of your time, I would really appreciate it. I've got a couple of personal questions concerning one of your members, Lou Maxie.

I don't know if my information is right about him, but I've heard some weird things. My only reason for asking you about this guy is to protect my company from booking a potential "undesirable" and buying a lawsuit. I hope that I am not stepping on your toes with this one. We've heard through the grapevine that this guy has announced that he was 'going to be the greatest African hunter ever,' and extending his North American hunting hype, he was already a candidate for next year's Weatherby Award. I know I'll encounter him on my visit, so I must be prepared to give him an answer if he wants to book with Hunters, Ltd. Can you tell me if he is for real or not?"

"He's real, all right, and that's unfortunate," Betty was quick to reply. "I've got an appointment in a few minutes, so be quick, and I'll try to help you out if I can."

"Okay, thanks. First, can he afford to come over here?"

"Martin, we've been friends for a long time, and I trust you, but I have a job to protect. You'll have to keep what I say in the strictest of confidence."

"Of course."

"Hell yes, he can afford to go over there; he can afford to go anywhere – with the court's permission that is."

"What do you mean, Betty?"

"Everyone knows he's presently under indictment for hiding income or something like that; it's in the paper every day! It's the IRS that's really after him, not to mention all the other people that he has screwed. I may be speaking out of turn, but they are just joining all the women I know in town that literally want bad things to happen to him."

"Hey, Betty, why don't you tell me how you feel about this guy?"

"Very funny, Martin. He's been all right with me when he calls here, but from what I've heard and read, he is a greasy sleazeball. I ought to say a prayer for his cute little wife every night. She's so nice. How can she stay married to that nut? I don't know. I don't know how you could exclude him from a hunt, but don't ask me to go with you."

"Betty, if I had known that you would come to Africa, I'd have asked you sooner."

"Aren't you sweet, Martin? I'm going pretty steady with someone right now – maybe next year."

"Betty, last question – what's his wife's name?"

"Sally."

"Betty, you're a doll, and you make better sense than most. I appreciate your time, and I'll see ya in a couple of months. I owe you a drink. Ciao."

Martin was excited about his chances of luring Sally Maxie into his plan. He had never met Sally, but if he could so arrange it, her circumstances could lead to a fruitful rendezvous. Martin forgot to ask Betty which dangerous African animal she thought Lou might want to pursue – but it didn't matter; he would have to take them all if he was going to be the new standard bearer of African hunting in Dallas.

A great deal of Martin's mornings from the previous week in London were spent in some of his favorite bookshops and the incomparable Holland and Holland Company, maker of the world's finest and most expensive rifles. The Holland and Holland side-by-side double .375 magnum with precision ejectors is the finest rifle known to an African safari sportsman. Martin was pleased to find out that Prince Charles, an avid hunter in his own right, had just ordered two. The price was over £80,000 each plus interest, and inflation carries until delivery in approximately two years. Although Martin yearned for one of these for himself, he knew that these guns weren't for everybody, and he was presently an everybody. Never in Martin's life had he envisioned even a chance to acquire the kind of money that he was now thinking about. If all went according to his plans, he would one day visit this shop again, and then he wouldn't even look at the price tags, he'd just tell the salesclerk what he wanted. Oh, he longed for that day to hurry and get here.

Smaller and less renowned gun shops were also "must" visits for Martin. And on each visit he would again imagine how his future success would impact future visits. In a couple of these, he was surprised to find three sets of detachable rifle mounts for his new Zeiss 1.5 x 6 scope that he planned to switch off between three of his favorite African rifles. *Next time, he would have the gunsmith do the mounting for him, and he would have three separate Zeiss scopes as well*, he thought.

For all of the beautiful secretaries that had been so gracious to help make arrangements for his accommodations in their various cities, he made a special stop by Rowland Ward, Ltd., for some appreciation gifts. There, the Bavarian crystal drinking glasses etched with authentic African wildlife was the order of the day. He made arrangements for the company to overnight deliver a dozen sets to his Houston office as soon as possible. He would then hand-carry the gifts to his appointments for a special presentation. As he left the store, he mentally thanked the new overseas delivery systems that were now in place to enable him to do these things; he reminded himself of the old times and that he was not getting any younger. Martin's USA-calling nights from his room were followed by hours of drinking scotch at the hottest spots in London and watching the short skirts scurry back to his hotel. However, his luck was just about equal to a lion's kill ratio, about one in ten.

The flight was ordinary and without any special passengers on board. Martin always looked for the rich and famous, and intercontinental flights were perfect for spotting such flamboyance, even if he was only flying tourist class.

As Martin stepped out of the baggage claim area at the George Bush Houston Intercontinental Airport, he was met by an old friend, one of the drivers for Hunters, Ltd. Despite his forecast of being absolutely beat from the plane ride, Martin felt almost refreshed; and he instructed his pal to go directly to the office. Out of a booking office of twenty people, only two secretaries had changed since his last visit; and Martin was quickly introduced to the new help. Frank Black was dressed in his typical leisure attire and had arranged his total day to be with Martin if he was up to it. The president of any company would want to know just what was going on in the field operations of his business, and Frank was no exception. Meaningless conversations were held with the rest of the employees before Martin sat down with his boss. Only one taxidermied head adorned Frank's walnut-paneled walls; it was a lesser kudu taken with Janet on one of their first safaris together in the Tsavo area of southwestern Kenya. *That trophy meant more to Frank than all of the heads on the walls of any other hunter in the world*, Martin thought.

Two thousand four had been a good year of bookings and operations, the smoothest year since the business was founded. Frank gave Martin a great deal of credit for this success but also pointed out to him that most of it was because of Frank's directions and reputation. Martin couldn't argue about that even if he wanted to. Frank was a good businessman, a tireless worker, and a man with impeccable credentials. The thought that Martin's upcoming venture might monetarily affect Frank negatively made him think. But the thought of cutting Frank in on his plans had never been an option. Frank wouldn't risk what he had so painstakingly built – plus, he just wouldn't consider the negative moral side of this equation. Besides, money wasn't something that Frank needed; he thrived on the success of the business. Martin didn't know how much Frank was worth, but he expected that it was considerable. As a hired hand, Martin knew he could never acquire much in the realm of wealth, but he had now suddenly found a sideline business niche to magnify his holdings.

Frank closed the door to his spacious office and pointed to the leather couch for Martin to have a seat. "The year is really over for 2004, Martin; what we're going to do from now to year's end will be for the benefit of 2005. It will be hard to improve on '04, but I think we can, even with the adverse publicity from our lion accident. We've got to turn that happening into a plus for us. There's no doubt that such an accident will enforce the hunters' stories about the dangers of safari life, and that should bring new players into our game. From my phone calls from our already booked clients, it is evident that everyone likes an adventure that is fraught with some type of unsuspected danger. The trophies that go on our clients' walls are proof that he or she took an unknown gamble with their own life. That sells!"

Martin was slowly running out of gas from his long flight, and Frank noticed his attempts to keep his head from dropping. After a few more minutes of going over the next year's business forecasts, Frank suggested that Martin retire to the new hotel down the street. "Martin, I have taken the liberty of booking you a suite at the new Ramada Inn down the road. Why don't you take one of the company cars and go get some sleep? If you feel up to it, we can have dinner around eight. I'll pick you up. All of the business talk can wait till then. I know you have got to be tired."

"Thanks, Frank, I am beginning to fade a bit. But I do want to discuss a couple of gun and camera club visits before I have to confirm them tomorrow. I guess we can accomplish that at dinner."

Frank pitched Martin a set of keys to one of the vans parked in one of the company parking spaces. "The white van. The same one Jimmy picked you up in from the airport. See you at eight; casual of course."

The evening meal at the River Oaks Home Town Grill was perfect as usual. Martin and Frank were on the same page on every business topic. At ten thirty, Frank asked for the check and took Martin back to his hotel.

The Houston Gun and Camera Club's September meeting was only two days away. Until then, Martin had to round up all his brochures, go over the new price guidelines, and check one more time with the Botswana game department to make sure that all of the animals that were on license were going to be available in the quantities that he was earlier told. After checking by telephone with the Botswana game department, with the exception of sable, every other animal seemed to be available in the exact number that he expected. Elephant was still closed, but a later determination on some new scientific game data might shed new light on the issuance of some new permits. No decision was to be made until the New Year. Lion and leopard restrictions to certain locals were dropped, so any lion or leopard within the company's operations borders was fair game. That was wonderful news; no more overnight sojourns to a far-off concession just for a chance at lion or leopard. Because of the time it took to get to neighboring concessions, bating with previous licensed kills was impossible. Now a client could spend that travel time in his or her own concession, improving immeasurably the chances for sighting one of the coveted cats. The professional hunters and the camp crews were going to love that!

3

The First Contract

It was time to put Lou Maxie and other potential clients out of mind and focus on a familiar face, Barbara Jones. On the morning of the day before the September meeting of the Houston Gun and Camera Club at the Sirloin Inn on Main Street near the old Astrodome area, Martin called Barbara at her travel agency to make a luncheon appointment. He requested an out-of-the-way restaurant where conversations could be kept private and where neither of them would likely be recognized. Barbara suggested a small cafe that was on a quaint little side street just off Kirby Drive near the Southwest Freeway. It was about a thirty-minute drive for both and readily convenient for them to extend their conversations there or at a nearby pub should the talks extend beyond their planned lunchtime expectations. Meeting time was set for 11:30 a.m., dress was typical Houston casual.

Martin had been in the company of Barbara on many other occasions but always with another person present. Thus, he was a little apprehensive about this rendezvous, particularly with its scheduled contents. Barbara couldn't have cared less about anything of the past, present, or future, she just wanted to extract herself from the maddening clutches of this tyrannical madman who, despite his money, was neither a lover nor pleasant company. He was just a bastard of the worst sort. She knew that certain parts of Martin's plan were going to be unethical and unlawful, but she felt it was her only option to change her life without going through a nasty divorce with cutthroat lawyers and whiny investigators and possibly losing her life in the process. She remembered Clifford had once told her that he'd never go through another divorce; he said that he would rather be tried for murder than be put through the rigors of another divorce proceeding. What was she supposed to think? Since there was no other paramour involved, Clifford's murder victim, if he was prone to have one, could only be her!

Martin arrived first and requested a table in a corner just to his liking. Barbara whirled in, showing evidence that she had been momentarily delayed from leaving the office as she had planned. Barbara was a pretty woman with every indication that she was her own boss and obviously fearful of nothing. She was certainly positive about her intentions, and Martin sensed that from the earlier telephone conversations and from his first look into her eyes this day. Barbara was dressed in a calf-length brown full skirt and a plain tailored white shirt. She wore khaki shoes and a lizard belt, and her hair was swept up in a bun. Her jewelry was a combination of Neiman-Marcus and Tiffany's. A lavish ten-carat deep green emerald dangled on a solid gold chain from her lovely neck. Of course she had matching but smaller emerald earrings. A half-dozen bracelets of gold covered her right wrist, while a thin opal-faced Piaget solid gold watch adorned her left wrist. She wore a simple gold wedding band, but God only knows how big the diamond was on her other ring. As pretty as it all was, Martin silently thought that all this jewelry and more were just presents from an old fart that was excusing his conduct for escapades with other women. It made him sick. She was thin as usual, and her tan gave away her liking for the outdoor sun. For forty-two, she was indeed something special both in looks and deeds, and Martin sincerely admired both.

"Martin" – a soft kiss on the cheek – "I've been waiting for this moment for nearly a year. I've been wishing for something like this since after the first week Clifford and I got married, but I've kept myself so busy that I've been able to ignore just how unhappy my life has been. I hope you have not 'chickened out.' You and I have been as close as a professional and a client can be, and I trust you. Please trust me. I don't want to go through a long divorce and all of its ramifications. The man means nothing to anybody. I'm not kidding, I mean to anybody, not even his kids. His ex-wives have all settled with him monetarily because they never want to see him again, and I think everyone else feels the same way. He's gone through six secretaries in the last four years, and the one he's got now is ready to leave. Keep in mind that he doesn't see them but an hour or so a day, that makes the turnover even more loathsome."

Martin was always reassuring when he spoke. At six feet one and a hundred and seventy pounds, he was fit and handsome. His blue eyes could stare right through you, or they could give you the comfort that the situation demanded. Martin was a cool customer who spoke only after careful thought, and he seldom said something that he would later regret. His attire was always a little more casual than one would expect for the occasion, but his confidence made anyone questioning such a feeling of inappropriate dress feel as if Martin was the one who was correct. If one were to cast a safari portrait for a safari magazine, the ideal subject would be Martin Smith.

"Sit down, Barbara. I haven't 'chickened out,' and I understand everything you've been telling me. I love you to death, and it would be my pleasure to make anyone pay for mistreating you. Our trust is mutual, so let's go over the situation step by step, and I'm sure we'll find the appropriate answers. Neither one of us is here to just talk. You are obviously wanting some action, and I am here to deliver what will help you.

"I hope you don't mind, but I've been doing a little private investigating myself on your behalf, and I've found your situation even more intolerable than you say. You mentioned to me that you had some photos and some letters or notes from your private eye that Clifford would find embarrassing; did you bring them?"

She opened her purse and pitched a stretched large rubber band full of photos and papers on the table. "They're copies because I've had to pay enough to my investigator for the originals, but they ought to be good enough for whatever you want them for."

"Fine, Barbara, I think we're in business. Let me move you a little closer so we won't have to talk quite so loud. I didn't remember this place being so noisy." Martin stood and helped her reseat herself next to him. Martin's manners were always superb, as were the manners of all the people in the safari business. "We've got a lot to talk about, and we've got to come to some solid agreements before we can both be sure this thing will be successful. I've made a few notes to joggle my mind, but I will destroy them immediately after we adjourn."

Martin removed the messily written papers from his pocket. "From now on, there must not be any unnecessary written material that passes between us, not a bit. In fact, no written material at all is the best policy! We must be equally as careful with our face-to-face meetings and our telephone conversations. We must always be aware of someone listening to us, following us, and seeing us. You never know when someone might be setting us up or at least trying to build a case for one reason or another. We have to play like they exist, and we have to limit their opportunities to discover anything.

"As I mentioned to you earlier on your call to me overseas, we must operate under an oral agreement. Not a written contract. 'Trust' is the byword between us. To unearth the contents of our agreement to others, should it be necessary, would bring both sides into the light of incrimination. For both sides to be scot-free after all is said and done requires both of us to do exactly what we say we are going to do, nothing more and nothing less. Normally, my partners and I would require some pretty hefty deposits from you to carry this thing through, but I have gone out on a limb to vouch for you in keeping with our agreement. That's because you first called me and because of our past relationships. I know that I am sounding a bit harsh and directive, but I am representing a couple of partners here, and it's best to start off with everyone knowing just where each other stands and what each other thinks. So if you want to back out, now is your last chance. From this day forward, we are both bound to whatever we agree upon today. Do you have any questions so far?"

Barbara shook her head negatively. Barbara knew when it was her time to speak and when it was her time to listen.

Martin picked up his notes and began to refer to them as needed. "First, we've got to get the money talk out of the way; if payments cannot be made, then we have already come to the end of the line. We need one hundred thousand U.S. up front to initiate the contract. Can you handle that?"

Barbara was devoid of any surprised expression. "I didn't bring a check book with me with that kind of money in it, if that is what you mean, but I can get that amount, given a couple of weeks' notice."

"Good, I suggest that you begin your preparations immediately so we can get my side of this thing off and running. You are going to have to transfer the money to a special account that I have set up in Switzerland, a 'no name' numbered account. I would suggest that you transfer it in two separate installments, as if you were going to pay for an expensive safari for one of your clients. Don't even think of using a wire transfer or anything that might be traced. I may be being a little too cautious in this instance, but wire transfers and big money transfers by mail scare me to death. You might just have to fly to Switzerland yourself to make the deposit. Keep in mind that your government demands a report on any check written or any deposit of an amount over ten thousand dollars. You will have to use a transfer method other than your personal check; and if you use your company check, you must make sure that it cannot be interpreted to be used for a safari for you with my company; that would be a red flag. In short, the transfer must be as close as possible to a business transfer of funds for a business reason. Just be careful! Your judgment in this instance is probably better than mine, plus you are privy to the ways and means of your type of business transactions.

"You have a perfect 'front' by using your travel business. What is the largest check that you have ever written on your company's account and for what? I know the question is awfully personal, but I think it is important for me to feel comfortable."

Barbara paused to answer while in deep thought. "I think that I wrote one for seventy-something thousand once to a bank in London for a party of thirty people that had booked a trip going all through Europe. The guide service had to have certified funds before the trip could commence."

"Fine, I'll leave it up to you to be creative enough to accomplish what we're after. Just be careful in your planning, and fill me in on all the details before you enact the actual transfer. Secondly, our final payment when the job is over will be nine hundred thousand U.S. dollars. We don't want any of this until all of the final knots are tied. As I mentioned to you over the phone, you must agree to move to Europe as soon as possible after your husband's affairs have been settled. It is a protection idea that should stymie any U.S. investigations should anyone be so inclined. When you move to Europe, predictably within three to six months after the job, we will instruct you where to send the balance owed us, probably to the same Swiss account. Even the big amount of money we're talking about will not be noticed if you are moving over there. Anyone would suspect that you are going to buy a house or something. Shouldn't be any problem at all. Nearly a million dollars will be hard to come by in certified funds, however, and that is another problem area that you will have to sort out yourself. I am not ruling out a transfer of some European personal or business check to our Swiss account, but that depends on how everything else is working out at that time.

"You're going to have to be lucky to sell your house that quick without settling for a 'fire sale' price, and I doubt that you can sell the business right away either. We'll be patient, but we're going to have our expenses to pay as well as you will. The obvious answer to this question is insurance. How about the insurance in force today on Clifford?"

"You asked me to find out all that I could concerning that, and I've been moderately successful. I didn't want to cause a red-flag alert, but I did find out the following" – she began to read from her scribbling on the back of a note pad – "he has a million-dollar policy that he has had for twenty years. It's paid up. Our agent says that it does have accidental death benefits for double the million plus a waiver of disability that I hope won't come into play," she finished as she looked over her half-rimmed reading glasses.

"He has another half-a-million-dollar policy that was pledged toward the latest improvement loan on the new distributor warehouse expansion. I think that loan has now been paid off, so I guess that policy is no longer encumbered. The policy is paid current and has been in force for about five years. I'm sure he would not let it lapse. It will take me a few more days to confirm that it is no longer pledged, but I see no problems finding out. He also has a four-hundred-thousand-dollar life policy in connection with our health insurance that is paid for by the company. I haven't figured out how I can find out about accidental death on it yet, and I may not be able to find that out without causing some suspicion, so I suggest we let that lie.

"Now, before you ask me about my business, the value of the house, and the value of the distributorship, let me give you my best guesses. On a forced sale, I could probably sell my travel agency to another agency in the same building complex for a hundred thousand, maybe more if I prolonged the negotiations. They have asked me to sell once before, but that was a year ago. I have sentimental misgivings about selling my business that I've worked so hard to please my loyal customers. But if I am going to sell it, I know I can work something out with the people in my building, and I can make sure they treat my old customers right. There would be no red flags at all in this transaction.

"The house should bring in a million or more after paying the real estate commission. My problem with the house is its contents. Except for a few of my things – the silver, china, and crystal – I'd love to sell everything or give it away. I want to start over. I don't want a damn thing from in there to remind me of my past miseries. I suppose that I would just list the house as soon as I could, and somehow I'd figure out what to do with the things I don't want. I could always put them in storage someplace, but that seems a terrible waste. As to the main business, the distributorship, I guess it is fortunate that we don't have any partners, but when you think about selling the thing, it would help if you could sell to someone who knew the day-to-day activities and knew how much it was worth. I simply don't know anyone who is on the inside that would have the money to pay for it."

Martin interrupted, "I have an idea about selling the business. I'd call your supplier shortly after the funeral, and I would tell them that you had no intention of running that business anymore and that you were going to move to Europe to avoid the crime in Houston. Ask them to find a buyer that you both would be mutually pleased with, and that you would pay them a finder's fee for their efforts. I think they would absolutely jump at the chance; they might even buy the damn thing themselves. Do you have an idea how much you would ask?"

Barbara shook her head again in the negative.

"I'd ask your accountant for starters but not until after the funeral. Maybe I can give you some 'guesstimate' now of what it's worth. My father used to be a business broker, and he drilled values into my head at every opportunity. He always reminded me of percentages and earnings. 'They never lie.' Most businesses are worth whatever they generate as income during a full year of business. In other words, the same value as the year's gross receipts, 100 percent. Another way is to multiply the monthly net earnings by a hundred or the year's net earnings by ten. All of this is for the business itself. The real estate or other like property would be extra. You will have to fill in the blanks. Sounds to me like you are going to go on easy street without a care in the world."

"Is that a guarantee, Martin?"

"I'm afraid not, but I sure know a bundle of people who would trade places with you."

"Are there any mortgages on the property where the business sits?"

"The big loans have all been paid off, for sure. The only one that I don't know about is the recent expansion project for the warehouse, and I'd bet that it is also paid off."

"Barbara, you are a strong person and an obviously astute businesswoman; if you just stop to think a minute before you make any decisions, I would bet that you will come out as good as anyone. Don't be pushed, and don't jump at the first offer unless the item you're selling is of little consequence. The insurance money will satisfy our obligations, and you'll still have enough to lead any kind of life you choose in Europe. Make sure that you find a qualified lawyer to represent you wherever you settle. Maybe your local lawyer here will recommend someone overseas for you.

"One last question regarding money. I hope there are no surprises that might be uncovered by a secret will or codicil that you are now not aware of."

Barbara thought a moment and then quite assuredly responded, "Not a chance, Martin, the two of us met only last month with Joel, our lawyer, at Joel's insistence to go over both our wills and any possible revisions. There were no changes. I actually saw Clifford's will; it's with Joel. Joel has a special feeling toward me. Don't get the wrong idea, the feelings are not mutual, but he cannot keep his hands off me. Every time I approach a door, sit down, or grab my coat, he is always there to assist. I think he knows how miserable I've been, and he thinks I'm some sort of 'trooper' or something to have stuck it out this long. It is good to know he is in my corner; for sure, he's in my corner."

"Good, Barbara, you deserve him. I think that we ought to order soon or we are going to be very suspicious sitting here doing nothing but talking. Let me get us some menus."

The strained faces of both Martin and Barbara immediately relaxed at the thought of food. The waiter gave them a few minutes to peruse the menu, then both ordered lightly – Barbara a chicken salad sandwich on toast, and Martin a tuna fish salad. Both had a small glass of the best house Chardonnay. Barbara couldn't help but think of the difference between the ordering of Martin and Captain Bullock. *Class*, she thought. *What defines "class"?* She was brought up in a small Texas town in the center of the state; her parents were not well-to-do, but she thought that somehow she'd always had class. She continued to wonder about class. Martin had class. It was funny, two classy individuals sitting there planning a murder with class.

After a few bites, Martin reestablished the conversation by politely asking her if she "would prefer to eat and then talk some more or discuss the rest of our business over the rest of lunch."

Waiting for her next bite to go down, Barbara motioned with her hand to continue. Then she confirmed her hand signal by saying, "Let's wind this thing up. I can talk and eat with no problem. Besides, you're the one doing all the talking!"

Martin took his cue. "I want to make sure that you understand my side of this agreement. I, we, or anyone else is not going to shoot your husband. We are going to set a stage where, if all goes right – and we will be damn sure that it will – your husband will be in a very hazardous position. A position where it will be almost impossible for him to extricate himself. Maybe a seasoned professional hunter might be lucky enough to come out of it alive, but chances are, not a client. We will then treat the whole thing as an accident. We'll report it as an accident, and we will cooperate with the authorities during any investigation. Our professional careers may be severely damaged by this accident, and that is why we are getting our inflated fees. You realize that we are paid to prevent accidents not assist in letting them happen. We will do our best to prevent any type of suffering, but this is going to be death by an animal not a kill by a human. If we were to even intervene to finalize the death, we both might be asking for trouble. Simply put, we won't do that."

Barbara had prepared herself for the description of the modus operandi, and although she could not be sure when a detailed explanation would occur, she hid her shuttering thoughts well. She made no visual or oral objections, and she held her breath to keep from trembling. She hoped with all her fervor that this would be the last time such a description would be necessary.

"You must book the safari with me as in the normal course of business. All flights, hotel bookings, etc., will be made as if it is going to be a completely successful trip of standard length. As in the past, you will handle all of that with Frank Black at our Houston office; you will suggest your choices of flights, hotels, food in camp, etc., as usual. Don't neglect to ask for your personal pleasures; that will make the booking absolutely flawless as to normal course of business. Frank will help you personally as he does with all preferred clients. You will have to pay for the safari over and above any of the fees that we have already discussed. I cannot assist you in payment, or it would invite questions. I will meet with Cliff at the gun and camera club meeting tomorrow. Does he know that you want to give him an elephant hunt? And for what occasion?"

Barbara smiled for the first time in the day. "I mentioned it to him when we were together at the lawyer's office. He knew that he couldn't decline in front of Joel or he'd lose face, and he'd have to explain just why he didn't want to accept his lovely wife's gift, particularly when I insisted on going with him. I told Joel that the gift was coming totally from my business income, and it was for his next birthday, but the real reason was to try and give us one more chance to discover what had brought us together in the first place. After we finished all the legal business, he asked me in front of Joel if I knew how hot it was going to be and how far I was going to have to walk. I answered with, 'How miserable would any other girl be if she went.' He just frowned and dared not answer. I told them both that I had already booked the hunt early for his birthday present. Joel complimented me on my thoughtfulness, and we left. While in the car on the way home, he agreed to go and take me. I told him that I would make all the reservations. He had only two concerns: that I book it with you and that we travel first class. Life's a bitch, isn't it?"

Martin was smiling all over his face when he said, "I'm really surprised that you have so much in place. You have really been busy."

"Not busy, just determined," Barbara shot back.

"It will not do you any good to know the details of our plans while on safari; in fact, the more you don't know, the better. It'll look more natural. Is that okay with you?"

This time Barbara nodded positively.

"I'll hand you a note with my bank account number on it when I see you tomorrow night. The number will be written exactly backward. I will tell you the bank's name and the town at the beginning of the meeting. If you forget it, then ask me again before you leave. It'll be our last chance to exchange this kind of information. You can call long-distance information for the number of the bank to begin your transfers, but please call from a nontraceable telephone. One last word. Don't be surprised by anything you hear or read. Our agreement is a done deal, and nothing is going to go wrong. I may play around with you and Cliff as I always do – denying any elephants are left in the concession, etc., but you know I'll just be kidding.

"I shouldn't tell you this, so I want you to swear that you'll never breathe a word."

"Okay," Barbara said with an inquisitive look on her face.

"No, I want you to swear it to me!"

After a short pause and with an evident smirk on her face, Barbara stated the obvious, "All right, Martin, I swear."

"There is someone else in your same predicament, and we are going to help her as well."

Barbara went suddenly berserk. "You are crazier than I thought you were; I guess that you are going to tell her about me? You are a money-hungry bastard."

"Wait, wait, wait," Martin jumped in. "I'm telling you this to soothe your thoughts when you get leery of our plan. It is bound to happen. I thought carefully about telling you. I sincerely care for you, and I don't want you to feel alone. This thing has also happened several times in the past. I have knowledge of a few of them, but I cannot divulge any particulars. I'm just trying to make you as comfortable as I possibly can."

"Well, Mr. Smith, I better not ever catch you telling anyone about this or anything else you know about me or I will personally cut your balls out and feed them to my cats! Is that clear?"

Martin had obviously made a mistake. Does he now deny what he had just told her as just a kidding remark, or does he continue to tell her that he told her only to help make her more comfortable? Sheepishly, Martin thought and then apologized. "I'm very sorry, Barbara. This person is far removed from Houston. No one you know knows either of them, I assure you. She is in a similar situation as you. She has been trampled on, spat on, and shit on, just like you. You of all people wouldn't want her to continue to survive under the same conditions as you. I'll say no more about her; the twain will never meet.

"I have told you things that I would never tell anyone else; I have vouched for you to my other partners, and I trust you more than any female that I have ever known. You've got to trust me."

Barbara sat silent. Both sat silent. Time stood still as each conversationalist waited for the other to end the silence. Finally, Martin called the waiter over for two more glasses of wine. "No," snapped Barbara, "bring us champagne, a half bottle if you have one, but a good one. What do you stock?" Satisfaction could not be had in a half bottle, so Barbara ordered a full bottle of the best in the house – Cure'e Dom Perignon. Not another word was to ever be uttered about any other clients of Martin, both agreed with a prolonged and multiglass toast.

The conversation now shifted to the more pleasant imaginations of life after the agreement had been fulfilled. Both were now approaching supreme alcoholic happiness, courtesy of Dom Perignon. After a last and final toast to their agreement, Martin left and went directly to his hotel to further celebrate by changing to Scotch whiskey. Barbara carefully drove home, pitched the butler the keys to her new Mercedes, and asked him to run down to the corner and bring her back a takeout plate of barbecue. *A common move for the spoiled rich folks when their cook had an off day*, she thought. By the time the butler reappeared, Barbara had showered and was dressed for bed. She opened a small bottle of diet coke, gathered her sack of food, and quietly retired to her upstairs bedroom with orders not to be disturbed. Although she had gone through the meeting with Martin just as she had planned, her stomach was in knots; and she could hardly eat a bite. Thank goodness the wine and champagne had made her sleepy. As she slept, she dreamed of future happiness in Europe, happiness that she knew she had dearly earned.

Ironically, while Barbara and Martin were meeting, Clifford had skipped his usual "gin" game at the club to take a new female model friend out to lunch. One of the country club's waiters was a roommate of a manager at one of the local strip joints, and he always knew when a new young face came to work. Traditionally, a starting girl would be short of cash and ripe for an interlude with some rich old man. The strip-joint manager rationalized his actions by telling himself that he was only helping a new friend in need. Of course he was splitting the "finder's fee" with his roommate.

On most occasions, the manager would secure a motel room and tell his accomplice to inform Clifford where he could pick up the key. However, last week's new face turned out to be not as great under sunlight as under spotlights, and Clifford now required a sight test before he would consummate a contract.

Today's date was beautiful. Clifford was so anxious to see her with her clothes off that he brushed off the waiter when he asked if there would be any desert. Clifford called for the check instead and suggested the two head for the hotel. On the way out of the restaurant, Cilfford slipped a hundred-dollar bill in the show-girl's hand and told her to "buy some gas." She was obviously pleased because she knew there would be more from where that came from. Clifford didn't come home that night. Didn't call. Same old same old for this marriage. It didn't matter to Barbara though, she had her plan rolling, and she went right to sleep.

The dress at the gun and camera club meeting was "coat and tie" for the gents and cocktail dresses for the ladies. Martin was in his latest European fashions, wing-tips, baggy pleated slacks, and a tweed sport coat. Barbara was just plain stunning. Her forty-two-year-old figure could have easily been mistaken for a figure fifteen years younger. Except for her Couch shoulder bag and her elegant pumps, her dress was plain – a long-sleeved off-white denim blouse and a matching midcalf skirt. Her jewelry was the same she had worn at lunch with Martin. Clifford Jones entered with his wife, but he quickly made for the other people with which he had more in common. The note concerning the bank account number was passed as soon as Cliff left Barbara's side. *What a tragedy*, all the rest of the wives thought. To be beautiful, nice, and unsuspecting (if only they knew). Barbara was a rare woman from the point of view of both sexes. As she amused herself going from small gathering to small gathering, Martin hung closely around Mr. Jones. He didn't enjoy the company, but it was business, double business. The date of the first available elephant hunt in Tanzania was offered to Clifford and he seemed extraordinarily pleased. Like the start of any hunting season, the first few days catch the animals more at ease. This makes the chances of success immeasurably better. Martin informed Cliff that elephant hunting might reopen in Botswana after the New Year, but he doubted it, so East Africa offered the best opportunity.

"Tanzania offers you the best prospect of taking a really good elephant, maybe even a hundred-pounder if you hunt in the Selous." Cliff knew all about where and when to hunt elephants in this day and time, and he longed for a real hundred-pounder.

The ears of a young man of about twenty listening in on the conversation perked at the mention of a hundred-pounder, and he politely interrupted, "Pardon my overhearing, but would one of you please tell me why an elephant is judged by being a hundred-pounder?"

Martin always jumped at the opportunity to explain something to a possible future client. "In the record books of the hunting world, young man, elephants are judged by the net weight of the heaviest tusk after the nerve has been extracted. Even a one-tusker whose single tusk weighed over a hundred pounds would qualify as a hundred-pounder. There have only been a few of these hundred-pounders taken in the last twenty years. The Selous is an elephant paradise in central Tanzania. It offers the best of elephants, but little else in the way of desirable game. The area is heavily infested with tsetse flies, so comfort is almost nonexistent." Then Martin turned to face Clifford again. "If you don't want to put up with the tsetse fly, then we can book you a couple of thousand miles south in Zimbabwe during the same time. Your choice."

Cliff finally acknowledged his going when he reached out for Martin's hand, shook it, and said, "I'm not getting any younger, you know; it would be nice to test my mettle one more time in that godforsaken territory of the Selous and have a reasonable chance at the coveted hundred-pounder."

Martin nodded in agreement. "It's all settled then, Cliff. I anticipated your desires, and I already made the arrangements for you this morning. I knew you would want the best, even if it will be difficult."

"Have you thought about how Barbara will take it?"

"Fuck no," was Cliff's typical answer, even in front of mixed company that he had never seen before. "She's got no goddamn right to be there anyway, but it looks like I'm going to be saddled with her. It'll be the last time, though, I won't have to intentionally make it rough for her; it'll just come naturally. Mark my word, she'll stay in camp about three days at the most, then I'll have to hire a helicopter to get her out of there. Martin, is there any way that I could then substitute another gal for her when she leaves?"

Martin had had enough when he replied, "Sure, Cliff, I'll send up a whole harem of AIDS-infested natives from the CAE [Central African Republic – formerly the Congo and the CAR] for you at no charge." Martin then excused himself and hustled over to another group of potential clients.

The program for the evening was given by a local member that had just returned from the Sudan. He had successfully hunted the famed bongo and he had the films to prove it. After the member's presentation, Martin was recognized and offered a few minutes at the podium to update the group on what his various camps offered for the next year. To further solidify Clifford Jones' hunt with him, he opened his remarks to the crowd by announcing that the famous Mr. Jones of the group had just booked the first elephant hunt in the Selous for the next season. He emphasized that Barbara had been the instigator of the hunt as a birthday present, and that she was going to accompany him. The crowd suddenly hushed, everyone could feel that this was going to be the time that this old bastard was probably going to kill pretty Barbara.

Martin then broke the silence by offering to the club a 10 percent commission for any hunt that would be booked tonight for the following year with his company. Frank Black beamed because he knew that everyone there knew it was his idea and his gift. Martin was mobbed by at least fifteen potential clients when he left the speaker's stand. Frank came over to help, and before the night was through, Hunters, Ltd. had booked a total of six safaris other than the Joneses.

Barbara decided to leave the gathering a little early and let Clifford "fin" for himself. She paid her respects to Frank and Martin and left. Martin gave special notice to her so that if she had any doubts about the city and bank that she was told to remember, he could restate their names.

There appeared to be no doubts.

4

Recruiting a New Client

The next month and a half proved rather uneventful for Martin Smith; that is, if one is not counting the everyday life of a person that is only committed to doing his or her job. Martin was an excellent employee as evidenced by his unusually high compliments that Hunters, Ltd. received following almost every safari. The people who went on these safaris were, for the most part, individual business people who were nearly always their own bosses. That meant that they were "chiefs" and not mere "Indians." When something good happens in business, it is usually the result of planning and good employees that carry out the plan. So, these "chiefs" were always quick to praise good planning and good work when they saw it. Because Martin Smith was usually their first and last contact with their safari, they correctly deduced that he was the one most responsible for their having such a fine time.

During the six weeks that followed the Houston meeting, Martin visited twelve different cities in an effort to book safaris for the coming year. He had good success in his normal safari-booking business in each city. But except for Lou Maxie, the Dallas womanizer he had yet to see, and Clifford Jones, who was already booked and enrolled in the "plan," none of his other new or old contacts held potential for his new elimination business. However, Martin made the most of his visits. He was constantly on the lookout for any hints of unhappy wives or business partners that might lead him to believe there was a possibility of adding a new name to his second vocation "hit" list. In the end, although there was no real prospect found, he did generate trust and confidence with all he met, and one could never tell when a prospect might suddenly arise.

It was in one of his lonely hotel rooms one night that Martin realized that his plan for eliminating unhappy wives' husbands might also be expanded to do the same for unhappy partners in a souring business relationship. He was not concerned about notifying his other partners that were still back on the "dark continent" of his possible new expansion plans; he would wait until a prospect of the like if it surfaced. His only reservation about his new concept was that there would be an extra person snooping for the truth other than the partner – a wife. "Too many cooks spoil the broth," came immediately to mind and his mind began to race. "She could cause plenty of trouble. If a business partner lost his partner to an accident, and he was well compensated for the loss, he would generally not make waves. But if the wife of the deceased was not in on the deal and the partner was eliminated, the surviving spouse was sure to cause trouble. She'd be emotional and all of her friends would be the same. If she didn't make the mess stink, then somebody would come to her rescue that would." Martin decided to only explore the partnership avenue if he could not put together enough unhappy wives to close out his plan. He knew he couldn't stretch the venture longer than one hunting season.

After concluding his grueling road trip that crisscrossed most of the contiguous Forty-eight, Martin was now back in Houston and had two full weeks before his next scheduled safari meeting in Dallas, 240 miles away. Because Dallas was a relatively short trip, he asked Frank Black if he could use one of the company cars to drive instead of fly. He lamented on his loss of desire to be in any more airports for a while, and insisted that he could use the extra time to court some new clients. The Dallas chapter of the national gun and camera club was embroiled in an intense new membership drive, and he thought he might make some headway with the new blood. Frank was a frequent visitor to the Dallas chapter and he knew the club's secretary, Betty Winslow. She would be willing to help Martin whenever he asked, so he wholeheartedly approved an early departure by car.

Martin spent the last couple of days in Houston tidying up his most recent bookings, and then donned a new pair of Italian leather driving shoes to drive straight away to Dallas. Martin could not wait to check into the downtown Adolphus Hotel. It was one of his favorite hotels in the entire world, in the center of everything, and it was old and historic – *just like his own classy profession,* he thought.

Its old real wood paneling, its high ceilings, and its valet parking with a whistling master valet in a top-hat, combined all the ingredients of class that he liked. He would save the elegant French Room that was adjacent to the main lobby for a very special dinner with, he hoped, a very special lady that was an applicant for his elimination plan.

Upon checking in, he immediately sought out the concierge; he handed him a crisp new fifty-dollar bill and his business card. He asked that he immediately be notified if anyone inquired about his stay, and suggested to the concierge that his services would also be needed a bit later for a few special occasions. Thanking him for his cooperation, Martin caught the elevator up to his room.

The first order of business was to select a good and doubly private "eye." He thumbed through the Yellow Pages until he found the section for private investigators. He dared not pick the biggest ad – they would be all talk and not undercover enough. He looked for a small ad without bold print. He found three. He called them all. The first one had an answering machine that received his call, so he immediately scratched that one. The other two were answered by secretaries who were obviously doing double duty typing as they answered the telephone. Martin asked both if the head man was in, if there was more than one investigator working there, and just how long they had been in business under that name. Both agencies he called had only one investigator. One had been in business for twelve years, and the other had been in business for nineteen years. The one that had been in business the longest and had its headman present became Martin's first choice, and Martin asked to speak to the boss.

Martin did not want to ever divulge his elimination plan to anyone outside the main loop of his partners and actual clients; instead, he would use the guise that a new potential client owed another safari company money from a previous safari and had caused them a hard time with other bookings because he had been so vociferous about his unhappiness. The same person had applied to his safari company for a similar booking, and he had to know more about him. Hunters, Ltd. was not in the business of refusing clients, but when they were alerted that a potential client might not be a paying one, they had to check him out. In this case, Martin also wanted to know about his personal life and that of his wife in case the guy tried something funny on him after he completed his safari. It was a fifty-thousand-dollar booking and Martin didn't want to lose any money, but more importantly, he didn't want to sully his reputation.

After a brief talk with the receptionist and the proprietor, Martin settled on John West; the name of his company was the same as his name except for the word "investigations" added to the end. When Mr. West initially picked up the phone, he hesitated to answer many questions, but he made it clear that he worked for no one without at least a thousand-dollar retainer.

Martin said, "Fine," and they agreed to meet for further discussions at the Adolphus' informal dining room for dinner.

The concierge in the hotel lobby was alerted by Martin to be on the lookout for Mr. West and to bring him personally to Martin's table in the dining room. Everything worked like clockwork. Martin showed the investigator the thousand dollars in his pocket, and said that he was most eager to cut a deal. Martin inquired first about how busy Mr. West was. After Mr. West instructed Martin to begin calling him John only, he answered, "I have my usual business clientele that I must take care of to keep my office doors open, but as of now, I don't have anything pressing that would hinder my doing some work for you right away."

"Good," Martin said, "because I will have to leave town in ten days, and I have to know all my answers by then."

John squirmed a bit, and then replied, "I give no guarantees, but I'll promise you a better than good-faith effort. Now tell me whom I am going to be calling on and just what do you want to know about them."

"The names are Sally and Lou Maxie."

"I quit," snapped John, "there are already so many federal and state investigators on their tails that I couldn't get close enough to them to find out anything."

Martin smiled and shot back, "I know, but I have to try to find out some answers, and anybody that I try to hire is going to have the same problem – right? I like your honesty, and all I'm asking is for you to do the best you can do. I don't need miracles; at least I don't think I do."

"Okay, as long as you know what we're getting into; I think I'm your man. Let me get out a legal pad from this old leather pouch and jot down some notes. You gave me your business card," he said while reaching into every pocket he owned to try to find it. "But I've already lost it; give me another and put your room number on it, and the name of that Iranian concierge. I suppose you're in pretty tight with him. I've noticed." John then opened his coat to reach for his pen. There was ink all over his shirt pocket where at least a thousand pens had been before.

Martin thought, *I like this guy – reminds me of Colombo on television.*

"Here is what I need, Mr. Colombo – oh! I mean, Mr. John West." They both laughed.

"In the next four days, I need to know all of the possible trouble that Lou is in; from the feds, the state, the IRS, partners, women – everything. I need to know if his wife has any possible incriminating connections where she might also be in trouble. I have gathered that he likes women. A different one every night, I'm told. If you can get me anything on them, I'd appreciate it, but we'll have time for most of that later. I need to know where he likes to dine, have drinks; and the same for his wife, Sally. I don't want to be running into either of them unnecessarily. If possible, I would like to know just who Sally's friends – main friends – are, and if she does any running around like her husband. In four days, you need to give me an update, and by then, I'll have figured out a few more questions. Do you think you can handle it?"

"Hey, man, there is only twenty-four hours in a day and you want all of this in four days? You must be crazy – but I'll have the most of it in three! Then I'll need some more money!"

"You name it, John, and you'll get it – within reason, of course."

"Martin – that is what I'm supposed to call you, isn't it?"

Martin nodded positively.

"I will probably get started tonight; do you happen to have either one of their driver's license numbers or their Social Security numbers?"

"I'm afraid not, John. What in the world would you use them for?"

John smiled. "You'd be surprised, Martin; I can find out almost everything anybody would want to know about a person from those two numbers and my computer. The Social Security number gives me all of a person's credit info. From that, I simply tie a certain part of that credit information to what other information I want next. For instance, if I wanted to know where our subject is dining tonight, I would pull up his credit-card file and enter each of his sub-file accounts to determine if there was any activity on any of the cards within the last few minutes or hours. Most people buy their meals at night by credit cards, so when our subject's card is submitted for verification of the night's meal, I know right where he is. As you can see, it makes my job a lot easier to know a subject's social number and his driver's license number."

Martin racked his brain for an answer to both numbers, but thought of no leads to get either. "Sorry, John, I can't help you there."

"That's okay, Martin, I can get them, but it'll be in the morning. I was hoping to get some of the work out tonight. Maybe I still can. If you will give me that retainer, I'll write you out a receipt on my napkin or this legal paper, whichever you choose. You can ask for credit on the rest of my food because I'm going to work!" Martin happily obliged and John was on his way. Martin called over the waiter and asked for a double Scotch to toast his believed success. Tomorrow, he too would begin his own little private investigation.

Rain greeted the morning wakeup call from the front desk for Martin; likewise for John West. John scoured the Maxie neighborhood for clues. He posed as an insurance investigator, and he managed to meet all of the Maxies' neighborhood acquaintances; the rain became a friend at keeping most of the neighborhood at home. He was quite persuasive and he obtained almost all the information that Martin had asked for that was unobtainable without his computer and the needed Social Security and driver's license numbers. His secretary back at the office was handling that part of the investigation. When John arrived back at the office late in the afternoon, his secretary greeted him with the news that she was confident she would acquire the information desired. Not only had she generated both of the subjects' Social Security and drivers' license numbers, she had also proceeded with other pertinent info on the case. She had printouts of all their telephone calls for the last three months – not just their mobile numbers which were easy to get, but their household calls as well. She expected to get Mr. Maxie's business calls before the day was over. She had typed out a summary sheet on the case that included the Maxies confidential insurance file (both life and casualty), their credit-card billings for the last three months, their utility bills, and when paid, their last income tax (filed two years ago), a copy of the grand jury's indictment against Mr. Maxie, copies of his recent bar and restaurant bills, his company's last quarterly payroll filing, and tax records for the subject's ownership of houses, cars, boats, a plane, etc.

The local newspapers were sending all copies of any articles or quotes from Mr. Maxie during the last year. "Good work, Dottie," John said. "Mr. Smith and I appreciate your diligence. Remind me to give you a bonus."

"Mr. West, I don't need any motivation for busting that sorry son-of-a-bitch's ass. Don't forget, I read the newspapers too, and I have a friend that knows one of his dancers. She says he is a real shit."

John was quite attentive, and then he said, "Dottie, we are working for an out-of-town client that demands secrecy of the highest regard. I know you'll be careful, but just because you hate this bastard so much, I better warn you. I'm going to need a lot of info from your sources before this is over, so watch your step! What have you found out about the subject's family?"

"There's not much there, boss," Dottie answered. "There are no kids, the Mr. has some family, but they're scattered all over hell. The Mrs. seems far more legit. She evidently met him at a city fundraiser, they had a short romance, he promised her everything, and she jumped. They are both Catholics, so a divorce, or the like, is much more difficult. Her parents are from Ft. Worth. They both teach at Texas Christian University. She has one brother, and I haven't been able to find anything on him except that he was in the army, may still be."

Martin awoke with a slight hangover from the three double Scotches that he had had after meeting with John West. He took a hot shower, downed a few antacid pills, and made himself a cup of coffee. The *Dallas Morning News* was delivered to his door and he began to catch up on the local news. There was nothing within on Mr. or Mrs. Maxie. He had already decided to wait until eleven o'clock to call Betty, the secretary for the gun and camera club of Dallas. By ten thirty, Martin was feeling like a new man and he decided to rush his contact with Betty a bit. "Hello, Betty, this is Martin Smith from Houston and all points beyond. I'm in love with your voice, your body, and your mother, will you trust me for lunch?"

"You are a crazy man, Mr. Smith. I already have plans; a girl in the office right under me. She works for British Airways, and we've promised each other for weeks that we'd get together."

"Good show, Betty; I'll just take the both of you to lunch. I'm sure I either owe British Airways something or they owe me, but it doesn't matter. I'll pick up the check, and I'll admit that I owe them, but only if the two of you will accept my invitation."

Betty laughed and replied, "Give me a few minutes to call her; what's your number so I can call you right back."

Martin wanted to give her his number anyway, so the sooner the better, he thought. He did. Both hung up, and Martin began to get dressed.

Martin's hotel room phone rang in exactly six minutes. Betty said, "You've got a date; or I should say, you've got two dates. I'll have to be the chaperon because I'm taken, but she is really cute. You better be on your best behavior."

"Say, what do you mean you're taken?"

"Martin, I told you the last time you called that I was seeing a guy on a pretty steady basis."

"Oh, thank God, I thought it was something serious to worry about. I'm in from out of town and steadies don't count when I come to town! You will always be fair game to me until you're wearing that little gold band, and then I might kill myself."

"Martin, you're out of it! My girlfriend's name is Diane, like Lady Di from London. It fits, doesn't it? With B/A and so."

"Where would you two like to dine? And don't give me that one-hour-lunch-limit business."

"We both like Cafe Pacific in the Highland Park Village."

Martin acknowledged with, "Fine, it's one of my favorites as well. Should I pick the two of you up or shall we just meet there? Remember, it's raining."

"We have underground parking, Martin, so I think we will just meet you there. Noon, okay?" "See you there, Betty."

Martin did not want to be late and he wanted to choose the table. He looked up the telephone number for Cafe Pacific and called for reservations.

"I'm sorry, we don't take reservations for lunch. Because of the rain, I doubt that you'll have any trouble, besides, we have a lovely bar." Martin didn't bother to reply. He absentmindedly slammed down the phone and began his rush to beat the crowd. Forty minutes later, he had the table he wanted and had already ordered his first drink. His wallet was thirty dollars lighter however. The girls arrived on schedule and were obviously excited at having a free lunch at such a fancy restaurant, the home of many restaurant settings for the episodes on the TV sitcom *Dallas*. After Betty made the proper introductions and after Martin made his usual mannerly compliments on the girl's good looks and after he properly seated them at his choice table, the conversation about Martin's being in town became the number-one topic. Right away, Martin inquired of Betty in front of Diane about what, if anything, had happened with the Maxies. "Judging from your past comments about them, Betty, and being that you and Diane are such good friends, I'm sure neither of you will mind discussing a little business. I would imagine that Diane shares your feelings about your town's number one womanizer. Huh?" Both girls were now sipping nonstop at their Ramos Gin Fizzes, but each came up for a breath and to nod their approval for a little business talk. "Any new dirt?"

Betty looked at Diane, and then answered, "Nothing new that I've heard about. How about you, Diane?"

Diane shied away from any involvement by quickly stating, "It's really none of my business, but I am sure that I know a lot less than Betty about those people. I just read about them in the papers like everyone else."

Martin came quickly to the rescue of the conversation. "Betty, has Lou shown any interest in booking any more hunts?"

Betty shook her head. "No."

"Well then, I guess we've got the business part out of the way," Martin said while passing out the menus.

The lunch lasted well over an hour. No more business was discussed, and surprisingly, Martin made no advances toward either girl. When lunch was finally over, Martin tipped the valet for both cars and returned to the hotel.

Martin decided to try his newly hired investigator at his office to see if he might have stumbled on something. It was about four o'clock. Dottie, the secretary, answered. Martin asked for John West, but Dottie told him that he was presently out of the office. When Martin left his name for call-back purposes, Dottie decided to jump the gun and give Martin some information. "Mr. Smith, I've been working on your case all day and so has Mr. West. We've struck pay dirt, I believe. I'm processing your case report for Mr. West now, and I just talked to him a few minutes ago. He seemed pleased with his part of the investigation. That's all I can tell you over the phone, but you're welcome to come by the office. I expect Mr. West within the hour."

It was now Martin's turn, "What did you say your name was?"

"Dottie."

"Well, Dottie, you are very nice to share your findings with me so soon; I really appreciate it very much. Just tell John that I called. If he needs me, I'll be at the hotel most of the evening, just give me a ring."

Martin was out of his room for dinner when John West called, so a message was left with the hotel operator for Martin to meet him at his office at ten o'clock the next morning.

Martin was always punctual and he was on time at John West's office. John filled Martin in on all of the investigation and gave him copies of the case report that Dottie had finalized. There was some "juicy" stuff in there, but he knew he would have to be judicious in using it. Martin asked if John needed any more money, and John said that it could wait until he got a little more information for him, probably tomorrow. Martin offered to take John and Dottie to lunch, but they refused. They simply had too much to do.

Martin arrived back at the hotel around 1:30 p.m. *It was now time to fish or cut bait,* Martin thought. The call that he was going to have to make wasn't going to get any easier by waiting. He had thought about what he was going to say at some time during every waking hour since he was last in Houston. Does he play it coy? Meet her in person? Pretend he is someone else and get to the safari channel another way? Or does he look for an opening in the first call, sense her needs, and hint of a fulfillment? Mrs. Maxie's unlisted telephone number was on the report that John had given him.

When the polite female voice answered, Martin said, "Mrs. Maxie, my name is Martin Smith. I am with Hunters, Ltd. out of Houston and Botswana, and I just tried to call your husband at his work, but I had no luck. I'm in town for next week's gun and camera club meeting, and I wonder if I might talk to you a few minutes about one of our special offers?"

"Mr. Smith," replied Mrs. Maxie, "what is it that you would like to talk to me about?"

"Mrs. Maxie, I am in town to book safaris for next year and I was told that Mr. Maxie might be interested in our company."

Mrs. Maxie interrupted, "That well may be, but I'm afraid you must talk to Lou about that."

"Please wait, Mrs. Maxie, I have a few clients whose wives actually book safaris for their husbands as a gift, birthday or something like that, and some secret mutual friend suggested that I might talk to you about such a 'gift' safari. It would give me great deal of pleasure to talk with you about such an arrangement."

"Mr. Smith, I do not wish to be rude, but I'm rather busy, and I don't think that now is the time for Lou or me to think about safaris. I am surprised that anyone that knows either of us would suggest such a thing. I'm not letting the cat-out-of-the-bag to suggest that anyone that knows anything about us knows we are going through some rather troubled waters presently."

"I appreciate your circumstances, Mrs. Maxie, and I try very hard to do my due-diligence on all of our clientele prior to any booking, but my friend tells me that your husband is truly trying to arrange an African safari, and he has stated that he is definitely going to Africa this year to hunt all sorts of dangerous game. I understand that everyone at the gun and camera club knows his intentions. Please understand that the safari business is my business, and I make my living through these types of referrals."

"Mr. Smith, I do know that we plan to attend the gun and camera club meeting next week because I personally sent in our reservations; couldn't we talk there? I am really quite bored with most of the people there anyway and you might give me a break in my boredom."

"Well, Mrs. Maxie, you are a toughie. I guess you give me no choice. Without stating anything but the best intentions of our mutual friend, I have learned a lot about your wonderful dedication to various charities, your classic demeanor in difficult circumstances, and to be honest, your less than rewards for all of these from one that should be your closest ally."

"Excuse me for butting in, but I think you already know too much about me. Again, I am terribly busy at the moment, and unless you can end this conversation immediately and civilly, I think that I would be a fool to encounter you at some safari get-together."

"You are exactly right, Mrs. Maxie. I don't often make a fool of myself. I was just so eager to meet and talk to you. Please, please forgive my forthrightness, my rudeness, and my apparent bullying. When you do meet me, you'll see that I have really been out of character."

"You are really very kind to be so interested in me, but it's my husband who's the hunter. I don't think that I would enjoy seeing an animal shot by Mr. Macho with some high-powered gun that has a scope so powerful that one cannot miss. Since it appears that you know so much about my husband and his intentions, please discuss this with him. I have so many problems of my own at present that I can't worry about my husband's doings."

"Mrs. Maxie, you have been the one that has been so kind to have talked with me this long. I represent a twenty-year-old company with a sterling reputation that I have sullied. Nevertheless, my intentions remain to try and meet you and talk to you in person. If you do not know of my company, please check us out on the web or through the Dallas Gun and Camera Club. I don't want to catch you off guard for an instant, but my company is the one that you might have heard about this last hunting season. We lost a client to a charging lion. It made all sorts of headlines in all of the news because of an interview with the wife that happened to be on safari with her older husband – she told everyone that she was thrilled it happened. She also mentioned that she had been treated like a rotten apple throughout her marriage. That sounds terrible, I know. But you'll only be able to know why I am telling you this fact if you meet with me. I promise you I won't bite!"

There was a protracted pause and Martin was thoroughly exasperated at what he had just mentioned.

"Mrs. Maxie, are you there?"

"Yes, I was just thinking. I have not heard of such a tragedy. I feel sorry for the wife."

"Well, again I thank you for your time; if you change your mind, please call me at my hotel, the Adolphus. My room is listed under Martin Smith and my company, Hunters, Ltd. Thank you again for hearing me out and I apologize again if I have made you in any way uncomfortable. I hope I haven't ruined your day. Please let me have the opportunity to make amends. I look forward to seeing you at the gun and camera club meeting next week. I'll be on my best behavior, I promise. Good-bye, Mrs. Maxie."

This time, Martin gently replaced the receiver on its cradle without even hearing whether Mrs. Maxie had said good-bye or not. Martin didn't know where to turn now. He felt that, under the circumstances, he had done very well for an introductory conversation but he had a rather sick feeling about being able to go any further. This job was going to be much harder than he had envisioned. His delusions of grandeur were crashing to earth with reality.

Sally had been standing while she was engaged in conversation with Martin. After the call was disconnected, she dropped like a wounded duck into the soft wingback chair that sat next to the telephone extension. She put her head back and began to think. Her imagination was running wild. "Was this Englishman for real? His accent certainly was. Did he mention that lousy husband's accident on purpose? If so, how could he be so brazen as to call me at home with such a teaser? Does he really work for a reputable outfit in Africa? How did he seem to know so much about me? I understand how he would know about Lou's hunting desires but he seemed to know everything about me. How? Do I really have a mutual friend with this guy? I forgot to ask who it was! Is he asking me if I want my husband killed? Maybe like that safari he was telling me about? God, is this a godsend to get out of this mess? Be calm; think of the consequences. Dad always said, 'think of the downside of any situation.' My charity work. My church. My respectful neighbors and friends. My family. Let's get some answers."

Sally raced into Lou's home office to find a phone number to verify this new mystery man in her life, Martin Smith. *Shazzam!* She was staring right at the written invitation to the next gun and camera club's meeting and their RSVP telephone number, 214/662-HUNT. "Was this another subtle hint from some ghost or something to inquire more about this thing? Am I correctly reading that there is such an off-the-wall offering?" Sally dialed the number. "Oops, I remember doing this same thing several days ago to confirm our attending the same meeting."

Betty answered the phone on the second ring. "Good afternoon, Gun and Camera Club."

Sally stumbled a split second and said, "Please forgive me, but I cannot remember whether or not I have confirmed my husband's and my attendance for your next meeting. My name is Sally Maxie."

Betty quickly responded, "Mrs. Maxie, I seem to remember your call; just let me check our confirmation sheet."

After a short pause, Betty said that indeed they were confirmed as going to be in attendance.

This gave Sally the much-needed time to think as to how she could find out if Martin is for real. "What is the program? I do hope there's going to be a program." Betty said that there was and told Sally that it was of African interest. Sally then asked who was putting on the program.

Betty told her but the names had no resemblance to Martin or his Hunters something-or-other company.

Sally was beginning to sink. "One last question, my husband is interested in going to Africa; will there be anyone there that will be able to enlighten us – him – on an African safari?"

Betty was trying to put two and two together. After all, she had just met with Martin, and his topic of interest had been Lou Maxie! Betty didn't believe in coincidences so she figured that now was the time she could help Martin. "Mrs. Maxie, there are so many good outfitters in Africa. Mind you, I have never been there, but I deal with their representatives almost every day; and I also deal with some of their complaints. I think you are in luck if you are going to the next meeting. There is a gentleman who is in town even as we talk who will be at the meeting. In fact, he will have a small part of our program. His name is Martin Smith, and his company is Hunters, Ltd., out of Houston, England, and Botswana. He is the best; and although his company is small, they give the personal attention that onesies and twosies really like. If you would like to contact him before the meeting so he would be expecting to see you, I can try to get his number for you if you would like. I think he is in one of the downtown hotels."

Sally's sunken feeling of a few minutes ago was gone. "I don't think I would feel comfortable calling a stranger at his hotel, but I appreciate the information. Lou and I will certainly look for him at the meeting. Thank you very much for your help."

As Betty hung up, she smiled at Sally's interest.

Sally had enough information to make her mind race with questions again. Was she being set up? Even the receptionist at the gun and camera club was in on this fiasco. Sally felt she had answered the ones about Martin and his company's authenticity. She had even gotten a good recommendation from someone that really counted. Why did Martin call her home in the first place, and why did he intentionally mention that husband's death? And the news about the wife's ordeal? Shouldn't he want to keep that quiet? She tried to clear her head and organize her thoughts. *Don't get in ahead of yourself. Piece this thing together one piece at a time. Martin surely didn't come to Dallas just to see her. He was on a legitimate business trip. If Betty knew him so well, he had to have been here many times before and he had to be doing business with Dallas clients. Obviously some of them told Martin about Lou's desire to go to Africa and Lou's and my troubles. Could he be an IRS plant? No, he was a foreigner. He had an unrehearsed accent, and he was a businessman with longtime credentials. Could he be working part-time for another government agency? No, same reasons. His livelihood depends on booking business, he admitted that. We shouldn't even be likely candidates for a safari considering our well-publicized problems. Maybe one of his clients put him onto us anyway. A mutual friend? Who? And why did he mention the lion kill of the husband? Why? There could be no downside risks if she didn't commit to something. She had to find out!*

After about forty-five minutes of lying on the bed, reading the paper, and thinking, Martin went over to the minibar to get a Coke when the phone rang. God, he hoped it was Sally Maxie but he knew it was John or his Houston office. "Hello."

"Mr. Smith?" It was a female and it sounded like Sally. "This is Sally Maxie, I had to go to the grocery store after I talked to you, and I've been thinking about your idea of a safari; maybe we should talk."

Martin could have been pushed over with a feather. "Certainly, Sally – may I call you Sally?"

"Certainly," she replied.

"I'm fairly knowledgeable about the Dallas area and of course I'm here with my company car, so you pick the site."

"How about ten in the morning at the lobby of the Hilton Hotel on Mockingbird Lane, just off the old Carpenter Freeway? I'll be wearing a blue suit and I have frosted hair – kinda short."

"The hair or your height? Just kidding, Sally."

"Both," she said with an obvious smile that Martin could not see. "I'll see you there."

The call was ended in the whispered tones of a normal disconnect. Perfect!

Quickly, Martin looked for John West's number and hurriedly dialed. John answered the office phone himself. "West Investigative Services."

"John, I've got a fish on the line. I'm meeting Sally in the morning at the lobby of the Hilton Hotel on Mockingbird Lane. Do you know the place?"

"Sure. What do you want me to do?"

"I need you to be there at least a half an hour early. I want you to make sure that she is not followed. I want you to stay behind the scenes while we're there and then I want you to follow her the rest of the day. You do have a cell phone, don't you?"

"Yep."

"I'll go immediately back to my hotel after our meeting. I want you to call me every hour until she beds down tomorrow night, okay?"

"Martin, I told you when we first met that everyone with a license was following the Maxies – maybe even some very undesirables. I don't know why you're going to talk with her, it doesn't seem to fit in the plan that you hired me for, but that's none of my business. You'll have to forgive my incessant hunches that go along with being in my kind of business so long. If things don't exactly line up, I'm trained to have a hunch. When all of this is over, I'll tell you what my hunch is for your wanting to see Mrs. Sally."

"John, it'll be interesting to hear your hunch on this one but I assure you that all I'm doing is protecting my company and our industry from unethical clients. I must confess, however, knowing what I know now about Sally's husband, I would sure like to help her. Although I have not met her in person, she surely doesn't deserve a man like Lou. And don't forget that I'm single. She might be an interesting mate if she got an unusually high divorce settlement, *ha, ha*! Just kidding, you know? By the way, your job is far from over. you've got to trust me that I'm doing the right thing. I'm not doing anything illegal! Please just continue to do as I ask and keep finding out all the information that you can on both of our subjects. You'll be well paid!"

"I figure that I'll get my money, but I want to know all of the details that I am entitled to know when I'm on a job. In my business, surprises are things we try to avoid."

"I'll fill you in, in time, John, nothing has really changed. I'm still trying to protect my company, but I'm also trying to book a hunt or two along the way. Hopefully, we'll recognize each other in the morning. Let's not blow our cover. See you at ten. Good-bye."

Martin was so happy that he didn't know what to do. If the plan continued to take shape, he and Rob and Jon-Keith were on the road to being set for life! He was so proud of himself. Rather than make a fool out of himself when he was in such a great mood, he decided to unwind at a movie across the street from the hotel. After the movie, he dined again in the casual dining room of the hotel, had a couple of drinks, and retired with eyes wide open.

Again Martin was better than Mr. Punctual at his meeting with Sally. He cased the place before her arrival, and then sat down in one of two chairs that faced each other in the darkest corner of the lobby. He had already picked up a newspaper and a fresh cup of coffee to bide the time if Sally was late. *Society women are always late*, he thought. At precisely ten o'clock, in walked Sally. Short hair she had, but it fit her perfectly. She wore an everyday dress, but it was clinging and it was stylish. She had an absolutely stunning figure for her age, nothing eye-catching on an individual note, but all packaged to perfection. Despite her had-to-be discomfort walking into a strange hotel lobby unescorted, she managed a delightful smile from the time she came through the door. Her jewelry was smart and high-class, but it was not ostentatious or gaudy. The scarf around her neck was fitting to tie her whole ensemble to the casual-but-elegant look. She wore makeup, but it wasn't noticeable. She was one of those fortunate females that hadn't lived her life always begging for more sun. Her skin and complexion were magazine quality. Martin was a "leg man," and from what Martin could see, Sally was nearly a ten in that department. It was obvious to Martin that Lou knew his women well and he had chosen a thoroughbred in Sally.

Martin peered over his morning paper to again case the situation. She appeared to be alone, and it was comforting to see John West not too far behind her. When she was looking around for a clue as to Martin's whereabouts and not looking in Martin's direction, John slyly gave Martin the thumbs-up sign and John walked out of sight. Martin rose in a casual fashion and walked over to meet her. With a broad smile that exuded confidence, Martin greeted her, "Mrs. Sally Maxie, I presume."

Sally was pleased to hear the English accent again. "That's right, Mr. Smith." And after a short pause, she added, "I presume." Then she extended her hand. In typical English fashion, Martin held on to her hand as he asked her if she was comfortable there. She replied that she was.

Martin then pointed over to the vacant table and two chairs that still housed his slightly smoking coffee and folded-up newspaper. Martin put his hand lightly on Sally's back and ushered her toward the prescribed sitting area. There was no one within twenty feet of them and it was unlikely that anyone would spoil their quiet little chat when there were other more comfortable and better-arranged chairs to be had.

It was evident that Sally was a woman of few words and liked to get straight to the point. Before another cup of coffee could be ordered and just after Sally was comfortably seated, she looked Martin straight in the eyes, and said, "Mr. Smith, I don't know why I should trust you; I certainly don't know you. And I don't know where you've gotten your information. But I think that you have correctly ascertained that I am a very unhappy person in my marriage; that my marriage is in fact in shambles and in all likelihood I'm about to undergo intense observations by the authorities. I think that you believe you have a way out of all this for me. Am I right? And for how much?"

"Jesus, Sally, you don't pull any punches, do you?"

"I don't have time to pull punches; I'm about at my wit's end now. I have options and I do want to do something soon. My concern is that I pick the right option. I would rather die than ruin all of the good things that I've accomplished in my charity work. And more than anything, I want to continue that work. There is so much more that needs to be done. However, the circumstances that are present in my home life are almost intolerable and they make my concentration on other more important things miserable."

"Okay, you better let me have the floor. My participation in your next gun and camera club meeting is legitimate. I am here on honest business. Since I've been here, however, I've been told by an anonymous acquaintance of yours, a former client, just how bad life has been for you the last few years. I do my homework. My research told me that your husband was looking for an outfitter to take him on safari, and I did a cursory investigation of him so that I would be in the best position to sell him on my company. During that investigation, it was pointed out to me that he was somewhat of a not-yet-proven scoundrel of sorts, and you were the unhappy recipient of his shenanigans. I've also been told how his indiscretions have absolutely affected you and your friends. I think I've been able to put two and two together.

"I happened to be in camp on the safari when Mr. B. F. Clark of San Antonio was killed. I was not actually on the specific hunt, but I was in the camp." Martin then paused for an inordinate length of time. Sally then rolled her hands in a manner to ask Martin to continue. "What I mentioned to you over the phone was a description of a controlled accident." Again Martin paused for a lengthy amount of time. "You are the only person other than the professional hunter who orchestrated the situation, me, and of course the wife who knows what really happened. She was terribly abused, at least that's true from all the factual information that I now know. After the accident, she inherited a great deal of money and all their community property. She's the happiest person in the world right now, living in London. And if I am not jumping the gun too much, I believe that you could be the second happiest person in the world if something similar would transpire.

"I don't want my story to come off as something that happens every day, it doesn't. But I'm in a business that offers an unusual solution for relationships that are irreparable and unbreakable because one person is being such a tyrant that he – or she, for that matter – is causing the other person constant misery from which he or she cannot escape by any other means. This is not a murder-for-hire scenario. It is a carefully constructed scene in the world of hunting that puts a knowledgeable paying client in a predictable but unusual situation of risk. The client can do all of the right things and extract himself, but the time to do so is extremely short and all the right moves must be made. It would be highly unlikely for a nonprofessional hunter to be able to escape. Because I think that I know your situation and I know it demands unusual remedies to solve, please listen to the rest of my story.

"Let me be brief so that I do not expose too many details at this time. If you are truly interested, I will initially cover your obligations to make this plan a reality."

Sally nodded her intent in continuing.

"As for cost, you and I will have to analyze your financial situation and see what you can afford. I assure you that the cost will be only a fraction of what you will eventually receive. I will require an oral agreement that neither of us can rescind, yet one that will benefit us both considerably; there will never be anything in writing. We will have certain rules by which we both must abide and all money transfers to effect this operation will be untraceable to a numbered account in Switzerland, except the actual safari part, and that must be paid to Hunters, Ltd. like any other safari. After the controlled accident – and I say 'controlled accident' because I know of no better description – you will be required to live the next part of your life in Europe, at least five years. And you must facilitate this within two to three months after your husband's funeral. Of course this is a flexible time limit designed to get you your best values for whatever you decide to sell – your house, your business, etc. We need to sit down together for about four or five hours and discuss the balance of this agreement if you are serious about my plan. The details have worked before, and they will work again, as long as both parties are loyal to each other and abide by all of the agreed-to rules and stipulations. The most important of which is a code of secrecy and silence to everyone but you and me.

"I will be here through your husband's club-meeting date and then I must return to my company's headquarters in Houston. I must mention, my company knows nothing of this sort of thing – the old happenings or the new. No one else will know of our plans until I pick the professional hunter to carry out our task, an old and trusted friend. I assure you – and myself, I might add – that he will be extremely trustworthy. His future will also be on the line. He will of course be paid handsomely for the possible tainting of his reputation as a professional hunter when one of his clients meets with an accidental disaster in the bush. I will handle his compensation, and you will probably never meet him unless you choose to go along on the safari. Now, if I have not already scared you off, then when is the best time for you and me to meet? I am at your service."

With her voice cracking from obvious concern, Sally Maxie began to speak. "I had no idea. Really, I had no idea." Sally was obviously dumbfounded but she yearned to know more and she had to know that there were outs to the plan if she got cold feet. "I am not making any commitment if we just talk. I didn't know that something like this could be an option, and I sure didn't know that it could be this complicated. You have my attention, but I don't know if I would ever be up to all of this."

"Sally, I know it seems a bit much now, but it won't in time; besides, all parties must be and will be protected. Believe it or not, this little plan has been done well over fifteen or twenty times that I am aware of. It's as fool proof as anything in the world. It's really a win-win situation for everyone except the guy that deserves what he is about to get. Neither I nor my professional hunters that work for me are hired killers – we will shoot no one. We will merely set up a situation that will be very dangerous for your intended. It will be so tough that even a highly trained professional would likely not be able to avoid succumbing to it. The probability of death is nearly 100 percent, and yet no one will even raise a question of it being other than an accident. The country in Africa where the stage will be set certainly doesn't want to uncover or publicize something that would hurt their precious tourism. My company will not investigate because I am the person in charge, and even if I weren't, they would shy away from this type of publicity all that they could – again, bad for business. The U.S. has no authority over there, so there can only be two movants that would be eligible to ask for an investigation. You would be one as a wife or next of kin, and a life-insurance company could be the other if the life policy in question was less than two years old, before the two-year incontestability clause has run its course for suicides, or for just general principles to delay the beneficiary's funding. They might have an interest to investigate for suicide. But this is certainly not a suicide case. Just think about it, there will be only two people in the bush at the time of the accident and only one will come out unscathed, and he would be part of the plan. How could they ever hope to reverse the finding that the death was an accident? From start to finish, only three people will be involved and all three will have been well paid – you, me, and the professional hunter. Other than answering questions from me, and making sure that you don't do anything that is traceable or linked to me or the accident, you have no job to do. You simply must just be careful. You may or may not wish to accompany your husband on this hunt; we have no objections either way. Now, that's enough. When do we meet again?"

"Martin, my apologies. I do not think I could do it. There is no way I could ever be a part of such a complicated plan. I would constantly be a nervous wreck in worrying about every detail. Secondly, I'm a religious woman who could never live with myself knowing that I had a part in killing someone, regardless of how I feel about the person, or the way it was done." Sally suddenly had a terrible thought. *My god, you are not recording this conversation, are you?*

"Heavens no, Sally. Believe me, I know where you are coming from. From all of my investigations, you are an exemplary wife, a true churchgoer, and a dedicated servant to charity. All these traits are noble. But where is there a life or a future for you and those noble deeds? How will those noble deeds continue? You could continue everything good that you do now if we implement this plan and you could do it better with a lot more money and no threat of an investigation hanging over your head for some illegal activity that your husband has done and you had no part of. The thought of being involved in a plan like this is bound to be uncomfortable. Let me see if I can make any sense of your actions if you decide to join me. First, you are strikingly beautiful but you are not getting any younger. Of course, this fact hinges on whether you might ever look again for a mate. It would indeed be unfortunate for you not to give a decent marriage a chance. I dare say, if your parents knew as much about your husband's problems and how they affect you as I do, they would vote overwhelmingly for you to take my offer. Secondly, you must somehow dodge your involvement in your husband's illegalities or you just might end up with some criminal record yourself, maybe even jail time, or certainly probation. I think my plan is your perfect out. Thirdly, I see no way short of an unexpected acquittal of your husband for you to end up with any money. You cannot stay involved with all of your charities, etc., if you have to go to work to support yourself. Sure, a divorce is the state's recommended way of calling it quits, but in your case, you will only get a piece of paper. And it will take years of tears and second guessing with nothing to show for it. You'll have nothing left of what you've truly earned. Fourthly, your husband is a well-known womanizer of the first degree, and he has set his and your life up solely for his own benefit. You must do something to get out of your marriage and you must do it soon. He's not going to change and things in general are going to get a lot worse. At least meet with me, discuss it some more; think about your future and think about how much good you could do for the rest of the world if you were without the burden of your no-good husband and if you had the funds to make a difference. If it is meant to be that he escapes this dangerous situation, then so be it. I refund everything. But if he is in fact killed – and quickly I might add, animals pride themselves over a quick kill – you will have no more to do with it than the scenario of renewing his car tag prior to a deadly automobile accident." Martin now figured he had better stop for fear of over-selling.

It seemed like an hour to Martin before Sally finally got the frog out of her throat and replied, "I bank right across the street from your hotel," Sally answered in almost a whisper. "I'll be at your room door at exactly ten in the morning, just as today."

"Okay, that makes me extremely happy. Just make sure that you are not followed, and that you have legitimate business being downtown. Think of a good reason for being here if something were to go amiss. I'm not trying to scare you, but we must get into the habit of contingent plans in case our first plans take a dirt road. I look forward to seeing you tomorrow. Have a good day and remember that I am truly in your corner. Despite my profiting from all of this – and heaven knows I need the money – I promise you that if push came to shove, I would set this thing up for nothing just to get your life back. You are an asset to this world and this plan is the only avenue left for you to continue being that wonderful asset."

The two of them rose together and each stared into the other's eyes. A bond of trust had already been cemented. Martin remained at the table as Sally walked across the lobby to the door. As she exited, she turned back to Martin and gave him a short one-swoop wave. John West was a few steps behind, carefully mingling in with the next group that was leaving the hotel.

Martin relaxed for the rest of the day in his hotel room while hoping that Sally would finally see the light. He was proud of his sales pitch and he gauged his hope for Sally's okay at over 50 percent. To break up the monotony of rest, he occasionally managed to scribble some notes on a legal pad that he got from John West the day earlier. He would later use these notes to guarantee that he had covered everything with Sally the next morning. John called pretty much on the hour, as he was instructed. He found nothing questionable or unusual about Sally's day, the places she visited, etc. John dismissed himself from his following act at nine o'clock when most of the lights in the Maxie house went out and it appeared that Sally had settled in for the night.

Martin did quiz himself about Sally's idea to meet him in his hotel room. Was she just trying to be secluded? Did she want to check out the authenticity of his being at the Adolphus? Or was she hell bent for a sexual encounter? He had to be ready for all scenarios, and despite Sally's attractiveness, he had to get those sexual fascinations out of his head.

Martin had his room cleaned early the next morning, courtesy of the well-paid concierge. He had a pot of coffee, hot tea, and two china cups and saucers waiting for an owner. He placed a newspaper clipping from the Johannesburg paper on the table that told of old BF's "accident," and then he put out a few of his company brochures that made a safari with his company look like a trip to fantasy land. He took care to put his own personal photo album of recent hunts on display within easy reach to heighten his own respectability. As a final touch, he was dressed in a casual khaki bush outfit with all of the safari accouterments.

Martin was impressed that Sally called from a house phone to make sure that the party she was about to meet was where he was supposed to be. The extremely light knock on the door signaled Sally's arrival at five past ten. Sally was again in casual attire, but she was equally as stunning today as she was yesterday. Martin never offered his hand to a lady until she first offered hers. Sally did exactly this. While Martin held her hand warmly and gently, he oozed the sincerity that had made him famous within his own business circles. His smile brought reassurances to Sally that she had missed for many years.

"I'm so glad you are here. We have a lot to discuss and I want you to be as comfortable as possible. Before we get into the heavy legal ease, I would like to answer any questions you might have about me or my company, or about the continent of Africa. Let's sit and have a cup of coffee or tea. What shall it be?"

Sally chose coffee while the British-educated Martin opted for his heritage, tea.

"Sally, I've got an idea; I need to run down to the lobby to fetch my mail, so why don't you peruse the photo album, the newspaper clipping, and our newest brochure on camp life, and I'll be back in a minute. I'll be just a few moments."

Sally was a little quizzical at such a departure, but it gave her time to let her heart rate return to a normal beat and it really did give her a chance to mull through some interesting material. She chose the newspaper article first.

Martin returned shortly in less than ten minutes with another soft knock on the door. He then used his key to open the door before Sally could accommodate. Sally had remained seated when he entered. *Was she still scared?* Martin thought. He wanted her to relax and he had to make the right moves to orchestrate it. "Sally, you are such a beautiful woman, I cannot imagine anyone not treating you like royalty. When you get to Europe, that is exactly what you can expect. Got any questions about the pictures or articles?"

"I do have a few. The camps look spacious and clean, but I don't see inside the tents. Are they the same way and are they comfortable?"

"You bet. The beds are innersprings. There is a hooked rug that covers 90 percent of the tent floor, and there are private reading lanterns on a bedside table at the head of each bed. There is a dirty-clothes basket and luggage racks for two suitcases per bed. You can see the outside of the tents in the pictures. Notice each tent has an insulating top tent on top of the main one that ensures a cool afternoon nap area. Under the veranda at the front door of the tents is a dressing table complete with a lighted makeup mirror and distilled water for drinking or brushing your teeth. In back of each client's tent is a toilet tent with an open ceiling and a real toilet seat mounted on a fifty-five gallon hollow drum that sits over a ten-foot-deep hole. Also in the back area of the client's tent is another tent of the same size, but it is equipped for taking a shower. There is an old Coca-Cola wooden box crate that is upside-down for the client to stand on and there is a shower head attached to a bucket that is hung at just the right height for each client. A small chain from the showerhead hangs down for the client to pull when he or she needs a rinse. The water is put in fresh and warm just before a client wants to use the shower. All you have to say is "majee moto." That's Swahili for hot water. The staff understands that you mean for the shower."

Sally again began thumbing through some of the pictures and folders.

"The animals look so close; isn't that a bit dangerous for the novice photographer?"

"Nope, the pictures that seem so close are probably taken with at least a two-hundred-millimeter lens that brings the subject up very close. No wild animal will let you get within fifty meters unless you are in a car. It will either run away, which is likely, or it will charge. Most of the animals are impervious to a vehicle within a park boundary, but out in the hunting areas, the animals treat the vehicle and its passengers as something suspicious and dangerous."

"I don't see any pictures that show any foul weather. It has got to rain over there. What do the animals do when it rains?"

"They get wet! And so do we and that is why we are not out taking pictures in the rain. Thank goodness it doesn't rain much in the early mornings and the late afternoons when game viewing is at its best."

"Well, can I reserve asking more questions later?"

"Certainly. In the mean time, if you don't have any more questions about safari life or me, then I have a few for you. Tell me about your family – I mean, *your* family, not Lou and his."

Martin listened intently to what he already knew. It was a short version, obviously designed to not include actual names. At the end, Sally asked Martin if she had left out anything that he thought might be important, so she was not really trying to hide anything. Satisfied that he got what he had asked for, Martin again asked her if she had any questions for him. There were none. She didn't even ask about his personal life; what a let down! She was obviously there for business, not sex. As attractive as she was,

Martin was pleased to know that she was now a serious player in his scheme. Sexual advances would have to wait, if they were ever to be tried at all.

Martin started off the conversation about the accident scheme in reverse order. Like a flashback book in reverse, he began by viewing Sally's life after she had settled down in Europe and then into what would probably happen on safari, and then what would have to be done to make it all come to fruition. Sally was attentive and Martin was thorough in going over all the plans and contingencies, just as he had been with Barbara Jones, except he didn't have to sell Barbara Jones; he did have to sell or convince Sally Maxie.

Sally seemed to understand everything quite well. She knew a lot about hunting by osmosis, even if she didn't approve of it. *Osmosis is a wonderful thing*, Martin thought. Life is going to seriously change for her and she now appeared up to it.

When Martin had finished, and when he had answered a few trivial questions regarding Sally's actual role, he suggested that Sally probably needed some time to think about making the real commitment. "There is just one final question I have to ask. If something in my life changes, and I can't imagine what that would be, to cause me to reconsider this whole thing, could I call it off?"

"Of course you can for any reason, Sally. Keep in mind that you would have already paid about 10 percent of the cost to me plus the safari and none of that could be returned because I would have had to secure our professional hunter and do other things that cost money. But it is your call right up to the moment the accident part of the plan is put into action. That might be a reason for you to accompany your husband on the safari."

"I don't think I could stomach myself being there when all of this happens. But I appreciate you giving me the option to cancel. The more I think of my present situation and what I could do with my life without my current distractions, the more I am sure that this is my out. I will forever be indebted to you, or I will hate you the rest of my life if something goes wrong!" Sally was dead serious.

Although there was nothing to sign, the oral agreement to go through with the entire plan was consummated. London, Sally's favorite European city in which to fantasize a new life was selected as her move site, and a similar plan for the disposal of her husband's assets as the one that Barbara Jones had chosen was likewise adopted for Sally. Lou was going to get a much-deserved vacation; a gift from his wife.

After a break for more coffee and tea, Martin now had to get specific about some of the details. Although Sally was to have the same payment for Martin's services as Barbara Jones', paying it was going to be much more complicated. Sally had no funds of her own and her bank account was used mainly to pay house bills and credit-card charges. They both had some work to do to figure out a way to handle the down payment. Martin had asked Sally to expound on what she knew about her husband's business, his lawyer, his accountant, and their personal-insurance agent. This was a tough order for Sally. She had been brought up knowing that talking about money was vain. She knew about her husband's business but she avoided talking about it with anybody. "If you know as much about me as you say, then you surely know about my husband's club business. His main income comes from owning the property and the building where that type of club exists. He has no part in the management. The reason he profits so much from the lease is that no one else would take such a risk in providing all of the niceties that the real owner of the club thinks are necessary.

"I think all of the property is worth somewhere around three million dollars. I understand that we make a million a year from our lease, but you cannot imagine all of the troubles that this lease brings to a relationship and I only receive barely enough money to run the house. If I ask for more, I am berated and looked upon with scorn. Maybe his expenses are as high as he says. If that is the case, then I don't know how we can afford giving him a safari."

Martin played along. He knew that the IRS was investigating because someone was skimming off the top. He also knew that Lou was the real brains behind the business end of the deal as well as the property; he just denied his operational part for personal reasons. His mere property ownership was really a front for the whole operation. Did Sally need to know this? He thought so.

"Sally, I'm afraid that my sources tell me that most of the tax investigations are from the belief that Lou is skimming cash off the books every night. He would have to be more than a property owner to do this, and you don't need to profit from such a ruse. I have done some investigating on his partner, his operations manager. He has yet to be indicted and that spells trouble. I'll be willing to bet that he has been offered some kind of immunity from prosecution, or he is setting up your husband for another reason. Maybe Lou is naive when it comes to his business partner. Whether any of this is true or not doesn't really matter. I just want you to know everything that I've heard, whether it's true or not. I know that you have already made up your mind about what you intend to do about your present situation; I do not need to fuel the fire. Let me ask you a couple of questions regarding your husband's activities and then we will get to the rest of my other questions. Does your husband stay out late at night?"

"Yes, every night that I am not with him."

"Does he always seem to have an abundance of cash, and would he rather spend that than charge something or write a check for it?"

"Yes to all of the above."

"Have you ever caught him in an affair?"

"No, but I expect that he has had a few and he is probably involved right now."

"Would you like for me to find out for you? I'd be very careful."

"I don't have any money to pay for such a thing. I went to a lawyer once, but when he saw that I had no chance of getting any money for him until I filed for divorce, he refused to take my case. If you will not expect an immediate payment, I would love to know the truth. Go ahead."

"Back to the earlier questions, are you friendly enough with your lawyer or accountant to get any information?"

"Absolutely not. Lou would know immediately, and he would probably have me killed."

"Does that mean that he is connected with the Mafia or something?"

"No, he would just have one of his goons that work for him do it."

"Sounds as if he has perfectly insulated himself from you. How about your personal insurance agent?"

"I don't think that would be a problem; we are in the same church, and I see him almost every Sunday. I could just ask him when I see him there. What do you want to know?"

"Ask him if all of your husband's policies are being paid currently, and try to find out what the limits are, the benefits, like accidental death, and with which company Lou is insured. There may be several policies. You need to know all of this anyway. You can tell the insurance guy that you are afraid of Lou's health with all of this adverse publicity."

"I'll get what you ask."

"Do you have any savings hidden away? Or would you feel comfortable in asking your family's help for the finances?"

"Double NO for both. My family didn't approve of my marrying the bastard – oh, please forgive my language, I am getting wrapped up in this too much to be civil. I absolutely cannot go to them with an admission of my mistake. I'd rather continue my life in torture than involve them."

"Sally, why don't you give the down payment money some thought; I have a few ideas of my own, but they will depend upon some more information that I expect to receive in a couple of days. Don't be alarmed or concerned that I'm in an information-gathering mode; I won't endanger our deal and I won't ever cause you any embarrassment. My work is cut out for me. You must find out all you can about just what you stand to inherit and the status of all your husband's insurance policies. We need to meet again in three days. That will give us another few of days to wind up our strategy before the gun and camera club meeting. In the meantime, if there is anything that I can do for you, or if you need me for anything, just call my hotel. Use the name of Betty instead of your own. Try to contact me at least once every night, including tonight. It is far less risky for you to call me than for me to call you. Your phones are probably bugged by someone, maybe even your own husband. We are clear so far; let's keep it that way."

The cordial handshake that started this meeting was substituted by a light kiss on the cheek.

5

Creative Financing

Martin issued a midafternoon invitation to his new friend, John West, for an evening out on the town. Dottie relayed the message to John and Martin received his confirmation of acceptance by telephone a few minutes later. They were to meet at Baxter's, the famous topless bar where the real estate was owned by Lou Maxie. John was to bring a photo for identification of Lou just in case they got lucky.

As expected, Martin was the first to arrive. As usual, he was European attired with Italian slacks, shirt, and shoes, but donning an obviously British sport coat with its usual hunting flare of leather patches on each sleeve at the elbow and a shoulder patch mimicking a pad for the shot-gunner. He asked the young lady with the push-up bra for a table for two and handed her a crisp new twenty-dollar bill that immediately went into hiding between her two mountains. He told her that he was from out of town and he had heard so much about the place that he had to come to see it for himself. He also asked her if she'd point out the owner and manager if they were present. She nodded in agreement but said neither was here at the moment, but she said that both were expected in later this evening. She said their names were Artie and Lou, and she really smiled when she said "Lou." Martin thought, *The damn guy can't keep his hand out of the till and he can't keep his peter out of the merchandise. The same would probably apply to Lou's manager.* John arrived a little late but had no trouble finding his client and neither did Martin. Despite the dim-lit room, Martin could pick out a well-worn ten-year-old suit and its manikin at almost any distance. They ordered drinks for starters and then planned to graduate to dinner and a desert menu of table-dances. Every time a waitress helped them, one of them would quiz her as to who she really worked for, how much she made each night, and if she was free for the evening. They're plan was to be somewhat inconspicuous, somewhat rowdy, and on an expense account. Martin told John that he desperately wanted to talk to Lou's manager. He told him that he suspected cooperation between the manager and the authorities because the manager had not yet been indicted. John agreed but he cautioned Martin on impersonating an officer or anything else illegal to gain his information.

There were at least ten cops in and around the place. Half were "rent-a-cops" and the other half were genuine city policemen. John excused himself for a few minutes to go to the bathroom and have a smoke. He returned after missing only one girl's stage dance.

"Martin, I found a policeman outside that used to do some work for me. I'm pretty sure of his loyalty to me even though he works a few nights a week here. He says that this place's days are numbered. He said that he likes the money he makes here, but he thinks both Lou and Artie, the manager, are crooks from way back. He seems embarrassed to be here. I asked about his wife and kids and then I slipped him a hundred – make sure you reimburse me. If I get too drunk, I'm holding you responsible for my reimbursements and my fees."

"Need not worry, my new buddy. You are wonderful and there will be no limit to my generosity."

After about an hour of watching hips and breasts bounce around on the stage, the policeman that knew John came by to introduce himself. He then asked to meet with John outside. To cover his exit, John asked the lone gentleman next to him for a cigarette and left for the door. Martin could see him lighting up just to the left of the double-glass entry doors. In a few moments, the policeman came over to John and they began to talk.

Their talking soon meandered out of sight and around the building. It was awhile before John returned. When he did, he was grinning from ear to ear. "I think we have struck pay dirt, big boy. Seems that my friend the 'fuzz' has just traded out with the regular policeman that closes things up around here. If things go true to form, the big bosses will be in shortly. They will be in the back office for about an hour and then they will each take their pick of the litter from the dancers and leave to more romantic spots. That is when the door opens for us. I will say I need a place for a very private telephone call. I am assured that you or me or we, can have at least an hour alone in their private office 'expecting a return long-distance phone call.' It's your call whether to have me with you in that office or have me follow one of the bosses to wherever he goes and let you know if trouble is brewing. Because of jeopardizing my license, I'd rather not be in that office alone."

After taking a few minutes to formulate a plan, Martin winked at John. "John, you are brilliant! But I've got another idea. Do you think that you could arrange for another two investigators to follow the bosses?"

"No, Martin, I work alone. Unfortunately, you cannot trust anyone in this business and I have plenty of scars to prove it." Both sat silently thinking about what was the best thing to do.

"Dottie!" John said. Then a long pause. "Dottie has been asking me for three years to let her try and follow someone for me and she always is in short supply of money. The idea this time is solid. If I can get in touch with her, she could wear something provocative and come here. There are a couple of broads in here already, so she could pass for a hustler. She would refuse any advances unless it was one of the bosses. If they didn't pick her for their fun times, then she could follow at least one of them. If she got caught, she would claim that she followed the guy because he hadn't picked her to go out with. You've seen her; I think she will stack up against all but a handful of the dancers, and she is much prettier than the strays that are in here now. Shall I try and give her a call?"

"You're damn right, John. Get on the horn 'pronto' – Martin had learned a little Spanish from his Mexican safari clients.

John returned from the outside phone booth in the parking lot. "We're in luck, she's on her way. I've already let our cop know to expect her. He remembers her from the times he came to my office to get paid. God, this is going to really cost you!"

Seven dancing girls performed their own special gyrating sex acts to music before another lone woman came through the glass front doors. "There she is, John. If the bosses don't show, I want a date with her!"

"Not on your life, Martin. I don't even get to handle that merchandise myself." John excused himself and headed for Dottie's table. He handed her a wadded up hundred-dollar bill for her expenses and then he returned to Martin. "It's getting dark outside now; I would bet that our big guys will soon be arriving."

John's forecast was the first thing that he had not correctly predicted. It was almost two full hours later when the two owners set their feet through the front door. They arrived within five minutes of each other. Artie, the manager, was the first to arrive, and he waited for Lou at a small back table before the two headed for the small back office. Artie sported an unbuttoned golf shirt and at least a size-48 pair of trousers to hide his obvious beer gut. Lou was much nicer dressed. He wore expensive slacks and shoes, an open-neck collared tan shirt and a silk sport coat. Lou had slicked-back hair while and Artie's hair looked like a bee's nest, unkempt for days. The office was obviously quite secluded. One had to pass through the entire kitchen to reach the door. The restrooms were located at the front of the building so there could be no snooping close to the office with an excuse that one got lost trying to find the head.

The two kingpins were in the office a little less than an hour. When they finally surfaced in the main entertainment area, both were smiling and both were obviously interested in meeting the new stock that was on display. Lou seemed to be the most careful. Although he did show an interest in Dottie when he finally noticed her, he opted for his private employee stock. Lou was the first of the two to move out, accompanied by the most beautiful gal there. She was draped all over him when the doorman opened the front door. Martin was so mesmerized with the events that he had not noticed that John was no longer at the table with him. Artie was now totally immersed in conversation with some gentlemen who were obviously his guests. There were three of them and they had five waitresses or dancers hanging all over them to supply their every need.

After about ten minutes, Martin became worried about the disappearance of his compadre. He went looking for him in the rest room but didn't find him. He then went outside to extend his search.

John was talking to his policeman friend and when he saw Martin, he motioned to him that he'd be inside in a minute.

The smirking grin that John had on his face when he returned to the table led Martin to immediately inquire, "What's so damn funny? I thought you left me."

"I should have. When I drink too much, and that is anything over one drink, I get to feeling invisible and then I start taking chances that otherwise would not be prudent. I did it again."

"What did you do, my friend, hustle more than you could handle?"

"Not quite. I had two tape recorders in my car that I use for secret recordings from time to time. I managed to get our police buddy to wear one while he escorted big Lou to his car with his new toy. I wore the other and I managed to follow them close enough to get some real juicy stuff on tape before I backed off and let Mr. Policeman take over."

"We were reviewing the tapes when you walked up. I didn't want him to know that you knew what I was doing. I can't let you hear them now, but I'll tell you that your pretty new friend Sally would give a million dollars for them if she wanted a divorce. Martin, we have been the luckiest duo in the world so far; I hope our horseshoes don't fall out of our asses."

"Speaking of luck, look over at Dottie's table right now."

"I'll be damned, my little secretary is about to charm the buns off Mr. Big-shot Bar Manager." Both ceased their conversation to devote their full attention to Dottie and her work. For about five minutes, Dottie and Artie talked in the company of one of Artie's friends. Then the friend was ushered off by one of the waitresses. In ten more minutes, Dottie was gathering her purse for a leave of absence with Mr. Got-rocks, the manager. John was up in a flash when he saw the two new love birds head for the door. In two minutes, John was back.

"Why did you follow them, John? Dottie will give us all the information we need from him. She probably has a recorder on, just like you and the cop."

"You are right on the last count, but I wanted to know that bastard's license number in case Dottie doesn't show back at the office in an hour or two; just a safety precaution. I've got to leave her a message on the office recorder since we are going office snooping in a little while. Please excuse me."

"You're a trip, pal. I'm sure glad you are on my side."

Martin and John had three more drinks and two more table dances before the crowd thinned out to less than ten customers. It was now 1:00 a.m. The bartender made the last call for alcohol. The top policeman came in from the parking lot and all of the lights came on. As if a fire alarm was sounded, all of the girls picked up their belongings and headed either for the dressing room or the door. The assistant manager all but frisked each one as she left the front entrance, either for hiding something stolen or just for his own pleasure. The back entrance was locked and barred. Soon, there was no one left in the house of lights except the assistant manager, the policeman, and Martin and John. The assistant manager came over to their table and politely told them that they would have to leave. Just as he was getting the last words out of his mouth, the policeman intervened and said that the two were his personal friends from out of town and in fact were his ride home. He asked the manager if they could stay until he secured the place and then he asked if it would be all right if Martin used the telephone in the office to make an overseas call, on his credit card, of course.

As the policeman knew, the assistant manager was always anxious to leave and if anyone would close up for him he would be very appreciative. The assistant gave a positive answer of "fine" to the call and the office use and left. The policeman stayed out front while Martin and John locked themselves in the office. John removed the telephone from its rest and dialed his office. There was no answer, so he held while the recorder advised him that no one was in. After this message, John punched in some numbers to activate his messages that had previously been left for him. There was only one and it was from Dottie. All she said was that she had the golden goose by the balls, that she was safe, and that she was going home. John smiled and set the receiver down without disconnecting the line.

"Dottie is okay; she evidently scored a hit with her companion. I don't want to disconnect the line, I want the red light to show if there are any other phones in the place. The extensions will show that we are on the phone. We are supposed to be making calls, so let's look like it."

"Look over there, Martin, a copying machine for our very own use, how kind of them. Look around for more copying paper. I want to leave the exact same amount of paper in the tray as when we got here. Take out the paper tray and remove the paper that's inside; we'll put it back when we leave, that way we can be sure of leaving the exact amount."

Martin shook his head negatively. "John, why don't you get the copy machine ready because I am the one who knows what we are looking for?"

Both men got to work. In thirty minutes, they had copied the last three months' receipts, the entire payroll record for the quarter, a supply list, a name and address book, and what looked like an informal partnership agreement. The safe was locked with the night's receipts already in it. "No use fiddling with that," John said. The two restored the place to as when they found it, wiped off any obvious finger prints except on the telephone, hung up the phone, and locked the door behind them. The officer out front was beginning to get a little nervous and he was glad to see them get out of there.

All three left at the same time, with the cop activating the alarm and locking the front door as usual. John asked his officer friend if he really needed a ride home, but the officer said that he had his wife's car. There were still several cars in the parking lot. Except for one, either the rest had trouble starting or they had been left there to be picked up later – after the money ran out or after the newfound romance had lost its flavor. John suggested that they meet with Dottie at his office at ten the next morning to go over the evidence. Martin agreed, but he wanted to take all of the copied papers that they had managed to get back to the hotel for a night of personal perusal. John agreed.

Martin could not sleep, no matter how tightly he closed his eyes. He had this Robin Hood complex that made him feel as if he were the New World's hero. He was going to profit off of his misdeeds, but the really good thing was that he was going to set free a beautiful woman from all of her daily nightmares. He had to sift through Lou's office evidence tonight. It could not wait until tomorrow. The partnership agreement was his first priority. It simply said that after paying all monthly bills, a lease figure of $81,000 a month should be paid to Lou Maxie. After that, Artie and Lou would split the excess. Attached to this agreement were about fifteen pages of numbers arranged in a T formation. At the bottom of each page, the totals on each side of the T were equal, but the entries on either side of the T from top to the bottom were of different amounts. Obviously, the numbers were an in-house record of nightly disbursements that only the two partners were privy to. The total on each page was approximately $31,000 for each side of the ledger for this month, and the month was just a little over one half used. "Boy, would the IRS like to get hold of these numbers, chances are they represent equal skimming."

The second piece of evidence that Martin chose to peruse was the name and address book. Almost all of the names were women. There were some descriptions of a few, but not anything that seemed very important except six names, they had asterisks by them and they had their passport numbers beside the asterisk. *Probably their out-of-the-country companions*, Martin thought. The payroll records seemed to be in order for filing by the fifteenth of the next month per the regulations. Later, Martin would compare this report with the tax returns but he saw no worthwhile information that either could bring him right now. The daily receipts were adding machine-tapes with a date written on them by hand. Oddly, they nearly always totaled just over $81,000.00 per month. "Very convenient if you want to skim all the take that was over the lease," Martin visualized. Lou was reporting his lease money to the IRS, but the two crooks were splitting whatever was taken in above that, and the other legitimate monthly expenses. They obviously had trouble remembering just how much the other one took each night, so they wrote it down together on separate sheets of paper. That explained why Artie waited for Lou to go into the office earlier that night. Sleep was now coming on rapidly, so Martin decided to retire.

Martin's wakeup call startled him. He must have been in deep slumber. He fumbled for the phone and then fumbled for his morning tea. He was a basket case of nerves. With too much to drink and only four hours of sleep, he understood his feelings. Nevertheless, he made it to John's office on time. Dottie was so excited to tell him about her fling that she refused to let them talk of anything else until she had her time on the stage. "We left the strip joint about eleven and the bastard wanted to check into the first hotel we came to. I told him that I didn't do those sorts of things on a first date. Only once before, I said, did I go to bed with a man on the first date and that was because he bought me a nice dinner. He then asked me where I would like to eat. We stopped at that cute little tin-roofed cafe on Travis Street just north of town.

"I was all plugged up and I knew that I was going to get all his memoirs. I did too. The tapes are full of petty garbage, but they also reveal a total dislike for his partner. He even confessed to trying to have him killed – in so many words, not exactly, but after you hear him you'll know he really did. When that didn't work, he said that he sicked the Feds on him. It's all on tape!

"He invited me to go to Bermuda with him next month with Lou and his new steady, I guess the gal he left with. He said that he could make two million a year clear profit if he didn't have a partner.

"Right after dinner but before dessert, I hurried to the rest room. When I got back, I told him that I had been breaking out all over my vagina and it itched constantly. I thought he was going to throw up. He got up, told me that he trusted me, and that I better not ever repeat any of his idle conversation because he really didn't mean a word of it. Then he paid the tab, flipped me a fifty for my cab ride, and left. Of course, that was fine with me. I told him that I could catch a cab, which I did, got in my car, went home, and here I am."

Martin couldn't wait to compliment her. "Dottie, you were great. There will be a lot of people forever indebted to you."

John then addressed Martin. "I've already duplicated all of the tapes and I'm giving you this player to use. I need a new one anyway, but I'm going to bill you for this one."

Everybody laughed.

"Martin, the policeman's tape and my tape together don't give you anything except a proven romance between Lou and Big Tits. However, combining all of the tapes, I think we slew the monster last night."

"I agree," came back Martin. "I brought you another two thousand dollars to apply to my bill; I'll settle up with you on the rest before I leave next week. I don't know of anything else for you to concentrate on right now, but please be at my beck and call tomorrow. We need to touch base with each other every day, no matter what. I'm going back to the hotel to get some sleep; I'll talk to you two later."

An hour after Martin had been back at the hotel, he received a call from Sally. "I'm glad you called, Sally. I've some very interesting information for you. I'm telling you for positive that I have evidence that your husband is indeed running around on you. He has been for some time and he and his partner are indeed skimming from their business. And to top all of that off, Lou's partner at one time tried to have Lou killed. I wouldn't blame you if you did not want to know any more of the details. But I have them in hand for you if you want them. I'm convinced that you must end your relationship totally with your husband, either by divorce or whatever. Nothing is going to get better, and quite frankly, I'm afraid for your life.

"Now, back to business; how did you make out on the insurance policies?"

Sally was floored with the results of Martin's cruel investigation, but she finally gathered herself and began her reply. "I have to ask you what you got in evidence that is such unerring proof, and how in the world did you get it?"

"The next time we meet, I will let you listen in on some taped conversations. I'm not stalling you. It's just that I don't want to divulge anything on the phone. You will be able to identify both your husband and Artie, and what they say will speak for itself. Until then, I need that information that I asked you to get."

"I did meet with our insurance agent, not at church, but at a cake-bake sale. We had a good long discussion and I'm sure he suspects nothing. Lou has three policies that are with him. One is for $700,000, one for $500,000, and the other is tied to the amortization of our house, somewhere around $350,000, he suspects. All have an accidental death benefit, except the house policy. All are paid in full for the rest of the year, and all have been in force for three years or better."

"Good job, Sally. Is there anything else of value that you stand to inherit other than the real estate where the business is located and the house? And of course the cars and personal property, but the later doesn't matter very much."

"Not that I can find. The country-club memberships are in his name and I don't think that I can sell them; that money is just gone."

"I understand; we'll find a way to solve everything. Believe me, I am committed to your future happiness. It makes me sick, all the things that I've discovered. If it's all right with you, I'd like to postpone our meeting for today until tomorrow morning at ten at my hotel. I want to check out something else for you. It'll be a big surprise for you in the morning! I'll have all the other evidence that I told you about together when you get here. It'll be your choice to see it or hear it. See ya tomorrow."

"I'll be there and thanks a lot for all you are doing for me, Martin."

Martin hung up and walked over to the table and picked up a piece of paper. He then dialed the scribbled telephone number that was on it. Using an alias, Martin felt comfortable about hiding which room he was calling from if and when Artie discovered that the call came from the Adolphus Hotel. He figured he might catch his party at this time of day on his cell phone in his automobile. He was right.

"Artie, my name is an alias, Uncle Sam. I was given your cell telephone number by the Bureau and the IRS. I want to talk with you. You are not in trouble and you are not in any danger, but there's a plot going on that might interest you. There seems to be a plan underway to eliminate one of your partners and I think you would want to discuss it with me. At this time, I do not want any notoriety or publicity, so I suggest that we meet at the Broken Promise lounge on the L.B.J. Freeway in one hour. I assure you that you will not be bothered any more than is necessary in this probe and you will never hear from us again if you continue to cooperate. Don't be late and be there alone! Needless to say, I cannot answer any questions over the telephone, so I'll see you at the restaurant. Good-bye."

Martin was proud of his firmness, but now he was having second thoughts about involving Lou's partner. Second thoughts or not, if he was going to help Sally and his other partners, there was no other choice but to involve Artie. If Martin's assumptions were true, that Artie was working with the government, then he would be there. If he was not working for the government, then it would be questionable whether he would show or not.

As usual, Martin was early for his appointment. He picked a secluded booth and waited for his guest. Promptly on schedule, Artie showed up. Martin went over to him and introduced himself as Uncle Sam, a private eye for the government. They sat down and Martin could see Artie' hate for being there. "I'm a part-time employee of the government; I have no credentials because I'm assigned to the most distasteful jobs on the docket. But, from my conversation, you will know that I speak the truth. I know all about your business; your partnership, the girls you go out with, the money you skim, and your previous attempt to hire a hit man. You are a certified louse, but it's not you I want. I want your partner that you couldn't get. I want him badly enough to leave you alone and let you be in complete control of the entire business, and let you go scot-free. You will make a mistake later, and then we'll get you. I don't think that you have too many scruples, so let me get directly to the point. I want to protect Lou's wife forever; both financially and in body. She is an innocent bystander in all of this, and she is deserving of much better, plus she is very cooperative with the authorities. And just in case you or anyone else is thinking about eliminating her, we've already got all the information from her that she could possibly give us.

"You are the key to taking care of Mrs. Maxie the way all of us want her to be taken care of. You see, unless we intervene, your partner is scheduled to have a tragic accident real soon. Right now, we can only sit and watch because having someone on a hit list is not against the law without further noticeable action."

"Why the accident part?" Artie finally opened his mouth.

"Because that is the way we understand the plan is designed, that's why. Listen, I'm the one that's here to do all of the talking, so you just take notes and perform when you're needed. Now, we know all of the property is in Lou's name and there is nothing that you can do about that. His present lease to your partnership is $81,000 plus per month. With my help, Sally is prepared to lease it to you for ten years at half of that, but it must be prepaid a quarter in advance, or you go back to $81,000 a month. The lease will begin the day after Lou Maxie is no longer with us, by accident or otherwise. She will assign to you all of the partnership holdings and she will not receive any further splits – that's a nice word for skimming – from that day forward."

"What do you want me to do for all that – kill him myself?"

"No, I'm afraid that has already been taken care of. You must simply arrange to pay Sally a hundred thousand dollars within the next three days to take advantage of the offer. I know that seems like a tough task, but look what you'll be getting. For one hundred thousand dollars up front, you are saving well over a million a year. I know. I've seen the 'splits/skim' sheets. You will never find me again if you do not participate, but I will find you, and you just might be on the same boat to the hereafter as Lou. On the other hand, if you perform as I think that you will, the business is yours for as long as you want it – without a partner. Once you pay Sally and activate this agreement, you will have another ally, strange as it may seem, and Sally is certainly in jeopardy from you if she doesn't live up to her part of the bargain. I will be around to make sure you and Sally do what you are supposed to do or all hell will break loose, courteous of me.

"Let me give you some confidence. Ask me a question about your last three months' income or your girlfriend's telephone number or where you were the last few nights or how much you and Lou 'skimmed' last month. I'm a creditable person and right now I'm on your side. Don't do anything to screw it up. I want you to meet Sally at her car in three days with the money. It's important that the two of you see each other and know of each other's participation. I'll tell you where in two days. I have your three telephone numbers. If anyone hears of our conversation or our deal, then it's off and so is your State's evidence pledge" – Martin knew he was taking somewhat of a chance in mentioning the State's evidence pledge but he was now more confident than ever that Artie must have been cooperating with the State to save his own hide. Otherwise, he would be under a current investigation just like Lou. By mentioning the State's evidence pledge, Martin gained the utmost in credibility from Artie because only someone close to the government could know about it. – "You must not talk to another government employee about this arrangement. Nobody, I mean nobody must know our deal or any part of it or you'll be locked up for life, if you're lucky. Now, you can run along and find the cash. I'll be in touch with you tomorrow or the next day."

Artie quietly got up and walked away. Then he came back. "How do I know you are real and how do I know Sally is in on this?"

Martin paused a full twenty seconds before answering. "Call her tomorrow night and ask her if the deal is a go. She will answer with four words, 'It is a deal.' As for me, try asking me some questions about either you or Lou."

"When is Lou's birthday?"

"Artie, you're dumber than I thought, you had a birthday party for him at the office two nights ago, right?"

After a protracted pause, Artie said, "Okay, I'm in. But you better not fuck with me either, okay?"

"Okay."

Martin called Sally the second he got into his hotel room. "Sally, there is nothing wrong, but I have a new idea to run by you. Please get to a pay phone right away and call me." While he was waiting for Sally's return call, Martin called John West to see if everything on his end was all right. John was out but Dottie answered and said that all of Martin's case reports were finished. She expressed her gratitude for allowing her to work in the field for once. And Martin again complimented her on her unusual night of expertise.

Martin let the phone ring twice and picked up the telephone receiver and answered, "Hi, Sally."

"Martin, I'm scared to death. Are you sure that nothing is wrong?"

"Nothing could be finer. And I think that I have all your money raised for my services, so you can forget about the down payment. I'm sorry to bother you, but I couldn't wait until tomorrow to tell you. You're going to know sooner or later. Artie's going to come up with the money because he thinks he is cooperating with the IRS, but he's really cooperating with us. Don't worry, we have so much on him that he has to cooperate. He's not one one-hundredth of the person you are, but he wants the same thing that you want, but of course for different reasons. Remember, he tried to have Lou killed. Besides, you are going to have to negotiate with him sooner or later. I certainly think that you have all of the cards to do it right now. I semi-negotiated a ten-year lease of the business for you – paid in advance quarterly, plus our down payment for initializing the deal. That way, no one will ever know that you are involved in the place. What do you think?"

The phone was silent.

"Sally, are you there?"

"Yes, I'm here, but I wish that I weren't. I'm afraid of that guy. I've only met him twice, but I'll be scared the rest of my life because he knows. I was beginning to have a world of confidence in you, but now that you've invoked Artie, well, I don't know."

"Believe me, Sally. You have absolutely nothing to worry about. He doesn't have the foggiest idea of who is after Lou; in fact he thinks that it is someone that he has never met, one of Lou's other business acquaintances. I assured him that you know no details at all, in fact, you are a 'doubting Thomas' on all of the information. But I told him that you had agreed to a negotiated settlement of his lease and partnership in case the information I have given you turns out to be correct. You know that you are at the mercy of whatever happens, and you know that you have no input or control of that info or the actions in any way. I told him that I'm stepping into this because I know about an underworld contract on Lou; and I want you, as an innocent party, protected and cared for. Again I reiterate, he knows that you have absolutely no part in any of this except in negotiating a business deal. Besides, we have the goods on him. We have him admitting, more or less, that he hired someone to try to take out Lou. We have him taped while he was out with another woman; his real girlfriend would kill him for that! He thinks this whole deal is being staged by the government to get Lou, and he has inside information that will make him believe that's true. He knows of no other enemy that Lou might have other than the government. Believe me, he is convinced. We have copies of him skimming. He has no choice but to cooperate, and he will benefit a bunch from it. His only risk is your down payment to me if the rest of the deal never happens, and that is small potatoes when you think of what amount of money he can make in the future.

"You're going to have all of the insurance proceeds. With accidental death benefits, you'll have over two and a half million minimum, plus the house closing. According to the deal that I have already presented him, you will agree to lease him that building 'as is' for ten years at half the current lease rate. You will deed him by quitclaim all your inherited ownership in that awful business that he is running. You could never lease that building for anywhere near that figure to a legitimate business, and you want him to have an advantage so that he will keep leasing from you. You will own the property forever if you want. He has to do two things to get what he wanted all along: he has to pay you a hundred grand up front, and he has to keep quiet for his own sake. He'll pay the money because it is a good deal for him. Remember, he was going to pay someone else to get rid of Lou. This way, he will feel safe. He'll be quiet because he will be involved and will profit from it. Remember also that sooner or later he would also have to negotiate with you if he were involved in Lou's death. Add to that, he truly believes that the whole thing is government orchestrated, except for the hit contract and its execution. I hate to use the words, but trust me."

"Martin, I guess that I have no other choice. I don't like it, but I'll sink or swim with you. I'll see you at ten; bye-bye."

Martin thought about using such descriptive words in his description of the business to Sally, and he felt a twinge of guilt, but he had to drive his points home with authority, even if Sally was a respected lady.

Martin opened the door at 10:00 a.m. for Sally. Both kissed each other on the cheeks this time. "Sally, you look beautiful, as usual. I have all the information from our scoop over there on the table. Before we get into that, I have to tell you that Artie is going to call you tonight to confirm our deal and to make sure that you're in agreement. He's going to ask you only one question: 'Is the deal a go?' You must answer in four words only, 'It is a deal!' Then hang up. He has no right to talk to you any further. When it comes time for you to answer, just take a deep breath and answer, 'It is a deal.' Can you do it?"

"I guess so. If my memory doesn't fail me."

For two hours the pair mused over the lifted material. Sally was very impressed at both how Martin had gotten all of the information and for specifically what he got. She was now convinced that she must go through with the deal. She now truly believed that she had run out of options if she was going to continue a life of charitable service. Her confidence in Martin had suddenly skyrocketed.

"Our last task before the meeting Wednesday night is to make sure that Lou accepts your gift to him of this safari. Got any ideas?"

Sally could not wait to show off her thought processes as well. "I brought a check with me from my account. I will simply write you a check for the full amount. He would be too embarrassed to let it bounce. And secondly, he wouldn't want to alert any more of the authorities to a new charge of check bouncing. I will explain to him that I thought the IRS would question a check of that size on his account, but they probably wouldn't even know if it were drawn on my account."

"Sally, you are brilliant. I'll hand him a receipt from our company at the meeting. He then can pick his dates for the safari and his campsite. The rest is up to me and I'll sell him.

"We have to cover the meeting between the two of us when you give me the check. It'll be easy to explain. The paper has given me a little write-up that was published two days ago in the sports section. You can say that you read it while skimming the sports section looking for the notice of the gun and camera club's upcoming meeting; that you remembered Lou talking about going to the very place that was in the article, where I hunt, and you called the gun and camera club office to get in touch with me."

After another short pause, Martin continued, "I've got it – then you can arrange to meet me at the gun and camera club office to give me the check. All fronts will be covered. Why don't you call the gun and camera club office right now and tell the secretary that you would like to set up a meeting with me."

Sally hesitated to make sure that she understood the plan; everything was happening so fast. Then she dialed the number that Martin gave her. Luckily, Betty was eating in this day, and she answered the phone. Betty was a little taken aback by Sally's introduction and further still when she asked how to get in touch with a man named Martin Smith from Hunters, Ltd. Sally told her that she had reconsidered her offer of giving out Martin Smith's phone number prior to the club meeting because she wanted to book a gift safari for her husband. Betty obligingly gave Sally the number and the hotel at which he was staying. The conversation was short, but just what it was supposed to be.

Martin then suggested that he order up some lunch and a bottle of wine to celebrate. Sally couldn't say no. Well-planned Martin already had a bottle of French Chardonnay chilled in the small bar refrigerator in his room. He took out two shiny wineglasses that he had managed to pilfer from his last visit to the main bar downstairs, and he poured a generous glass of wine for each.

Small talk filled the void between the ordering of room-service lunch and the time that it arrived. The waiter who brought the food recognized Martin from earlier dinners and complimented him on his always-neat attire. Martin tipped him grandly and ushered him out.

Martin proposed a toast to Sally. "To one of the most beautiful women in the world, and soon to be the happiest." Not wanting to mix pleasure with business, nothing else of importance happened.

That night, Sally answered the telephone, and when a strange voice asked her the expected question, she replied as instructed, "It is a deal," and hung up.

The next day, Martin called Artie at his home at seven o'clock in the morning. He instructed Artie to meet Sally at the drive-in window parking lot at the NCNB bank beside the Meadows Building off the Northwest Freeway at ten o'clock. Martin waited for a rebuttal, but Artie sleepily said that he would be there with the cash.

Martin was waiting three parking spaces down from Sally when Artie arrived. Artie recognized Sally's car and came over to Sally's driver's-side window and asked to sit inside. Sally politely declined and asked him if he brought the bag of money for her. He said yes, but he wanted a receipt. Sally told him that this deal was a way out for both of them and that they better play along with Mr. Uncle Sam of the IRS and a receipt had not been discussed. Artie still insisted on a receipt. Sally then looked Artie straight into the eye and began to blow her horn. This obviously frightened Artie and he turned around to see who was watching and listening. Martin climbed out of his car and strolled over to Sally's vehicle. "Any trouble ma'am?"

"I don't think so, sir, other than this guy wanting a receipt for his money."

"Well, I'll give him a receipt for you, but I'll have to sign it Mr. Uncle Sam. Is that all right, Artie?"

Artie was dumbfounded. "I didn't really expect you to be here; a receipt from you would be worthless."

"You are dead right, Artie. I don't want to twist your arm, but we have a wire to make and we must go now; either you're in or you're out. We can work either way."

Martin told Sally to meet him at her bank and turned to leave.

"Hold on, Mr. Government Man. I'm giving up a hundred grand here and all I want is to be sure that we have a completed deal. Don't we need to sign some papers?"

"Nope, Artie. There are three of us here that know what's going on. You and Sally are, in effect, partners now through Lou, and you're agreeing to continue the partnership after Lou's gone, but for a different amount of money. You have the goods on Sally if she reneges, and she has the goods on you if you somehow screw up and tell somebody. The deal is good for both of you, and if you give her that money, I will be the enforcer for both of you."

"It's getting hot outside now, Artie, and I have to be presentable to my bosses within the hour, so I have little time to waste. Sally, tell him how much rent or lease payment he is to make when his new contract starts and tell him how long it is going to run."

Sally looked up at Artie and said, "One-half of the $81,000 per month that you are paying now and for ten years. You also get all of the actual operation."

"That's enough, Sally. We're going the extra mile for this clown, as it is. We're truthful and faithful to our agreed obligations. I speak for the government and Sally. Do we have a deal, Artie, or are you going to spend your out-of-prison life running from me?"

Sally was now about to wet her pants; she loved the excitement, but she was scared to death.

"You win. Here's your money, but you, Government Man, better carry this thing off or you'll be running from me."

Martin closed the conversation with, "I wouldn't waste your time planning to find me, it won't be necessary!" All cars then departed.

Martin followed Sally to her bank, at least about halfway. When he turned on his headlights and then flashed them, she pulled over in the next street. Martin got out of his car and slid into the passenger seat of Sally's and they began to count the money. "Sally, you can have all this money if you want it and I'll walk away without even so much as a whimper. But if you want me to complete our plans I'll put it to good use."

"It's yours, darlin'," chided Sally. "I wouldn't have any use for it as long as I am married to the biggest bum that ever walked the face of the earth." They both laughed and Martin took the brown paper bag of crisp new bills to his car.

Betty and Martin sought out one another during cocktails at the gun and camera club meeting just as planned. For once, Martin wore a tie – a classic hunting tie from the famed Rowland and Wards in London. Lou was in another silk jacket with another open-collared shirt. Betty was conservatively dressed as an employee of the club and Sally was simply stunning in a Neiman Marcus pantsuit that seemed to point to her lovely blue eyes. Together, Martin and Betty accompanied each other arm-to-arm to find Sally. Sally faked the respective introduction by Betty in such convincing fashion that Betty had absolutely no idea that the two could have previously met. Sally did mention, however, that the two had talked by telephone to get the booking process started. With Betty watching, Martin gave Sally several choices of safaris to give her husband. And after a short discussion on each, he recommended the one in Zimbabwe over the ones in Botswana because it offered the most variety of game for a first safari. Sally appreciated Martin's judgment and she tendered a check to him for the full amount of the gift hunt. Betty stood by in quiet amazement. But for Martin and Sally, she stood by as an unsuspecting witness.

Sally then strolled over to Lou to tell him that she had a surprise for him and that he was going to go on a real-life safari, in Africa! Martin stood casually by to watch the unfolding of what might be a scene of bad taste, or jubilation.

"Sally, what a surprise. I truly didn't know you had any idea that I wanted to go on a real-life safari. It's my dream! How generous you are with my money! And how thoughtful you are to resurrect our relationship. I can't imagine what has come over you. Am I dreaming? Or did you do this in sincere admiration of our staying together?"

What could Sally say in view of such sarcastic comments? "Since you have everything that anyone could want except for the bragging rights that go with the hunting experience of having been on a safari, I thought that it would be fitting for you to go. Besides, while you are in Africa, I will be free from your scrutinizing my charitable work. We both win!"

For once, Lou was without a comment.

Martin interjected, "Mr. Maxie, I knew you must have a lot of money or were very handsome to rate such a woman. We don't get many beautiful women that want to buy their husbands safaris. My hat is off to you." Then Martin gave his famous hand-roll from the tip of his nose down to his knees.

"Martin Jones, I recall," said Lou. "I remember you from Las Vegas a few conventions past. We dined together in one of the posh hotels, did we not?"

"Maybe my memory is failing me, but as I remember it, we had breakfast together with a great number of people late one morning, or is my memory failing me? Regardless, it is a pleasure to be with you again." Everyone that could hear the conversation immediately went into uncontrollable laughter. "I do hope you are pleased with your wife's selection, both the safari company and your destination. I'm sure you will have an exceptional time, and I promise you a successful safari as to the game you wish to take. In fact, I guarantee your success!"

"I reiterate, it was a great surprise; she just told me about it. I'm elated, and I'm particularly pleased that I get to go with your company. I've heard nothing but praises from everyone that has ever been with Hunters, Ltd. It's probably a bad time for me to be going, business wise, but I'll manage. How about showing me some of your pictures and brochures? Might you have them handy?"

Martin was quick to respond, "Indeed. May I buy you a drink? I think we have some dates to set and some animals to pick out."

Sally excused herself and roamed over to a group of her make-believe safari friends – they were so ostentatious compared to her Cancer Society comrades.

Martin managed to set an early date for Lou's safari in Zimbabwe. May of the next year. He sensed total excitement in Lou when he mentioned that this was the ideal place to start an African collection of that continent's big game. He would be able to take impala, zebra, waterbuck, wildebeest, warthog, buffalo, leopard, and a huge lion if all went as planned. All without having to endure the dreaded tsetse fly. Martin indicated that he would like to join Lou for a day or two while on his safari just to make sure that things were going as well as they should. After an hour of detailed discussions concerning game, weather, bugs, guns, ammo, and travel arrangements, Martin and Lou exchanged business cards for correspondence reasons and the night came to a close. Lou was not the only client of record that Martin saw and recruited for next year's hunting season; it just seemed that way to Martin. He did manage to book two other safaris that were both longer and more profitable to the company than the Lou Maxie sojourn. It was a successful evening and a very successful trip from Houston. Frank Black would be pleased.

Martin called Sally at ten the next morning to wish her well and to leave her his telephone numbers in Houston, London, and Johannesburg. He reminded her that she would have to let Frank Black know by January whether she was going to accompany Lou on safari or not. Then he called John West to ask him for a final billing amount for his investigative services. John said that he would send him a bill in Houston. Martin thanked him, but asked him to mark the envelope "Personal" and make sure that the bill inside did not refer to anyone by name. They then thanked each other for their great experience together and hung up. Martin checked out of the hotel, thanked his concierge, called for his car, and headed for Houston. Never had that six-hour trip gone so quickly. He daydreamed all the way about Sally Maxie, and how utterly wonderful she was going to have it when his plan had finally unfolded. He simply couldn't wait to make it happen.

6

Travels and Spas for the Last Client

Martin was showing signs of cabin fever after being cooped up in the same hotel room in Houston for nearly all of November. He had made only one gun and camera club meeting since Dallas, and that was a short trip to St. Louis, Missouri. The trip could have best been described as a baseball meeting where he went down on three straight strikes. No bookings and no prospects for his elimination plan, and no sign of real potential interest for either in the foreseeable future.

While in Houston, he began to think that the telephone was actually part of his anatomy; he was on it constantly. This was the PR part of being in business that he didn't like. Via the long lines, he paid his respects to all of his recent clients, and he made contacts with all other past ones who were still alive. Again, he thought, *What a shame people couldn't enjoy safaris when they're younger, but they probably couldn't afford it then; he was obviously in a nearly dying business in more ways than one.* Nevertheless, he had to conjure up business some way, and telemarketing was essential. He called nearly every officer of every chapter of Gun and Camera Club International all over the States for their ideas on chapter members that might be interested in traveling to Africa. This amounted to over 320 calls in itself. Martin was becoming a very tired telephone operator. He could not wait for December, because that signaled a bit of vacation time. He regularly visited one of his old clients' condos in Vail, Colorado, for his second favorite pastime, skiing. Hunting was still his first love, but skiing the white powdery stuff in Vail was a close second, particularly after being in that Houston office for a month plus.

After the first week of January, Martin would make most of his West Coast stops before ending his sales tour in Las Vegas the second week of February. The Las Vegas meeting would always coincide with the International Gun and Camera Club Convention that was held alternatively each year in Reno and Vegas. This year, Las Vegas had the whole shooting match. After attending the five-day convention, it would be back to Africa to set up camps for the coming season. An enjoyable grind that he welcomed after being held captive in the States.

Before Vegas, though, he had a number of stops to make. Seattle was wet and it always rained buckets every day while he was there. But that didn't stop him from visiting with the Klineburgers, old friends famous for their safaris and taxidermy. Although they were competitors in every realm of the safari business, they were always friendly and enjoyable to socialize with. Like Martin and his company, the unspoken ethics of the industry prohibited them from coveting another company's clients; at least that is the way it was supposed to work. The gun and camera club meeting's program was traditionally shared by both companies, and thankfully, there was never a hitch.

San Diego was perfect; the best weather on the planet, but only one booking. Los Angeles was "Star Time." Tales of previous African safari adventures by the kin and friends of Robert Stack, Clint Eastwood, Jeff Chandler, Roy Rogers, Carroll Shelby, and many others added spice to his visit. Seldom did Martin leave the City of Angels without cornering a big-time screen star for a safari. This time was no exception; he booked two for a month apiece. The sad part was that they wanted to go incognito to stay away from protesters. That really pissed off Martin. He had to book them with their aliases. "What you see in Hollywood is not necessarily what you get!" Martin lamented.

Phoenix was wonderful. While the rest of the country was chilling out, the temperature was 70 degrees there – perfect safari weather. Business was not quite so hot, but the West was something to behold around Phoenix. Santa Fe was Martin's last stop before February's trip to Las Vegas.

Maybe, the Santa Fe area north to Chama was America's most beautiful scenery; only Vail could compare in the eyes of Martin Smith. While eating at the Pink Adobe in Santa Fe, Martin ran into the old star of Monday-night football, "Dandy" Don Meredith himself. Don had hunted Africa several times, and was once the featured hunter on the old *American Sportsman* series with Curt Gowdy. Martin happened to have seen that *American Sportsman* adventure that was filmed in Southern Africa, and he had also watched old Number 17 throw the football many times on TV. Don's waitress had originally called Martin's attention to the celebrity, and after a while, Martin couldn't help himself from going over to Dandy Don's table to meet him. Don's party was intrigued by a professional hunter from Africa being in Santa Fe, and Martin was invited to join their table. The conversation naturally got around to just why Martin was in the area, and Martin told them about the gun and camera club meeting that was to be held at the downtown Hilton Hotel on the square the next evening. Martin asked the entire table to be his guests at the meeting, and all were delighted to take him up on the offer.

Martin wasn't stupid, he invited everyone he could find that had even a remote interest in carrying a rifle or a gun on an African safari to be at that month's meeting, and he dangled Dandy Don as a guest that was bound to be there. The crowd was the biggest that chapter had seen in its history. After the cocktail hour where everyone was delighted to meet and see Don Meredith, Martin introduced each and every one of last night's dinner group prior to his portion of the program. Martin was sure such introductions would give him more than added respectability from the community. He was right because he had never envisioned booking three twenty-one-day safaris for the next two seasons. Old "Turn Out the Lights" was always a pleasure to be around, and for this night, he was one valuable asset.

Martin returned to Houston to finalize his office duties before his last trip on his western booking circuit. His plans called for him to leave directly for Johannesburg by way of London as soon as the Las Vegas convention was over. As he was preparing for his departure from Houston, his mind was constantly on his elimination plans, and he was sweating his last booking that he so desperately needed to satisfy his promises to his other two partners. Every hour he would remind himself that he needed one more contestant for this business, and time was indeed running short. Vegas held some promise simply because so many African hunters and their wives would be present – nearly ten thousand! And the local chapter there had another potential client that he remembered, a doctor that had taken all of the twenty-seven species of North American game and had announced that he wanted to be the only doctor to bag the "big four" (lion, leopard, elephant, and buffalo) in a single African safari. *For sure, this egotistical bastard must have wife problems,* he thought, *at least that was the rumor. He would check it out, but he would do so very carefully.*

Being that this was the year that the Gun and Camera Club International Convention was in Las Vegas (Lost Wages, for Martin), he was always excited to make his multiple presentations, and he relished talking to all the other outfitters to swap stories. With all of nearly ten thousand safari-goers dressed in their high-fashion safari outfits and their animal jewelry, the place was a costume jungle all its own. Martin kept his eyes and ears open for any and all comments and suspecting demeanors that might indicate that somebody might have an interest in having one's spouse chewed on or stomped upon. The convention lasted five days, so even if he struck out on the first day in searching for a client, he had only used 20 percent of his time there. And that is exactly what happened. Likewise for the local chapter's meeting on the first night of the convention. The one guy who was going to set new records for big game hunting for a doctor proved also to be a bust. He was happily married to some artificial blonde bimbo who was perfectly happy to just spend his money whether he was with her or not, a perfect rich combo.

Most safari clientele brought along their wives to the convention, and it was hard as hell to tell if there was a marital spat brewing or not. The few younger couples that were there always seemed so enamored with each other that there was no chance of spotting a major tiff, and the older couples were smart enough to not show their disenchantment. After two days of listening and mingling with every person he could, Martin decided his best potential client was not the guy who brought his wife but the one present without her. It was impossible to judge the sanctity of marriage for most of the couples present because they were usually on their best behavior. He either had to have inside information or he had to use another tactic. He put his new thoughts into high gear. He approached every chapter president he could find, and to each he found a way to ask if all of their chapter's safari travelers that were there were with their wives. He was such good friends with all of them that they saw no harm in playing his game. They knew Martin was single, and they just figured that he wanted information for flirtatious reasons.

How could I have been so stupid? he thought. He had obviously found the key to new potential clients. Six different presidents gave him all of the names of members that were there without their spouses for the expressed condition of enjoying either their brought-along mistresses or the prostitutes that were so readily available. Upon further examination, two of these brought along a "toy" from home. "Gotta have a lot of nerve to do that," imagined Martin, "especially intermingling with all of their own chapter's members and such."

As quickly as he could and as inconspicuously as he could, he amassed a rather large dossier on each of these two potentials from conversations with all of their fellow chapter members. Things were beginning to fall into place. One chap, the one from Atlanta, seemed to be having more than his share of self-induced marital strife. Supposedly, his wife had actually caught him with another woman while out to dinner with several of his hunting buddies and their wives. Obviously, no one appreciated the encounter that took place, and it was rather nasty; a lot of yelling in a public place was quite annoying and the episode didn't endear better friendships among those that were present. Martin was quick to pounce on this lead and stepped up his inquiries as to this couple's wealth, their health, and business activities. The guy's name was Dennis Kyle, and his wife's name was Mary. According to the information supplied, both were in their late forties, and the wife had more than suspicions.

Mary was a socialite active in the Atlanta Symphony, the American Cancer Society, and was an officer at Piney Creek Country Club. Recent memories of Sally jumped into Martin's head. He was well aware of the typical charity contacts most of these well-to-do women were into. Dennis was a businessman who owned a series of health spas around the Atlanta metropolitan area. He appeared to be active in nothing but hunting, animals, and women, and not necessarily in that order. Dennis and Mary had been separated at least three times, but the story was that Mary could not go any further with her divorce plans because every time she got close to a trial, Dennis would file a Chapter-11 proceeding to tie up all of his assets, and then Mary's lawyer would advise her to back away for his own selfish monetary reasons knowing that he would have to fight too hard to get his fees. Her last attorney reasoned with her that if she had proceeded, she would have gotten nothing from or during the divorce, and she didn't have any separate funds to maintain her lifestyle. She was in a damned-if-you-do, damned-if-you-don't relationship. Her best option was to stay put and bide the time away until something in her favor happened.

Perfect for Martin. Martin could envision himself riding in on his great white steed with his shining silver armor to rescue this pretty middle-aged damsel. He hadn't inquired as to her beauty, but Martin took it for granted that she must be at the very least well-groomed to have such an active social life.

Martin decided to nix his earlier thought of plans to call another private investigator into play. Everyone at the convention had cameras, so he would get some high-speed black-and-white film for his own camera and do the work himself. In the safari business, every professional was a proficient photographer, and although he rarely led any safaris on his own anymore, he still possessed great skill with a camera, even indoors with or without glittering show lights. If he could keep his shutter from energizing the flash mechanism, he could get as many incriminating pictures as he needed, and that was the purpose of low-light black-and-white film. Dennis Kyle was his target's name and he would have to find out the name of the "toy" when they met. He decided that he could even pal around with the duo, and if he were discreet, they would never know when their pictures were being taken. Within an hour after his thoughts became a plan, Martin had his camera around his neck, had inquired about the goings on of Dennis Kyle, and intentionally made a point for a rendezvous with Dennis and the toy post haste. It wasn't an hour and a half until he was sharing the same table with Dennis and his out-of-town toy at lunch.

Martin was a master at making himself at home with strangers, and he quickly drew out all of the names of everyone at the table. He cared little about what others thought about his sudden clutch to them. He told Dennis that he had been asking everyone at the convention about the beautiful girl that Dennis carried on his arm. Jokingly, Martin chided Dennis that he thought Dennis was married, just to see what kind of rise he would get. Martin thought his best approach would be a bold one, and he was up to the task. He knew that most of the conventioneers thought Dennis had not been divorced, but everyone that knew Dennis at all knew his marriage was, per se, null and void. That explained the noncaring rumor of Jennifer Miller being a constant companion of Dennis's in and out of town.

Martin let everyone know that he could think of nothing finer than the two of them enjoying a safari at one of his camps. They would certainly lighten up the place, and the company could always benefit from plenty of pictures of the handsome couple for their new photo album. Martin was thinking ahead and he was covering his ass ahead of time. Dennis knew of Martin and his company from his appearance in various hunting periodicals and from former clients within his gun and camera club chapter. He had even met him once at an earlier gun and camera club meeting back in Atlanta, so he relished the safari talk, especially since he was the center of attention.

Occasionally the conversation would slip to another subject, but then Martin would put the safari subject again front and center. Martin continued to express his interest again in the two being a photo draw while on safari in Hunters, Ltd.'s new brochure. Right away, Jennifer liked the plan; if there was a possibility of being in front of a camera, Jennifer liked the idea. Besides, she had always wanted to go on safari. She was always enamored over the taxidermy that adorned the office walls of Dennis's luxurious office as well as those of her other friends that had been on safari. She didn't know African game from American game, but she knew she liked the adventure behind every letter of the word "safari."

Dennis was less enthusiastic. Martin could sense his concern about a trip that would include Jennifer, and how it might look in the eyes of a judge should a divorce proceeding really come to fruition. So Martin changed his bold strategy to one that was a little more conciliatory. Quietly, Martin mentioned that he had arranged for many a safari that was designed especially so that no one knew anything about the entire trip. He cited some various movie stars as an example of his successes in that regard, and even mentioned the two safaris that he had just booked with Los Angeles clients that intended to travel incognito, without the stars' names of course. Dennis became a little more interested.

"Dennis, just what animals would you like to add to your trophy collection?"

"I really haven't given it much thought, Martin. I haven't been back to Africa in several years, you know, and I've only been once."

"Why?" quizzed Martin.

"To be honest, I was scared to death one night when I thought a lion was going to eat me alive."

"Tell me about it," Martin said.

"Jennifer has heard me tell it a thousand times, so I guess one more time won't hurt.

I was in South Africa, hunting with Jon Cronje on his farm near the Timbavati River that borders Kruger National Park. Jon was a game rancher and he had an overabundance of impala, wildebeest, kudu, and zebra. The lions in Kruger were quick to learn that their chances of success in making a kill on Jon's place were significantly better than in the park. So, at night, the lions would sneak under the barbed-wire fences that surrounded the farm and come in for a kill to fill their bellies." Dennis couldn't help an abundance of hand gestures to further describe his ordeal. "They would fill their bellies and return to the safety of the park before daylight. It was a real problem for Jon. A ritual that had to be stopped. It was like someone walking into your store at night and lifting part of your merchandise. Jon got permission from the game department to take a few of these beasts in hopes that their practice would cease.

"I happened to be there when the first permits were issued. I hadn't really wanted to hunt anything dangerous; I just wanted the experience of going on an African hunting safari. Anyway, Jon enticed me to try to take a lion. We killed some bait, and placed it in several places around the farm, forty-eight hundred hectares as I recall. A big place, the equivalent of over ten thousand acres. The lions hit every bait every night we put it out. It was like food stamps to them.

"We would try to spot-light 'em, but they were too clever. Every time we would get close to them, they would sink down in that tall grass and disappear. To make a long story short, we decided to hang a bait from a tree and then sit up in the same tree and wait for them. The bait would mask our scent. As the lion came to snatch the meat, we would have a close and easy shot. Well, it didn't turn out to be quite that simple.

As Dennis continued, his voice changed from an informative voice to one that was reliving a time of great concern. One could tell that he had suffered from plenty of nightmares about the incident. It was evident that Dennis was not comfortable with his life in the hands of someone he had just met, and Martin sensed concern that he might never accept those conditions ever again.

"The lion came, all right, but always to our backsides. We couldn't turn around enough to get the rifle in position to shoot. But that was not the scary part. Once the lion figured out that we couldn't face him, he would literally try to climb up the tree trunk between the bait and the bark to get at us. Luckily we were about fifteen feet off the ground, but he got to at least a foot from us. I thought that I was a goner," said Dennis as he wiped his brow.

"After the first night's close call, we put some chicken wire below us to ward the lion off if he tried to get us again; and we moved the bait to the other side of the tree so we could maneuver to get a shot without falling down from our perch if he persisted his aggressive nature. On thinking about that chicken wire later, I imagine it was about as safe as being wrapped in cellophane. Anyway, on this last occasion, we also lowered the bait so his interest would be more on eating the bait than on us two hunters. Well, the damn thing disregarded the bait entirely, and climbed up even higher this time to get at us. He even clawed down all the wire, but he couldn't quite get to us. Thank God he was too big to be a very good tree climber. I don't know how he figured out where he wasn't vulnerable to our guns, but he did. Again, we couldn't rearrange ourselves to get off a shot despite our careful planning. Even Jon was scared; I think more from that damn lion's intelligence than from the thought of really being attacked.

"Well, that's the story. No more hunting dangerous game for me unless I'm in a tank. Would you give this up for dying in the claws of some cat?" he said, pointing to Jennifer. "I'll just stick to the good eating game animals. They don't fight back as hard. I'm not into macho mania, at least in Africa."

"I guess you have a point there, Dennis. But what about buffalo or elephant? Buffalo is plenty good eating."

"You forget, Martin, that I am with all these African hunters at every safari meeting, and I hear their grisly tales about buffalo and elephant. About the guy that was treed by a buffalo but couldn't pull his feet up high enough into the tree and the buff licked off his boots and all the skin off his feet with that raspy tongue of his. And about that poor Montana man who was hunting elephant when the damn thing charged him and grabbed him with his trunk and threw him nearly fifty yards up and into the top of a thorn tree. Then the big brute pushed down the tree, pulled the hunter out of the thorns, knelt down on him, and pulled off his head, arms, and legs, and scattered them over an area the size of a football field. Nope, not for me. I like to live to eat the meat. I'll stick to kudu, impala, and the likes."

"I understand, Dennis, and I don't blame you. We professionals have to stop telling all these danger stories. They really don't depict the true African-safari life. However, I know both of your last two stories, and I know them to be mostly fact. So what about a nice cozy safari that will include nothing but plains game?"

"I might be interested in that, but not for over a week or ten days."

"We can mold one for you any way you like. For that period of time, I could probably get you into any camp you wanted, plus we could spend a couple of days in one of the parks taking pictures. And for sure we'd get in some super bird hunting that Jennifer could equally enjoy."

Since Jennifer had heard the gruesome stories before, she was immune to the normally perceived horror. She just wanted to go on safari. She wasn't scared; she thought she was impervious to danger. But listening to both Dennis and Martin had her sitting on the edge of her chair, keen with interest, and hoping that Dennis would take her. "Please, please," she coaxed and pleaded with Dennis. Martin was beginning to suspect that Ms. Jennifer was a total airhead. But he had to be careful; her actions might be purposely deceiving.

"Looks as if you've got a problem, Dennis. I think she means business. A safari makes the heart grow fonder!"

"You are the one with the problem, Martin, I'm too busy starting two new spas to spend any of my time over there."

Martin winked at Jennifer, and said, "Oh, I see, business is more important than what Jenny wants, eh?"

"Listen, Martin, if I get some good lovin' tonight and in the morning, we'll talk about it over breakfast tomorrow, huh?"

"You got it," Martin said with a smile. "Looks like your work is cut out for you, Jennifer."

The conversation then switched to Jennifer's choice of shows for the evening. She was now in an animal mood, and she begged to see Siegfried and Roy, the magicians who could make tigers and elephants disappear. Dennis and Jennifer made that show while Martin opted for the bar shows that could be enjoyed with a stiff drink and wiggling miniskirts. Bedtime for all was late as usual in Las Vegas.

The next morning at the convention breakfast, Martin nudged into the Kyle group at table number five on the dining room floor. Pleasant good mornings were exchanged, and the talk about last night's shows commenced. Everyone liked the magician show, and no one could imagine how the illusions were accomplished.

As if it were planned, all of the other people at the table except Dennis, Jennifer, and Martin finished their breakfast early and excused themselves. This gave Martin the opening that he had hoped for. "Dennis, I talked to my office this morning and I have tentatively reserved the most beautiful camp in Africa for you two in the Okavango Delta for mid-April. This is where most of the migratory birds from all over Africa come to raise their young. The climate is great. There are no bugs, not even a tsetse fly. And the animals that are there are completely different from any you have encountered before. It is a romantic site so beautiful that even Hollywood can't do it justice. Expanses of clear water that gently flow over a sandy base makes fishing a delight. Tiger fishing is the best fresh-water sport fishing in the world. Palm trees on every little island makes you swear you are in a tropical paradise. I am telling you, it is a virtual Garden of Eden.

"You fly directly into Johannesburg, take a short flight to Maun, Botswana, to clear customs, and then another short flight into camp. The scenery from the air is fantastic, and the camp food is nothing short of exquisite. We'll fly in anything you wish for food and drinks, and we'll even arrange a short trip to the local game park for some close-up pictures. If Jenny plays her cards right with you, I will personally take the two of you to see Victoria Falls, and spend a night at the Victoria Falls Casino and Hotel. However, I won't stand for your gambling losses, I guarantee all of the tables and slots there are fixed. This would add to the trip of a lifetime for the two of you."

Jennifer was all over poor Dennis with kisses and hugs. "Please, please, please," came the sounds from her beautiful red lips.

While squirming in his unarmed straight-back breakfast chair, as if he was trying to weasel out of something that he didn't want, Dennis bent over the table toward Martin and whispered, "I had a pretty good night last night, my friend, so I guess you can book it. I'll have to confirm the dates when I get back to Atlanta, but I don't really see a problem. I assume that we will have to be out of the country for the standard fourteen days to take advantage of the excursion air fares, right?"

Martin was quick to answer, "That's right, and that means that you'll need to pick a night or two at your favorite European city for a stay on the trip over, or a couple of days in Cape Town or at Sun City. I always recommend that you take a slow journey over and a quick one back. I'll also guarantee you that the whole jaunt will be as secret as you wish."

"Maybe my wife will die of food poisoning by then and Jennifer and I can use the trip for a honeymoon," Dennis's true side was again starting to surface. Martin paused before he said, "I wouldn't wish that on anyone; I've had food poisoning."

Jennifer jumped in with, "You don't know his wife!"

Martin then reached into his pocket for a pen and piece of paper to jot down Dennis's proper contact numbers and his office mailing address. Dennis was hesitant to give out Jennifer's numbers, but when Jennifer insisted on all of the brochures and pamphlets on the area and on the game be sent to her, Dennis acquiesced. Martin was having a hard time figuring out the true Jennifer, but he envisioned that time would soon give him a clue.

With Dennis's booking verbally committed to, with a check to be held in hand, and with all of the proper contact numbers exchanged, Martin was more anxious than ever to know more about the lives of other relatives of these apparently single-minded people that were going to share his company's facilities. "Jennifer, how did you two get together in the first place? Does your family know about Dennis? Would you tell me something about your family, and something about your earlier life before Dennis?"

"I'm glad you asked me those questions, now I can take part in some meaningful conversation. Dennis was pointed out to me by one of my girlfriends one night at a club in Buckhead, you know Buckhead, it's that ritzy inner-city night-life area in 'Hotlanta.' He was with this gorgeous brunette and they were dancing every dance that the band played. I love to dance and I am naturally attracted to good-lookin' men who dance a lot. My girlfriend knew Dennis's name and his business from being introduced to him at a private party a year or so earlier. She said that she had seen him several times with different girls at other parties and clubs, so I asked her to introduce me to him the next time his date got up to go to the restroom. It's been a romantic thriller ever since!

"As for my family, I have no brothers or sisters, but I have the most wonderful Mommy and Daddy in the world in Texas. They are retired. My dad was with the intelligence department of the coast guard for many years. He got several medals for his special service. I don't get to see them as much as I'd like, but we try to talk on the telephone at least once a week. They usually call me. I know they wanted me to be an educated school teacher or something like that, but I knew my limitations, and I knew what else I had going for me. So, I got in the dancing business, and I proceeded to make a pretty good living for myself. I have never had to ask my family for one dime. I bet you don't know many girls my age that can say that."

Dennis had held his tongue as long as he could. "See, she has always been a starlet and she has always been was conniving and she's still at it. Just like this safari I've just committed to just to keep her quiet!"

"I'm just accustomed to getting what I want, and I don't mind working for it. A girl doesn't get to keep this kind of figure forever, so she has to use her charms while she can. Anyway, Martin, after my girlfriend introduced me to Dennis, I promptly told him that blondes have more fun. He liked my comment and he asked me out the next evening.

"We met at his office and he showed me around his business. He showed me some pictures of his hunting trips and I really got interested in him – he was so good-looking in his safari outfit and everything. He took me to Chops for dinner, and then we hit a few clubs. He danced me off my feet! We went back to his apartment for a nightcap. I delicately informed him that I was not going to go to bed with him, but the night had been very special and I hoped that there would be many more just like it. I like to make sure that I'm the only woman in a man's black book before I go to bed with him. That was nearly two years ago, and his old black book has vanished."

"Now, Jennifer, I've been out of town a lot since we met. I still have a black book for traveling. Just kiddin'. You know that you're my only squeeze. Well, Martin knows what I mean."

It was Martin's turn for more questions. "Where do you go from here?"

Inquisitively, Jennifer answered, "I don't know what you mean."

"Are you two going to get 'hitched,' as they say out here in the West?"

"Of course we are, as soon as Dennis can get rid of his wife. Don't get me wrong, she is easy to work around, but she just won't let go. Dennis and his legal beagles are working on it, though."

Dennis began his squirming act again. "Are these questions a prerequisite to our safari with you?"

"Absolutely not, I just like to know as much about my clients as they choose to tell me so I can personalize their needs when they are in camp. It helps me entertain them better."

"Let's just say that my wife and I don't have much in common. We got married too fast before we could check each other out. From what you've just heard, a divorce seems natural but there are complications. I've had some very good years in the spa business and her attorney expects that trend to continue. Based on that, she stands to settle for several million. That's not reasonable. What if competition comes in and blows me away? My lawyer and I have a plan. I routinely take each of my spas into Chapter 11 to take advantage of reorganization. They are separate corporations with separate partners, and I can funnel pretty much all of the money taken in to wherever I choose as long as I make my token partners happy. That holds her off for a while. And during the Chapter-11 time, I'm perceived as not quite having it all together. At the same time, I'm reducing her monthly allowances. That hurts her charity and social life. Our guess is, within the next year, she'll be frustrated and she'll want out at any price. Then we can talk business."

Martin didn't like what he was hearing, but he had to ask another question. "What if she doesn't succumb to the pressures?"

"She'll succumb; we just have to keep tightening the screws."

Martin kept his thoughts to himself, but he recognized they were a two-edged sword. "I hate that bastard for his flaunting of Jennifer and his greedy attitude toward his wife, but he might be making my elimination plan a success. I realize I'm rationalizing a bit, but whether I'm involved or not, Dennis is a sorry son of a bitch and even his best friends know it. If I can make it happen, I'm going to be the best thing that ever happened to Dennis's wife."

"Well, I think that I've pried enough – didn't mean to, but I did. I'm going to show you two the neatest and best time that any two lovebirds have ever had on a safari. The whole operation will be alerted for your extra pleasures." With that, Martin politely excused himself, and indicated that he had a plane to catch. As he rose, he managed to snap one last picture.

With all of his bookings secure and his elimination prospect on the line, Martin decided to leave the convention a day early – not to celebrate, but to make sure that he had ample time to do the rest of his elimination business in Atlanta. He contacted his office to tell Frank Black about his booking successes and that he needed to rearrange his flight schedule to include a day or two's layover in Atlanta.

Martin's Delta 727 landed smoothly at Atlanta's Hartsfield International Airport. He had acquired a fake mustache from one of the "fun" shops at the Las Vegas airport and he was going to make good use of it. God forbid, if he ran into Dennis or Jennifer.

After a thirty-minute limousine ride to the Buckhead Ritz-Carlton Hotel, he began his search for the home phone number of Mr. and Mrs. Dennis Kyle. The number was unlisted. He hadn't planned for that, but he then remembered that he was in the United States, and everyone over here seemed to cherish that anonymity. He dared not call Dennis's office for fear of alerting him that something unusual was happening. He checked through his notes for a hint of how to get in touch with the wife. In his little black appointment book, he found that he had scribbled down the Cancer Society and Piney Creek Country Club next to Dennis Kyle's name. He remembered getting the names from Dennis's gun and camera club chapter president.

Of course, it would be a snap to call the secretary at the Atlanta Gun and Camera Club for the phone numbers, but he just could not take a chance of being known to be in town.

He decided to call Piney Creek Country Club for the house number. The answering person was very nice, but she refused to give out Mrs. Kyle's number but she did offer to have her return the call. Martin thanked her for her protection, but said that he had not checked into a hotel as yet and he did not have a number to leave.

He next tried the Atlanta Cancer Society. He claimed to have a check for a new ad in their upcoming program; the check was solicited by Mary Kyle, and he thought it would be nice to give it to her personally. The Cancer Society always seemed to have a new shindig planned or in the making and that meant a new fund-raiser of some sort. His luck turned ripe for a change. They not only gave him her number, but her mailing address as well in case Martin was unable to reach her by phone. At the end of the brief conversation, Martin asked for the person's name that had been so kind to help him. "My name is Mack Hall, and I came in contact with Mary through one of our volunteers back at my old home in Houston. She has turned out to be one of our finest assets here at the society. You wouldn't want to join our society down here would you?" Martin politely declined, but he said he was proud of the fact that he had the opportunity to help the Atlanta organization with their new fund-raiser.

After hanging up, Martin began to mull over his plan for his initial contact with potentially his final lady client. The pressure was on; his time constraints would have to be kept undercover and close to his vest, yet he had to make a deal within thirty-six hours, or blow away what seemed to be an excellent opportunity.

It was two o'clock in the afternoon when the telephone rang at the Kyle house. Oops, a man answered. Martin hung up. All he could think of for the next few minutes was whether they had that new telephone gadget that recorded the number from which the call had come from, caller ID. With the Kyles having an unlisted number, that likelihood was indeed more than a possibility. He quickly called again. This time, when the man answered, he would give him a false name and say that he was in from out of town to address the Cancer Society to promote a new fund-raiser or something. The phone rang for six rings before the man answered again. Martin's heart was almost in his mouth. "I beg your pardon, my name is Roger Bryan, and I am here from out of town on Cancer Society business. I just called your home a few minutes ago, but was disconnected. It must be these inferior hotel telephones. Could I speak to the Mrs.?"

"Sure, please hold on and I will get Mary for you."

Whew, that was a close one; it almost sounded like Dennis, Martin thought.

Mrs. Kyle came to the phone and politely answered with the expected, "Hello, this is Mary Kyle."

"Mrs. Kyle, my name is Roger Bryan; I hate to interrupt your present meeting and I had no idea that you might be so involved. I'm in town from Europe, and I've just called on your local Cancer Society for some pertinent information that we might use on the other side of the Atlantic in regards to some of our fund-raisers and membership drives. Your local society receptionist was very generous with her help and she was kind enough to give me your number for further assistance. I understand that you wrote the book on charity fund-raising." Martin hid the fact that he had actually talked to a man, Mack Hall, just in case Mary decided to verify the person that gave out her number.

"I will be in town for only a short time, on some non-Cancer Society business, and I wondered if you might spare a minute or two of your time to help me out a bit. I would be glad to call you back or meet you at your convenience."

"Mr. Bryan, that is right, isn't it?"

"Yes, Mrs. Kyle, I'm sorry that I rambled so long to allow you to almost forget my name."

"I pride myself on remembering names. One has to in charity work, or one doesn't get much accomplished. Not seeing your face leaves my memory techniques without a referral, so I wanted to make sure that I was correct. My meeting here is just about to conclude; would you like to give me a call in a half hour or so? I plan to be here for the afternoon. If I cannot answer your questions over the phone, then maybe you could drop by for a bit of your accustomed tea" – she remembered that he was from Europe, and his accent certainly supported his allegation – "Or should I arrange to meet you at our Cancer Society building?"

"You are so accommodating, Mrs. Kyle. Since I've already been by your Cancer Society office, I would feel better if I didn't disturb them again."

"So please give me a call in a few minutes and we will see if we can arrange a short meeting here at my home."

"Mrs. Kyle, I will think about my schedule and call you back in thirty minutes."

"That'll be just fine, Mr. Bryan. In fact, wouldn't it be easier if I called you back as soon as my present guests have left?"

"Thank you, but I have not yet checked into my hotel, so if you don't mind, I will give you a ring in thirty minutes or so. Will that give you enough time to conclude your meeting?"

"Yes, that'll be just fine. I look forward to your call. Good-bye."

Mrs. Kyle returned to her dining area just as her guests were rising to leave. "I just talked to the most interesting gentleman from England; you can tell that lovely accent anywhere. He's here for some Cancer Society information, so I guess my day is still not over." She politely wished her guests a formal good-bye and quickly instructed the maid that a hurried cleanup was in order.

Showing off her newly decorated house was one of her favorite things to do, and now she had a chance to show it off to someone from Europe. Being ostentatious or nouveau rich was not her forte, but her house was something that she was proud of and she certainly enjoyed sharing it with new acquaintances. "Maybe he will be so impressed with my decorating skills and my varied interests that I'll be invited over there to give them some assistance in their Cancer Society projects." What a callous and selfish thought that was, and Mary giggled to herself. She was entitled to a little selfishness every once in a while. In approximately thirty minutes, Mrs. Kyle's telephone rang and Mrs. Kyle answered.

"Mrs. Kyle, this is Roger Bryan again, and now I am in the midst of checking into the Ritz-Carlton Hotel in your famous Buckhead. Unfortunately, I'm missing a bag from the limousine, and I must stick around here to identify it when it comes. Are you anywhere close to this hotel? If so, would you entertain the thought of having a cup of tea or a drink with me here in this beautiful lobby?"

Mary paused an inordinate amount of time. "Mr. Bryan, I do not regularly meet people I do not even know in a hotel, but because of Cancer Society business, I think I might make an exception. I am already dressed, so I could be on my way in ten minutes or so. It will take me about thirty minutes to get there. You are at the Ritz across from the Lennox Mall, are you not?" "I think so. Let me ask the bellman." Martin held the telephone receiver away from his mouth as he politely asked the bellman to confirm the Ritz's location. "Mrs. Kyle, I am right across the street from the Lennox Mall, on Peachtree."

Mary had already heard the bellman speak. "All right, I will be there in about thirty minutes, depending upon traffic."

As soon as she had finished that sentence, Martin interrupted. "I will have the concierge or the doorman reserve a parking spot for you out front. What kind of car will you be driving?"

"Gosh, that is so thoughtful of you. I will be arriving in a blue Cadillac with a white roof. I'm also wearing a blue dress. And if you will meet me as I come into the lobby, I would appreciate it. By the way, what are you wearing?"

"I have on brown slacks with an open shirt and a light brown jacket. See you in a few minutes."

Mary Kyle ran up the stairs to her bedroom to change shoes and put on some less formal jewelry still matching her exquisite attire. She shouted to the maid, "Never mind the cleanup, I'm going to meet a Mr. Bryan at the Ritz in Buckhead. I'll do the cleanup when I get back. There's no need for you to stay around; go home and enjoy your family. I appreciate your help with the meeting."

"This is going to be fun, too bad that I'm not sharing it with my buddy Helen." Then she thought, *Why not?* Mary grabbed her portable phone and dialed the memory call number of Helen Beasley. "Helen, I won't take no for an answer, I am driving out of my driveway right now to meet the most charming person from England. I don't know whether he is cute or not, but he is here on Cancer Society business and he is waiting for me at the Ritz-Carlton in Buckhead. I am going to pick you up in five minutes so hurry and get dressed – a cocktail dress."

"Mary, you are a lunatic. I have just been watering my plants. I look like hell and I probably smell worse."

"No use, Helen, I'm coming to get you. Just think of it as protection for me meeting this strange bozo that might not be a bozo."

Helen didn't have a choice and she reluctantly said, "I'll be as close to ready as possible."

After exiting her driveway, Mary dialed information for the Buckhead Ritz-Carlton Hotel. She was given a direct connection by the operator and she asked to speak to a just checked-in guest named Mr. Bryan. The hotel operator referred her to the front desk. "May I help you?" "I would like to speak to Mr. Bryan, please. He has just checked in, and he is probably waiting in the lobby for a lost bag that didn't arrive with his limo."

"My pleasure. I will be glad to check." After a couple of minutes, the clerk came back on the line. "Ma'am, I'm afraid that we have no Mr. Bryan in the house; at least no one of that name has recently checked in."

Mary was taken by surprise. "Ah . . . ah . . . would you be so kind to check with the concierge?"

"My pleasure."

In less than a minute Mr. Bryan was saying hello from the concierge's desk. Martin had fortunately gone to him to arrange the parking for Mrs. Kyle, and he also mentioned that he was using an assumed name, Mr. Roger Bryan. That cost him a quick fifty to the concierge. Mary Kyle was reassured of the authenticity of Mr. Bryan once again, and informed him that she was bringing another Cancer Society volunteer with her and she would be a few minutes late. This caught Martin by surprise, but he had no choice but to laugh and say that was just fine.

Martin went immediately to the bar for a quick toddy to settle his nerves and to think of a new approach to Mary regarding his elimination for hire scheme. Somehow he must be able to converse with Mary alone; he would just have to wing it depending upon the circumstances.

The doorman recognized Mary's car the instant it pulled into the circular driveway, and he motioned her to a special parking spot right beside the main door to the lobby. Just on the inside of the circling round doors at the entry stood Martin to greet his guests. After the proper introductions, Martin guided the two women to a cozy three-chaired table in the corner of the bar. "I hope you have no objections to being seated in the bar?"

Mary was first to reply. "After that hurried drive, I think that I need something more than a spot of tea. I need a drink!" In a reversal of form, Helen dittoed the same order, but with more composure. Martin waved for the waiter and drinks were served. Both of the women had vodkas straight up and Martin had a short malt Scotch.

As if he had another choice in opening the conversation, Martin suggested that they leave the Cancer Society business alone for a while and asked each lady all the right questions about herself, her families, and her special interests. No new facts were divulged that could assist Martin in the conquest of his final client.

Soon, the conversation turned to Martin with both of the women dying to know all about how such a handsome, debonair Englishman got involved with the Cancer Society. Martin could hide no more; it was time to come clean.

"Actually, I'm not as involved as it might appear, or as I might have led Mary to believe." Both ladies seemed to edge to the front of their chairs.

"My company president is an ardent backer of the society and I help him with certain aspects of his involvement when I'm available, but my personal contributions have been quite limited. My president asked me to check on each Society chapter in each of the American cities that I was to visit on this trip, with special instructions that I was to bring him back some good information on the Atlanta group. He does chair a committee for fund-raising, but he is mostly involved in the membership drives that we have in London and he thinks that you Atlantans have all the answers. Otherwise, you wouldn't have landed the Olympics in 1996!"

Helen decided that this charade, if it was one, had gone too far. "Just what business are you in, Mr. Bryan, and what honestly brings you to our fair city?"

Martin took a healthy swig of his Scotch and began his shortly rehearsed oratory. "I really have two pieces of business with Mary; let me speak first about the one that involves your local chapter of the Cancer Society. For the sake of all people, I want to bring back as much information as I can regarding the specific needs of recruitment and fund-raising within your society. If the two of you can help me in this regard, I would be most grateful. Do you solicit new members by functions, direct mail, local advertising, or by purchasing lists of potential members? Or maybe all of the above?"

Mary answered with somewhat less enthusiasm than in the earlier conversations. "Mr. Bryan – "

"Please, Mary, call me Roger as I have already taken the liberty of calling you and Helen by your first names."

"Very well, Roger. We have been very successful in recruiting worthwhile members for our Atlanta organization. I do not mean to sound snobbish with the use of the word 'worthwhile,' but mere member bodies will not facilitate our needs. We must recruit people who have time or money to help us, or they must have the connections to do the same. That does not mean that we will not take a dedicated servant that does not have much time or money to give, but we try to concentrate on those that can give the most. Just good business and a judicial use of our time. I am not sure whether our recent success stories are because of the temperament and will to succeed of most Atlantans today, or the result of our own aggressive work. We lead the nation in percentage of membership increases, and we are proud of that regardless of the reasons. We seem to have our most productive efforts in our special functions, Halloween parties, pre-Christmas mixers, a July Fourth fireworks display, and introductory parties that involve the participants in the local symphony, ballet, and the various home sports. By sports, I mean our Braves in baseball, the Hawks in basketball, and the Falcons in football. By having all of the players present with their wives, we draw unbelievable crowds to each of the preseason functions for all of the sports teams that I have just mentioned. At each, we meet our guests personally at the door to compile a special mailing list with office and home telephone numbers. If we fail to sell a guest by personal communication during the function, then we get back in touch with him or her the next week by telephone. On our follow-up call, we compliment him or her for coming to our function, and we try to be expressive about a personal item, like his or her work or other special thing that we have newly learned about the person. It is amazing how much people like to hear compliments about themselves, and we accent that the most. Needless to say, because the figures speak for themselves, we are very successful."

"Mary, I had no idea that a local organization would be that thoughtful, that resourceful, and that hardworking. All of you must be very proud. I cannot wait to relay these innovations to my boss. I should have been taking notes so I may ask you to review your solicitation methods once again before I have to leave."

"I'm not sure that I would describe our efforts as innovative because all of these techniques have certainly been used before, but we combine them in what we think is a very special way. Now, if you do not have any other questions regarding the society, tell us more about why you are really here, and something about you and your work."

"As distasteful as you might believe, I'm a semiretired professional hunter in Africa – Botswana, to be exact. I currently hold the title of field manager for the safari firm of Hunters, Ltd. It is our off-season at this time of year, so I travel to the various cities around Europe and America to solicit old and new clientele for the upcoming year's safaris. I will be the keynote speaker at the Atlanta chapter's Gun and Camera Club International meeting here in a few days.

"I must confess to both of you another misrepresentation. I have an ulterior motive for my call, and for that, I must see Mary alone to discuss it. My real name is Martin Smith and not Roger Bryan." Both women took a short gasp of air and looked at each other with inquisitive faces. Martin, of course, noticed the change in demeanor and quickly proceeded with his explanations. "My reason for misnaming myself was that I did not want to take the chance of Mary recognizing my name in connection with the gun and camera club until I had a chance to explain just why I was begging her to talk to me. I know Dennis Kyle and I have just conducted some business with him. I would like to discuss this business with you, Mary, as I'm afraid the business is very personal. I hope you will forgive me, Helen."

Mary could hold her tongue no longer. "Mr. Smith, if that is the name you want to currently use, I am appalled at you brazenness to gain a meeting with me under false pretenses. Never has anyone had to use such a ruse or unethical means to talk to me about anything."

"I sincerely apologize, but – "

"I am not yet finished, Mr. Smith," Mary reinterrupted with an obviously agitated demeanor. Then she tried to protect her friend and her suggestion that she come along. "Anything that you have to say or inform me of may certainly be said in front of my very best friend. Before you waste any more of your time and ours, please get to the point that obviously brought you here."

Helen interrupted. "Mary, maybe we should not jump to conclusions about the real reasons that we, or you, are here. Maybe Roger, or Martin, has something important for you. I can take my drink over to some of those display windows over there and give him a chance to state his reasons for being here, or I can just go to the restroom. That wouldn't be a bad idea, anyway."

"Nonsense, Helen, you know everything there is to know about me, and I would feel more comfortable with you here."

"All right, Mary, let's compromise. I need to go to the restroom anyway, so Martin can give you the short version of why he is here; and when I come back, you can tell me to go visit the windows or to join the two of you again. Won't that solve everything?"

Mary did not seem to have another alternative. "All right, Helen."

Martin knew his time was short, so he blurted right out as soon as Helen Beasley had left the hearing range of the table. "Again, I apologize for any inconvenience or misgivings, but I know that you will want to hear me out, regardless of whether you will be pleased with my discovery or my suggestions. I come from the most reputable safari organization in the world, and I hold the most important job in that organization which deals with its success and credibility. May I suggest that Mrs. Beasley herself decide whether she should be with you or not in the next part of my discussion? It being a given that Mrs. Beasley is your best friend, I am sure that she knows already about your husband's alleged illegal allegations and what I would describe as his womanizing. That part alone is, of course, none of my business. However, he has just booked a safari with me that includes another woman going along as his guest.

"I have just returned from Las Vegas, and I have in my room a series of pictures of your husband with this other woman named Jennifer Miller, also of Atlanta. I know that you and Mrs. Beasley have better things to do than listen to fictitious gossip or idle rumors, but my time is precious as well, and the evidence I hold in my room is unequivocal and certain."

Mary tried to be disinterested while looking in the direction of Helen and the women's restroom. "I do not think that you can tell me anything that I do not already know, Mr. Martin. I have a louse for a husband, but I am trying to make the best of it, and my time for worthwhile events is significant because we are estranged. All things considered, I kinda like it that way."

At this moment, Martin invited Mary and Helen to the reading area on the same floor as his room in hopes of making the two more comfortable to view his newly gathered photos, the company's safari picture album, and a copy of the Johannesburg newspaper story on the death of B. F. Clark. But Mary stood her ground and insisted that he break down all of his information by voice sitting right where they were.

Helen was thoughtfully taking her slow time in returning. Per Mary's insistence, Martin began his sales job; he knew that he would have only one chance, and the pressure was really on. "I met several of your friends, Jim Bullock and his wife from Charlotte, Chris Franklin and his wife Carolyn from here in Atlanta, and others that know you, at the recent Gun and Camera Club International Convention in Las Vegas. I was there to give some presentations for my company. While there, not only did I meet your husband but also many of his acquaintances. I was intrigued to learn of your troubles with your husband. Your friends did not volunteer anything. They are very protective of you, and from what I gathered, they admire you immensely. I inquired of them when I saw your husband with this Jennifer after knowing your husband had an interest in booking a safari with us. In fact, your husband did, immediately thereafter, book a safari with my company on which he is planning to take Jennifer. Dennis Kyle seemed to be the talk of the show, and all of his transgressions, whether deserved or not, were the topic of conversation. I am aware of your justified unhappiness, the potential legal problems that must be associated with such, and your husband's partners who are really all partners in crime as well. At least that is what I have been told. By that I mean that all are under severe scrutiny from the IRS as well as local authorities. I will explain later how such information was given me, if you care to know. Much more information is at my fingertips, but I hesitate to bore you unless you hear my solution. Shall I continue, or have I reached your tolerable limits?"

"I am going back to calling you by your first name. Martin, I am shocked at what you have just told me. I can't help but wonder how you got your information, but I must confess that your information thus far is substantially correct. Please go on, but with the understanding that I might interrupt or totally disregard your information. I might even just get up and leave."

"Before I get into my ulterior motives, I would like very much for you to read the article that I have in my hotel room from the main Johannesburg newspaper, to look at our pictorial album, and then I will show you the pictures of your husband's latest escapade if you desire. May I be excused for a moment to get these from my room? You can examine them here at the table if you do not want more seclusion in the reading area on my room floor. This is not smut; it is a means to possibly answering most of your life's problems."

Helen was now slowly approaching the table. She stopped for her eye-contact orders before attempting to be seated.

"Helen, you were exactly right, I apologize. Please give us a few more minutes and I will fill you in when we get into the car."

Helen responded. "I'll just mosey around. Just give me a wave when you're ready to leave."

As Helen left the table for the second time, Mary turned to Martin and said, "Please hurry; I do not want to keep Helen waiting any longer than is necessary; I'll look at what you have right here."

With that, Martin said, "Excuse me, I'll be less than two minutes," then he walked briskly to the first open elevator to fetch his printed and photographed assemblage concerning his plan for Dennis Kyle.

When Martin returned, Mary didn't say a word, she just held out her hand for what she was supposed to read. While she was beginning to read, Martin interrupted her thoughts with, "It would be my pleasure to buy you another drink; the waiter is waiting."

"Thank you, I'll switch to a glass of Chardonnay, the best house wine by the glass. Please send another over to my friend. I see her next to the jewelry store window." She then buried her thoughts in the newspaper article that she was supposed to digest, and Martin motioned for the waiter.

Obviously Mrs. Kyle was a smart woman, but she was either a slow reader or she was memorizing the clipping word for word. After concentrating on print, she switched to the picture album. It took her less time to thumb through it than it did to read the newspaper item. After closing the album, she looked toward her friend that was now seated across the room and brushed her hair with her hand. It was an obvious signal of some sort or another. Martin picked up on it and inquired, "I hope that was a signal that everything is fine?"

She nodded approvingly. "Martin, I'm puzzled about why you are here. You obviously know a lot about me and my husband, and maybe more than I about our legal shortcomings, but why the pictures – that you have not yet showed me, I might add."

"Mrs. Kyle, that newspaper clipping told facts, but it did not tell the whole story. Mr. Clark was intentionally put in harm's way to acquire a result. The desired result was achieved."

From her facial expression, Martin could tell Mrs. Kyle was not comprehending. "Mr. Clark was intentionally killed by a wild beast, by a plan that cannot be detected. There were only two people in the bush together hunting lion; one got killed by the lion, and the other earned money for the setup. Other than myself and the now happy wife of that deceased individual, no one else knows, and never will know about the plan. I'm being presumptuous and I don't know any other way to say it, but it seems to me that you need the same service applied to your husband." Martin hated to use the BF incident to his advantage, especially since it had not happened the way he was portraying it, but it was an ideal story to drive home his points, and it added credibility to his overall plan.

Mrs. Kyle sat in stunned silence. Her pupils became dilated and she had two big gulping swallows of wine before she could open her voice box. "God knows I need the same scenario for me to live out a happy life, but there's no way that I could be part of a plan like that. All my life, I have abhorred violence of any kind; I don't even support your still legal occupation. My charity work – "

Martin rudely interrupted, but he knew that he must to prevent her from saying something that she later could not retract. "Mrs. Kyle, as I have previously stated, I've already booked your husband and Jennifer on a safari together in March of next year. I had no legal right to refuse them. You don't have to arrange a thing. You just have to stay out of the way, and you have to compensate my efforts for the loss of our reliability in losing a client, if it so happens just the way I have described to you. Might you reconsider thinking about what it might bring you? It might get your life back, and it would certainly enhance your charity work. You'd live the rest of your life making a difference to a lot of people, and you'd never have to worry about finances."

"I think I'll have to talk to somebody, maybe my friend" – she nodded in Helen's direction.

"Absolutely not. There must not be another person that knows of this, other than those who are participating; otherwise we are bound to have leaks. In fact, I have some other requirements that might be pretty hard on you; particularly with your intense involvement with your various charities and your country-club work. I require a down payment to cover our setup expenses. After the accident, you must immediately sell your house and move to Europe for an agreed-upon time, to let the interest and idle chatter of the accident die down. And I will require an agreement to protect us both, one that binds us both. Not one in writing. There can be no traceable evidence of our undertaking, but an ironclad understanding of all the particulars. In addition to all of that, I'll require a million-dollar payment to be transferred to a Swiss bank within three months after the funeral and after your settling sales of your inherited business interests and your home. I know it is a high price for happiness, but most of my requirements are for permanent protection for all of us. And I might add, this is a tried and true arrangement that has been successfully used many times. And, all of my widows are extremely happy with their new lives, and neither of them know any of the others.

"You're not the only person that will have chosen this route to escape torture. You do not deserve your tarnished life that will only get worse. I have heard your husband tell me, and others, just how he intends to make you settle for a pittance in a divorce proceeding, and I am sure he has better legal advice than you can pay for. He has mentioned that he has bankrupted several of his spas before just to make you squirm. He is ruthless, and it is going to get worse, and I am appalled by it all. Some of my past lady clients have even remarried, and I might add, none of these have made the same bad husband choice again. Time is of the essence, or I would not expose their happiness to someone I have just met. I know your circumstances maybe better than you, and I am guided by those facts by your quality friends. They say that you are a trusting person; please don't think of exposing this conversation to the detriment of others that were once in your same shoes.

"From what I know, you're never going to get a divorce with any worthwhile proceeds going to you because your husband will continue to protect his assets by Chapter-11 filings. When the torture becomes unbearable, you'll divorce him anyway, but you will virtually be broke, and your lifestyle will be gone, and by then, this opportunity won't be around with a perfect solution.

"And your generosity of time and money to your charities will cease. Believe it or not; this is your husband's present plan, to make you suffer long enough to accept his divorce terms. You now have another choice. This is not a plot for a hired killing, or murder; it's a plan whereby someone is simply put in harm's way by his own desires, and no one else tries to get him out of it.

"I'll be leaving for England at midnight day after tomorrow. Plans must be made immediately. At some time in the near future, after you have checked me out, and after I have answered every one of your questions, I will need approximately one hundred thousand dollars as a down payment. I know this is sudden and I've had little time to convince you of my authenticity, but somehow you desperately need to take advantage of this safari that has already been booked. Considering your purse strings are being held by your selfish husband, do you think you could possibly come up with the kind of money I just mentioned?"

"I'm out. I couldn't raise that kind of money to keep my mother alive, and I would do anything to do that."

Mrs. Kyle started to get up, but Martin eased his arm over to hers and softly said, "Mary, I believe you. This meeting has been so shocking for you. I've known my role for several days, and I have no right to expect you to unconditionally believe in me so quickly. Because I'm asking for money up front, I can imagine your doubts, but I'm as truthful as the day is long. In fact, I will go on just your word alone for three weeks. Starting three days from now, I will be in London for one day, and then on to Johannesburg for a short rest before going into Botswana and inspecting all of our camps for the upcoming hunting season. I can be reached at any of my stops. If you want my services, you must notify me as soon as you can and then find a way to send me whatever money you can. I promise you that the finances can be worked out. I am so distraught about your circumstances, and after seeing you and hearing more about how you touch so many lives for the better, I will not let finances get in the way of helping you. We professionals don't have a lot of money lying around to help solve other people's problems. However, if I had the money, I would perform my plan for you for nothing, just to get you out of your trap. Unfortunately, I'm not the only decision-maker and my other professional partner insists that we are adequately paid. We are really giving up part of our hard-earned reputation for future business when an accident happens as I've described. As a starter, I will leave the amount up to you. Whatever you do not pay toward the one hundred thousand up front, I will collect additionally to the million after the funeral. Others in your situation have totally relied on insurance proceeds to solve the money problem. I'll be glad to help you with that at a later date if you choose. Incidentally, my help will only be a guide, your lawyer and your insurance agent will make all of your decisions with you. Until you have thought about this some more and until you are ready to make some sort of a commitment, just forget the money end of the deal right now."

"About that million-dollar payment at the end. I'm not sure that I could come up with that or your down payment! I have no idea what insurance policies are now in place. What am I saying? Your plan is preposterous; I cannot even think about such a thing."

"I know your feelings. I know your doubts. And I also know your unenviable position with your lousy husband. He made me sick just being with him and that girl for five hours. I can imagine your distaste. You must rectify your tranquility. Listen, Mary. I don't need a commitment signed in blood. I want you to have all of the time you need to make sure you will have no second thoughts. In the meantime, just in case you finally agree on a plan with me, certain things that need to be discovered before we can go forward will have to be done. Nothing that is unusual, like updating your information on your husband's life insurance, your home worth, and if possible, his businesses' worth. All of this can be obtained secretly with no chance that anyone knows what you are doing. I will be at your beck and call for any help. Remember we are on a short time fuse because the safari has already been booked and the dates are virtually set.

"Go ahead and take the next step, you have nothing to lose. For the next few weeks, you need to find out how much life insurance – including accidental-death benefits – you stand to inherit. That won't be an unreasonable question to ask your insurance agent. You have a right to know those things. Dennis might even tell you, but I would verify whatever he might say with the insurance agent. Add to that your accountant's estimate of your husband's businesses values with a deduction of his known debts. Then call me at my Houston office. Talk to Gloria; she is my secretary when I'm in town. She'll know where to reach me, either in London, Jo'burg, or in Botswana. Don't give her any details, just tell her that you have to speak to me. Remember to be careful about your calls being traced or overheard. In fact, be extra careful with all of your research as well. I don't think your husband is suspecting anything, but other evildoers out there might be interested, people like you've never dreamed of, like the IRS or some of your husband's disgruntled partners."

"You said you have a partner. That scares me to death."

"I should have better explained that detail. My hunting business has been in existence for nearly twenty years. All of it with a professional understudy that I have grown up with since our childhood days in Kenya. He is closer to me than a brother, if I had one. He has taken part in several plans like this before with me, and he is completely loyal and trustworthy. You will never meet him or talk with him. He just exists and he will be the only other person that will know our secret. I need him for certain things to make this happen flawlessly. He will be the professional that actually carries out the plan. We want everything to look natural and adjustable to camp life and like a typical safari. He will always know what to do in any set of circumstances, as will I. You have a right to know everyone that will be in the know!"

"Okay, would you go over your contacts and the names one more time, and I will write them down. Again, I am not giving you the go ahead with this God-awful plan, but I will keep my options open for a short time." Martin obliged, and then proceeded with the details requested by Mary. Mary wrote the names and numbers down on a bar napkin, and put it away in her purse.

"If my guess is right, I'll bet that your husband has a couple of million in insurance with double indemnity for accidental death. His banks would probably require it. The policies may even be assigned to a bank. Try to find out. If they are, then find out what the loan balances are that they secure. I doubt if his business ventures are worth much to anyone but a competitor, but even then, they may be substantial. You might secretly inquire as to a competitor's interest if you have an entree, but you have to be careful. They might add two and two together after the accident. Now, what are you going to tell Mrs. Beasley that we have been talking about?"

"I'll simply tell her that you are taking Dennis on a safari and you wanted me to know with whom he was going, that girl. I won't divulge the pictures. Let me see the pictures." Mary spent a total of fifteen seconds staring at all twenty exposures. She would tend to them later. She stuffed them in her purse when she was sure that her friend wasn't looking. "I suppose you have copies." She looked at Martin. "This thing is so against my nature. I cannot believe that this kind of option even exists."

"Mary, I've heard him say that he is going to squeeze your budget until you say 'uncle.'

He and his lawyer have a plan to slowly restrict your funds until you can't stand it anymore, then you'll settle your divorce for much less than you deserve. While your suffering will go on magnifying, he will not skip a beat on doing exactly what he wants to do. You're too smart to be played as a fool. You have to do something, and I don't see many options."

"Let me think about this thing tonight; I will get back to you in the morning. Maybe we can meet around ten here again if I feel as I do now."

"Swell, Mary. I sincerely believe that this might be your last chance to reward yourself for the life you have been living. I know it will be the safest way out for you. Do not even give it a second thought that we are participating in a hired killing or anything else illegal. I'm going to set a stage where your husband could theoretically extract himself alive. But if he doesn't make all the right moves, at all the right times, the accident will be fatal. Nobody is going to shoot him. There will be nothing for an inquisitive mind to go on. The setup is only a setup, not a guaranteed injury or death; that is why you must never believe you caused something to happen. He has been injuring you for a long time. Now you are giving him a better chance than you've had, and if he gets killed on his own booked safari with another woman, so be it. From the people I've met, he won't have many folks feeling sorry for him. You go home now, and get some rest so that we can think clearly tomorrow."

"Stand up with me, Mr. Smith, and lean over toward my face." Mary then kissed him on the cheek. "I hope Helen is looking this way because that has to be a good signal that I'm all right and that everything else is as well." And then she left.

That night, Martin donned his mustache in case he ran into some of his Atlanta clients, and toured the Buckhead nightspots that he had heard so much about. He wanted to be alone and he didn't want to have to explain why he wasn't visiting with certain safari people in the area.

For some reason, ten o'clock the next morning came earlier than normal for Martin because of his semilate evening in Buckhead. Nevertheless, he responded to Mary's early-morning call by again getting the same table and chairs ready for their meeting – less one that had previously been set for Helen. If he didn't get all the necessities accomplished at this time, then the chances of working a deal with this client were indeed slim. Pressure on Martin seemed to follow this prospective client and their meetings at every turn.

Mary strode through the double doors into the lobby with an assurance that would please the pope. "Good morning, Mr. Smith. What good news do you have for me today?"

"Good morning to you, you are especially beautiful this morning but you are the one that has the good or bad news."

"Surprisingly, I slept quite well last night and I didn't worry about a thing. Based on that, I think that we have some mutual interests to consider. I still have a lot of questions that I need answering from you and from me. But my choices for getting out of my present situation unscathed and with the ability to continue my service work make me look at your terrible plan with more than a casual interest. I apologize for my peculiar behavior yesterday, but I was really caught off guard with some stranger presenting me with such a scenario, even if you had the best of intentions for me."

"Wonderful, Mary. Let me order you some tea or coffee. Do you care for something to eat?" They both opted for hot tea with a little sugar and a little cream. Both declined breakfast of any description.

"Martin, I already have some good news for us. I stopped by the bank on my way here and I checked our safety-deposit box. I found four life insurance policies. One was on me and the other three were on Dennis. On the way from the bank to here, I called from my cell phone to our insurance agent to inquire about a silly question concerning my mother's life policy. While I had my agent on the hook, I casually asked him about all our health and life policies. Unbeknownst to him, I pulled over into a parking lot to take notes. Here they are," she said as she pulled them from her purse. "I have a half a million on me."

"That scares me, Mary. If your husband gets into a tight spot, you call me!"

"You are a bigger scaredy cat than I am. Dennis has three identical million-dollar policies, all with accidental-death benefits. Two were bought within the last two years, and the other is six years old. All are paid current. I told the agent that he was to let me know if any of our present policies ever became past due."

"Mary, you're a quick thinker. We're going to be all right with this approach, I promise you. Do you, by chance, know exactly how old the recently issued policies are by months?"

"Not exactly, but he told me that they were bought just before he opened the last two spas. That would make them at least twenty-three months old."

Martin smiled and said, "That will make them over two years old by the time they are needed."

"I also asked him if either of the policies were pledged and where they were located. He said no to them being pledged, and that we had possession of them either at home or in our safety-deposit box because Dennis would never keep anything like that at the office and the agent said that he didn't have them. I never told him that I already found them. He said that there had never been a request through him for an assignment or pledge. I asked him if an assignment of any kind would show on the policy and he said that in this case I would have to actually sign the assignment or pledge papers because all of the policies were owned by me, and I was the beneficiary. There is nothing about any type of assignment on the policies and I would remember if I had signed something like that in another instrument. I think that we are home-free concerning the insurance policies."

"I hope that your husband hasn't forged your signature. But if he has, you could probably prove through a handwriting expert that you didn't sign them. I agree with you, we are just about home-free. I know that you can get something for his spas and I know that you have some equity in your house, so you are going to be far from destitute. Even after you pay me, you'll be a multimillionaire with no one to spend it on but yourself and your charities."

The rest of the meeting was not as sober as Martin was expecting. It was almost joyous.

It reminded him somewhat of the aftermath of BF's accident and his wife's joyous mood. Yet he remembered how scared he had been at BF's widow's demeanor.

There were no disagreements to any of Martin's requests in an abbreviated review of his elimination agreement. The bond of agreement was formed and the next move was Mary's raising what money she could for a deposit in Martin's bank in Switzerland. After that, Martin was to make sure that Dennis met his last surprise as planned.

7

London, Dreams, and the "Big Four"

Martin boarded a Delta Atlanta to London flight at 11:00 p.m. the same night as his final meeting with Mary Kyle. On the flight over, he reminisced about the dates and circumstances for each of his elimination clients to which he would have to accommodate.

As the sleek AIRBUS 300 reached thirty-thousand feet, the Fasten Your Seat Belt sign went off. Martin pushed back his seat and began to think about the coming year in safari land. He had a lot of work and planning to do to ensure there would be no slip-ups in his elimination venture. Now was a good time to sit back and think about some of the necessary details.

"The first hunt in this connection will be for my latest sign-up, Mary Kyle; the victim will be Dennis. He will be joined by his steady companion, big Chi-Chis Jennifer, and they will be on safari for ten days. Seven days and nights will be in a camp in Botswana's Okavango Delta, and the other three will be split between a game park, probably Savuti, and the Victoria Falls Casino and Hotel in Zimbabwe." He made a written note to himself for his two clients to get the additional visas if needed for Zimbabwe.

"Dennis was keen on only hunting plains game and game birds. He didn't want any unnecessary risk to spoil his enjoyably flagrant everyday life at home. On my last talk to Dennis, he requested that he not even bring a gun. Clients usually bring their own .375 H&H or larger. He wanted to use one of the camp's firearms and our ammunition, probably a .300 Weatherby or the like. That is not totally unusual, but it probably points out what a disingenuous hunter Dennis must be." Martin didn't like disingenuous hunters; they gave the sport a bad name. But in this case, it gave Martin one more reason for caring less about the guy that he was about to help finalize. "I must make arrangements for an extra gun and ammo. The camp must apply and obtain licenses for impala, zebra, wildebeest, kudu, lechwe, and tsessebe for Dennis, along with bird licenses for both Dennis and Jennifer. After these licenses arrive, then we must apply for an added buffalo permit. I won't expose it until we corner a buff, and since the license will be on a separate piece of paper, Dennis will never know we've received it. There were no special requests for beer, food, or particular spices. I must remember to book reservations for everyone at the park lodge and the hotel after the main safari, even though by design they are not ever to be used. Air transportation from Zimbabwe back to Jo'burg must be ticketed, and arrangements need to be made for getting the Land Rover back to camp in the Okavango. I have got to make this thing look good, as in standard procedure.

"I can assign one of the new assistant professional hunters to assist me in conducting the safari. I will carefully plan the unsuspecting encounter with a Cape buffalo while hunting kudu, but I will have to make sure my assistant is not on the hunt with me that day. The final plans will have to be made on the fly, spur of the moment, because there is no way to predict where we will find buffalo, and there is no way to predict the animal's reactions once one has been found and wounded.

That will all depend on the day's weather, the terrain, and many other obscure things that a novice like Dennis would never be able to pick up on. That will be my advantage. I know I will have to be the one to wound the buff and then somehow manage to get Dennis to go in after it with me, but I can figure that out later. I can use one of the less experienced trackers and the same for a gun bearer – they will always wait for orders while an experienced crew would take the matter into their own hands. Ah, inexperience is the key."

Martin's mind then turned totally to the bush and the actual follow-up of the buffalo. "I'll search for high grass, and the odds for that were nearly a hundred percent for an early hunt such as this. The natives don't start burning the countryside grasses until May." This is a practice that is followed all over game country in Africa to concentrate the game near watering holes; this makes it easier for the natives to make their kills. Hunting-conservation groups are trying to reeducate the arsonist culprits into not burning such big areas by local government order, but the governments say that they have no money to widely enforce such decrees. Rather typical for Africa.

"After an intentionally missed first shot by me, too far back from the heart and lungs. I must be within close proximity of Dennis, hopefully less than a hundred yards to make Dennis believe that this is going to be everybody's problem. Dennis will have no choice but to accompany me on the follow up. It would be far safer for him to go with me than to return to the vehicle. I would then tell Dennis that the brute was badly hurt and there was little chance, if any, that the buff would charge. After a very careful stalk, when the wounded buffalo is found, I would pull Dennis up beside me and tell him that the buffalo is dying and that he should put it out of its misery by shooting it behind the shoulder. I'll have to compute the angle of the shot to ensure Dennis hits the thing too far back again. He will try extra hard to place the bullet right where I tell him. I would quickly explain to him that I would then be the backup if the brute should charge, even though it is a very unlikely scenario. I shouldn't get any argument from Dennis in such a dangerous situation.

"As Dennis would take aim, I could quietly back off to a predetermined hiding place. At less than thirty yards, like a heat-seeking missile flying into a hot engine, the buffalo will be on top of Dennis in less than four seconds after his shot. I've got to pray that he doesn't miss badly enough to actually kill the buff. God, what a mess-up that would be. I'll have to make sure I get him to shoot even farther back behind the shoulder than normal. Unless Dennis could jack in another shell and place a bullet squarely between the eyes and just under the boss of the horns of that rumbling, snorting beast within a four-second time frame, Dennis would be a goner." The "boss" is that thick horn structure that covers a Cape buffalo's forehead like a helmet; it is usually ten to twenty inches wide – from just over his eyes to the back of his skull – and is two to three inches thick. It is part of the entire horn structure and is virtually impenetrable by standard hunting rifle bullets. Unless with a solid and a direct perpendicular hit.

"The evidence would show that Dennis had a change of heart and wanted to take a broadside shot at a Cape buffalo, the first shot. The evidence would also show that I tried to stop the charging beast with the only shot that I had, the second shot. Both bullets and entry wounds would tell the perfect story! We will be using the same type of guns and ammo to further bolster my story. Who could possibly tell who shot which shot? After the buff is through with poor Dennis, I will let the buff lie down, lose some blood, and stiffen up a bit before going in to finally dispatch him.

"Jennifer will be in the Land Rover a mile away and will vouch for the mishap, actually hearing the proper number of shots to fit the story. The tracker and gun bearer will offer no advisory comments. First, they will probably have vanished from the area before any investigation can get there. But if they're found, they could only support my set of facts because they actually saw shots. Added to any investigating problems would be the huge language barrier. Any investigator will much prefer to get the story from only me and Jennifer. No one else would be present to offer an alternative conclusion." Martin would have slapped himself on the back for such a crafty plan, but there were people on either side of him in the rather cramped quarters of his economy section of the airplane.

They would probably not understand and the 'needs assistance' light would certainly start to flash, Martin thought.

"After collecting the remains of Dennis, I will radio the camp to prepare an immediate flight into camp by the Flying Doctor. The accident needs to take place in the morning's hunt in order to get the plane in with daylight." Martin was beginning to smile. The thoughts were a little morbid, so Martin couldn't help wondering just how he was going to comfort poor Jenny. At least her postdeath actions would show whether or not she was sincerely in love with her paramour, or just after his money and good times. He made a slight wager that the latter was the case.

"When the Flying Doctor takes off for Maun, I will notify the game department and the local police of the accident. There will be a minimum of two days of paperwork to be filled out, but there should be no ill will or controversy. I have to carry this first deal off with style; I have to set the example for the other two to follow. I have only three weeks to get ready; Dennis's hunt will start on April 15.

"The second programmed death will be for Rob Manson to orchestrate. It will commence on April 25 in Tanzania, some fifteen hundred miles to the northeast from the Botswana camps. I plan to make a cameo appearance at their camp, but only for a day or so. I'll have to make a charter flight in a small plane to get into his camp. Tanzania paperwork is such a hassle. I wish I could drive, but it is a seven-day round trip just to be there for one day – no way, I'll have to fly. It would be nice if all of the dirty work would already be done by the time I arrive. Camp life there should be a real "hoot." There will have to be a lot of drinking by everyone just to survive the verbal blows between the proposed victim, Clifford Jones, and the designated beneficiary, Barbara Jones. Cliff is one sorry son of a bitch.

"He will be hunting big elephant in the God-forsaken bowels of the Selous. The tsetse fly will be horrendous." Martin remembered the last time he was there. While he and a client had been after a big tusker, he turned to see if his client was where he was supposed to be during the stalk. He had had to take a second look when he saw his poor client literally covered with tsetse flies. Only his eyes were visible. What an ugly scene. There's no bug spray when elephant hunting; they can smell that stuff a good five miles away. "Barbara will be a basket case with the tsetse, but it will all be worth it for her. I will inform Rob that she can always be counted on if he needs any help; she is quite a lady! Aside from the necessity for camp meat, there will be no need for any other licenses except elephant. In the Selous, there is never anyone to check any licenses or permits. No human could live there by choice.

"The only part of the Joneses's safari that has not been decided upon is the transportation from Dar es Salaam to camp. For Barbara's sake, they better charter a bush pilot. It's a three-day drive in a Land Rover and petrol will be a scarcity. As to camp supplies, Cliff will insist on J&B Scotch, plenty of Tabasco sauce, and crystal wine glasses. He will not bathe if there is harsh soap, so we have to have something soft and smelly – same with toilet paper. He will always forget something, so we better make sure that we have another chartered plane ready to fly over camp and parachute drop what he's forgotten. He uses a Browning .458 Magnum rifle, so we better have some spare ammunition in case he forgets his solids or softs. And we've got to get enough fly spray for Barbara in camp.

"It's Rob's business, but I would leave Barbara at camp the day I planned the 'coup.' Because Cliff is such a good shot, with all the experience that a client could have, he is going to have a tough time setting up a provoked elephant charge. He cannot count on Cliff to be flustered. Maybe he can loosen the main screw on the bottom of the stock and adjust the spring that feeds the cartridges into the barrel. Once Cliff fires his first shot, shells will start dropping all over the place from the kick. Cliff will be defenseless. But how will Rob get the elephant to charge and how will he get it to zero-in on Cliff? Simple. Rob will have to abandon the traditional heart shot. Cliff will not be up on the skull anatomy of an elephant. The brain lies between the eyes head on, and between the eye and the ear hole from the side. But if the elephant is quartering and not straight on or broadside, Rob could easily instruct Cliff to shoot slightly to one side or the other. The elephant's head is the size of a refrigerator, but the brain is only the size of a football! The rest of the skull is a light porous bone. When the elephant turns to charge the report of the rifle, Rob would have already slipped away. Cliff would try to run, but the elephant would zero in on his movement and grab him. The rest would be sheer horror. When the elephant is through, Rob would emerge and dispatch the tusker with one well-aimed solid-jacketed bullet. The aftermath will be easy with Barbara. She will take care of her end of the deal with no problems. Her business experience will be a plus. After she wires our money to us in Switzerland, I'll go to London or wherever to meet her for a celebration."

Martin awakened from his close-eyed dreaming and pontificating by the noisy meal cart ricocheting down the isle. It was time for his first airplane food of his long flight. After a bottle of white wine and a grilled-chicken dinner, Martin returned to his thoughts of his latest business venture. "The last elimination plot involves Lou and Sally Maxie. At last word, Sally was a 'no go' for the actual safari. That meant that Lou would be traveling alone or with one of his hired bunnies at his topless joint, Baxter's. The Houston office will know sooner than I will about the end result of who's going and who's not. Thank God, I can leave that problem to Houston. Lou's safari will begin May 6 at the Kudu Hills ranch in the Matetse area of northern Zimbabwe. Peter Smit is the current manager of the ranch, and it is good to know that he will move heaven and earth for me if I ask. Up to now, there are no special orders for food, spices, or anything else.

"It will be Lou's first African safari. Jon-Keith will be our professional, and he always has gotten along real well with Pete. Jon-Keith will bring his own Land Rover and hunting crew with him from Botswana. He will only need a tracker from Pete who is familiar with the ranch and its boundaries. Jon-Keith hunted there once last year when our sable permits ran out, so he should be familiar with all of the game department rules and regulations. I don't think there are any new ones that have hit the books since last year. It's a twenty-one-day hunt for all of the plains game plus buffalo, lion, and possible leopard, so Jon-Keith has his work cut out for him.

"Jon-Keith has his choice as to which animal he wishes to use for the alleged accident. If it were me, I'd choose the lion. It would be the easiest to orchestrate. The leopard is more certain to maul and injure a person, but not many people have died from a leopard's efforts while hunting him. Not so with either buffalo or lion. Unfortunately, when a client is hunting with a qualified professional, one is more likely to suffer paralysis from a buffalo encounter than death because the pro will be level-headed enough to shoot the buff off a client if he is in trouble. Naturally, that wouldn't happen in this case. The odds are almost reversed when hunting lion, you either escape without paralysis, or you are severely scratched or mauled; maybe even dead meat if the lion stays with you for a while. If I were Jon-Keith, I'd suggest a shot behind the shoulder of a lion. With a proper line-up of a quartering lion, that would mean a reverse Texas Heart Shot – a gut shot! This pisses a lion off more than just about anything. He'll retreat to a dense hiding place and wait for the inflictor of such pain to follow.

"The key here is identifying the lion before anyone else in the party does. That should be duck soup for Jon-Keith. He will then move so close to the lion that he provokes a charge. He will have instructed Lou to kneel down and fire into the lion's mouth if he charges – that is easier said than done, and damned near impossible for an amateur. Jon-Keith will somehow have to get out of the way of all this action. After the blood-letting, Jon-Keith will have to follow up the wounded cat and dispose of it – that, too, is easier said than done. But in this case, I'd rather have Jon-Keith than almost anybody to do it. The trackers and gun bearers will be on their own. They won't get hurt unless they try to be heroes. That is not likely unless Jon-Keith's life is in danger.

The hard part of this scenario will be explaining it to Pete Smit. He will want to return to the scene and reconstruct the "accident." Jon-Keith will have to be extremely careful not to leave any evidence that would lead Pete to a conclusion other than that it had been a pure accident. I know Jon-Keith will be able to handle it. I can't wait to see Sally's face when all of this is over. I bet she takes Europe by storm. Maybe I can fit into her plans a little bit."

After Martin had daydreamed his last elimination safari, he fell asleep. He slept right through the movie. Just as it was beginning to get light outside his window, he awoke to a different aroma of fresh orange juice and coffee. Breakfast was served soon thereafter. The line at the rest room was particularly long after breakfast because the flight was completely full. Martin managed to endure, however, without wetting his pants. Touchdown at Heathrow International Airport was as smooth as a baby's butt – a greaser. After collecting his baggage, Martin piled into one of the standard big black cabs out front and headed for the Hilton at Hyde Park.

The desk clerk had no messages for him, so he went straight to his room. "Man! It is good to lie down." Martin slept for four hours without moving. After he freshened up a bit, he went downstairs to dine at the world-famous Trader Vic's Restaurant. Polynesian food was one of his favorites, and this night he had his fill. The rum punches went straight to his head, but he didn't care; he had twenty-four hours to burn, and starting off with a mild alcoholic hangover was not a problem. Besides, he needed the liquor as a substitute for a sleeping pill he did not have.

Martin was up and dressed at 6:00 a.m. He put on the biggest coat he had and went for a morning stroll through Hyde Park. As always, it was beautiful and clean. The rest of the day was spent inside his room making follow-up calls to various clients that had some loose ends to tie together before their safaris commenced. He asked for a late checkout and took advantage of the hotel's generosity by taking another nap. Catching up on his missed sleep from the past month was now a pleasure, but it was fast becoming a habit. The front desk called for him at 5:00 p.m. That gave him three hours until his flight was to depart for Jo'burg. He wondered just how he was going to survive an eight-hour-plus flight without needing to go to sleep; he was now cursing his past little naps. Except for being as uncomfortable as a human could be, Martin found the flight uneventful.

Rob and Jon-Keith were on hand to meet Martin's flight that arrived in Jo'burg just before dawn. After clearing customs and being processed through baggage claim, they all went directly to Rob's midtown apartment. Martin begged off any immediate detailed conversations until he had another nap; this time for only three hours. He got up in time to join the other two professional hunters for lunch at a cafe down the street from the apartment.

Over a hot meal, Martin thought, *is the time to tell Rob and Jon-Keith where their assignments for the elimination sequences would be.* Rob was going to Tanzania to guide Clifford Jones on an elephant hunt and Rob was going to Zimbabwe to guide Lou Maxie on a mixed-bag hunt that included leopard, buffalo, and lion. Each had received a short version of the happenings from the States, and each had tentative knowledge of their future assignments. Now was their first real chance to ask some questions and get some detailed answers.

There was no sour reaction from either pro about their respective assignments, but both wanted the full scoop on how the plans had progressed for all three accidents waiting to happen. They wanted to know all about their clients, the beneficiaries, just who was coming on each safari, and how and when the money from the operation was to be transferred. Martin explained it all to them, and then they returned to Rob's apartment. There, Martin gave each one of them ten thousand dollars American in cash. He itemized his already-spent expenses and he charted his expected ones. He offered to divide more money if they wished, but he cautioned them that if their expenses exceeded what they thought, they would have to return the overages to make up for them. Both

Rob and Jon-Keith decided to let Martin keep the remainder in escrow for unexpected costs. And besides, the extra money wouldn't draw questions as to where they had gotten such a windfall.

They went over every detail on each of their safaris like adolescent boys looking at their first Playboy magazine. All offered input that would make the plans easier and safer. When all was said and done, the three went out to celebrate. Rob expressed it best. "Never did I imagine that I would be doing someone in need such a favor, and never did I think I would be so confident that everything would go so smoothly." For the next two days, all three of them again went over every detail of each proposed accident. By the time they had gone over all of the plans at least three times, they all thought that all the holes were plugged. Arrangements were made from Jo'burg at their offices and from Lanseria Airport for all of their upcoming travels, and then the three of them boarded a company plane for Maun, Botswana. After a night there at the local company office, they joined one of the company's bush pilots to fly into each of the company's eight camps in the Okavango Delta to check on their readiness. Without exception, all of the camps passed with a high grade. The three then were flown back to the base camp to finalize any necessary business before clients began arriving.

Rob decided to stick around the base camp for another week before he would have to abandon its comforts for a miserable journey to Tanzania. He was going to postpone the inevitable for as long as possible. Jon-Keith's Zimbabwe safari was not to begin until May, so he would function as a professional hunter at some of the other camps in Botswana until a few days or so before the starting time of Mr. Maxie's safari.

On his first morning in base camp since he got back, Martin received an urgent message to get in touch with Frank Black back in Houston as soon as possible.

What a wake-up surprise, he thought. He had the native camp crew rig up his high radio antenna and tried to make a connection with Frank.

After thirty minutes, Frank was on the air. "Martin, I know it is still a little warm down there, and I know that you have plenty to do before the regular scheduled safaris start to roll, but we are committed to a special favor that we can't say no to. The editor-in-chief of a nationally syndicated magazine that appears in almost every big newspaper in the U.S. has asked us for a promotional safari for one week. He intends to write about the business and our company in the June issue. He wants to bring a photographer from the *New York Times* as well. I think we would be a fool not to oblige him. Can you fit him in?"

"Sure, Rob will be here, and he can help me entertain them as well as lighten my load around the other camps – *hakuna metata* (no problem). Anything else, boss?"

"Nope, the guy's name is Chris Doogles. I will get the secretary at the Lanseria office to meet his plane and then get him to Maun. You will have to arrange with one of our fly-boys to bring him out to camp. Let him ride with the supplies in a supply plane.

"Treat his thoughts with kid gloves. I don't know whether he is an anti or not. From what I can surmise from one telephone call with him, he seems excited to be going. We'll hope for the best. Take care, and give my regards to all the hands." Martin was relieved that the sudden call was not related to his new venture.

Rob and Martin met Chris Doogles and his photographer, Mike Sims, at the main camp's grass landing strip. As usual, first-timers always bring too many clothes and too much other paraphernalia. This was certainly the case for the two new arrivals. Rob showed them to their tent and helped them unpack cameras, laptop computers, film sacks, lighting, tripods, and tape recorders. Their tent looked more like a television studio than what it was supposed to be, a rest spot. Chris's first question was, "When do we get to go see some animals?" Rob promised them an afternoon game drive starting about three o'clock. Until then, he recommended that they take a nap, or familiarize themselves with the campsite.

Chris's second question was, "Rob, I need a description of all the dangerous game from a professional's perspective, and I would love to compare the dangerous aspects of each with the others. Can you help me?"

"Tonight, Chris. I've got a few chores to get out of the way before we go out this evening." With that, Rob excused himself.

The game drive was typically spectacular for a first-timer, from the view of the first animal, a warthog, to the magnificent sunset that paints the pure blue sky with strokes of amber, purple, and orange. The sun seemed to take an unusual amount of time getting to the sunset position, but when it was there, it was awesome. Unfortunately, it fell so fast over the horizon in its final stages that the beautiful view lasted for only a few minutes. As the newcomers headed for camp, they could see the distant campfire spitting its bright yellow flames into the treetops that ringed the campsite, always a spectacular view. The light dust and sudden curves of the camp's dirt road were never an inconvenience to first-timers, they seem to drink in the whole picture and they are always thankful just to be there.

Rob helped them unload their gear from the Land Rover and told them that their showers would be ready when they got to their tent. The two emerged from that well-earned shower, put on their light jogging suits, and headed for the campfire. The serving waiter met them with their preordered cocktails. Each pulled up one of the director chairs that ringed the campfire, and propped up his feet on a big log that was dutifully placed to rest weary legs and feet on. The serving lad then offered them some tidbits of red-eyed dove wrapped in bacon, some fried fish chips, and potato skins. "What a life," Mike said to Chris.

After another drink, the two were joined by Martin and then Rob.

Mike wanted to know what to dream about during the night. "What is a typical day like on a safari in the Okavango?" Martin knew that Rob had already been quizzed to death on the afternoon game drive, so he was the first to answer. "It's not much different here than in any other part of the bush; you'll be awakened around seven in the morning. Your cabin boy will tap on your tent and then he will unzip it and bring you either coffee or hot tea at your bedside. You'll need to let me know which sometime tonight. He will also have a tray of biscuits or cookies to get your stomach churning. If it is cold, he'll put some shoe warmers in your shoes for you; otherwise, he'll just light the lantern between your beds and leave. Breakfast to your order will be served about half an hour later. We load up the vehicles for the morning hunt a half-hour after breakfast.

"You'll need to dress in layers. Put on some shorts – no underwear, unless you want the 'jock-itch.' A nonwhite T-shirt is preferable over a button-up shirt. Put your jogging suit over these for the early-morning chill in the safari vehicle. In fact, if you have light gloves and a hat, I'd bring them. We generally ride for about two hours. We usually see several thousand game animals in the morning session; what we see will depend on where we go. You get to pick which animals you would like to find, and we'll try to accommodate. Around noon, we'll find a quaint little water hole with a shade tree in just the right place, and we'll stop for a bit of lunch. A morning of bouncing around in a Land Rover can create quite an appetite. Lunch will consist of a cold meat sandwich or so, some fruit – banana, apple, pear, or oranges. You can wash it down with your choice of beer, wine, or Coke. The natives will set up a small table that we carry under the vehicle. We'll dine on a linen tablecloth with linen napkins and crystal wine glasses for the winos. After lunch, we'll all take a short siesta, except the crew, and they'll clean everything up. We'll give them a chance to finish their lunch after they cleanup, and then we'll be off to see more game.

"At around three thirty or four, we'll stop again for a light snack and drinks. At each stop, the crew will raise our portable antenna into the tallest tree so that we can call back to camp. We do that to just check in. If we don't, they'll come looking for us. We'll finish our last game-viewing trip much like today, then we'll head for camp. Dinner is usually a seven-course meal starting with a soup dish and ending with some of the cook's special desert, usually peaches and something that would go well with the sweet fruit. Notice our native server always is dressed in a tux and fez, and his serving manners are always five star. He will put the food over your left shoulder and then you spoon out what you like. The serving dish will never hit the table until everyone has had his first serving. If there's a particular drink, spice, or food that you would prefer, just ask. The same routine is repeated day after day – kinda boring from our end unless we are with interesting clients, so the key to us having a good time is you two! *Ha! Ha!* I guess you've noticed the shower buckets with their welded shower heads. They are preset to each of your heights. If they're not set correctly, please let your cabin boy know.

"Now, you know that we have to eat meat around here; the camp crew loves meat and there are eleven of 'em. We have to take something for the pot now and then, and tomorrow is the day. Would either or both of you like to shoot an animal for the pot? It would be greatly appreciated, and we'll send you the horns and back skins for trophies by year's end."

"Gosh," Mike said. "I didn't know we would be able to hunt."

"I think we'd both would like a try at it," chimed in Chris. "What animals are the best eating?"

"Buffalo, of course," said Rob with a laugh. "I pass."

"Me too," came back duo retorts.

"Just kidding, we'll try for an impala and maybe a lechwe."

"That's more like it. Mike and I need to get our feet wet on something that won't kill us."

"There've been authenticated deaths from impala and lechwe, guys."

"Well, not tomorrow. I won a medal for shooting in basic at Ft. Bragg. I'll bust him a good one!"

"Same here, but I never received any special accommodations for marksmanship."

"I hear the dinner bell; let's have some nourishment."

Dinner was begun with a liver pate and crackers; it was quickly followed by cream of mushroom soup. A chilled bit of sorbet to clean the palate was then served in just the right dish. impala Stroganoff was the main course. Green beans and cooked carrots were the main vegetables. Peaches and cream were the cook's private selection for desert. A red and a white South African wine was always opened prior to dinner for proper breathing and chilling. Douglas Green was the red for the evening, while a Nederburg was chosen as the desired white. For the true soup du jours and the folks that like things a bit hot and spicy, Martin had his own mixture of Pouli-Pouli. God only knows what was in it, but Martin added something hot to that old wine bottle every night. The mixture of every hot sauce known to man was kept in that old corked wine bottle, and someone had to change the cork every few nights or so because the mere fumes would eat the cork right up. Oddly, no one ever refused it. Welcome toasts were intermingled with the meal, and a final shot of Grand Marnier at the end sealed the fine dinner. With glasses in hand, all adjourned to the flickering flames of the adjacent campfire.

"Okay, I know that we are the novices of all novices, but we are not only here to write a story; we want to learn. Naturally, everyone who thinks of Africa thinks of lion, elephant, rhino, buffalo, and leopard, the 'Big Five' I believe. I know you're both tired of educating us, but if you have a few more words left in your mouths, please tell us about these."

Again, Martin remembered that Rob had taken the two out earlier on a game drive, so he thought it only fair that he would again start the talking. "Let me start off by saying that several hunters have actually taken the big five on one safari. I think it's possible to get them all in one day in some places. But the point of a good hunter is to search out the largest male of the species in the huntable area.

"There is no reason to hunt anything anymore unless you are taking an animal that has been deemed to die by licensing for the good of the herd. In other words, there is only so much food and water available – the maximum-yield theory. Once the animals exceed that supply, they all die a miserable starving death. No longer can we expect nature to take its own course; to put it succinctly, we have fucked up nature beyond its capability to resurrect itself. Never again will animal life be safe as a species unless man helps it.

"As to these dangerous animals, I consider it a far more gratifying feat for a hunter to collect all of the spiral antelope of Africa than all of the dangerous game. I think the same for all of the duikers as well. Africa is so big and the various species are so spread out that to accomplish the two collections I have just mentioned would take a person at least ten years of hard hunting in over twenty separate countries of distinct areas to have a chance at completing such a chore. Not so with the big five or the big four. I mention the big four now because any professional worth his salt would kill the son of a bitch that tried to take one of our last surviving black rhinos, so that leaves only four. I am supposing that you two know the difference between the white and the black rhino?"

"Not really," chimed one of the guests. "I know there is an Indian rhino from India, but I didn't know there were two African species. What's the difference?"

Martin again to the rescue. "There is a huge difference. The 'white' rhino is almost twice the size of a 'black,' maybe a difference of nearly a ton! The white is a grasser while the black is a browser. That means one eats only grass and the other eats thorns, bark, etc. The black's reputation is thwarted by his eating habits. He is the mean one of the two, and that would figure if your diet was mostly thorns. Keep in mind they have to go in and go out. I wouldn't want that challenge every day. I'd be pretty damn mean as well. The white is almost docile. I swear I'd rather ride a white rhino than one of those American rodeo bulls I see on television. The black is one mean machine. It seems that his brain never turns on. Red-and-black-billed tick birds always adorn his back and shoulders. The damn thing can't see and the tick birds are his warning center. Funny how nature figures all this out. The rhino always has broken skin around its shoulders and it bleeds incessantly, and that attracts ticks and they attract the tick birds, and the tick birds warn the rhino. Kinda like a team sport, I'd say. One of my hates in this game of hunting is that the white rhino counts as a big five member. I grant that the black rhino is very much deserving of its inclusion because it is hard to stalk, very dangerous, and quick on its feet. The damn white rhino is like shooting your mailbox. It is easily found, it is slow afoot compared to the black, and it is about as dangerous as a giraffe. Mind you, they both can kill you, but the black is a formidable quarry and the white is not. Because the black is truly endangered, no sportsman can fill his quota of the big five unless he shoots a white. Unfortunately, the best way to hunt the white is on a ranch hunt in Zimbabwe or South Africa – or Texas, for that matter. In fact, there are more white rhino in Texas than in Africa – at least, so I've read. To pay ten grand or so to shoot a fenced-in bloated cowlike animal to fill out one of the most prestigious accomplishments in the sporting world makes me sick! And I have expressed that feeling to the hunting powers that be until I'm hoarse. Maybe someday the powers will wake up. If you really want me to give you the extras on this safari, promise me you'll mention the rhino saga that I've just told you."

Martin didn't have to ask twice, both of the guests eagerly made solemn promises to do just that.

"I understand the romance with dangerous game, and I will tell you what you want to know about them, but remember the other game animals as well because they too are a real treat to hunt. And I might add, it takes a darn lot more skill to hunt most of them than to hunt the more popular man-killers.

"We'll see a lot of kudu on this trip, but remember it if we get close enough for a shot, someone has done some good work, it takes some expert tracking to get close to those buggers. The kudu is an example of hard and dedicated hunting to acquire him. That is not to demean the big four, because most of the time a hunter has to go through a prolonged tracking nightmare to get one of those as well.

"Now, I'm not trying to evade your questions concerning the big four or the big five, so which man-killer do you want to discuss first?"

"Martin, the night is young and we've got all night. I've got the tape recorder going with plenty of tape and batteries. Let's just go in alphabetical order, that makes the Cape buffalo first."

"Okay, the buffalo is by far the most numerous. Both sexes have horns, but the bull's horns meet in the middle of his forehead in about a ten – to twenty-inch-wide mass of impenetrable armor, called the boss. He is terribly thick boned and a shot through the shoulder area to get to the heart vitals must be made with a steel-jacketed bullet and with nothing lighter than a .375 magnum bullet. Out of a hundred buffalo taken with good well-placed first shots, only one in that hundred will succumb to the first single shot. I have literally blown the heart out of a bull out here, and he ran over a mile after the shot to get to his ambush spot.

"They cling tenaciously to life, more than any other animal known to man. After they've been shot, the wounded one will head straight for the densest cover he can find. He has been known to back up on his tracks to throw off the pursuing hunter. When you least expect it, he comes tearing out of the cover straight for you. The charge is usually only fifteen yards or so and he covers that length in just a couple of seconds. His head will be out and nose up when he comes; the only way to stop him then is to wait until he lowers his head to toss you, then you must give it to him right through the boss. If you know that, you have time for two shots. You can try to kneel down and shoot the first one through his nose and into his brain. The odds of stopping him with this shot are about one in three because the target area is so small and the damn thing will be coming like a freight train. If you have failed to stop him with either shot, he will knock you down and pound his boss all over you until nothing is left of you but your shoes. You are literally ground into the earth; only a bloody spot in the soil will remain. Needless to say, I have never known anyone to escape a 'pounding.'

"The big bulls go nearly three thousand pounds, and their horns are in excess of fifty inches from outside to outside; obviously, most buffalo taken are much smaller. They're a great animal to hunt – they have excellent hearing, an excellent sense of smell, and their eyesight is certainly above average. It's funny. You can ride a vehicle right up to them in a herd, even run with them, and there will be no repercussions; but when one is wounded or one is alone, you better watch out for your life. Robert Ruark once described their look as 'as if you owed them money.' I think he was right on.

If you polled all of the professional hunters about their choice of the most dangerous animal that they hunt with clients, I'm sure 50 percent would say the Cape buffalo was the most dangerous.

"I guess the elephant is next if we are going to stick to the alphabet. The African elephant may grow to thirteen feet high. In fact, he grows all of his life. Most go through seven sets of teeth, and then when they can't chew their food anymore, they get emaciated and die a miserable starving death. They consume about three hundred pounds of vegetation a day, along with forty-plus gallons of water. They sleep for only a few hours each night, and they always take a catnap of about two hours around noon each day. When you are tracking a big bull, it is unusual to catch up to him before his midday siesta. The fastest that a man has ever run is twenty-six miles per hour, and an elephant can walk at twenty-nine! The standard first shot is through one of his shoulders and into the boiler room of the heart area. This will partially immobilize him and may kill him within a few minutes. Always be uphill from a dangerous animal when you first shoot him because his path of least resistance is to retreat downhill. When an elephant that weighs six to eight tons comes rolling down on you, it doesn't matter whether he meant to or not. You are still smushed.

"In a crunch, sometimes we have to go for a brain shot. The brute's head is the size of a refrigerator, and the brain is the size of a large grapefruit. It is equally suspended between the eyes and the ear holes. This is fine to say, but his head is usually jerking around; and you are not always level with him at the time you fire, so the brain shot is very difficult for the inexperienced. When an inexperienced client opts for a brain shot, it can result more often than not in somebody dying. There are two types of African elephant that we hunt – the rain forest variety, smaller in body with larger ears and straighter ivory; and the savanna one with smaller ears, bigger body, and thicker but shorter tusks. Both have excellent hearing. I'm told that in an experiment, an elephant could hear a watch tick downwind at a distance of one hundred meters. They've been known to smell water underground at ten miles, so they have the most finely developed smell and hearing senses in the books. Where we are, the elephants are extremely ill tempered, and they are the largest in the world. We try not to get in any embarrassing spots. One more thing. Many people disguised as do-gooders try and make money off contributions from illiterate folks who buy their story of the African elephant being endangered. That is pure poppycock! There are confirmed game department estimates of over two million African elephants south of the Sahara. The elephant lives to about fifty years of age. If every year one-fiftieth of the population dies, that would be forty thousand elephants. Because old elephants tend to get a disease called musk, they tend to go mad and destroy habitat, farms, and the occasional person. And because there is a tremendous amount of hunters who want an ivory hunt, most elephant are culled or sport hunted after they reach fifty. It takes no mathematician to figure that we have to take upward of thirty thousand elephants a year in culling and hunting. And still, there are more elephants in Southern Africa today than in the history of man! Make sure you put that tidbit in your article as well, but make sure you verify my statistics with some game departments."

Both guests again nodded their approval.

"Rob, why don't you give me a break for a minute and tell old leopard's tale?"

"You got it. If you were to ask every professional hunter which animal did he think was the most dangerous to wound you, I am sure that most would vote for the leopard. The most prolific man-killers of our time have been leopards, but they were all in India – the record for a single man-eating leopard there is over three hundred fifty people – virtually the same cat as here, just a different locale. In Africa, it is fairly rare to ever hear of a man-eating leopard. When you hunt him, if you are going to enjoy any success ratio at all, you must bait him. Once he has come to the bait, usually about a hundred pounds of meat of warthog or impala or something else that size, you will probably get a shot at him if you have a decent blind.

"The leopard can see almost as well as wild mountain sheep. He cannot smell very well, so you will have to put the bait almost under his nose for him to find it. He can hear very well, but he really depends on his eyesight. He will come to the bait most often just before dusk. He will circle the area several times to scope out any trouble. It is a must for the hunter to be absolutely still, sometimes for two or three hours at a time. Believe me, no one ever sees him go up the tree to get his bait; he just mystically appears. You let him get comfortable and begin eating before you adjust your aim from the blind. Then you shoot for the chest area.

"Now comes the fun. Usually you bring along a thick sweater to wrap around your neck to ward off his bite. You condition yourself to fall back on your back and hold his hind legs off you with your rifle if he springs at you, and then you pray that one of the other hunters will wedge his rifle between you and the cat to shoot him off you. This saves your stomach and abdomen from his whirling back feet and claws. That is the safest follow-up method. If the leopard has vanished, you got a shitload of problems. When a lion is hiding, you can throw a rock in his direction; and he will growl but not a leopard. He is not going to move or utter a sound until he knows that he can get somebody. I've searched an open glade the size of less than a football field with six men for five hours, knowing from his blood spoor that he was in there, and still not make him charge until we were almost literally on top of him. Once he gets you, it is just razor-sharp claws churning like a saw. You're going to get cut up pretty bad, but you probably won't die; thanks to the Flying Doctor and penicillin.

"Let me tell you about the baiting and the blind you must construct. Leopard range around rivers and creeks, so you hang the bait off a big tree limb high enough where the bait can dangle down a foot or so, so other smaller cats, owls, and eagles can't sit on the limb and eat. The lowest part of the bait must be at least twelve feet off the ground. That is so because you don't want a lion jumping up and pulling it down for himself. After the bait is correctly hung, we place a tracker up by the bait to have the same view as the leopard will have. Then we construct the blind about forty meters away with the setting sun to our backs, and downwind if possible; but the sun is the main culprit we have to satisfy. If the leopard comes as the sun is setting, you don't want to risk a shot shooting into the face of the sun. The rest of the trackers will construct the blind. A complete enclosure with a grass door for entry. They will make a small hole for the rifle, and they'll put a gun rest made of branches to hold the rifle on target. When you run your baits at midmorning and you've got a hit, then you construct the blind. You enter the blind about two hours before sunset so your noise and smell will be dissipated long before the leopard comes for his free meal. Your rifle will be secured to the rest branches so that you will only have to move it very slightly to get your target. Then you wait and wait and wait. You can hear the leopard coming – not really him, but the birds and other animals try to give notice by sound that danger is approaching. Then, *whoosh*, he's on the bait. Then you pray for more sunlight to see the crosshairs before you shoot. That's it, he'll fall right off that limb if you've given him a good shot, then no more worries."

Martin paused a few minutes to let the guests catch up on their notes and to install new batteries in the recorder and then grabbed a drinking glass of scotch and wet his whistle for more stories.

"While I'm on the cats, I might as well take the lion."

"Go to it, brother," Rob said with encouragement.

"The biggest thing to remember about a lion is his speed. If the world's fastest animal, the cheetah, is within twenty yards of a lion, he is as dead as a doornail! The lion has been timed in the hundred-meter dash at 3.9 seconds. Compare that to the fastest man ever at 9.8. My best advice: don't run! Like the leopard, he is very soft skinned, so most pros use an expanding bullet. The shoulder shot is the only first shot. Period! You must have planned carefully to make this happen. You must slow down his inevitable charge by knocking down at least one of his shoulders; then you have a chance if he isn't dead from the first shot.

"As in hunting all dangerous game, you get as close as you can get for the first shot and then get ten yards closer. The first shot is everything. One sees fifty times more lion in the wild than leopard, but the best way to get them is still like the leopard – by baiting. But here in Botswana, it is illegal to bait. So we watch for circling vultures every morning and listen for roars every night. Those two things get us started in the right direction when we leave camp on a lion hunt. Lions in this part of Africa don't climb trees; so where baiting is legal, it becomes a little difficult. You have to hang a good-sized animal from a tree where the leopard can't reach it from the tree limb and where the hyenas can't reach it from the ground. Again, as with all dangerous game, you learn everything that you can about them and their habitats, and then you try to stack the odds significantly in your favor, then there is less likelihood for serious trouble. A lion weighs upward of five hundred pounds, and his muscle power is said to be sixteen to eighteen times that of man. He is one powerful bunch of raging feline. His roar has been heard for over ten miles. When he charges, he comes with mouth agape and his lungs roaring. I am sure that he has literally scared some hunters to death. Even hell would feel like heaven after being mauled to death by a lion."

Rob couldn't hold his tongue any longer. "Let me give you a few confirmed facts about the big four populations. There are more leopard south of the Sahara Desert than ever before in the history of man. They are plentiful and a downright nuisance to the baboon population. The lion is holding his own. They are still plentiful but not as many as the leopard. Very much different from what you read in the papers in the U.S., huh?

"The elephant is about to eat and breed his way out of house and home in Southern Africa – Botswana, Zimbabwe, Namibia, and the Republic of South Africa. I reiterate what Martin has said, we have to cull or hunt at least thirty thousand a year to keep their numbers in check. In East Africa, the poaching is still going unchecked in most countries, but a new movement headed by Dr. Leakey's son in Kenya seems to be making some headway. The buffalo is so numerous that we are all scared to death of another outbreak of hoof and mouth or rinderpest disease. When animals of one species overpopulate, they all become weak and susceptible to disease. This is where licensed hunting is a tool of wildlife conservation that must be used. Otherwise, the resulting famine is unbelievable. Okay, I'm getting a bit sleepy. Why don't we continue this in the morning?"

All drank up. All said good night and departed for the sack.

Rob was the first to meet the two newcomers the next morning at the dining tent. The new safari-ites didn't sleep very well on their first night in the bush. Despite their well-planned dreams, each wondered what the hell all the noises were.

Rob casually replied, "At least two elephants, a lioness with cubs, and a hyena came calling during the night. Frequently, a lioness will stroll through camp with her cubs to teach them the scent of man. You have a flashlight in your tent; make sure that you shine it around a bit before you step out to the toilet tent. Given a choice between a rifle and a flashlight to ward off animals in the bush at night, always opt for the light. All of the animals are scared to death of light in their eyes. Think about it – it limits their sense of sight; so unless they are mesmerized by its beams, they will turn and run away. The elephants that came by were just feeding; sometimes they grab the tent ropes, thinking they're a thick strand of grass, but they quickly figure out that they have a trunk full of rope instead and then they let go. Again, they are also afraid of the light, so use that torch!

"Hyenas are going to come by every night. They scavenge the whole countryside trying to pick up a free meal. They will eat the leather seats out of a vehicle or airplane if you leave it open. Tonight, after we bring in new meat, they will be in abundance. That's just life out here; you'll get used to it."

Breakfast of steak and eggs – real chicken eggs – were a morning hit. Cereals and cream were also available. Guava juice was the fruit juice of choice, followed by the traditional hot tea.

After the morning bathroom duties were completed, the Land Rover was loaded; and Rob beckoned for his writer and photographer to jump in. Rob's tracker and gun bearer climbed in the back standing area of the open vehicle; the guns were secured in their racks behind the front seat, and all heads jerked back from Rob's quick acceleration to get out of camp.

Less than a mile out, Rob stopped the car to "glass" a small herd of impala not more than two hundred yards away. "I think we should get one meat source out of the way; who's first to shoot?"

Chris and Mike flipped a coin at breakfast, and Mike had won. "I've loaded a .270 there on top for the 'light' work. Grab it, and follow me. Always stay right behind me as related to the animal we are going after. We only want to give one silhouette to our quarry. If I squat down, you do the same. I will give you plenty of time to get beside me to shoot when the time comes; until then, stay right on my heels and do as I do."

The stalk was surprisingly easy. Mike pulled up beside Rob at approximately seventy yards from the herd. By now, many of the herd had their eyes trained on the two hunters. Chris saw the smoke from the shot through his binoculars a full second before he heard the rifle's report. The shot was true, and the lone male impala in the herd fell quickly. Rob arose from his squatting position and surveyed the place for any trouble, there was none.

"Congratulations, my friend; quite a nice shot. Not often do we get clients that take their first animal with a one-shot kill."

The impala was loaded into the back of the Rover, and all headed back to camp. The impala was off-loaded; the blood was washed out of the back; and with the crew intact, Rob resumed his driving duties. "We'll let the cook butcher that impala, and we'll bring him another impala or warthog later in the afternoon. Until then, let's try to find a lion or two to photograph. Keep a good lookout for vultures coming down from the sky; it's a good bet that they are after a fresh kill, probably last night's."

The fivesome rode for another hour before they saw a hundred vultures or more landing in the tops of some trees that circled a small island in the middle of the delta about a mile in front of them and to the right. They circled the spot to find the best way across the water. They elected to cross a little farther away from the evident kill. The wind would be better for their approach. "Ordinarily, I would insist that we walk, but because neither of you has a lion license, I think we will ride in. Besides, there's water all around the site, and felines don't like to get wet. We could very easily provoke a charge. Hand me that bottom rifle." Rob took the gun from his gun bearer and checked it over. All was well. He opened the bolt and jacked in a soft-point shell. The two natives in the back climbed higher on the back scaffolding for better views. Slowly the Land Rover crept closer to the vulture-outlined site while Rob held the rifle with his right hand and drove with his left. All hunting vehicles in southern Africa are right-hand drives.

The vultures started to scatter when the vehicle was within twenty yards of them. Obviously, there was something guarding the kill. Cyclops, the gun bearer, was the first to spot him – a beautiful male lion with an absolutely gorgeous mane crouched under a small bush to the right of the kill. The prey was a tsessebe, an antelope of about four hundred pounds; and both sexes have small horns. The reason no hyenas were present was that there was no escape route for them with all the water around; the same was true for the present intruders. Rob stopped the vehicle and shouldered his rifle. With a bloody face, the cat just stared at them. Mike's camera clicks sounded like atom bombs; and every time he snapped a picture, the lion's ears would stiffen. Rob eased the gear box into reverse and slowly backed up. As he did so, he angled the vehicle so that it didn't exactly face the still-crouched lion. He did this for two reasons: First, to keep the lion from thinking that they were going to come closer. Almost all full-grown lions have had encounters with man in vehicles, and they damn sure knew the front meant more serious business than the rear or the side. Secondly, at an angle, Rob would be better fit to handle his rifle in case of a charge. After a staring match of over ten minutes, the lion got up and lumbered over to his kill. He was now confident that his intruders meant no harm. He hunched down beside the rear end of the tsessebe and began to shear off chunks of meat.

Shortly after leaving the lion, the other tracker, James, spotted a distant small herd of elephants. As the crow flies, they were about three miles away, but by way of bush trails and the dodging of deep water, the trip would be well over ten miles for them. They were lucky to catch them in the open, and Mike got some spectacular pictures.

The afternoon ended with Chris duplicating his partner's shot, but this time on an animal a little bit bigger, the lechwe. After the carcass was loaded in the back of the Rover, the trackers guided Rob back to camp via a few shortcuts. The campfire was again waiting for them on their return. Hors d'oeuvres were varied; but the guests could not have imagined, of all things, smoked oysters. Supper was mainly liver and onions with mashed potatoes, and desert was brandied peaches. The campfire discussion was held at a minimum because of the lack of sleep from the night before, and all retired early.

The rest of the safari was ditto the fist day and a half – spectacular pictures, good food, and plenty of drinks. On the last evening at the campfire, Chris managed to get Rob to compare his thoughts on each of the dangerous animals and to state why one was more dangerous than the other.

"When comparing the dangers of one of the big four to the others, one has to set some parameters. If you are alone, without another gun at your side – like a professional hunter – and if you're in open country, the elephant is certainly the least dangerous. He can't see worth a tinker's damn; and if you are quiet and watch the wind, you can almost stalk right up to him and slap him on his ass. Believe it or not, I have seen that very thing done in the CAE. If you're in thick bush and the elephant knows you are there, he is definitely the more formidable of the lot. In that case, you probably have no more than a fifty-fifty chance of surviving an all-out charge.

"As to lion, if the lion has not been chased to the point of exhaustion, if he has not been wounded, and if it is daylight, he will nearly always run away from you unless he is guarding a kill or a hot female. But at night, he flips into his Dr. Jekyll and Mr. Hyde uniforms, as the case may be, and he is extremely dangerous in the open or in thick bush. If you ever encounter a male and a female together and you shoot the male, the female will come for you most every time. If you shoot the female first, the male will always tuck his tail and run away. Kinda male chauvinism of the worst order. Like an elephant or a buffalo, if a lion gets you one on one without another gun handy, you better not make a mistake or you are as good as dead. As we discussed the other day, the lion's charge is unreal – the sound, the speed, and the muscle power are all awesome.

"The leopard is 'Mr. Stealth.' Everything that he does is secretive and quiet. He is a loner, and he likes it that way. You are not going to catch him out in the open very many times. When he is wounded, he is certainly the one of the four that is most likely to hurt back. If you are fortunate enough to have on hand a shotgun loaded with double-ought buckshot, then you have the best stopping power that you can get; if you wait until he's very close, it won't be a long wait. If you are stuck with just a rifle, then you are probably not going to stop his initial charge. He doesn't come straight at you like a lion does; he zigzags, so he's very difficult to hit. If you're not alone and if your companion has any guts at all, both of you will survive.

"The Cape buffalo is only dangerous when he's alone or wounded. That sounds simple; but if you shoot a buffalo, you're most likely going to be dealing with a wounded one. You just can't kill them with one shot as a general rule. In the open or in thick bush, he will have drawn the line in the sand if he is wounded. It is either you or him, and he will stick to it until the conclusion. More people have been gored and killed by the Cape buffalo than all of the other big four or five combined, but of course more of them are hunted. As a professional, I would detest stopping a buffalo for a client more than any other of the big four, mainly because I don't think that the client could handle him if I went down.

"Please put in your article that you have seen neither hide nor hair of any snake. This is a well-documented problem that we have. Everyone is afraid of snakes, and they think we have them crawling all over the place. I doubt if I see three a year, and then they are going as fast as they can to get out of sight. Also bugs; when there are ten thousand animals around you at any one time, at least within a five-mile radius, if you were a bug, wouldn't you opt for all those shit piles instead of going over to bother a poor human? Get the picture?"

Martin and Rob bid adios to their new media twins the next day, and then they began final preparations for the first hunt of their new venture.

Martin was due on center stage in only a week.

8

Marking Time

While Martin was readying his campsite for the arrival of Dennis Kyle and his girlfriend Jennifer Miller in a week, all of the other indispensable parties in all of the upcoming plots of death were also preparing for their coming attractions.

Jon-Keith had talked to his friend and ranch manager, Peter Smit, on three different occasions about the May safari of Lou Maxie and whoever might join him. It was easier on a ranch-type safari to adjust plans at the last minute for an additional nonhunter. The camp layout usually used at the Kudu Hills Ranch would suffice for the Maxie safari. All the licenses and permits had been applied for, and there had not been any game department surprises regarding the game, the permits, or licenses. The country of Zimbabwe was still the same as South Africa and Botswana as far as inoculations and pills to be taken were concerned. Yet there were always some crazy U.S. government doctors that were not on the reasonable side of life, and they recommended a shot for everything. Thank goodness the state department quashed most of their recommendations to encourage tourism. Only a tetanus shot was classified as "highly" recommended in the shot department; and as is all over Africa south of the Sahara Desert, malaria pills that dissuade both strains of the disease are an absolute must, particularly in South Africa's low veldt.

Peter Smit told Jon-Keith that there were lots of lions in the area. He said he'd been hearing them every night for four weeks. That was the only game animal that Jon-Keith was sweating. If the lion prospects were not good, then he would have to switch to another of the dangerous species indigenous to the area to culminate his plan. Petrol was readily available according to Peter, so Jon-Keith would not have to overload his Land Rover by bringing his own. Peter said there were four safaris scheduled at the ranch before Mr. Maxie. Usually, on ranch hunts, most safaris finished a day or two early, and then they adjourned to a rest-up place like the Victoria Falls Hotel and Casino. If that happened to the safari that was there just before Lou Maxie, Peter had offered to quietly set out a few baits for Jon-Keith to keep the lions around. Lion baiting is legal in Zimbabwe, and Peter's thoughtfulness was greatly appreciated by Jon-Keith.

Rob was biding his time with Martin at the main camp in the Okavango dreading every minute of his scheduled long drive to the Selous in Tanzania. Having just helped entertain the novice newspaper writers, Rob was now relegated to overseeing the details of camp painting, the relocating of toilets and showers, and general repairs that must precede the upcoming client visits at this camp. He too had had multiple contacts within his safari area in the Selous in Tanzania. The Arusha office in Tanzania of Hunters, Ltd., had handled all of the arrangements necessary for him and his client Clifford Jones. They had sufficient warning to provide all of the wishes and contingencies for this demanding client. Special attention was made by that office to ensure as much as possible a comfortable stay for Barbara Jones, courtesy of Martin Smith. Backup ammo, an extra rifle for Mr. Jones, and his special orders of food, drink, spice, and soap were already in camp. Rob was insistent on the extra rifle because the company was furnishing Rob's firearm there as well. This way he would have two choices in case one rifle was preferred over the other. April 5 was only a little over three weeks away. Until then, Rob would stay with Martin and help with the Okavango operation for another two weeks.

Barbara and Clifford Jones were still in Houston immersed in their usual routines. Cliff was still coming in "drunk late," and Barbara was attending to her travel business. Quite naturally, Barbara subconsciously was reducing her workload with an eye on the "easy street" that soon would materialize. She had made two contacts with rival travel agencies to see if any interest existed in acquiring her business, and one of them was a hot prospect. Although she was eager to pursue a sale, she let the lead cool so that she would not show that she was too anxious. She was an astute businesswoman. She had always been too proud to ever ask her rich husband for assistance in the money department, so she had to be shrewd and energy efficient with her time. Hers was one of only a few agencies her size in Houston that made a profit, and that was due solely to her management. Exercising her expertise on her own sojourn, all of the travel arrangements had already been confirmed; and the tickets were issued through her agency.

Her only obligation toward Martin's plan was to send him the down payment funds. Barbara had two certificates of deposit in her bank. Both were in her name only. One was for eighty thousand, and the other was for sixty five. They represented the last two years' profit after taxes from her travel business. She talked her banker into combining the two CDs and withdrawing temporarily a hundred thousand for a booking that she had to pay up front for a group trip to England. The balance would be held in another CD until she got her hundred thousand back from her committed clients. As few business people can do, she talked the banker out of any penalties for the modifications. She then sent the hundred thousand by wire to an agency in London that she had frequently worked with. They in turn wired the same amount to Martin's no-name account number at his bank in Switzerland. Her reason for doing this was to have that money available in Europe when she was to personally take a party over there in May. She didn't want any hang-ups with funds because she was taking some very wealthy and influential clients that could send her lots of business in the future. As was usual in the travel business, she would dole out the money for their entire trip as it progressed, and she needed no-hassle funds in Europe to make the transactions easier. Everybody bought the story, and the deposit was transferred into Martin's account as agreed.

Barbara was going to try to treat the days left before departure just as she would for the days before any other trip. No one was going to have a hint that anything mischievous was going to happen.

Mary Kyle, in contrast to Barbara Jones, fought to keep herself busier than ever. She just didn't want to think about what she was now a part of. She thought about backing out of the deal. But every time such thoughts occurred, she would remember the strangest thing – not the pictures of her husband's escapades, but the kiss that she had given Martin when Helen was there with them. It had only been a signal, but it meant more to her than that. She could never go back on her word to Martin. She was now beginning to like the idea of living a spontaneous life, maybe Martin could even fit in. She was going to be free, with her own money, with her own time, and without a louse to share it with. But she wasn't going to let herself sit and think about it until the cards were played. If there wasn't a meeting scheduled for her on a particular day, then she would call one, either at the Piney Creek Country Club at the Cancer Society or for the Atlanta Symphony. She made herself stay busy from dawn to midnight. She wasn't going to let herself be drawn into dreams until they were certain.

Dennis Kyle never noticed his wife's daily routines before, so now was nothing different. When he did stay overnight at the house, he left early for his office every day but Sunday. And on that day he had a standard tee time at the golf course at 7:30 a.m. To his credit, he did make one trip to the local library to read up on Botswana and its neighboring countries. He ordered the new *Current Records of African Big Game* from Gun and Camera Club International to see which animals were recently listed from the area where he was going to hunt and with which professional hunter they were acquired. His research in business helped him get the jump on the competition in opening the spas in Atlanta, and he carried over the same aggressive thoughts of due diligence into this safari.

This was his second African safari, and he had learned from the first that it was prudent to try to get every animal that was on license in the area if he could – all but the dangerous game, that is. He even managed to go by several of his gun and camera club members' offices to familiarize himself with the looks of the heads that were on their walls from Botswana. Dennis was one of those people one didn't refuse, but that broad group of acquaintances would never give a thought to being the first to invite Dennis to anything. So Dennis was welcome at his fellow hunters' offices, but he was never asked to stay very long. Almost every one of his chosen members had been to Botswana fairly recently; it was a popular place for safari-goers. *It was nearly six weeks until he would be an African legend*, he thought. No matter how many spa businesses he opened, he could never reach a high like he was going to reach on this safari. His main squeeze was Jennifer, had been for nearly two years, and she was going to share this tremendous experience with him.

The most excited person in Atlanta about going on safari was the only one who was not going to hunt, Jennifer Miller. She had broadcast her trip to everyone she knew and many she didn't. She couldn't spell "Botswana" or "Okavango," so she didn't write many letters, but she did an okay job on pronouncing them to all those who would listen. She loved her new passport, and her picture inside was the United States' first to show three-dimensional imaginary cleavage! She had a new Canon digital camera that zoomed up to ninety millimeters. It cost nearly three hundred dollars! Every past safari client she knew recommended diskettes, extra batteries, short dresses, sun suits, bathing suits, thongs, and new tennies. Everyone who had ever been to Africa who talked to her couldn't help wondering just how many bugs and how much dirt that long, frizzy blonde hair would hold. Even Dennis wondered occasionally if he was doing the right thing in taking her. She was great in Atlanta. She would come and go at his command. But over there he would be saddled with her every minute of the time. He had made a promise, though, and she would certainly make trouble if he reneged on it now.

Sally Maxie was the woman with concern. She often thought, *Just what have I done? What have I committed to?* Then she would think of that day in the parking lot next to the NCNB Bank in Dallas. She would think of Martin parked a few spaces down from her when that bastard of a guy named Artie came over to her car and tried to pull a fast one on her. That receipt business. She thought about honking the horn and calling for Martin. What a tremendous pleasure it was to have Artie by the balls. Thanks to Martin, she had experienced the time of her life in that impromptu meeting with Artie. She and Martin did him in. She could never let Martin down for showing so much interest in her. She didn't want to get caught up in what could happen between them, so she had to stay busy to keep those thoughts out of her mind. Despite all of the evidence she had been shown by Martin of her husband's flings, she was now calm, cool, and collected about her plans. For someone who really didn't have a specific hourly job, she kept busy. Martin had his down payment, thanks to Artie, so all she had to do until the accident materialized was to be her calm, cool, and pleasant self.

Lou Maxie was the one in turmoil. Sally was still not certain whether or not she was going to accompany Lou on his fateful safari, but understandably, she didn't want to be there when the accident happened. No doubt she had more than a "crush" on Martin, and she hoped that someday she might get to go on a safari that Martin himself conducted – there would be no question, wild horses couldn't keep her from going then. She was more than apprehensive about joining Lou on this trip, but she had to make it look like it was her wish to go. After all, it was she that surprised Lou with the booking, and she was going to be part of it. However, complications had arisen, and she knew she could make a substituted reason for not going, especially at the last moment. Lou wasn't making things any easier for her, and she could tell he wanted some advance notice if she wasn't going so he could take a replacement "toy." He made it perfectly clear that he did not want her to go, and he concocted horror story after horror story to try to dissuade her from thinking any further about it. Her days were numbered for her to make a decision; and right now she was heavily leaning toward not going, but she didn't want to please Lou with her decision too soon. She would let him know at the last possible moment Night after night Lou would cast his eyes upon the merchandise in and around his business; he was beginning to question his current number-one companion's age. Was she getting a bit old? At least, a bit old for him? In his mind he was already grooming her replacement, a new sport model that had quickly become the number-one attraction at Baxter's. There were several potential conflicts with a new arrangement. Under present conditions, all he had to do was call his old number-one gal, and she would go on a moment's notice to wherever he wished. She and a couple of others already had their passports ready for any and all sojourns. The new one would be playing that old role of being a little hard to get. If Sally finally chose not to go with him, he could only take one company asset to Africa with him; and he silently dreamed of taking a new toy. There were several viable candidates for this position, and each one knew what she was vying for. Several times two or more would call him at the same time to stay in touch. Once he forgot his prior conversation and made a date with two at the same time. Life was becoming rather confusing for Lou. His mind stayed jumbled with the thoughts of his business turmoil, the upcoming safari, and whether he should chance taking a new toy with him or not. The thought occurred to him that his old gal might go to the Feds if he dumped her without taking her on the safari, and he often tried to think just how much she knew of his operations for blackmail purposes. Maybe his best bet was to just go alone, or heaven forbid, with his Sally.

Lou had about three weeks to cure all of these problems. He was to be in camp in six weeks. There were passports and visas to get if he entertained new blood. There were clothes, cameras, and hunting paraphernalia that had to be obtained. He had to do all of this and still watch over his business with Artie. Artie, not girls, was the biggest problem. How much would he steal while he was away? Probably more than the cost of the safari. New guidelines and safeguards must be in place before he left. He set an appointment with his accountant for his advice. He also wanted to hire one of his regular patrons to watch Artie as best he could and then report back to him when he returned. Up to now, he had not found the right guy.

9

The Killing Begins – Botswana

Jennifer Miller and Dennis Kyle deplaned from their London to Johannesburg flight at Johannesburg International Airport shortly after dawn on April 14. They were met by a twosome from the local Lanseria airport office of Hunters, Ltd.: Anna Marie, the top secretary and general girl-Friday; and Bishop, one of the company's drivers. Bishop took care of the luggage, while Anna Marie performed her usual but high-class welcoming service. Customs was well organized, thorough, and reasonably quick. In less than forty-five minutes after they touched down, Dennis and Jennifer were being whisked away as honored guests to a luxurious hotel room that was waiting for them at the Carlton Center. On the way, Anna Marie sensed the tiredness from the long plane ride for both of them and made simple conversation that was designed for yes and no answers. She wanted them to know she was available for information and conversation, but she wanted them to choose their dosage. The four arrived at the hotel in less than thirty minutes. Anna Marie personally checked them in, and then, if they were up to it, suggested a short walk-through of the various shops that surrounded the hotel and underground ice rink.

Dennis and Jennifer seemed to get their second wind, and they both were eager to see the mall that reminded them of the gallerias in Houston and Dallas. On the promised quick walk-through, Anna Marie pointed out the shops that most first-time South Africa visitors enjoy. And then she escorted them back to the enormous hotel lobby to say good day. Despite the pleasant aroma of the coffee from the lobby coffee shop, Jennifer and Dennis were winding down from their second wind and now were longing for a shower and a nap after such an arduous flight.

The lobby had been redecorated and was something special, even for such a fine hotel; and they were expectant that their room would be equally as exquisitely furnished and decorated. They were not disappointed. It was small compared to U.S. standards but was larger than those they were accustomed to in Europe. After alternating showers, the king-sized bed was just too inviting to turn down for a short nap. Instead, they slept for three straight hours.

Upon awakening, Dennis made reservations at the Three Ships Restaurant at the top of the hotel for the evening, and then they caught an elevator down to the shops. Curio shops were the vogue for Jennifer, and she headed straight for the currency exchange. Although the messy curio shops were the delight for Jennifer, Dennis was more at home in the C&S Bookstore and Rowland Ward's big game shop. For four hours, they gawked and bought. They had forgotten to ask Anna Marie if there would be time for some shopping when they returned, so they sat down at one of the restaurants to reexamine their itinerary. They were convinced that there would be no time available for any worthwhile shopping when they came out of the bush. This fact rationalized their extensive shopping spree. The connections were strained at best for their flight from Maun to Jo'burg and then to Jan Smuts for their home departure. They decided to limit their purchases to all they could carry in hopes that such an agreement would keep them from having to lug the stuff on safari. This bright idea of Dennis's soon was quashed by Jennifer when she saw two outfits that she just had to have: one leopard-print skirt and blouse, and a zebra-print dress, plus an enormous wooden carving of an old witch doctor – all of the aforementioned easily put her over their prescribed limits. She convinced Dennis that she could leave any of their purchases at the Lanseria airport office, and all would be safe until they returned. By the time that they were through with the shopping spree, Jennifer had six bags that were as big as she, and Dennis was light at least two thousand dollars.

After another short nap, Dennis and Jennifer dressed in the finest clothes they had brought for an evening at one of the best restaurants in the world. Complete with special chamber music right at their table, they enjoyed the most delightful meal anyone could imagine. The wines were suggested by the wine steward to match their specially table-prepared orders, and they expertly complemented every morsel. After a desert of bananas Foster, the two danced to the harmonic strings of a twelve-piece orchestra. Champagne and the dancing proved fatal to their thoughts of a late evening, so they retired at just past midnight.

As is typical of seven-hour time changes, they were both wide awake at 4:00 a.m. Before Jennifer knew it, she had been politely stripped of her new sexy gown and lay next to a quietly satisfied Dennis Kyle. Jennifer was truly in love with Dennis despite his current marital status and his often-wandering eyes. She was confident that she could be happy with him the rest of her life, and she knew she could make him just as happy for as long as they were together. The jury was still out on just how long Dennis would value Jennifer's company. He knew that he had special feelings for her, but he also knew that it would be hard for him to stick with any one woman for a lifetime. When he told her that he loved her, it certainly had a time limit on it.

At 8:30 a.m., Anna Marie was ringing. Jennifer was about to answer it but was shouted away from the instrument by Dennis. Before Dennis lifted the receiver, he rebuked Jennifer for attempting to answer, no matter how nice she was trying to be. "The trip must be confidential," he said. Dennis then answered pleasantly, as if nothing had just happened. "We'll be ready," he said as he hung up the phone. Jennifer knew when to argue and when to take her whipping, and now wasn't the time to turn the start of a lifelong dream vacation into a nightmare. So, without a word, she retreated to the bathroom and locked the door.

Through the locked door and above the noisy water that was running in the sink, Jennifer was warned that they would be picked up at 10:00 a.m. That left them a little less than an hour and a half to get dressed, pack, organize their new purchases, and have breakfast. The rush was on.

Bishop unloaded all the safari baggage directly from his van to the chartered aircraft, a Piper Navajo. He placed the newly purchased curio items in the office in a specially locked storage compartment that Hunters, Ltd., had designed for just such an occasion. Dennis and Jennifer finished their bathroom duties inside the airport lounge, and then they boarded the Navajo. Dennis had warned Jennifer that there was no place to "go" on a small aircraft. The pilot's name was Johan, and he was a most pleasant chap. He pointed out all of the scenery and monuments they flew over and generally gave them an education on South Africa and Botswana.

Another secretary, this time from the Maun office of Hunters, Ltd., met their plane at the end of the short but paved one-strip runway at Maun. The unloading of gear took almost an hour because the safari company had brought in supplies for all of the camps with them. The first uncomfortable situation of their trip came from the uppity customs official that would not grant them temporary visitors' rights until everything was off the plane. The secretary explained that all of the Botswana customs officials seemed to have a chip on their shoulder. It was their one chance at superiority, and they were damned well going to use it. After finally perfecting all of the credentials that the customs official demanded, they debarked to the Duck Inn for lunch. The restaurant was once owned by a professional hunter and his wife; it was now owned only by his wife, a result of a somewhat amicable divorce. Dennis picked up all of his licenses and gun permits from the Hunters, Ltd., company office and then headed back to the Maun Airport. The baggage had already been transferred to a Cessna 206 for the short flight to camp. Johan was replaced as captain on this smaller bird by a young gentleman from the States, Pat Herold.

No one can adequately describe the low-level flight from Maun to the Okavango Delta camps. One begins to see game in less than ten minutes from takeoff. The water below is crystal clear; and its azure blue tint, mixed with the green grasses and palm trees, makes an indelible picture in the mind. Giraffe, elephants, herds of buffalo, and zebra are all visible from the plane. Several times during the short flight, Pat dropped down to just above treetop level to buzz herds of buffalo and the occasional lone elephant. Even smaller game such as impala were visible when Pat brought the plane down low. Jennifer was snapping pictures at the rate of four a minute. She went through five diskettes in two cameras. When she got so excited about seeing a small herd of giraffe, Pat nearly wrapped the plane around their necks. He banked the plane at such an angle that Jennifer was looking right down on their heads. "If being on the ground and seeing all of this is better than flying and seeing all of this, then I am really going to be in heaven!"

The plane ride of her lifetime ended in less than an hour when Pat asked everyone to look out of the windows to help him spot the grass landing strip. The grass landing strip was hardly discernible to the inexperienced eye, but Mr. Herold knew where it was. He was just playing a game. He made one low pass over it to make forebodingly clear to all animals that he was coming in, and then he banked for his final approach. The wind was negligible, but he checked the grazing animals in a nearby open field just to make sure. Their tails were swatting flies and were not being blown in one direction or the other. All of the animals were grazing downwind to keep the chaff and dust from blowing up their snouts and into their eyes – an old bush trick to determine wind direction. Pat knew everything he needed to know to make a perfect landing.

Two Land Rovers were waiting next to the strip. Martin greeted Jennifer first with a cold glass of champagne and a kiss, then only champagne for Dennis. "Welcome to paradise, you two!" At least five Botswana native helpers scurried around the plane and the Rover, getting things on and off. Before they were through, Martin yelled at Dennis and Jennifer to jump in his vehicle, and off to camp they went. "Let them eat the dust. It's always important to be the first vehicle; it's the only way to stay clean."

At thirty-five miles an hour, even an open vehicle normally seems safe. But with all the twisting and turning, bumping and rolling, even that low speed caught the two new clients by surprise. "With all of the land so flat, why are there so many turns in the road to get from here to there?" Dennis said as he pointed to a make-believe spot.

"You two have a lot to learn about this part of Africa – it's going to be fun. The reason for all of the winding roads is simple. If a tree has fallen or if an animal or something else is dead in the road, it's always easier for the native to go around it than it is for him to get out and move it. We give them that consideration, and as a result, all of the roads are crooked. A road in a straight line from A to B doesn't exist in Africa! Camp's just over that next patch of palm trees; you can barely see the smoke from the cook's kitchen just over the right edge of the trees." Martin was pointing and describing everything in sight as he fought the wheel.

Before the Land Rover could come to a complete stop, the rest of the camp crew encircled the vehicle to welcome the new arrivals. Martin took them on a short tour of the camp while their belongings were being placed in their tent. "If you are not too exhausted, we might take a short game drive in about an hour, if you like. We will have about two hours of daylight left. Gus, your gun bearer, will ready your rifle for a little target practice if you'll kindly give it to him along with some ammo, preferably some .270-grain softs. By the way, what other kind of cartridges did you bring?"

"All .375 H&H soft point – .270 grain," Dennis replied.

Martin then suggested, "I'll get Gus to put a few solids in your pouch for good measure, can't tell what we might run into, you know?"

"Bullshit, Martin. I told you quite clearly that I didn't want to hunt any dangerous game."

"I know, Dennis, but if I get in a fix, I want you to have something to bail me out, okay? Besides, if we see a big eland bull, I know you would want to have a go at it, wouldn't you? They are rare here, but the possibility exists. The eland around here will weigh upward of two thousand pounds, and success in bagging one depends on getting that bullet all the way to the heart or lungs, a soft will just mushroom too early, you'll need solids if we see an eland."

"I guess I can conform, but don't get me into anything that I'm not accustomed to," murmured Dennis.

The afternoon was still warm when they set off for the target range. Martin had a favorite old tree that he used to sight in all of his and his clients' rifles. He had already marked off one-hundred- and two-hundred-yard ranges. Gus put up two separate targets for Dennis to use. "Just get it on the paper, Dennis," Martin yelled from a safe hiding place near the targets. Dennis fired, and Martin watched his head yank back at the recoil. *He doesn't have the rifle tight enough against his shoulder,* Martin thought. *He also has a rather pronounced jerk instead of a squeeze on the trigger. He would get by but barely.* Dennis fired off three more rounds – two hit the target paper, and one was two inches high. They were not grouped well enough to adjust the scope with any certainty.

Martin then moved a new target paper out to two hundred yards. Again, Martin sought a big tree for protection and signaled Martin to give it a go. Martin had previously told Dennis to hold two inches above the bull's eye at this distance. Three more shots were fired. This time, only one got any paper, and that was just inside the right lower corner, a sure sign of a trigger jerk. The other two rounds were each a foot away from the bull.

Martin gathered the targets and brought then back to the firing site. "Dennis, I wouldn't worry about a thing. For someone who stepped right off a plane and was thrust on to an unfamiliar firing range, you have done remarkably well. I don't think your scope suffered any knocks at all; I think it is just fine. You may not have hit the bull every time, but you would have killed the animal you were after every time." Gus took a shell out of the chamber, slid the rifle back in the scabbard, and tied it up in the gun rack behind the front seats. Martin told Dennis that Gus would always leave three cartridges in the magazine, but he would never have one in the chamber. He would clean his gun every night, and it would be loaded in the vehicle every morning for the first hunt. "We will always have time to unsheathe the gun and jack a shell in the chamber on this safari. Even if we are out for a walk. If we are seriously tracking something, I'll tell you when to put one up the spout. We'll always be taking it slow and easy; there is rarely any excuse for rushing a shot out here."

The campfire was ablaze when they turned the final curve into camp. The serving boy was nattily attired in his formal outfit, and hors d'oeuvres were steaming from the pan in his hand. Hot sausages wrapped in bacon were the first course. Martin talked Dennis into some cool – not cold – beer, and Jennifer opted for white wine. Jennifer brought out her diary to make sure she listed all of the animals that they saw – warthog, zebra, lechwe, impala, blue wildebeest, silver backed jackal, hyena, and tsessebe. They thought that they heard a lion, but they couldn't find it. They saw plenty of elephant sign, but no pachyderms up front. Martin insisted on her listing the bird life that they saw as well – a secretary bird, ground hornbill, lilac-breasted roller, lapse vultures, guinea fowl, Egyptian geese, black-and-white kingfisher, and two beautiful fish eagles – all of this on a short two-hour expedition.

Spaghetti and buffalo meatballs were the main dish for dinner. Prior to that, an Italian soup and salad were served. And following the main course came peach melba for desert.

Jennifer and Dennis were still suffering from jet lag, so the after-dinner campfire would have to wait until another night.

Martin set the pattern early for this safari's normal vehicle work crew. On other safaris, he usually took three natives with him every time he went out, but he had to reduce that number on this one if his elimination plan was going to work. Yesterday he took only Gus, the gun bearer, out with him. Today he would take Gus and one other. He would never take all three on this safari. This arrangement wouldn't arouse suspicions among the crew because there was a woman involved. He was bound to run into buffalo at some time, and he had to have as few people as possible with him to carry out his coup.

The next morning hunt yielded an impala and a record-book lechwe for Dennis, and he was ecstatic. Both hunts demanded an abnormally long stalk, and both offered only an offhand shot. Even Martin was impressed with Dennis's coolness under fire. The shots on both animals were slightly high and back of the ideal spot, but they were both fatal. Pictures and horn measurements were always the routine after a trophy was taken, and both clients on this safari enjoyed posing.

After at least ten pictures were snapped with each trophy, the animals were gutted and loaded into the rear of the Land Rover for the trip back to camp.

Jennifer never realized how much blood she was going to see, and at times she became slightly nauseous. Whenever they were downwind and traveling slower than that wind, the smell from the open carcasses in back nearly gagged her. She proved to be a better trooper than Martin had thought, though, and she finally got used to it. During the morning stint, they saw plenty of buffalo, but none in small bands that they could approach. Jennifer did get some pictures of a few elephants and a gorgeous cheetah with two cubs. Because of Dennis's good fortune in bagging an impala and a lechwe, Martin opted for a camp lunch instead of the traditional picnic. That way, he could leave the kills off for the cook and skinner to process without having to carry the smell around with them all day.

After a nap of about an hour and a half, Martin blew the horn in a short burst to notify all that it was time for another sojourn. Jennifer was again tardy getting ready. Why she had to have makeup on for a game drive was beyond the comprehension of everybody. The evening hunt began almost an hour later than usual. Still, they had nearly three hours of tolerable hunting light. With the Rover properly loaded, Martin took off in the best direction he knew for Cape buffalo.

The hunting portion of this safari in this area was to be only seven days, and one-seventh of his time was now down the drain to carry out his contract. Martin was getting a little antsy, but he knew he still had plenty of time; and he didn't want to show any concern. About two hours away from sundown, he spotted a small herd of buffalo near a familiar lagoon that he knew quite well. He coolly turned in their direction without calling out their sighting. "Great country for kudu, Dennis. I wouldn't want you to leave here without a record one; there are some really fine specimens in this part of the delta." Luck was with him. As he got to within about five hundred yards of the buffalo, he saw two of them split and go into some brush on the right; the others remained in the open to the left. He closed another two hundred yards, and then he stopped the vehicle to glass the game.

Martin carried a pair of Leitz ten-power fold-up binoculars in his top shirt pocket. While everyone else was now looking at the buffalo to their left, Martin was glassing to his right. "Gus, did you see that kudu bull go into that brush there on the right?"

"No, baas." The word is pronounced "boss" and means the same thing as "sir."

"I'm a little afraid of the wind, so we're going to have to keep our numbers down. Give me my rifle and hand Dennis his; I think it's time to bag a kudu." Dennis was riding a high now from his earlier shootings, so he was easily enticed to go after a kudu.

"Gus, you stay here with Jennifer just in case there are some hidden lions following that bunch of buffalo." Martin got a kick out of that statement that was clearly meant to get Jennifer's attention. Gus seemed bewildered, but Jennifer started looking all around for the lions. Martin motioned for his other tracker, nicknamed Bugsy for his protruding eyes, to come with him. Bugsy was indeed a good tracker, but as of yet, no professional hunter had commandeered him for his own. He was the spare that Martin wanted to have with him. One of the reasons was that Bugsy didn't speak much English at all. The professional hunters could easily communicate with him in his native tongue, but a client had no chance. This made the clients a bit uneasy. But for Martin, in this case, it was ideal. Martin positioned Dennis behind him and brought up Bugsy beside him. They slowly entered the moderately thick brush about three hundred yards from the vehicle.

Penetrating even this foliage was tough, but they moved as quietly as they could through some shoulder-high grass. They continued to search for signs – Martin for buffalo and Bugsy and Dennis for kudu. The shadows from the near-setting sun were now casting false images at nearly every turn. Martin sensed that Bugsy was feeling very uncomfortable with the situation. He knew that there was no kudu sign, and there was fresh buffalo sign. It was getting very dangerous. Bugsy reached over and put his hand on Martin's shoulder. Martin ignored it. Bugsy then grabbed Martin by the arm and whispered in his ear. He warned Martin of buffalo and no kudu. Martin indicated that he understood, but that he knew what he was doing. Just about the time that Martin had finished his whispered answer, Bugsy pointed to a dark blob in the bush ahead. It was a lone buffalo bull only twenty yards in front of them. His nose was low, and he was very alert to their presence. He was looking under the brush instead of over or through it.

Martin knew he would have to think fast in this situation to carry out his elimination plan, but for some reason, a quick decision like he was now facing was not already programmed in his brain. He was used to stacking the odds of survival in his favor, not doing the opposite. He knelt down and wondered if he would ever get a better chance to carry out his plan than this. No. The light was bad, and that was good; the buffalo was perfect in size, and he was alone. The tracker did not have a clue as to what was going on, and that was bad; but it was good! All of the people were in the right spots, and the buffalo was too. Darkness that was well on the way offered further cover if anything went wrong. Martin knew he would never again get such an ideal setup. He looked at Bugsy and told him that he thought that the buffalo was going to charge; otherwise, why wasn't he with the rest of the herd? Bugsy replied that there were two that had split off from the herd when they approached in the Land Rover. Martin said that he too had seen the other one, but where's his ass now? Bugsy shrugged his shoulders in an "I don't know" manner. Martin turned to Dennis and told him to crawl up even with him. He asked Dennis if he had a cartridge in the chamber. Dennis whispered, "No."

Martin then whispered to Dennis, "There is a buffalo straight ahead of us; do you see it?"

"No," Dennis said as softly as he could with a trembling larynx.

"He's backed up into a corner, and so are we. If he lifts his head to charge, I've got to nail him. You better put one up the spout; we can't turn our backs to him."

Martin knew that the noise that Dennis was about to make, by maneuvering his bolt to put a round in the chamber, would be enough to make the buff either raise his head to charge or run away to join his brother. Either would accomplish Martin's objective. At the sound of Dennis's clumsiness in releasing the bolt, the big buffalo shot out of the brush. He was not heading directly at Martin, but Martin seized the moment and fired. The bull stumbled as the bullet raked through his stomach and gut. A perfect shot for what Martin was after. In five seconds, the tearing brush from the running buffalo became silent once again. An eerie silence that all could feel.

"The buffalo has turned around, and somewhere he is waiting for us," Martin cautioned. "We can't retreat, or he will bushwhack us from the side. We've got to go after him, and we don't have much daylight left to work with."

"Goddamn it, Martin, I told you not to get me into anything like this. I ought to shoot your dumb ass. I'm heading back to the car even if I have to go alone."

"Grab hold of yourself, man. I don't like the situation any better than you. We were trying to get you a bloody kudu, and we ran into some bad luck; that's hunting. If you want to try and get out of here on your own, then be my guest; otherwise, you better damn well do as I say. Surely you realize that the buffalo is right in the direction of the vehicle. If we were to skirt the buffalo to get you to the vehicle, it would take us a good two hours, and we don't even have half an hour's daylight left. Besides, neither of us wants to leave a possibly wounded buffalo out here to kill some unsuspecting unarmed native, do we?"

Martin then turned to Bugsy and spoke in his native language. "Bugsy, I want you to go out the opposite way the buffalo has just gone. Walk around the area until you can get up a tree to spot, Gus. You and Gus then position yourselves around our backside to see if the wounded one backtracks and tries to get away. If so, one of you follow it, but leave sign for me to follow as well. Watch out for the other buffalo that was with this one. Got it?"

Bugsy didn't answer, but he nodded in the affirmative and crawled away.

Martin then grabbed Dennis. "Dennis, we are going to be all right, but we have to work together. I've sent Bugsy to fetch Gus. They will know that we are following the buffalo on his own trail. It will be easier walking, and at least we will know from what direction he might come, if he were to come. This time, you stay right next to me, not behind me. If he were to charge, you shoot him until you run out of shells; but remember, do not run. You have no chance if you run. Okay, let's go. It's not getting any lighter."

A speed of three steps per minute is a fast stalk when you are after a wounded buffalo in thick bush, Martin thought. But everything was going just as planned, and Martin knew that he had to spot the buffalo soon enough to set up the next stage. They moved at double the normal pace in this type of situation. Martin's eyes were literally out on stems. He carefully studied every patch of grass and every dark clump of bush. He dared himself to not even blink. Darkness was now less than a half an hour away. The light was worsening every minute. The rifles with scopes and crosshairs would only be good for another thirty minutes at the most, then Martin would have to unsnap his scope and opt for the fold-up open sights. This thought actually scared Martin; he had not practiced with open sights in years.

The brush area that they were in was about the size of two football fields; it was thicker in some places than others, and occasionally, there would be a small patch of grass about three feet tall. Not quite tall enough to hide a buffalo even if it were crouched. They hurried through the grass. They had gone in a little less than a hundred yards from where they first spotted the buff when they began to pick up fresh sign. The wounded bovine was now heading at a right angle to their original entry. That meant that he had over a hundred yards of cover to work with or hide under before he left the thick brush boundaries. The vehicle was almost quartering from their intended target, so there was no concern about a stray bullet causing any harm to the occupants.

At approximately 150 yards from where the buff was first shot, Martin spotted a black mass hidden in a clump of brush on Dennis's left. He physically grabbed Dennis by the arm and turned him to face the buffalo. Martin then whispered in Dennis's ear. "You see him?"

Shakily, Dennis whispered back, "I think so."

"Dennis, you have to take the first shot. That will give me the killing shot when he breaks into the open. It doesn't matter where you hit him because it's my shot that will count." Dennis raised his rifle and aimed in the middle of the black blob of darkness some forty meters ahead. Martin had eased his way behind Dennis to give the charging buffalo only one target. He would postpone his getaway until the buff was busy on Dennis. At first, Dennis tried to pull the trigger with the safety still on. Then he figured out what was wrong and clicked off the safety. The fire from the end of the rifle barrel completely blinded Dennis. It even semiblinded Martin. But it gave a clear indication to the buffalo of his impending target. The buffalo had drawn the proverbial line in the sand for somebody's death, either his or the blasted hunter that was giving him such pain for the second time. With a well-defined target lighted by fire and sound focused in his brain, now was his time to move.

With the boiling fire of pain in his abdomen and adrenaline pumped to its maximum in his heart, with his nose stretched in search of his enemy, the bloodshot eyes of this raging fury of buffalo guided his heavy boss of armor into Dennis's torso in less than five seconds. He had covered the last twenty meters in less than two seconds. Martin had stepped aside and had barely gotten behind the nearest tree, about five steps away, when he caught sight of Dennis's body that literally bounced off the palm tree closest to him. Then after a few seconds that seemed like an eternity, the enraged buffalo spun on his fallen target. He trampled every part of Dennis's body with his hooves and pounded him incessantly with his big boss of a horn. Then he stood over it to acknowledge his conquering. With blood flowing freely from his dilated nostrils, the buffalo continued the pounding. Martin watched from a close five yards. The buff was totally engrossed in the surliest of his activities. When Martin knew that there could be no life left in poor Dennis, he shouldered his rifle and fired. The buffalo's attention was still entirely on his prone enemy. He chose a shot through the big bull's left shoulder and right through his heart. The buffalo rocked backward at the impact and went down on all fours. As he tried to regain his feet, Martin again fired; this time through the other front shoulder. The buff tried to rise again, but it was no use. He had no front legs to hold him. He was permanently anchored. With his last shot, Martin moved in front of him and put it right between his eyes. The traditional death groan of the last air escaping through this great beast's lungs was sounded and signified the end to this moment of madness. Just at that moment, Bugsy and Gus arrived.

Dennis's rifle stock was broken in two jagged pieces. The rifle barrel was noticeably bent to the conforming body of Dennis. *God, what a force*, Martin imagined. Dennis's body was a limp piece of rags. It appeared that every bone was smashed. Blood was everywhere, and it was impossible to distinguish which blood was whose. Death was so sudden that the terrified expression was still adorning Dennis's face, and Martin had to physically close Dennis's frightened eyes.

Both trackers just stood there in amazement. They had both seen buffalo-induced death before but never to a white man. They thought they were invincible. Martin slithered around the tree that was in back of him and sat quietly on the ground for a minute or two. Soon he looked up at the amazed trackers and asked, "Which way to the vehicle?" After figuring out which way was the shortest route around the densest portion of the bush to where they could meet the vehicle, Bugsy was instructed to hack a trail in that direction. "For God's sake, watch out for that other buff, he is surely in here somewhere." Martin instructed Gus to go with Bugsy to bring Jennifer and the vehicle to the closest spot where they could load the dead combatants. Martin loaded the smashed body of Dennis over his shoulder and determinedly began to carry his client out to the edge of the thick brush. It was a tough trek because of all of the blood all over Dennis's body and clothing. Several times Martin had to let the body go and adjust his hold. The thorns were a menace, always grabbing Dennis's torn clothing, yet Martin still made it to the clearing.

Gus was too scared to answer any of Jennifer's questions and that made Jennifer all the more apprehensive. When Gus stopped the vehicle at the prescribed place, the suspicious Jennifer saw Martin heading her way and tried to run into the dark brush to see what had happened. Gus grabbed her and begged her to wait. As Martin broke through the last cover, Jennifer could be held no longer. On the run, she met Martin the second that he stepped out. "My god, my god, what happened?"

Martin laid the body down with the help of his two trackers that had reached his side. He then knelt down beside it, but he said nothing for several seconds. "I am so sorry. Neither of us thought that there was any danger in there. We came face to face with a big buffalo bull. Inadvertently, we had pushed him into a corner and then he charged. I got one shot in him, but it was a bit far back. Dennis shot him once the second time he charged. I was blocked, and I couldn't get my shot away for fear of hitting Dennis. I think the bull's first hit on Dennis must have killed him instantly. It was a ferocious charge; the worst I've ever seen. I doubt if anyone could have stopped him at that distance. It was so thick in there; I was thrown over to one side when the buff hit Dennis. I was standing almost shoulder to shoulder to him. If the damn thing had come from the right instead of the left, it would have been me. God, why couldn't it have been me? I still doubt if I could have stopped him any better than Dennis though. I really can't remember, but somehow my rifle got away from me when the bull hit Dennis. I had to grope around through the brush to find it. By that time, Dennis was . . . well, even if he was still alive, he didn't have a chance. As soon as I got my rifle back, I busted that son of a bitch with everything I had. He was lying nearly on top of Dennis. The impact broke Dennis's gun stock right in half. It even twisted the barrel around part of Dennis's body. Gus, please go back in there and fetch Mr. Kyle's gun."

Suddenly Jennifer was awestruck at Martin's grief, and she rushed into his arms. They held each other tightly while Bugsy turned away. With her female-inherited motherly charms taking over, Jennifer put aside her own grief and began to console Martin. She somehow began to realize that Martin being there when this terrible tragedy took place was more tragic than what she was now seeing. Without a word said, the two just continued hugging each other until Gus returned. Martin finally came to his senses and told everyone that night was fast approaching, and they had work to do to get Dennis back to camp. After the three men loaded the body into the back of the Rover, Jennifer slumped into the seat next to Martin; and they drove slowly back to camp.

It's eerie, but a camp staff seems to know the score even before they are told. They must detect it from the way the driver drives coming into camp. As the Rover pulled in, Martin and Jennifer could see the deep concern on their faces despite the dim light that flickered from the campfire. The whole crew knew that trouble had found this safari. Martin had already given instructions to Gus on how to handle the body, so Martin escorted Jennifer into the mess tent where the radio transmitter was kept. Martin had reported very few accidents during his tenure as a professional, and never an accident in the late hours of a day; but he had to now.

One of the other professional hunters in the area heard the Mayday call. Peter Winston recognized Martin's voice immediately. "Martin, this is Peter, are you all right?"

"Peter, thank God it's you. We've had a tragic accident at the main camp. Dennis Kyle has been killed by a buffalo."

"My god, how did it happen?"

"I'll fill you in on the details later, but we were tracking a wounded buff in some really thick stuff. When it came, I was blocked out by Dennis. He gave it some lead, but it was too close. I'm sure that it killed him on the initial contact. After I found my gun that it had knocked away, I killed it; but it was too late. Can you get someone to fly in and help us? Rob Manson is in camp with us, and he will be here a few minutes. He can set some fires along the strip; do you think we can get a plane in here at this time of night?"

"You're damned right we can. I'll get Pat, and we'll be on the way in thirty minutes. Can we bring anything to you – do you need anything?"

"No, just get here as soon as you can."

"Martin, you stay cool. I know you, and I know you did all you could have done. Drive around the strip several times with your lights on when you hear us – that will get rid of the animals that might be grazing or lurking on the runway. See you in an hour!"

Peter contacted Pat, and the plans were put in high gear. Peter also called the local game ranger for that territory and informed him of the accident. He even asked him if he would like to accompany them on the immediate flight. The ranger declined, saying he was busy.

Rob had come into camp just as Martin had disconnected from Peter. Gus apprised him of the circumstances, and then Rob ran to the mess tent. Martin told Rob that he would tell him the whole story on the way to the landing strip, but for now he was to load both vehicles with everything necessary to light up that runway. They would transport the body to the plane after the plane landed.

Martin paid his respects to a crying Jennifer in her tent and then suggested that she would probably want to accompany Dennis back to Maun. Arrangements past Maun would have to wait until tomorrow because of crossing a country's demarcation line. The secretary in Maun would take care of her until the morning flight was arranged. Jennifer agreed and began frantically packing all of hers and Dennis's things.

The Cessna 206 landed on schedule. Peter and Pat showed great care for Martin. They tried to prop him up in every way they thought possible, and Martin was most appreciative. Even though Martin had caused this whole thing, he relished the sincere friendship that he was being shown. He wished that he could tell Peter and Pat that he had done a good deed, but he knew that was impossible – no one would understand except Mary Kyle. He also knew that Rob was aware of the setup, and he was a guideline for Rob's future encounter under similar circumstances. He couldn't let Rob down. Martin had to summon all of his energies and thoughts to make this whole ordeal seem as natural and unexpected as possible. It was harder to do than when he had planned this whole thing, but he had to make it real. And despite its difficulties, he knew he was up to the challenge.

When all assembled back in camp, Peter and Rob took over all the decision making. They decided to wait until they got back to Maun to try to place any more calls, and they decided to save all the arrangements for the body until Jo'burg if the Botswana government would allow them to do so. Jennifer and all of the baggage were put in Martin's Rover with Rob driving, and everyone else rode with Pat and Martin in another vehicle. The body was loaded in the plane first, and then came Jennifer and all the luggage. When all this was secure, Martin asked if there was enough room for him to go. "Sure, Martin," Pat said. "Weight limits are no problem – jump in."

After the plane departed, Rob wound down the camp from its high-pitched fever and set a schedule for everyone to follow that would keep them busy for several days. He watched very carefully all of the commotion and grief because he knew he was soon going to be put in the exact same set of circumstances. He thought he could handle it.

Peter took the body directly to the Maun Hospital for any postmortem work that might be necessary. Jennifer and Martin went directly to the offices of Hunters, Ltd. The office complex there had four spare bedrooms for clients to use when necessary. As soon as they entered, Martin insisted that he be the one to call Mary Kyle and inform her of the accident. The secretary made the connection and then left the room so Martin could talk in private. There was nothing said in their conversation that would give any suspicion of a prearranged plan. There was merely a description of the accident and condolences. With the office personnel in support, Jennifer and Martin then drank themselves to sleep. When morning broke, Peter retrieved the body of Dennis Kyle from the Maun hospital. After all the necessary palms were greased, the Botswana government acquiesced to allow the body to be flown to South Africa. They did, however, insist that a complete autopsy be performed there and that they get a certified copy of the results. Martin personally called the local game official in charge to make himself available when needed. The officer was appreciative of his gesture and suggested that he wrap up all of his other needs before it would be necessary to see him. He even gave Martin permission to leave the country for a short while if he thought it appropriate.

After that call, Martin asked Peter to make the dreaded call to Frank Black back in Houston. During all this, Pat the pilot made the proper arrangements with both countries' officials to fly the body to Jo'burg. He also informed the Lanseria office of the accident and asked them to take care of the body transfer to the morgue.

Martin elected not to accompany Jennifer on to Jo'burg. He felt that Pat would look after her as well as anyone could. He also didn't relish the thought of facing all the other professional hunters that he would surely meet at Lanseria. Time would cure a lot of ills, he hoped.

After the body was transferred from the plane to the hearse, Pat assisted the office secretary, Anna Marie, with a news release about the accident. Within six hours, every reporting agency in the world had its contents. Breaking news flashes hit every radio and television station in Dennis's hometown of Atlanta. The gun and camera club president there called an emergency meeting of the board via telephone to send flowers and offer their personal condolences to Mary. Neighbors of Mary and Dennis were on their doorstep within an hour. Representatives of the symphony, the Cancer Society, and Pine Creek Country Club made their special appearances as well.

After answering at least twenty more calls of condolences, Mary began to call the necessary people that she would have to work with to wind up Dennis's affairs. *Affairs*, she thought, *double entendre*. She would stick to the business ones for now. She had long had a semicrush on the handsome bachelor lawyer that was on the board at Pine Creek Country Club, she dialed his office number. The receptionist answered by the telephone number alone. Mary gave her name and said that she needed to talk to Mr. Mark Trent as soon as possible about a very urgent matter. She was asked to hold. Mr. Trent's personal secretary was soon on the line. "Mrs. Kyle, I am Mr. Trent's secretary. I recognize your name from the board at Pine Creek. May I assume that this is Pine Creek business?"

"No, madam. This is urgent personal business."

"I'm sorry, Mrs. Kyle. Mr. Trent is in court, but he will be calling in at his next break. May I have him call you?" Mary thanked her and left her home phone number.

Thank goodness she had caller ID, she thought. She didn't want to miss Mark's return call. She then looked up the number for the funeral home that she had been thinking about using for some time and dialed it. She could not yet give the kind man who answered all the information that he needed concerning the day of the body's arrival, but minus that, she made all the other arrangements.

She next placed a long-distance call to Frank Black at the Houston office of Hunters, Ltd. Frank could hardly carry on a conversation. He was shocked by the accident and especially shocked that such an unbelievable event could happen twice in one year to his company. At the same time, he was deeply sorrowful for Mrs. Kyle and all involved. Mary made it very easy for him, and that made the conversation reasonably bearable. Frank told her that he would take care of all arrangements in getting the body to Atlanta. At the end of the conversation, Frank cleared his throat and asked, "Mary, do you know that Dennis was not alone on this safari?"

"Frank, Martin told me when he called me last night. I understand from some of my friends that things like this have been going on for some time, but I was just a wimp; and I didn't pursue the allegations. I guess that I was too busy with my charity and social work. Obviously, you can guess that we didn't really have a normal marriage. Nevertheless, Dennis deserves a decent funeral and all the respect that I can muster. After sleeping on his latest actions, I cannot harbor any bad will at this time. Maybe I'm at fault for spending so much time with the society and things."

"Mary, you are a very special person, and one I admire very much." On that note, the conversation ended.

Mr. Trent had already heard the tragic news when he called Mary back. "Mary, I am so sorry; I didn't know Dennis well, but I know you and he had to be a fine gentleman if he was married to you."

"Mark, I have suddenly become a businesswoman, and I'm afraid that I will have to talk to you in that manner. I appreciate your condolences, and I know they are sincere; but that is not why I called. I want you to represent me in a lot of ways. I want you to be my attorney. I don't know how busy you are at the present, but I'm going to need you for a good amount of time. Can you help me?"

"I cannot be too busy to help you. I'll finish my court duties this afternoon. I'm not due back in court for another three weeks, so I'm all yours. When would you like to meet?"

"Tonight, Mark. There are all sorts of complications regarding the business. You have to meet Dennis's lawyer and accountant at ten o'clock tomorrow if you can. If not, then we'll need to reschedule at your convenience. From what I know, which might prove to be very little, I believe we had a very fragile business. A hands-on business, and if I am going to salvage anything from it, then we better move as fast and as careful as we can.

"Dennis was with another woman on safari, so we will have to sort that out. I haven't talked to our insurance agent as yet, and I prefer that you do that. I have made some tentative arrangements at the funeral home, but they are going to need some legal documents. Then, of course, there is the will. I think it is in the safety deposit box, and I will get it in the morning. There will still be people coming by tonight, but I would still like you to come over."

Mark politely waited for Mary to finish her thoughts and catch her breath. "I'll be there at seven-thirty. Is there anything that I can bring?"

"No, I have plenty of food, thanks to all my neighbors. I'll see you then."

Mary and her lawyer handled everything as scheduled. Dennis was buried; and even Jennifer was received as warmly as possible at the funeral, although Mary and Jennifer never met face to face. Mary and Dennis had no offspring; but Dennis's mother was still alive, and she attended the funeral. Almost all the other attendees were on Mary's side. Except for Mary's side of the family, most of the others in attendance didn't know one another, and all were present with an uncomfortable feeling. The actual funeral was short. It was composed of a eulogy, several prayers, several organ hymns, and Mary's preacher paying tribute to Dennis and the calling for prayers and condolences for Mary. The graveside service was well attended by Mary's friends and social and charity workers. The ordeal passed slowly for Mary, but she had prepared herself well; and there was no hint of impropriety.

The next morning, Mark Trent met with Dennis's old attorney and accountant as scheduled, and all the business contracts and procedures were handled in proper business fashion. A business broker was contacted, and the spas were put on the market for a quick sale. Prudent business sense dictated a fast turnover because of the nature of the business. The insurance proceeds were exactly as Mary had perceived, and thanks to Mark, their funding was accelerated. Mary's charity officers understood her wishes for moving out of town, even to Europe. She assured them all that her charity work would continue but just in different offices. Mark put Mary's house up for sale and sent her off to Europe to find a new life. She was doubly confident that her newly found attorney would handle everything. Thinking and hoping that all of her problems were over, Mary was eager to get started anew – a new land, new charity offices, and a new life.

10

Keeping Up with the Joneses

Thanks to Rob Manson's cleverly disguised demeanor regarding Dennis Kyle's death, the main camp in the Okavango Delta was about back to normal. Everyone that had been present when Dennis's body was brought in was now gone except for Rob and the basic camp crew. Martin Smith was days away from returning from Johannesburg to that camp because he was still winding up the complicated affairs for the company following Dennis's death. Plaudits were in order for Rob who had done all that he could to bring this camp back to normality. Now he was feeling an inward pressure to get to Tanzania as quickly as possible. There were sure to be questions there that had to be answered surrounding Dennis's accident. Word travels fast in the bush, particularly in safari circles, and assurances about the accident to the game department in Tanzania, his camp crew there, and to any other inquiring minds had to be handled personally, speedily, and genuinely. He knew that if and when his plans for a similar accident were to materialize, he did not want to deal with compounded debacles at the same time. Rob's reputation all over Africa as a true professional hunter would serve him well in explaining to whoever inquired as to just how such an accident could have happened. He was eager to get all of the questioning over with.

Rob said good-bye to this Botswana camp on April 21 and climbed into his slightly overloaded Toyota Land Cruiser for his five-day jaunt west to the oldest wildlife hunting refuge in Africa, the Selous. One of the reasons that Rob chose to drive rather than fly via a bush plane was to have some time to himself so that he could finalize his impending plans on how to rid this world of Clifford Jones.

Rob Manson had grown up in the neighboring land of Kenya several hundred miles to the north. His father was a farmer, and his mother was a farmer by osmosis. They were never rich as far as money was concerned. They earned what they had from the toils of the earth, and everyone who did that was rich in character. Still, the kids never really wanted for anything. Rob, his sister, and two brothers worked long hours on the family farm, but such work never interfered with schooling. The private school system for Europeans in Kenya was especially good. Even at a young age, Rob garnered respect from everyone who knew him. He was always respectful, always had good manners, and was always willing to work harder than most. His outdoor adventures of farming and boyhood hunting took its toll on his body and the smoothness of his skin. He had scars all over him from his many scrapes and falls. If anyone ever asked him if he would have traded his childhood for anyone else's, he would surely choose the life he had led, just where and how he had led it.

Because of his upbringing, Rob had great respect for nature; and he knew how hunting benefited the whole scheme. His only childhood fights came not from arguments with other guys concerning girls, but because of another guy's interpretation of the benefits of hunting. Although he was almost "one" with nature and although he respected all of nature's creatures to the highest degree, he had an exception. That exception was any human being that didn't respect the nature he loved or the tool of hunting that preserved it.

He had met Clifford Jones before, and he knew quite well of his selfishness. He was not a hunter in the true sense but merely a bragger who really skirted danger whenever it was known to exist. Sure he endured various hardships to collect his trophies, but he never showed that extra respect for either the animal or the natural habitat that a true sportsman and lover of hunting should have. He hated the likes of Clifford Jones, and the only thing better than causing his death would be to fight him with his fists. But of course he could not do that. He was relegated to settle his distaste for Clifford Jones with his death plan, and he was not about to mess it up.

The drive through the northeastern portion of Botswana was much more pleasurable than he had hoped. Game was abundant, and the long stretches of pure wilderness gave him plenty of time to think. He absolutely relished the vista of flora and fauna. It had been a long time since he had been able to absorb such scenery without having to teach a client about it.

Soon he was going to be nearly back home in Namanga, Kenya, just three hundred miles or so south in adjoining Tanzania. There, the types of game would be nearly the same as in Kenya, but they would be happier than in his old homeland because they didn't have to share their home with nearly as many humans. There were fewer people to screw things up. His upcoming job that he had willingly contracted to do was now tucked far away in the back of his mind. His mind was vacillating between the symphonic views he was now experiencing and his winding road trip through Tanzania. He had always been mesmerized by the totality of nature, and this drive was rekindling those rare moments of childhood when he was last so totally mesmerized. As a child he was so inquisitive about all of the facets of nature, and this drive renewed his earlier commitments to continue his learning efforts about the same.

As soon as he crossed into Zimbabwe, the wildness began to change. From the open wildlife areas of Botswana to the human population crisis of Zimbabwe made him grateful that he had chosen Botswana for his vocational homeland. The roads were somewhat better in Zimbabwe, and petrol stations were more numerous; but those were about all of the kind thoughts that he could muster about Dr. Mugabe's raping of an old fine country. Water was apparently in very short supply, and the panorama of the countryside told a man of Rob's outdoors experience that a coming disaster was imminent. Since the conversion to "Black Rule," the infrastructure of the entire country was a short-fused time bomb ready to detonate, and this included the limited water supply.

Taking over a country is more than transferring leadership to a majority; it also takes on added responsibility to the future, for human inhabitants as well as for the fauna, flora, and wildlife. Thus far, all of the new colonial-supported governments that have achieved their rightful independence have failed to maintain their country's infrastructure and other typical government functions, Rob thought. *God, I hope the new African leaders in South Africa don't make the same obvious mistakes.*

When his newly topped-off petrol tanks crossed into Zambia from his short trip through Zimbabwe, he could feel the return to openness. There was a reason for this openness. No country in Africa can claim backwardness like Zambia. And the reason is, from the top of their various government agencies to their poorest tribal councils, the land is fraught with graft, sickness, stagnation, and AIDS, and no one seems to want to help make the necessary changes to bring this country into modern times.

Things were just exactly as Rob had predicted. Roads were makeshift. Petrol stations were buildings to hang a sign on; they never had any petrol unless you were willing to pay three times the customary price. Places to spend the night were unheard of, and stores that were designed for the people to buy their bare necessities from all had empty shelves. Nevertheless, the country and its people somehow adjusted, and to drive through their land and marvel at their existence was a lesson in humility. Think-time quickly outweighed pleasures for the time being.

Zambia was a driver's nightmare, but finally Rob crossed into Tanzania at the Zambian border town of Mwenz. What a relief! He now had only four hundred kilometers to go until he reached the outskirts of the Selous. Driving in this open and almost desolate land gave Rob plenty of time to turn his thoughts to Tanzania's past. Rob's inquisitive nature of his past made him remember the great Dr. Louis Leakey and Mary Leakey who personally elevated the Charles Darwin Theory of Evolution to its zenith when they discovered the first of some thirty-one hominids there in 1979. Paleontology evidence showed they were hirsute people about five feet tall with low foreheads, and they ambled continuously for more than a hundred years throughout the Oldovia Gorge. Their carbon-dated bones told their age at 1.75 million years. Little has been discovered and little is known about the early Stone Age descendants that followed these people. But we do know that from them came Homo Erectus who introduced upright bypedalism and the use of hand-axes and other primitive tools. As Rob Manson thought of these old discoveries, he patted himself on the back because he was continuing their early tradition as a hunter-gatherer himself.

From then to now, a lot of muddy water had gone under the bridge. Tanzania was now a crossbreed of natives and Arabs. The old native tribes still existed as they had for thousands of years, but in the towns, the influence of the Muslim Arabs was apparent everywhere. Mosques were springing up in all but the smallest towns. Signs were written not only in English or the native language, but in Arabic as well. Like the Sudan of yesteryear, Tanzania was on the verge of getting a new basis of religion.

Rob's thoughts soon turned back to the problems at hand, and that meant elephants. *The Selous was chockfull of them, upward of a hundred thousand or so. The area could support even more,* Rob thought, "and had it not been for Tanzania's President Julius K. Nyerere's decision to trade elephant tusks to the Chinese for their labor in constructing the country's relatively new railroad system, the country would be teeming with them." It was hard for Rob to understand the socialist government of Nyerere that would bring in outsiders from another country to work when his own people were starving for the same positions. The key to his decision had to be the trade-off of ivory for a labor force that the country would not have to pay for – false economy when you are destroying such a valuable renewable asset as the country's elephant population. True, the elephants are a reoccurring resource, but they have to be harvested in accordance with the maximum use of the food and water supply and not because you want to build a railroad. Rob seethed at the government's reasoning.

As Rob traveled deeper and deeper into the hot wilderness, the roads became narrower and more twisting. He was reminded of the old axiom that was present in every country south of the Sahara, the sudden turns were made because someone was too lazy to get out of whatever vehicle he was in to move whatever obstacle was blocking the road. He had told that story to every hunter he had guided, but he still laughed at its factual nature. As he neared the Rufiji River that bordered the great Selous, the tsetse flies began to take serious notice of his Toyota. The flies were attracted to anything that was big and moving. Both people and vehicles suited those requirements. The temperature was above ninety degrees in the shade, but Rob was sensible in opting for more heat with closed windows than suffering the awful bites of the tsetse.

Their bite is reminiscent of pinching oneself with a pair of pliers, he thought as he grimaced. A horse will die from a single bite, but the indigenous wildlife is not affected. Humans still suffer from an occasional transferred disease by them, but basically they're just a big pest to people. It was once thought that almost all African wildlife plagues were the result of the tsetse fly. In many affected countries, herds of animals were slaughtered with hope that such a procedure would rid the region of the tsetse. Caught in the center of this misguided project were the vast herds of Cape buffalo. Now, such radical measures are tempered by scientific conclusions that favor the existence of this unpopular pest. In fact, wildlife is the primary beneficiary of the tsetse. Where the fly has been eradicated, human population has been quick to move in and take over. Soon domestic cattle and goats run out all of the preexisting game species. Where the tsetse has been allowed to remain, the game flourishes without threat of conflict with humans. The wildlife nurtures and seeds the land; domestic animals eat the grass to the quick and cause erosion and soil loss. Habitat and wildlife actually depend on this bothersome nuisance, the tsetse fly.

Soon Rob crossed the Rufiji River and he was in the hunting reserve named for the incomparable Frederick Courteney Selous, every hunter's idol. Immediately, Rob's memory of reading two of Selous's great books on hunting in this area, *A Hunter's Wanderings in Africa* and *Sunshine & Storm,* jumped into his mind. He tried to remember all of Selous's accomplishments. "Conservationists the world over revere this great sportsman. It's true that F. C. Selous bagged over a thousand animals from this location, but despite the largeness of that number and the insensitivity that such a number suggests, Selous was Tanzania's – then Tanganyika – first real game warden. He was a true conservationist. The number of kills that he made must be measured against the fantastic numbers of game that inhabited the area at the time and the good deeds that permeated the area because he was there. Everything is relative," Rob silently judged. "Several old-time elephant hunters bagged more ivory than Selous did, but no one ever amassed a bigger collection of the various game than he. He literally fed villages with his rifle and he detested waste.

"He was always the one who was called on to rid the fears of the villagers from man-eating lions, rogue elephants, rhinos, hippos, and buffalos. He was a medicine man, a substitute priest, a teacher, and a generally good Samaritan. He died in 1917 at age sixty-five fighting the Germans for his beloved England as a member of England's Royal Fusiliers to save Tanganyika. He was born in England in 1851, and he was hunting in Africa in 1872, at twenty-one years of age. By the time he was twenty-five, he was the number-one renowned elephant hunter of the entire continent. No wonder that the twenty-one thousand-square-mile reserve was named in his honor for his superlative exploits and deeds." Although no one was present in the vehicle with Rob, he wanted to verbally shout and tell someone of his remembrances of the old scout.

His trip was timed perfectly. Rob arrived at his company's camp just in time for supper. The professional hunter that usually used this campsite was still there. Rob brought him a personal gift, two bottles of Scotch whiskey, rare in this neck of these woods. Finn Moss was most appreciative. Finn introduced Rob to all of the camp crew and then he invited the resident black professional hunter of the camp to join them at the dinner table. As required by law, every foreign professional hunter in Tanzania must be in constant companionship with a native professional. All licenses and reports must include the native professional's signature as well as the foreigner's. The Tanzanian Game Department tried unsuccessfully to sell hunts all around the world using their own native professional hunters, but few clients bought the idea. They then let in the qualified white European professional as long as he was shadowed by a native one. *Surely someone high up in the Tanzania Game Department knew that heavy-spending clients are almost always Caucasian, over 99 percent so. There was no way that they were going to pay large sums of money to have their life guarded by someone of native decent,* Rob thought. *It had nothing to do with race, just with the law and order of protectionism that they are accustomed to. It didn't take them long to realize the true facts of life, and the government sure didn't want to lose any more money by not attracting clients. Their answer was a mandatory native assistant.*

For Rob, this was an excellent idea, and it fit his upcoming plan perfectly. The native hunter would know where all the game was at the moment and he would know their habits, where they were going, and how to get there. Departing from form, instead of all the camp employees reporting to the chief professional hunter, the trackers and gun bearers worked for and reported to the native professional. The camp life, the vehicles, and the contact with the clients remained the responsibility of the white hunter. It was a workable relationship.

Finn relished this particular safari of Rob's. It was literally going to be a vacation for him. He planned to stay in camp for a day or two to familiarize Rob with all of the subtle nuances there and then he was going to set sail for the coast. With the young native professional at hand, there would be very little difference between this camp and the ones back in Botswana, as far as management went. The real differences were logistic – where to buy vegetables and when to order petrol and other necessities from as far away as Dar es Salaam. Having been reared in neighboring Kenya, Rob spoke the native language of the Masai as well as his own English, plus the conglomerate language of Swahili, so communication was not going to be a problem. After only one day of orientation from Finn, Rob shooed Finn off a day early to enjoy his vacation on the coast.

Mulwa Mbogo was the native professional. He had gone through all of the traditional schools and training for this specialized job. He held a high school diploma, he spoke English fluently, and he was an expert mechanic for all types of vehicles in camp. In addition to this, he had been required to hunt and kill by himself, in a fair-chase manner, all of the dangerous game except hippopotamus and rhino. He passed tests concerning the habits and habitats of all the game in Tanzania and he periodically passed tests on his shooting skills with both shotguns and rifles. Except for the almost college degree in professional hunting as a requirement for the imported white professionals, he was equally as well trained as his imported cohort. To both Mulwa's and Rob's credit, they immediately hit it off.

With four days remaining before the Joneses arrived, Mulwa and Rob scouted the concession daily for their own pleasure and for their next client. Each took a couple of impala for the pot, and Mulwa also made a magnificent shot on a running warthog from over a hundred yards to add in a little pork flavor. They searched diligently for sign of big tuskers. They followed tracks from the dry riverbeds to the high hills for glimpses of out-of-the-herd bulls. Glassing with their binoculars every morning from daybreak to around 10:00 a.m., they sighted several "keepers." Each time they spotted one, they would follow it for several miles to judge its habits. By the time day 3 was over, they had plenty of good ideas as to where the best elephants would likely be found.

On the afternoon before the day the Joneses' plane was to arrive, Rob rechecked his order list for supplies from Dar es Salaam. It was critical that he not overlook anything, the next plane could not be dispatched for another three days. All seemed to be in order when the radio operator in Dar read back the list. With that comforting thought now out of the way, Rob and Mulwa had dinner together with six old friends, commonly known in the area as bottles of Tusker Beer.

The radio came to life the next morning at 9:30 a.m. The plane seemed to have the usual delay for one reason or the other in departing Dar for camp. "There's a new guy at the airport tower, and he wants his share of hold-up money before he will allow the plane to depart," Rob told Mulwa. "When is someone going to realize that before long the government's inattentiveness to its tourists will result in their going elsewhere?"

"That's why I'm here and not there, Rob. Everyone left in that God-forsaken place tries to screw somebody out of something all the time," answered Mulwa. "Someone will sort it out, and the clients will be here this afternoon. That airplane has to make money too."

Sure enough, the chartered Piper circled camp to announce its arrival shortly after 3:00 p.m. Mulwa, Rob, and two bearers immediately jumped into two of the Land Rovers and scurried to meet their party at the airstrip. As soon as the Piper had come to a full stop and the engine was throttled down, Clifford Jones burst the passenger door open and shouted, "Who the fuck recommended these clowns to bring us in here?" Rob pretended that he didn't hear and he extended his hand to help the old geezer down. The bearers were already unloading the bags when Rob stuck his head through the passenger door to assist Barbara in exiting from the backseat.

"You must be Rob Manson, the good-looking professional that Martin Smith always talks about?"

"I don't know about the good-looking part, but I am at your service, Mrs. Jones," came Rob's reply.

"Listen, young fellow, you call me Barbara. And one other thing, I'm so tired of listening to that old fart's bitchin' that you better have a separate car for me to ride in or I might kill him before you do." Rob didn't know how to answer. He knew that she was privy to the plan, but he hadn't expected her to talk to him about it. It had been a Freudian slip.

Rob swallowed a big gulp of air, and said, "Welcome to nature's ninth wonder of the world, the Selous. Camp is a delight and all of the crew is most anxious to please you. The weather is as good as we can expect at this time of year and we have plenty of bug spray for the tsetses."

"I'll be all right, Rob. I'm just exhausted from the trip. Please forgive my untidy manners for the moment, and I promise you that I will be most cooperative person ever with whatever you suggest in the future."

"Mulwa, why don't you show Mr. Jones to camp with their baggage and I'll bring Mrs. Jones in with the supplies?"

Rough and ready Cliff was showing his age since Rob had last met him. He was now slightly over six feet tall with an overhanging beer gut that had to be at least a forty-eight-inch belt size. He wheezed when he struggled out of the plane and his eyes seemed so droopy that it would be a wonder if he could locate anything through a rifle scope. His rugged complexion mirrored the rest of his worn body. His hair was almost gone and his gruff voice was sure to scare all of the native help. He always wore the typical safari khaki clothing, including a snap-sided wide-brim hat. His dependency on alcohol was apparent when his first order to the camp crew was a cold beer. He never offered to help in any way, and he was quick to grumble when everything didn't go his way.

Barbara was the opposite of Cliff in almost every respect, plus she was very attractive and she looked much younger than her passport declared. She hid her disdain for being there, but it was apparent to Rob by her previous comment and her other actions that she was ready for her final chapter of marriage to Cliff to come to a close.

The ride to camp was only five minutes, but within that time Mulwa was completely indoctrinated to Clifford Jones's constant griping. When the camp crew surrounded the vehicle to welcome Mr. Jones and assist with the baggage, he pointed to the youngest native girl and told Mulwa, "That one's for me. Have her meet me in one of those tents tonight. I'll pay her well."

Mulwa just smiled and continued to unload. "Your tent is over there," Mulwa said as he gestured in the proper direction. "There is cool water in the basin and your favorite beer you just ordered is on the dressing table. If you wish to take a shower, I will have one of the crew put some hot water up for you."

Mr. Jones didn't even answer; he just walked toward his tent.

Rob drove slower than usual to camp from the airstrip. "I could arrange separate tents for the two of you if you would like, Barbara."

"That won't be necessary, Rob. I have my cross to bear. Maybe I'll get sick around the second night or so, and then you can move him out of my way."

Rob just laughed. The same crew met Mrs. Jones as she rode into camp, but pleasant exchanges were the vogue instead of sullen remarks. Barbara did request a shower, but she passed on any beverage for the time being.

As soon as Barbara was in the shower tent, Cliff went looking for Rob. He found him just outside of the maintenance shed. "Rob, how about a tour of the countryside while my congenial wife is taking a shower and can't join us?"

"Sure, Cliff. Just give me a couple of minutes to talk to the cook about what we are going to have for dinner. Do you have any requests?"

"No."

"Please tell Mulwa to get your rifle and we can sight it in while we're out."

Mulwa and Cliff were already in the Toyota when Rob emerged from the cook's compound. Mulwa had an uncanny knack for reading Rob's mind as to whether Rob wanted to ride or drive – he immediately switched from the driver's seat to the rear without being asked. Cliff rode shotgun while the two bearers stood in the back behind Mulwa.

Rob began a narrative on the area of the Selous and how it was so different from most hunting areas of Africa. "Game in the Selous is not nearly as concentrated as in the plains. Here there are more trees and considerably more underbrush. Because of this, there are more hiding places for predators, and thus less plains-type of game. There are warthogs and impala, but there are not many other species of smaller game. Zebras, giraffe, wildebeest – of the Nyasaland variety – an occasional hartebeest, hippo, Cape buffalo, and elephant make up the species of the larger herbivores. Cheetahs are very seldom seen; and when they are, they're usually in the bordering areas of the plains. Lion, leopard, crocodiles, and hyenas are the main predators. I know you're not interested in predators at this time, so elephant is our only real concern except for camp meat; and it's up to you whether you want to bag the table meat or you want Mulwa or me to shoot it. If we come across an obvious record-book animal of another species, we might want to reconsider taking out a quick 'radio' license. Mulwa is an expert at getting additional licenses in a hurry.

"The firing range that the camp uses for rifle sighting is a good hour away. During our drive, everybody look for elephant sign. Can't tell when that big one might cross our path, or vice versa." Cliff was encouraged by the numerous signs of elephant – limbs were pulled down on many trees, bark was stripped from the larger trees, and fresh dung was almost everywhere. Although they saw only a few cows and calves in their direction, sign was obvious that there were big bulls around someplace. Rob wheeled the Toyota around broadside to the target tree for Cliff to shoot. One of the bearers placed a large target midway up the trunk and sought shelter behind another tree some fifty yards diagonally away from the target. Rob rolled up his jacket and placed it on the hood of the perpendicular Toyota for Cliff to use as a rest. Cliff was dead on with his first round. He proved that his first shot was not luck when he successfully bull's-eyed the next three.

Rob acknowledged the feat. "I see we have no amateur here." Then it was Rob's turn. Although Rob had taken an impala the day before, he motioned the bearer for a new target so that he could make sure his rifle had not been knocked off ever so slightly during his trip from Botswana. Like Cliff, Rob's rifle was also right on. Mulwa declined to show his skills, opting to save his ammo for the time when it really counted.

The group took the long route back to camp in order to cover some different territory. A couple of good bulls were spotted, but Rob indicated that they would be his last choice; he had seen considerably better during the last few days. Mulwa spotted a giraffe that had lain down just after giving birth to a calf. Several vultures were already circling for a place to land to devour the placenta. Mulwa knew that hyenas would soon be at hand, so he asked that the fivesome wait a few minutes for the newborn to gain enough strength and mobility to follow his mother. Grudgingly, Cliff agreed. After ten minutes, the calf was licked clean by his mother and his wobbly legs began to stiffen. After fifteen minutes, the little rascal was coordinated enough to run and jump. The wait now was for his mother to regain her strength to fend off the usual predators that would home-in on the new calf at first chance. The hyenas were quick to arrive and were already starting to dart in to steal the placenta before the vultures had their turn. And if the predators were lucky, they had a chance to separate the youngster from his mother. Of course, that was the real reason Mulwa wanted to stick around, he was going to play god and jury. Soon the mother's adrenaline was beginning to flow, and with this energy aid, she nearly made mincemeat of at least three hyenas with her big slashing hooves. So cocky and strong was she now that she merely moseyed away with her newborn, not giving a second thought to those evil two-hundred-pound predators. Even Cliff finally enjoyed the drama.

Because there was really no intention of hunting elephant the first evening, all the occupants of the vehicle wore an extra dose of bug spray for the ever present tsetses. In camp, Barbara was trying out a new remedy for the dreaded flies, a bottle of Skin So Soft. Her friend at the local zoo had recommended it to her. Unbelievably, it worked to perfection. She couldn't wait until Cliff came back to tell him. *The sorry bastard had virtually guaranteed her that the people at the zoo were crazy if they thought that that stuff would keep a tsetse at bay,* she thought. *I'll show him!*

Just about the time that the sun was split in half by the hills beyond, the sound of the approaching Toyota began to get louder. As the hunting party rode into camp, Barbara sat pleasantly outside the mess tent sipping her favorite vodka. She never waved at a fly, and at this time of evening, the tsetse seemed intent on devouring everybody. All of the former occupants of the vehicle dashed into the supply tent for more spray. Casually, Barbara told Rob, "There's some Skin So Soft over there on the table. Unless you're skin is materially different from mine, I think you'll like the results." Rob looked confused, so Barbara got up and fetched the spray bottle herself. "Stick your arms out and I'll show you." She sprayed Rob's arms, legs, and his back. Mulwa was skeptical, so he just watched. In five minutes, all of the personnel that were in the vicinity were literally covered with tsetse except Rob and Barbara.

"Gimme some of that goddamn stuff," Cliff was disparate.

Barbara couldn't wait to retort, "I didn't bring enough for you because you said that my friends that gave it to me were crazy. You go get some more of your Off." Her searing smile was as wide as the nearest river!

"I just didn't want you to get your hopes up; everyone's got a remedy, but very few work."

"Oh, I see," Barbara said as she smiled again and sarcastically passed the bottle to Cliff.

Rob and Mulwa tried to carry on civil conversations at the dinner table that night, but despite their noteworthy intentions, the tension between Cliff and nearly everyone there was insurmountable. After generous helpings of egg-custard dessert were consumed, dinner was finally over. Barbara opted to retire to the confines of her mosquito-netted tent while Cliff preferred to sit and drink at the campfire. Thanks to the Skin So Soft, the tsetses had gone to bed for the time being. Mulwa politely excused himself to tend to chores. And that left a non-too-happy Rob to entertain his client, Mr. Jones. But Rob knew that was part of what he was being paid to do.

Rob tried to steer the conversation to hunting and the animal life that abounded in the area. But most of the time Cliff preferred to talk about other things; namely, available native women, the sorry bastards that engaged in the hunting fraternity, and the outlaw outfitters that stole his money on hunts such as this one. Rob had once said that he would relish the time between his initial assignment to the task at hand and the actual time when the plan was to be carried through for the building of hatred for the guy he was supposed to dispose of. Well, he had already had a head-start for that mad-on from his past meetings with him, but all that was now doubly reinforced by just being around the campfire with Mr. Jones for a little while.

The night finally came to an end when Mr. Jones was too drunk to get back to his tent alone. Because of all of the earlier day's activities, Rob was already too annoyed with Clifford to be with him another second so he summoned a cook's helper to assist Clifford to bed.

The next morning came early for the elephant hunters, 5:00 a.m. After a short breakfast, Mulwa, a tracker, a gun bearer, Rob, and Clifford Jones loaded themselves into the Toyota Land Cruiser. The top had been removed for better vision, but the front windshield remained locked in place. Normally, the client preferred the second seat in the back because it was slightly raised above the driver and front passenger seat, but not today; Cliff wanted the comfort of no wind in his face, he wanted a front seat.

At just before six, the headlights picked up fresh tracks in the dirt road of a small herd of elephant bulls. The tracker and gun bearer jumped out to take a look. They followed the tracks a good hundred yards into the bush before they returned with their analysis. There was one pretty good bull with four askaris. "Cliff, they say one is not a bad bull, but the askaris will make a stalk very difficult. You remember that the young bulls guarding the old man are called askaris in Swahili?"

"Yea," was Cliff's muffled answer.

One native estimated the big bull at over fifty years of age and the other native thought that forty might be more realistic. The footprints were large and the big one seemed to travel without any impediments. Mulwa and Rob asked several other questions. "How old are the tracks?"

"Two hours."

"Were they traveling or feeding?"

"Feeding."

"Any sign of females or young ones, 'totos'?"

"No."

"How high were the branches disturbed?"

"Ten feet."

"How big are the teeth?"

"Maybe seventy pounds."

Rob looked at Cliff and asked, "It's up to you. It's early and I think we can do better, but it might be bigger than we think."

Cliff's response could have been predictable, "How long a walk do you think it would take to catch up with them?"

"About four hours if we don't have to cross any streams and if we don't run into any other elephants."

Cliff turned his head and said, "Let's ride awhile."

Because of the first sighting, Rob slowed the pace of the Land Cruiser down to about fifteen miles an hour. One good sign usually meant that there would be other sign nearby.

Cliff surprised Rob with his first question, "How can they be so sure as to age and tusk weight?"

Rob was honor-bound to give him a competent answer. "First of all, these natives know little else but the bush and its surroundings, yet they are really the professionals, not Mulwa and not me. Although I have tracked many an elephant and I can read sign as well as any white man, they just see and feel things that I cannot comprehend. You know as well as I do that all elephants grow in size until they die, so the older an elephant is, the bigger his tusks should be and the more likely that one is broken. In fact, usually the tusks are directly proportionate to the circumference of the feet. It stands to reason that if their feet are growing, so will their teeth. Sometimes, a small elephant will have big tusks for his age, so that's why I asked him how high the branches had been disturbed while he was eating. In this case, he indicated ten feet. Considering the foliage in the area, I doubt if an elephant would reach any higher than he had to, to get to his favorite morsels. That trunk and those tusks are awfully heavy to lift, you know. Sometimes he resorts to the lazy way of feeding on the higher branches. He uses his trunk and sometimes his tusks to push over a tree to get to the high stuff. I imagine it gets rather tiring holding up that five-hundred-pound trunk just like it tires us to hold up our arms. So, if you measure the distance from his footprints to the trunk of the tree that he is trying to fell and if he uses his tusks to do the job, then you have a good idea about how long the tusks are. The natives digest the information from their findings on tusk length and foot circumference, and they can be ungodly with their accuracy on weight and length. This is reinforced by measuring the distance of the spoor from the tree where an elephant has tried to pull down vegetation and by the marks on the tree's trunk that are made to begin stripping the bark for food.

"Another point to remember when hunting a hundred-pounder or so is that they sometimes rest their head and neck muscles by leaning on their tusks. If we catch one that has done that, we can tell still more about him – how big the tips are, how wide a spread they have, and whether he is right or left tusked. Elephants are right or left tusked just like we are right or left handed. Depending on how deep the indentation was in the ground when he rested his head on the tusks, we can determine how much they weigh. By measuring their width, tip to tip, at the ground, we can tell by the comparison of other elephants in the gene pool of the area how old he is to have tusks that wide. Generally, the older he is, the wider his tusks will be at their points.

"If our quarry is feeding rather than just out strolling along, we'll have a much shorter time getting to him. Remember, an elephant can walk at twenty-nine miles per hour and the fastest a man has ever run is twenty-six. He feeds while moving at about three miles an hour on average, so we'll be fortunate if we catch a feeding one. Our chances in that regard are good, however, because he must consume upward of three to four hundred pounds of vegetation a day to maintain his body weight and growth pattern. He also must drink upward of forty gallons of water a day to keep his radiator in good working order. He's gotta stand still to drink, so that gives us more closing time if he's thirsty. If we're really lucky, we'll find our big one sleeping. They usually sleep a couple of hours every midday. While sleeping, they continue to flap their ears; it's their dual radiator system. All of their blood flows through them every ninety seconds to cool themselves down, and those ear flapping noises will likely be the first sounds we hear from our big bull if we catch him snoozing.

"I've only hunted elephant in the Selous a couple of times, but when I did, I noticed that they're extremely smart; more so than the ones in Botswana. They're also much cleverer when they feel pursued. I think the Botswana elephant is more aggressive, but the Selous elephant is certainly cleverer. The foliage is thicker here so he has more opportunity to be clever. Because of such thick growth of the vegetation, it is almost impossible to just glass for them unless you can find a really high and negotiable hill; you can see that we usually find the big ones only by tracking because there aren't many mountains around here. Mornings are the best time for tracking because you have the whole day to catch up to him and because we can make use of his nap-time at midday. It's very disheartening to follow one of these giants starting in the afternoon and then run out of daylight. If we're unsuccessful in our morning hunts, then we'll usually rest until after they finish their midday naps and glass, for whatever that is worth, during the afternoon. We'll try to find a close one, providing we can find a high-enough hill to spot anything."

One of the trackers snapped his fingers to signal Rob to stop. This time it wasn't for tracks, it was to take a leak. Vervet monkeys and olive baboons seemed to be everywhere. "I guess the leopard population must be down because there are so many baboons," Rob said laughingly. "They will be a damned nuisance when we get close to our bull; we'll have to dodge them somehow. Their chatter will alert the whole countryside."

While the boys were out after their big pachyderm, Barbara got up from her beauty sleep to enjoy a leisurely breakfast of bacon and eggs. "The East African coffee was tremendous, and so was the food." She directed her pleasant comments to the server. After breakfast, she decided to tour the cook shack and pick up some pointers on how to make all of these "Julia Child" meals on nothing but a pile of coals. The cook took her through his entire kitchen. It was about twenty by twenty feet. There was a lean-to that housed the can goods, bottles, linens, and dishes. There was the raised coal hearthstone around which the cook stoked his coals. The dimension of his stove of coals was about four feet long by eighteen inches wide at the bottom and then sloped upward in a trapezoidal effect to a top of one foot by three feet. One end of the stove was kept significantly hotter than the other end, and only the cook knew the temperatures in between.

Barbara really got a kick out of his buried oven; fresh bread was offered every day but she wondered how he managed to produce it out of that. The refrigerator was an old gas Servel like her grandmother used to have. It had been remodeled to run on bottled gas, but other than that, it was still the same. Keeping it level was the key to its working properly. Barbara thought about how much she had taken for granted back home.

Her next stop was the wash area. There was no cover here, just clotheslines. Two young girls tended to all the wash. All of the client's clothes were washed and scrubbed daily whether they were dirty or not; it gave them something consistent to do. The girls also ironed daily for the same reason. They were responsible for going to the river every day to fetch their needed water, and the river was over a hundred yards away. They carried the uncovered liquid in five-gallon buckets on their heads without any arm or hand support and they never spilled a drop. Barbara was amazed.

Despite the apparent difficulties in performing all of these mundane tasks, all the personnel seemed especially happy with their jobs and their conditions. But Barbara was glad she didn't have to put up with such antiquated means. She considered it a trade-off by having the world's most modern conveniences but having to put up with Cliff. Throughout all of her observations, Barbara continued to think about what was supposed to happen to her husband and how all these people would take it. She was making everyone here share her misery by unknowingly consenting to the "accident," and for that she was sorry.

Rob and his entourage stopped for lunch at noon under a shade tree in an open glade. The tsetse lived in the thick bush, so it was always wise to get as far away from their living quarters as possible when it came time to rest or eat. The tree that was chosen to dine under had fresh scratch marks from a recent visitor of the feline family. Mulwa indicated that the marks were from an old male lion. "Since when do big cats climb trees?" Cliff asked.

"This is the one of the few places in Africa that I know of where they do this most of the time," Rob answered. "They want to get away from the tsetse as badly as we do. If getting to a higher perch means less flies, then we should take notice. Maybe we should construct our camps here on stilts. How about that idea, Mulwa?"

Mulwa nodded in agreement.

The vehicle was parked a hundred feet away to hopefully attract the flies that were meant for its masters, but the tactic was of little success. A nap was the usual order after lunch but Cliff knew that it was going to be hard to rest with those biting flies trying to take him away. "Give me some of that spray; the damned elephants will just have to get used to the smell. I can't stand this any longer." Mulwa dug into the wooden picnic box and grabbed a can of Off for him. Rob then asked for a shot for himself. "If you are going to broadcast our scent, then we all might as well do the same."

An hour later, Mulwa roused the bunch for their afternoon drive. He indicated to Rob that there was a good glassing hill about five miles from where they were, and if they got a move on it, they could be there about the time that elephants usually passed below it to go to water. There was even a good salt lick that was visible from his favorite glassing area. In fifteen minutes, the Toyota was loaded and on its way. Very few animals were stirring at this time of day, so the drive to the glassing area was without amusement.

There was a worn vehicle path up the north side of the hill away from the usual migratory route of the elephants, and Mulwa directed Rob right to it. Mulwa positioned everyone of the party out to different glassing views and all began looking for the fabled big tusker. More than a hundred elephants were spotted but most were cows and calves. With an hour of sunlight left, Rob called the party together for departure. "We don't want to be caught out at night as a target for some rogue tusker waiting to vent his anger on us for some other trouble he had with other humans."

The Toyota rolled into camp just as the sun was falling behind the westward trees. Showers were in order for all. Cliff didn't even stop for his usual drink – he was hot, tired, bitten, and sore from the rough riding. Barbara, who had been in camp all day, had already showered and doused herself with Skin So Soft, and kindly left the bottle out for Cliff when he finished his shower. Tsetses are not usually active at night, but Cliff wasn't going to take any chances.

Supper was divine but nobody was in the mood for stuffing a stomach. Everyone ate a little and then began a drinking parade that lasted for another two hours. Barbara was drowning her thoughts about what was about to happen, an event that she had sanctioned, while poor old Cliff just wanted relief from sore muscles. Somehow, she thought the two observations had a timely fit. Barbara had planned her sickness routine for the following evening, so if things went as they were supposed to go, this would be her last night to sleep in the same room or tent with her miserable husband. That thought should have kept her awake, but she didn't fret a bit about it and she went sound asleep without giving it a second thought. Maybe it was the liquor?

Wake-up and breakfast at two hours before sunup were standard procedure for elephant-hunting days. Mulwa readied the rifles and the vehicle for departure and the loaded Toyota left camp an hour prior to sunrise. Heading north out of camp, the first destination was a salt lick that was frequently visited by the big elephants of the area. Clifford Jones and all of his hired hands were well concealed in a makeshift ground blind when light first appeared. There were no elephants, but sign was everywhere; they had been there earlier that morning. Most of the tracks were from cows and calves, but there was one very impressive set of tracks that had to belong to a giant bull. As the trackers followed these big footprints, it was apparent that there was only one other bull with him, a lone askari. The decision was easy to make; everyone gathered their belongings and they all set off for a potentially long walk. The tracks were probably two or three hours old and catching up to him would take a strong pace for at least five hours. The task ahead was arduous but everyone seemed up to the challenge. About an hour after the crew started their trek, they crossed another good track of another big bull with two askaris. The separate set of tracks pointed in ninety-degree angles.

They had to choose which one to follow. The main tracker and the gun bearer were at odds, so Rob made the choice for them – they would continue on with the first bull that had only one askari.

For three hours they dodged the other animals of the bush while keeping close to the tracks of the bull they were after. This bull was a smart one. Every time he would have to cross an open area, he would send his askari first and then he would quicken his pace until he was within the confines of the bush again. He never dallied in the open and his walk was always in a serpentine pattern.

At precisely eleven o'clock, the lead tracker heard a branch break in front of them. They were close. Rob got out his old and dirty wind sock that had once adorned his feet. It was full of campfire ashes and he shook it to test the wind. It was quartering over their left shoulders and heading to the right of the sound. They had to get downwind and they had to do it fast. Cliff was definitely the weak link in this maneuver but they made it. Again Rob tested the wind with his trusty sock. "Okay." Rob motioned to the others to remain hidden while he took Cliff in to have a look. Rob could now hear the big one breathing with that raspy, guttural sound that is so familiar with full-grown elephants. It sounded like he had gallstones in his windpipe. Duck-walking to stay as low as possible, the two got to within fifteen yards of the largest bull. The smaller askari bull was on the opposite side. Perfect! What an easy shot! But there was to be no shot. The big bull had only one tooth! Although the one tusk was gigantic and certainly over a hundred pounds, Cliff wanted a trophy with the traditional two tusks. Dangerously, the two crawled backward with their backsides to the grazing twosome to get out and away from the two sleeping giants.

Upon reconnoitering with the others, it was decided that they would angle back toward the other big track that they had earlier rejected. By taking a sixty-degree cut, they thought they had a reasonable chance of running into him. After a quick two-hour fast walk, they again heard elephants feeding just ahead of them. The wind was checked and they moved slightly to their right again to get below downwind. The three bulls were feeding on high branches and their tusks could easily be judged from fifty yards away. The two askari bulls had nearly identical teeth, about fifty pounds apiece – large for askaris. The big bull had at least seventy-five-pounders. He was quite a trophy but they all knew that Cliff had come here for something more spectacular. They left them in peace.

After lunch, they again returned to the high hill to glass the afternoon away. Again they saw plenty of elephants, but nothing worth following.

When they rolled into camp, the cabin girl came to meet their vehicle. She said that Mrs. Jones was sick. Rob judged it to be a stomach virus and suggested that Cliff take the unused tent that was always erected for just this purpose. Barbara skipped supper, and it was a good thing. Cliff ate his and her share; he was famished from walking for ten hours. Campfire stories were short and all retired at a little past ten. A small rain shower peppered the tents most of the night and that made sleeping delightful.

The next morning brought Barbara a better sense of well-being, but she was not well enough to cohabit with Cliff again. She silently hoped that this would be her day of atonement. The safari was scheduled to last over two weeks and today was just their third day, but that didn't stop her from hoping. She pretended that she was sicker than she actually was, and she elected to try her breakfast after the men had departed.

The men had breakfast early as usual. They had to be in the bush before daybreak if they were going to get a jump on tracking their elephant. It was just after daylight that they crossed a nice bull track on the smooth dirt road. In fact, the old bull walked on the road for almost a mile before exiting to the north. Oddly, he seemed alone – no askaris. Rob suggested that they give this bull a go, so all bailed out of the vehicle in anticipation of a fruitful walk. The Land Cruiser was pulled under a tree and locked up to prevent the odd wanderer from helping himself or herself to whatever was inside. Canteens were filled from the outboard water bag that was carried draped over the front fender and the rifles were shouldered in walking style, held by the barrel over the shoulder while the butt of the rifle protruded out back. Freeze-dried food packages were put in the tracker knapsacks and candy bars were stuffed in everyone's empty pockets.

This area of pristine wilderness was a favorite of Mulwa's. It was the only tree-dwelling portion of the company's concession that held the African Blackwood tree known as the Mpingo. According to the last *National Geographic* figures, there are less than three million of these trees left on earth. They are primarily used for the black carvings that the natives in this area are so famous for, but some of them make it to the worldwide institution of music. Mpingo is the only wood out of which are made clarinets.

"Unfortunately, they are carving up their own very existence – so what is new in Africa?" Rob thought as he gazed through the endangered forest, thinking only of the wasteful practice of carvings for curio shops. As they passed another one of these black-grained trees, Rob thought back to the times he had tried to play the clarinet when he was a child. "There are a lot of clarinets and other black woodwind instruments in the world and they all came from the Mpingo tree right here in Tanzania," Rob visualized. "When they are gone, so goes Mozart, Benny Goodman, and Kenny G. See, a professional hunter is not just all killing and skinning!" Rob continued his silent thoughts as the party continued their silent stalk.

They had been walking for only two hours when the head tracker caught high-limb movement about a hundred yards in front of them. It was an elephant, but it appeared off the tracking path they were following. Their tracks slanted to the right and the limb moved ahead to the left. Mulwa whispered, "Maybe he joined up with another bull." Rob acknowledged this as he brought out his ash-filled sock out again to test the wind. They were in luck. The wind was perfect for them to circle to the left to check out the new arrival. Everyone put a shell up their respective spouts and brought their rifles to the ready. Carrying them in one hand with their hand gripped around the trigger guard. All rifles had their safety on, but they were only a millisecond from action.

As they eased forward, they could now hear the new bull feeding off to their right. When the head tracker pulled away the last leafy branch to get a glimpse of the new bull, they were standing less than ten yards from him. His tusks were shiny white, but they were also skimpy and short, about thirty-pounders. Mulwa motioned to withdraw for a consensus. They could not approach the original bull from this point because the new one was directly upwind from the original one.

They opted to follow them at a short distance for a while until there was an opening to get to the yet-unseen elephant. The two bulls proceeded to feed crosswind, so the fivesome in pursuit walked another two miles before they had a chance to view their original quarry.

He was a dandy – perfectly symmetrical tusks that were exceptionally long. "I can't tell how heavy they are," whispered Rob to Mulwa. "They look a bit thin but they are sure long enough. What do you think?" Mulwa pondered the situation and tried to remember other elephants that he had previously judged from this distance, about twenty yards.

"I think that they are thin, also. Maybe over seventy pounds; definitely not over ninety pounds." Rob motioned all to move back. When they were out of downwind hearing range of the two monsters, Rob posed the question of whether to take him or not to Cliff.

Rob began by stating, "You will never find a more beautifully matched pair of ivories in all your life but they are only seventy to eighty pounds."

"Let's take him," came Cliff's reply.

Mulwa dropped back with the gun bearer to offer the elephants less chance of smell. Rob took Cliff by the arm and positioned him the exact distance behind him that he wanted Cliff to follow. The tracker led the way. They could have easily taken the big bull just a few minutes ago when they sneaked in to judge him, but now he had moved closer to the other bull and the wind had shifted; it was awful. Patiently, they followed the twosome for nearly another mile before the tracker thought it safe to move closer. The sun was now beating down on the forest bush at nearly a hundred degrees. Gnats were fighting with tsetse flies for a piece of everyone's flesh; they were as plentiful as stars in the night and they were matted around everyone's eyes. Although each had a hand free to swat them, that action was strictly taboo. Any sound or unnecessary movement might quash their stalk and give them away.

With their hearts pounding in their earlobes and with beads of sweat rolling down their arms and faces, the three pursuers crouched and crawled as close to the ground as possible to gain distance on their quarry. They were well within range for a heart shot if the bull would cooperate with a broadside view, but all they could see was elephant ass. The wind was right, but the damned elephant would not give them a shoulder to shoot. They continued their tracking. Finally, the bull quartered just enough to offer a decent shot. Rob had his plan in mind when he whispered to Cliff to abandon the heart shot and shoot him just behind his right eye.

Cliff's face told of his disbelieving ears. "I can get him behind the shoulder – " The elephant screamed. Trumpet. Scream. More screams and the pounding of earth as branches and trees gave way to the startled elephants.

"You blew it," shouted Rob. "Let's try and catch them. Follow me," he said as he began to run. It was no use, the elephants had already put two hundred yards between them and they were pulling away. Cliff ran about as fast as a turtle. Rob had no choice but to abandon the chase. Because of the circumstances, the walk back to the vehicle was solemn and gloomy. No one said a word for over two hours. Such a waste of energy when it had been about to pay off infuriated everyone. There was no love in this hunting party!

Mulwa didn't need an explanation; he had seen it happen a hundred times before. Somebody moved, got caught talking too loud, or stepped on a twig that cracked its "I'm here" noise. Mulwa knew there would be another day, but the rest of the party didn't like to waste such a stalk, particularly with such a beautiful creature at the end of it.

The cloudy day had decreased the tsetse activity for the day, so Rob suggested that they have a bite of lunch and then go glassing for a while.

Cliff was disillusioned so he protested. "You should have let me select the shot I wanted when I was in position."

"Maybe you are right, Mr. Jones, but I had to make that decision in a matter of seconds and I thought we would lose him if we didn't anchor him with a brain shot. Are you telling me that you aren't good enough to handle a brain shot?"

Cliff looked up from his reclining position and snorted, "I can damn well outshoot you and I can damn well hit a brain at twenty yards. I've always been taught to elect a shoulder shot when it's available, that's all." Mulwa started the Toyota's engine and all climbed aboard.

The afternoon glassing was cut short because there was little activity. "Maybe today was not meant to be," said Mulwa as he rounded up the glassing rests and other paraphernalia. "Let's go home and have a shower."

After a rather silent supper, Cliff retired early in favor of a book. Barbara joined Mulwa and Rob at the campfire for a nightcap. "How did it go?" Barbara inquired as she toasted by the fire.

Rob was first to reply, "I gather that you can tell. We had a few problems. We had a dandy on the line but he got away. Cliff was all set to fire but they spooked and we didn't stand a prayer of getting back up with them. You never like for a day to end that way but that's hunting."

Mulwa turned to Barbara and added, "Tomorrow will be another day. I believe the big ones are moving now; the clouds are keeping it a little cooler and sign is everywhere. Tomorrow will be our lucky day."

"Hope so." Barbara smiled.

Breakfast was again rather silent but Mulwa managed to get a smile out of everyone when he absolutely guaranteed the big one this morning. "I can feel it," he said. "I sneaked over to the closest village last night and I managed to pay a visit to the witch doctor's hut. He rattled some bones for us; you can bet we are going to be lucky today!"

The witch doctor must have known something because as soon as the hunting party was a mile from camp, there were fresh elephant tracks everywhere. It was difficult to pick the right one to follow. After studying several bull spoors at approximately three miles from camp, they decided to follow the biggest print found. They parked and locked the vehicle and began their march. In less than a mile, they switched to an even bigger footprint. In less than a mile from there, they switched again. In comparison to all of the other previous tracks they had observed, they all knew they were now onto a whopper Mulwa was the first to spot the small group of bulls ahead of them. There were four – three askaris and the big one. The thick cloud cover prompted increased winds, and that was a plus for getting close. Unfortunately, the bulls were feeding, and that meant that they were in thick brush. Rob motioned Mulwa over to him for a powwow.

"I think I better take this bastard alone with Cliff. Can you keep the tracker and gun bearer with you at a safe distance behind?"

"Sure, Rob, but for what reason?" "None other than to keep the scent down if we have to move suddenly. There are a lot of bulls in the immediate area. If one gets our scent, they all will scatter."

"Okay, but you be careful; there might be other elephants we haven't seen."

"Thanks, Mulwa."

Rob came back to Cliff who was left with the tracker and gun bearer to watch the small herd while Rob and Mulwa conversed. "Mulwa and I think you and I should go in alone, no tracker or bearer. Can you handle it?"

Cliff didn't bother to answer; he just shouldered his rifle and began to walk toward the herd. Rob grabbed him by the shoulder and pulled him back as he strode past and yanked him behind. The askari bulls were surrounding the big one, but the wind was in the stalkers' favor. They closed to within forty yards before they were repelled by the presence of one of the askari bulls turning their way. They were not seen or noticed, but they didn't want to be, either. As the herd moved slowly though their feeding patch, Rob and Cliff kept pace. Rob led another crouched stalk while Cliff was carefully in Rob's shadow and conscious not to give their quarry another silhouette to spot. Part of Rob's designed plan was to make sure that Cliff was tired and tense when it came time to fire. Rob pursued the stalk for nearly two miles to accomplish this, and Cliff was bushed in more ways than one.

When the foliage thickened, Rob took Cliff in for the kill. The wind was in their face and the sun was nearly directly overhead – no shadows to throw off a shot. As Rob pulled Cliff up to him, he could feel Cliff's heart pumping abnormally. "He is the one we've been after – at least ninety pounds apiece, maybe more. I would not be surprised if they were hundred-pounders. With him facing us as he is, you can either prove your marksmanship with a brain shot or we can wait for a heart shot later down the line."

"I'll take him from here; right between the eyes?"

"No, his head is down and we're slightly above him compared to ground level. Aim almost a foot over his eyes." It was a clear shot. There was nothing between the elephant and Cliff but twenty empty yards of space. Even with open sights, this was not going to be a difficult shot. Cliff rose to a bent-over posture leaning slightly left on a dead tree trunk. He was weak from the stalk and he was panting from the lack of oxygen, but when he shouldered the rifle, he seemed as steady as the Rock of Gibraltar. As the rifle roared, the bull was knocked back on his haunches. All of the askaris screamed in deafening unison and each looked for something to charge.

As designed, the bullet struck the choice bull high on the forehead, a foot above the eyes. Cliff had hit his mark but the mark was intentionally miss-given. The steel-jacketed projectile scorched through the bull's skull with hot searing pain, but it found no brain. Although the elephant's head is a mass of spongy bone to lighten his load, the bullet gave the big bull an awful, sudden headache. As he regained his balance on all fours, his eyes became instantly bloodshot and they focused in on just where the sound had come from. His trunk stretched out in the same direction, searching for a scent to charge. Surely he smelled the cordite explosion of the shot. Rocking forward from his haunches, the bull hit full stride in the first ten yards. Cliff was using a Browning .458 bolt action, and he ejected his spent cartridge and jacked in a new one. The big bull had to hear the ejection and the slamming of a new cartridge going into position. Cliff knew he had time for only one remaining shot. He glanced around to Rob for help, but Rob was nowhere in sight. The bull had not found his tormentor during the first part of his charge, but he picked up Cliff's movement as Cliff turned to look for Rob. There was less than a second for Cliff to react. He shouldered the Browning and fired again, upward at a sixty-degree angle, but like his first shot, he was high again. The crunch of twelve thousand pounds of muscle and bone hitting a hundred-and-seventy-pound man was eerily quiet. The momentum of the bull carried him over his target and into a big Mpingo tree. Despite the big bull's weight, he bounced off the tree and spun around for another charge. Cliff was now lying prone in death from the first smash.

Rob witnessed the entire episode. His plan had worked to perfection and he was caught up in the moment of his success. As the wounded bull hovered over his fallen enemy, Rob slithered through the brush to put the poor beast out of his misery. While watching the bull and trying to move through the brush at the same time, Rob unintentionally made a sudden movement when his foot slipped on a wet exposed root. The bull caught Rob's movement and whirled to face him. As suddenly as he had charged Cliff, the bull came for Rob. Rob shouldered his own .458 and squeezed off his equalizing round. Just as Rob fired, the big bull stumbled in a warthog hole – the bullet went high again. Seeing his misfortune, Rob ducked behind the tree from whence he had fired, but it was no use. The elephant had him in sight and smell. The tree actually hampered Rob from ejecting his first round and shoving another one in. The bull reached out with his trunk and knocked Rob down as he sped past. The blow stunned Rob for a quick moment as he lay waiting for more destruction. The bull wheeled back to his newly downed enemy and reached for him again with his trunk, but Rob was not moving. The bull hesitated. Suddenly, Rob awoke to find himself straddled by the front legs of the elephant and boxed in by the adjacent tree. All the while the big hunk of mass was studying trying and to stab him with his tusks. Dazed and half-crippled from the earlier trunk whipping, Rob tried to crawl back to safety between the elephant's hind legs, but the bull was too quick. It grabbed him by the left foot with its trunk. With one big jerk, the bull snatched Rob out from underneath him and slammed him into a tree. Rob's life was over. Next, the bull slung Rob's lifeless body over his shoulder and into a nearby scrub bush. When the body fell through the bush and hit the ground, the big bull turned to get into position to kneel down on the now blood-soaked body of his enemy, but at that moment another shot rang out.

Mulwa proved to be a better shot than his predecessors. The bull staggered sideways and then fell in a clump. The accompanying tracker and bearer searched vainly for the other askari bulls for they now posed the greatest danger. The crashing of brush to their right told their story. They were getting out of "Dodge" as fast as they could.

Mulwa knelt down over each body in complete amazement. He began to cry. He cried so emotionally that the two natives could not make him quit. For an hour, the three stayed with the bodies, not knowing just what to do. Finally, the tracker suggested that he go and fetch the vehicle. He began to run. After he was nearly out of shouting range, Mulwa summoned all his strength and yelled for him to come back. The bearer ran after the tracker. In ten minutes they both returned.

"The keys, they are in Mr. Rob's pocket," Mulwa cried. The tracker rolled over the dead body and extracted the bloody keys.

It took three hours to get the Ranger close enough to retrieve Mulwa and the two bodies. The two natives loaded the corpses while Mulwa attended to the guns and other paraphernalia. Mulwa cut off the tail of the elephant in hopes that whoever found it would know that the deed was done by a legitimate licensed hunter and not a poacher, and that the licensee would return shortly to claim his prize. This was what was done in the old days to claim a downed elephant. *If this carcass is found*, Mulwa thought, *hopefully it will be found by someone who knows the past.*

The saddened hunters were two hours later than usual in turning into camp. The camp crew met them with hushed silence. Mulwa motioned to the cook and cabin boys to remove the bodies while he walked nervously to the campfire to console Barbara.

At the end of his narrative, Barbara was in shock. She was literally dumbfounded. She asked herself, "Am I to blame? Certainly so!" Mulwa held her and offered her consolation, but she was now in a trance of blameful shame. One of the women attendants took over for Mulwa while he tried to raise someone on the radio. It was impossible to get a plane in that night, but one would be sent first thing in the morning. The radio operator for the company assured Mulwa that she would notify all the necessary authorities and the main company office of the accident. All of the arrangements in Dar es Salaam would be taken care of in the morning as well. Mulwa returned to Barbara at the open fire.

Barbara had prepared herself for Cliff's demise but she had never given thought that someone else might also succumb. After a while, she began to rationalize. "Rob knew what he was doing; he was doing it for money. He knew the dangers." This reasoning seemed trite. Finally, Barbara got hold of herself and realized that the facts were not going to change. They were set in stone and she was going to have to live or die with them. She would choose to live. Mulwa sat up all night with her at the campfire. They both dozed off a few times, but in each case, the other would bring the conversation back to life with a "why" or "how."

The next morning showed the bodies in full rigor mortis. They had been wrapped in sheets for transportation. The whole camp crew readied Mrs. Jones for her departure, and that included all the baggage, guns, etc. The plane arrived just short of noon. After the buzzing of the camp by the hired bush pilot, the camp crew loaded the bodies and the other paraphernalia into two vehicles and drove the almost two miles to the grass landing strip. There, the bodies were loaded first in the plane and then Barbara was put in the copilot's seat. The rest of the stuff was crammed in the back around the two bodies. It was a grotesque sight. By now, the bodies were beginning to smell. It was the most awful plane ride that anyone could imagine.

The company secretary and a pair of Tanzania Game Department officials meet the plane as it landed in Dar. Barbara was helped out of the plane and escorted to a waiting car for a ride to the company offices. She was told that she must submit to a government interview but it could be done at the safari company office. The kind young secretary, Joanne, had already arranged for her and the bodies to be flown to Nairobi for final procedures. From there, Barbara would escort Cliff's body back to Houston for burial and the company would have Rob's body flown to Johannesburg. The later arrangements were subject to change when the next of kin was finally notified.

The government interview went as smoothly as one could expect. Making the best of what was available, Barbara took a short sponge bath and applied new makeup. She was then shuttled back to the airport by Joanne for a departure on the rather unreliable East African Airways jet to Nairobi. The unreliability was in reference to time only. The plane finally departed two hours later than scheduled.

Upon deplaning, Barbara was met by security officials from the Kenyan government as well as a representative from Hunters, Ltd.'s office in Nairobi. She was given a temporary visa before the officials of the government tended to the task of taking care of the bodies, then a young man from the Hunters, Ltd. office ferried Barbara to the downtown Hilton Hotel. She was informed that the next flight to Europe that she and her husband's body could make was in two days. This stopover was not in her plans. But it was all right; this was not her first visit to Nairobi. In fact, she had several acquaintances there and they would certainly be disappointed if she did not call on them in this time of sorrow.

She called on Simone and Joe Cheffing, who owned and operated the Bateleur Safari Company of Kenya first. The Bateleur offices were in the adjacent Hilton office complex and they immediately rushed over to Barbara's aid.

After the traditional hugs, Simone questioned Barbara as to why they were not given prior notice of her arrival, after all, Barbara and Cliff had been on three safaris with them. Everyone was severely stretched. Barbara invited her hosts to sit down, and then she began her story. "Cliff was killed by an elephant in the Selous yesterday."

"My god," both Joe and Simone said in semiunison. Barbara continued with the details until everything that was of any importance was out. Joe insisted that Barbara stay with them for the next two nights and he sent one of his company employees to fetch her belongings from the hotel baggage area.

Joe and Simone took a sabbatical from their daily business routines to comfort Barbara. They visited Nairobi Park for some leisurely game viewing by day and they dined at the Carnivore Restaurant the first night and at the Nairobi Casino the next night. The idea was to get what had happened off Barbara's mind as much as possible. When it was time for Barbara to leave, Joe took charge of getting Barbara to the airport while the Hunters, Ltd. office took care of having Cliff's body loaded on to the plane. Joanne had been able to make straight-through flights all the way to Houston once Barbara left Nairobi – for this, Barbara was most grateful. She arrived in Houston early in the morning. Frank Black, from the main office of Hunters, Ltd., met her at the deplaning gate. They hugged for a few minutes before either could say a word. Then they verbally consoled each other; Frank to Barbara for her husband's accident, and Barbara to Frank for the loss of a fine professional hunter. "This represents three people this year that we have lost, Barbara. Do you see anything different in the way we are operating?"

"Absolutely not, Frank. Everything was just as well organized and everyone was just as caring. You have a splendid company. I'm afraid it was just one of those things."

Frank took Barbara home, but before he could drive away, the driveway was packed with sympathizers and well-wishers from the neighborhood. Other friends showed up within the hour, and soon came Barbara's lawyer and insurance agent. Barbara handled everyone in typically gracious fashion. When she had time in-between guests, she discussed the business aspects of the accident with her lawyer and her insurance agent and she was assisted by both in making the necessary funeral arrangements. Although most of the members were not fond of Cliff, almost the entire gun and camera club chapter showed up to express their sorrows. Again, Barbara was grateful and gracious.

At the funeral, an odd person came up to Barbara to offer her condolences. It was Jennifer Miller, and she was accompanied by a member of the gun and camera club chapter from Atlanta, named Chuck something or other. She indicated that she had lost someone quite special last month in the same sort of accident, also on safari with the same company, but at the hands of a lion. Barbara then remembered hearing about it from Cliff. Barbara returned the especially kind condolences and turned to receive other well-wishers.

None of Clifford Jones's children or grandchildren accepted Barbara's invitation to come to the funeral. Barbara called them all personally to inform them of the accident, but all of them had long given up on any relationship with the old man and they didn't want to rekindle old wounds. They were, however, very concerned about the health and happiness of Barbara. She thanked them for their concerns and told them that she would be all right. She indicated to each part of the family that she would soon be in touch with them as to where she planned to live and she hinted strongly that she was going to move to Europe.

After the funeral, Barbara tried to remember the fellow's name that escorted Jennifer but couldn't. She remembered the name, Jennifer, and remembered that she was from Atlanta, but that was all that she could remember. Then she thought, *If I need it, she just might be someone I might commiserate with. If I need to know his or her name later, I can always go to someone in Cliff's old gun and camera club chapter and get him to help me. For sure, they'll recall the other accident.* She then dismissed it from her mind.

In a week's time, her lawyer had everything under control and suggested to Barbara that she get out of town for a while. He had her recently executed power of attorney and Barbara had the utmost trust in him for all of her affairs, and he already knew them well. That idea sounded good to her, so she turned over the keys to her office to her competitor with the idea that they could better assess her travel company's value if they sat in the office a while. They jumped at the chance. She left, prepared bank deposit slips with both her accountant and her lawyer in case any insurance proceeds came in, and then she caught a plane to London to go house-hunting.

11

The Burlesque Lion

Martin Smith expected to hear about the tragic death of Clifford Jones, but he, like Barbara Jones, had never envisioned that Cliff's death would be coupled with Rob Manson's. Martin was more than shocked; he was bewildered and almost incoherent when Frank Black called him from Houston to break the news. Martin had rehearsed his disbelief well in anticipation of such a call, but when Frank mentioned Rob's accident as well, Martin went comatose. It was several seconds before he could even answer his boss. He instinctively knew what happened, so he did not bother to ask any questions about the debacle. He knew that Frank would fill him in anyway. Mulwa had reconstructed the scene with the help of the trackers that were present during and after the accident and told Frank the gory details. "After the bull had killed Clifford, Mulwa said that Rob made a traditional attempt at a brain shot from about fifteen yards, but the elephant charged as soon as Rob broke cover to make the shot. The big bull tripped in a warthog hole just as the shot came off and the bullet went high. There was no second chance. He was using his bolt-action .458 because he was running low on ammunition for his .500 side-by-side. What a pity he was caught with the wrong rifle for the occasion. His .500 Nitro would have at least stopped the charge even if the shot wasn't perfectly placed. Rob was just too good a professional not to have stopped that elephant."

Frank informed Martin of the tentative plans to fly Rob's body to Jo'burg from Nairobi in a day or two. Martin finally mustered enough breath to take part in the conversation. "What about Barbara? God, I'm sorry for her, but you understand my more extreme grief of losing Rob. We had been together in one form or the other for nearly thirty years. It would have to have been something queer for an animal to get to Rob. He was a great professional and a great shot under pressure. I just can't believe it."

Neither spoke for a moment until Frank broke the silence. "I've talked to Barbara, and she seems to be fine. It'll probably take a few days for what has happened to sink in, but as you've told me before, she is a strong lady and she'll be all right. Martin, are there any special instructions that I should know about concerning Rob's body and where it might be shipped? Secondly, do you think that you should get to Tanzania as quickly as possible to assist Peter Moss? I haven't been able to find him. I know that he went to the beach somewhere, but I have no idea where, do you? Maybe Melindi, about an hour away from Mombassa?"

"Frank, I'm going to have to ring you back concerning Rob's arrangements. I'm just drawing blanks right now. As for Peter, he usually liked to go to a little spot just south of Dar, but I doubt that there are any telephones down there. We're going to have to wait until he hears something and then gets back in touch with us. When was he due back?"

"At the end of the Joneses' safari, I suppose. Get your wits together and call me back this afternoon. I'll be waiting for your, and hopefully, Peter's calls. By the way, I don't want to send you away from where you are until I know that you have Lou Maxie's safari all lined up over in Zimbabwe. At a time like this I hate to even think of business, but I have to. Do you still plan to use the Kudu Hills ranch for most of the safari?"

"Sure do, Frank, and as far as I know, everything is in place. Jon-Keith has handled most of the details, but I've checked behind him. I'm satisfied that we are ready. Do you know whether Mr. Maxie is bringing anyone else or not?"

"He's coming alone. His wife has some sort of society function that she's in charge of and she just can't miss it. Thank God he isn't bringing one of his burlesque employees. I've had enough foiled relationships for one year."

Martin went immediately from the radiophone to the bar, and he proceeded to mix the world's strongest double Scotch and water. He had convinced himself long ago that he was doing the right thing by entering into these three contracts. Now, he wasn't so sure. As of the moment, he was going to be richer than he ever imagined, but it was at the expense of his friend's life. That was hard to rationalize. After closing his eyes and thinking about the situation for a good thirty minutes, Martin concluded that he must go on and he must orchestrate his third contract. He thought about Rob some more; in fact, he couldn't make his mind quit thinking about Rob. He remembered that Rob's last girlfriend had told him that Rob wanted to be buried in the bush if something ever happened to him before he got a family. He had to get in touch with his Jo'burg office immediately.

Anna Marie answered the phone on the second ring. She was aware of the accident and she knew she was in for a long day on the phone from government officials, friends, and the news media. She was glad the person on the other end of the line on this call was Martin. After consoling each other again for a few minutes, Martin asked her to try and get in touch with Rob's last "love" for details that the office might have overlooked. Special mention was made of Martin's remembrance of where Rob had indicated he would like to be buried. Anna Marie was ready to cooperate post haste. She was as shocked as anyone over the latest accident, even more so because she had a natural affection for Rob and she wanted to do something special to help. Rob was respected by everyone in the organization and Anna Marie cared for him beyond the mere respect she had for him. It wasn't a silent infatuation for him, it was because he had such a love for all of nature. Anna Marie loved Rob because he was a real man that wasn't motivated by money, but by nature itself. It was his life and his death.

Rob's "ex" was at home when Anna Marie called. Word travels fast and she had already heard the terrible news. In fact, she was presently conjuring up enough presence of mind to call the office for more details when Anna Marie rang. She explained to Anna Marie about their relationship. It had been one that wasn't designed to last into marriage, but it filled a void for both until others would come along. Nevertheless, she was heartbroken. She remembered the spot vividly where Rob talked about lying if he met death at an early age. It was outside of the main camp in the Okavango Delta, next to the only baobab tree in the region. It was high ground, it was shaded, and it offered a high-water escape for all kinds of animals when the area was prone to flood. He especially didn't want his grave fenced; he wanted to be as close to the animals as he could be. Anna Marie relayed her findings to Martin and then called the Nairobi office to ensure that Rob's body was coming home.

Martin radioed Houston as soon as he disconnected from Anna Marie. He was put right through to Frank Black. "Rob wanted to be buried next to the main camp, under the Baobab tree, and I think we ought to grant his wish."

"I wholeheartedly agree. You make the necessary arrangements. If there are any friends or relatives in Jo'burg or Maun that want to attend, make sure that we provide air transportation. Rob was a good man and he helped this company more than we all know. Spare no effort or expense to do it right. God knows that I wish that I could be there, but it is impossible. I've got to take care of the wounded here. Say something special for me at the graveside, and I mean really special."

"I'll make sure that everything goes as you would want. He was special to all of us. Frank, after the funeral, I think that I need a rest. All of the camps are in good shape and all of the next few safaris are well planned. You can dock me for whatever as far as pay is concerned, but I have to get away for a while. I don't know whether it will take two or three weeks for me to get my spirit back, but I can see myself growing useless at present."

"Martin, it has been trying on all of us. I can't tell you how many calls we have received from our competitors offering their condolences. We've been hit harder than any outfit in the history of big-game hunting. I don't understand it, but we have too much invested to quit. If we survive all of this, we'll have even a bigger edge on our competition. Take what leave you think is necessary, but for god's sake stay in touch. I have to know where you are just in case."

"Thanks Frank, I'll make it up to you."

Jon-Keith Haley was leisurely taking a few days off himself at his apartment in Jo'burg when he heard the news of Rob's untimely demise. He dared not make too big a deal of it to Martin because one of them might get too emotional and forget the rules that they had agreed on in their hired-killing affair. Instead, he decided to drive up to the Lanseria Airport Lounge to get more details. If the other professionals there didn't know the circumstances, then Anna Marie at the company airport office would. Time was running short until his next safari and he must be able to explain the past accident without causing any undue alarm. He was to meet Lou Maxie in two days to fly to Victoria Falls; his turn was up next for the performance of the last contract.

The lounge was abuzz with the speculations of just how Rob met his maker. Anna Marie gave Jon-Keith all of the information that she knew, which wasn't much, but he was appreciative. Rob had been a regular at the lounge whenever possible, so all of the "pros" there were righteously forlorn for him as well as for his longtime buddies, Martin and Jon-Keith. Jon-Keith made number six of the professional hunters that were present, plus two bush pilots who knew Rob equally as well as his hunting cohorts did. The impromptu "wake" at the airport lasted until nearly midnight, then the saddened group scattered for their homes.

Jon-Keith's following day was spent making sure that all contingencies were met in Zimbabwe for the next safari. The people at Kudu Hills were always appreciative to leasing concessionaires, especially the ones that gave them continued business, like Hunters, Ltd. They were always well stocked with food, petrol, ammunition, and almost anything else that a professional hunter might need for himself or his client. Jon-Keith was especially pleased that the camp manager was outraged at the number of lions in the area at the time. They usually didn't sell many lion permits, so the overabundance of the felines would signal a reduction in other game species if the lion numbers were not thinned out soon. He was glad that Jon-Keith was coming to take at least one, and maybe scare away a few more.

While Jon-Keith was at the airport lounge the day before to mourn Rob's unfortunate death, Anna Marie had given him the itinerary for his incoming client, Lou Maxie. If there were no delays, Lou would arrive at Johannesburg International Airport in Jo'burg at ten o'clock the next morning. Martin had briefed him on what a sorry son of a bitch Lou was. Evidently, he had a wonderful wife but he treated her like shit. He owned and ran a topless club that was one of the biggest and most successful in the country. It was so successful that he was under indictment from the Internal Revenue Service to explain lost receipts. Jon-Keith wondered how he could get out of the country in such circumstances. "Must have one of those high-powered lawyers," Jon-Keith supposed. "I guess that the same lawyer represents him against his wife as well." Martin told Jon-Keith about Lou's new "toy" that he took out every night when he came to his office to siphon off some of the cash. Martin also told him about his wife trying to divorce him, but she was denied a fair hearing each time because he filed Chapter-11 Bankruptcy every time to freeze his assets.

His wife's name was Sally, and not only was she quite attractive, she was a true socialite. She was not a social climber that yearned for credit whether she deserved it or not. She was unobtrusive in her activities with her various charities, and she was never heard complaining of her home-life situation. In fact, most of her protégés didn't even have an idea that she was unhappily married. The offices and tributes given her for her unselfish work were neither sought nor desired. Sure, this life that she was leading was somewhat an escape from her lacking home life, but she was sincere in her work and she never solicited recognition. She was trapped with a man she didn't respect or love and didn't complain – an admirable quality for anyone, but in this case, one certainly not deserved. Obviously, she had food, clothing, and shelter – all the best of each. But she was lied to, cheated on, and denied a better existence, all because Lou Maxie wanted to have his cake and eat it too. As Rob did for his last client, Jon-Keith was likewise building up his hate for the sorry SOB he was about to eliminate.

Lou Maxie arrived via South African Airways' 747-B on schedule. Customs was a breeze, and immediately after clearing such, he was met by his professional hunter, Jon-Keith Haley. From the second Lou was introduced to Jon-Keith, he was asking questions – if not about the animals, it was about camp, the terrain, the weather, and firearms. Actually, Jon-Keith found Lou very amusing; at least he showed a keen interest in all of the inner workings of a safari, particularly because this was to be his first. Lou demonstrated his homework as well; it was obvious that he had studied the animals and the country. Thanks to the advice of his gun and camera club brothers, he brought all the right things – a .375 H&H Sako bolt-action rifle, the expensive Safari Grade no less, the proper clothing, and even a gift of a new pair of ten-power Leitz binoculars for his professional. Jon-Keith's intentional distaste for this chap was beginning to wane instead of grow. He had to correct that problem in a hurry.

Lou had even done some research into his professional's past life. Lou had called all of the references that Frank Black had given him, and three of them had been on safari with Jon-Keith more than once. He learned that Jon-Keith had been a boyhood friend of Martin and Rob's back in Kenya. His father worked in the Game Conservation Department, and they lived on the outskirts of Nairobi. Jon-Keith stood nearly six feet in height, and he was a trim one hundred and eighty pounds. All of his past clients complimented him on his special caring for his clients and his always-present manners. He liked his Scotch whiskey after a hard day's hunting, but besides that, he appeared to have no other vices. His marriage was never mentioned, but all assumed that it was a good one. He had no children but he was especially caring when any clients' children accompanied their parents. His calling card was an ascot that he always wore after his shower for dinner and sun-downers. He was a stickler for punctuality and he was always prepared for any eventualities. In short, everyone thought that he was an ideal professional hunter that quickly developed special caring for his clients.

Arrangements had been made out of the Jo'burg office by Anna Marie to have Lou and Jon-Keith flown directly into Victoria Falls, Zimbabwe, for Lou's first night in Africa. Accompanied by Jon-Keith, they arrived at midafternoon and were met by a native representative of Kudu Hills. Rather than drive through the countryside in darkness for the last half of their automobile ride to camp, the three opted to spend the night at the Victoria Falls Hotel and Casino. The dinner and floor show at the hotel were just what the doctor ordered for Lou – pretty women and a lot to drink.

From his most recent experiences, Lou told Jon-Keith just which dancers had "fake boobs," and which ones were real. He even guaranteed the cup size for most of them. The night told dearly of Lou's lifestyle and Jon-Keith was certainly not jealous of it. Jon-Keith was a one-woman man and all he could think of was Lou's miserable wife. Few people and very few things impressed Jon-Keith and Lou didn't. Jon-Keith's disdain for Lou was growing. The threesome checked out of the hotel at seven the next morning and were off on their four-hour dusty drive through the bush toward camp.

Kudu Hills was situated in Matabeleland just southeast of Wankie National Park in Zimbabwe. The area was named for its occupying tribe, the Matabele. Jon-Keith explained to Lou on the way, "These are fierce hunter-gatherer types that take their war-prone ancestry quite seriously. They are the tribe that waged war so effectively during the political bouts between their leader, Joshua Nkomo, and the more populous tribal leader Robert Mugabe to be Zimbabwe's first black president. Atrocities occurred from each tribe to the other, but Nkomo's Matabeles did more than their share of damage. The final election was won by Mugabe, an outright communist, I might add, and he is still having trouble controlling Nkomo's people."

"Who owns the ranch where we'll be hunting?" Lou changed the subject.

Jon-Keith waited for the driver to answer, but when he didn't, Jon-Keith took charge. "It's privately owned by some old Rhodesians that have taken up their everyday life in England, but they still keep tabs on the overall operations as if they were still here. The manager, Peter Smit, runs the place for them and he does a damn fine job. The ranch covers fifty square miles and it is still one of the largest in Southern Africa. It offers hilly landscapes that jut up to small mountains that reach nearly four thousand feet, and yet it offers low-veldt sand rivers below a thousand feet. The temperatures for this time of year range from the midsixties at night to the midnineties at midday. Naturally, the higher hills give some relief from the higher temps.

"Camp-life is confined to rondavels. Substituting for tents, these fifteen-foot-diameter circular buildings are the vogue in this part of Africa. With their grass roofs, they are cool at night and in the day. The sides are made of thick concrete block, and each rondavel is equipped with a commode and lavatory. The open windows at night still allow each inhabitant to hear all of the night noises that game country is so famous for. It's not quite like a real tented safari, but the conveniences make up for it. I promise you one thing, you are really going to like it."

The camp crew unloaded the camp vehicle and placed all of Lou's baggage in his rondavel immediately upon arrival. After a short lunch snack, Jon-Keith took Lou out to sight in his rifle. Unlike the primitive sighting setups in typical bush safaris, Kudu Hills had a permanent firing range for just such purpose. That way the game was only disturbed by the noise in one area. When Jon-Keith was satisfied that Lou was on target, he suggested that they go out for an impala or warthog to initiate the safari. "It's always good to let a new safari client try his hand at one of the lighter animals before he comes face to face with something that could hurt," Jon-Keith mused. "Besides, some folks that come over from the U.S. tell me that the light is completely different over here. I can't find any scientific justification for such, but it damned well might be true. You didn't seem to be having any trouble when you were sighting in, though."

Just about the time that Jon-Keith had finished his sentence, the vehicle came around a bend; and there stood a gigantic warthog right in the middle of the dirt road. Jon-Keith slammed on his brakes and told Lou to hurry and get his rifle. Someone had forgotten to screw down the front windshield when the top was removed after coming into camp from Victoria Falls, so the whole windscreen came slamming down on the hood when the brakes were so suddenly applied. Because of Jon-Keith's yelling and the windshield's crashing noise, the poor old warthog stood stunned. It had never heard such noises, and it didn't have a clue as to what to do. Lou jumped down, took two steps away from the vehicle, and fired. One warthog for the pot was down. After pictures and congratulations, the accompanying tracker and gun bearer loaded the "poor man's rhino" into the back, and the safari recommenced.

Within several miles of camp, Jon-Keith looked over five herds of impala before he decided on a male that was of record-book quality and thus worth taking. The horns had to exceed twenty-two inches to make the book and they needed to diverge at the tips to make a good-looking trophy mount. Judging the quality of animals is a major job for any professional because there are usually no second chances. When the difference in horn length is only an inch or two and when one has to judge it quickly from over a hundred yards or so, it takes real smarts and experience to know when to tell a client to shoot or not to shoot.

When the right impala was spotted for Lou, it was apparent that the herd that he was in was in too much open country to try for a normal stalk, so Jon-Keith decided to employ a little ingenuity. "Try to slide out of the vehicle as inconspicuously as possible when I slow to almost a stop next to the single bush up ahead. Animals can't count and they won't miss a passenger that has mysteriously evaporated behind a bush. When it's clear that the herd is watching the vehicle move off, then take your time and fire. There is only one impala in the heard with horns. Please try and shoot that one," Jon-Keith said sardonically. Jon-Keith slowed down to almost a stop for Lou to exit away from their quarry's view. Lou scrambled behind the appropriate bush and then Jon-Keith kept motoring. As designed, all of the impala's eyes in the herd kept following the car. Since there is only one male impala in a normal breeding herd, Lou had no difficulty in picking the right animal to shoot – the horned one. John-Keith noticed that Lou was taking his time, securing a good rest for his rife, and positioned himself so that he had a comfortable shot. At the sound of the shot, Jon-Keith turned the vehicle around to pick up Lou. The plan worked to perfection and Lou had his second one-shot kill of the afternoon.

After the impala was piled in the back on top of the warthog, the hunting party headed for camp. The food was just as good as Lou was told it would be and it was just as good as Jon-Keith had grown to expect. Because markets were within driving distance, the burden of having to be a dietitian did not fall on the professional hunter at Kudu Hills, and that gave Jon-Keith extra time to be with his client. That was good news and bad news. Normally, that was a plus, but with the thought of having to eliminate his client soon down the line, Jon-Keith had mixed emotions about getting too close to Lou. Instead, Jon-Keith managed to fabricate other jobs so that he could be away from Lou as quickly as possible.

The second day of this ranch-type safari was spent in pursuit of zebra, blue wildebeest, waterbuck, and tsessebe. Only the tsessebe proved elusive enough not to be bagged by Lou that day.

The third day was spent hanging leopard baits from the unused meat supply from the previous day. Once an adequate tree was found where there had been some leopard sign, the bait was hoisted into place. The bait was tied by rope on a limb where the leopard could lazily lie down to consume his gift. Jon-Keith had to properly predict just how the leopard would react so that his client would have an easy shot. A blind was then constructed that was "see in" proof from the leopard's perspective, and convenient enough to walk into without causing a ruckus on the approach. In all, Jon-Keith placed four baits, all along a slow-flowing creek that offered plenty of cover for the leopard to approach his free meal. Between placing these baits, Jon-Keith and his cohorts were in constant vigil for a tsessebe. Just before sunset, a lone tsessebe was spotted lying on an anthill not far from camp. Leaving the tracker and gun bearer behind, Jon-Keith personally guided Lou to within forty yards of the unaware animal. Resting his .375 H&H in the fork of a mopani scrub tree, Lou took the tsessebe with a clean shoulder shot that dropped him on the spot. Actually, the tsessebe stood stark still for a good five seconds after the bullet hit, then it just keeled over without another movement. It took all four of the occupants of the vehicle to load the four-hundred-pound antelope into the back of the Land Rover.

As Jon-Keith steered the loaded Rover through the camp gates, Lou asked him when they were going to try for buffalo and lion. Jon-Keith replied, "Tomorrow morning, we will run the leopard baits to see if we have had a hit. After we check the last one, we will look skyward for any tale of vultures that might put us on a lion kill. You know Swahili? 'Simba' is Swahili for lion. We'll look for old simba the rest of the day. Buffalo seems to be so numerous, that I would rather wait until we have filled our quota of lion and leopard before we get after Mbogo – that's Swahili for buffalo. If we have a fresh hit on one of our leopard baits in the morning, we'll still hunt for lion the rest of the day; except we'll knock off a little earlier from hunting lion to get to the leopard bait in time for our dusk ambush. We have to be in place in the blind two hours before sunset, that's a little before 4 p.m."

The days had been extremely hot for the first four days of the safari and the new cool winds from down south were refreshing, producing a cooler than normal sleep on that fourth evening.

The exception for enjoying the cool sleeping weather was Jon-Keith Haley. Sleep was becoming harder to come by every night that passed because of the pressure to make the accident happen. He thought about Lou Maxie's private life, his terrible treatment of his wife, his IRS indictment, his estranged partner and his embattled partnership, and finally, how everyone that depended upon Lou would fare if he lived or if he died. The projections were clear – everyone would be better off with Lou pushing up daisies than having him continue taking advantage of everyone he touched. *He has to be a sorry person,* Jon-Keith thought. Over and over Jon-Keith reenacted the planned accident. The time and the circumstances necessary to make the accident look like an accident just hadn't materialized during the last four days. Time was slipping away; he had to make it happen soon.

The next morning came particularly early for the nonsleeping Jon-Keith. Despite his lack of shut-eye, Jon-Keith was prepared to carry out his assignment that he had agreed to do. Hurriedly, Jon-Keith's hunting party gobbled down breakfast and scurried to the newly hung baits. None of the four had been hit by a leopard, but there appeared to be a large lion that had tried to climb the tree on the lowest-hung bait to snatch it. But there was no evidence that the beast had a mane which would qualify it as a true trophy lion.

The next order of business was to get to an open area and begin to glass for vultures. The tracker knew just such a place. Within ten minutes, the foursome was out of the vehicle and searching the skies. Off to the north, there was some activity. At first, it was hard to tell whether the descending vultures were just riding a low sinking thermal or were serious about a cleanup job. Soon they were joined by too many other vultures to be out only as searchers. More and more of them started dropping out of the skies. It looked as if they were heading toward a big rock kopje. "Hey, Lou, do you know what a kopje is?" Lou nodded in the negative. "Well, it is an Afrikaans word for a small mountain of rock that exudes out of an otherwise plains area. It is a favorite resting place for lions and leopards. The rocks are pretty cool and the sight vantage point keeps them entertained. But it is hard as hell for us professionals to sneak up on either of them when they have that high sight advantage. Look, those vultures are going down right by that kopje over there" – Jon-Keith pointed out the area – "if it's our lion, there's no time to waste. Let's get going before he finishes eating and heads for water," Jon-Keith said.

The Land Rover was already moving away when the gun bearer and tracker ran to jump aboard. It was about a five-mile jaunt to the vultures' drop point. The last half-mile or so was downhill. Jon-Keith radioed the main camp and all of the listening vehicles in the area that they were on a "hot" lion or leopard prospect, and to steer clear. He stopped on top of the hill from which he would descend and made sure that everyone was ready in case they encountered their expected quarry ahead of time. He then cut off the engine and pushed in the clutch to coast downhill without a sound.

The vultures were still in the trees and no other animals were around. Two things could be surmised from this – first, that something was still on the prey; and second, that the kill was fresh enough to have not yet attracted the customary hyenas and jackals. The vehicle was stopped about a hundred yards from the kill site. Jon-Keith then sent out the tracker to one side of the kopje and the gun bearer to the other. They were to circle the area and meet on the other side. When they had gotten enough evidence as to what was happening, they were then to report back to the vehicle.

It took the two natives thirty minutes to return with the news. Lion, big lion, tracks went into the thick bush on the right, and he was dragging a half-grown zebra between his front legs. It was obvious that he had tried to hide his kill from potential sharers and intruders.

Jon-Keith seized the scene as his moment to invoke "the plan." He ordered the tracker to perch himself up in a tree to the far left of the circled area. He ordered the gun bearer to do the same on the right. They were to keep a sharp eye out for any disturbances or a retreating lion. Their signal of alarm was a red-eyed dove call – a soft *cooh, cooh*. The air was still and the entire scene was noiseless except for the whistling wings of the dropping vultures. Jon-Keith whispered his instructions to Lou. "You stay right on my right hip. Don't look for the lion, I'll spot him before you can. Watch your step and don't make a sound. Place your footsteps into mine. When we are ready for action, I'll tell you. Only give one silhouette to our quarry, keep me between you and the lion, and be quiet! *Shhh!* Put one up the spout with the safety on and let's go."

The two hunters entered the thick brush exactly between the two tree-dwellers that were their watchdogs in case something unexpected happened. Walking upright soon became a bent-over walk. The bent-over walk soon became a duck-walk, and soon the duck-walk became a slow crawl. The smell was becoming noticeably stronger when Jon-Keith motioned Lou to lie flat. The wind was perfect. Jon-Keith sensed that they were close. He reached into his shirt pocket for his folded-up binoculars. When he had surveyed the lion's obvious hiding places through the thick brush in the immediate area, he determined that all was safe for the moment and he signaled by hand to Lou to move out with him. Sweat was now oozing out of every pore in every inch of skin on both stalkers. Tension was at an all-time high for both men. The sun was baking down its rays of heat and the stillness of the air made breathing laborious. The guns were slick with perspiration and the visibility was limited to only a few feet. Jon-Keith motioned Lou to crawl up beside him. At a rate of less than a yard a minute, the two slithered on their bellies in the direction of the smell. A freshly gutted zebra had a smell all its own when one was directly downwind of it. The total area of the thick brush containing their lion was slightly over fifty yards square. They had opted not to follow the drag because there the lion is more conscious of what might be following him than in any other direction. The element of surprise was their key to success and they were downwind to make the plan work.

Suddenly, but not quickly, Jon-Keith pointed in the direction of a dark spot under the most densely shaded area yet encountered. He could see the hind legs of a small zebra. Lying beside it was a tawny-colored shape that was obviously a sleepy lion. He lay on his side, and despite seeing one of the lion's legs stuck up in the air, it was impossible to determine which way the lion's head was facing. Less than 10 percent of the lion was visible. Jon-Keith knew that a lion in this position was extremely dangerous. The lion would want to protect his kill and he would be doubly irritable if he were suddenly awakened. Jon-Keith guessed that there was an 80 percent chance of a charge and calculated that figure into his plan. Jon-Keith grabbed Lou's hand and pushed it slightly forward toward the sleeping giant to make sure Lou was clear as to the direction they were to move. Each closed the gap between themselves and the lion about two feet. Going only a foot farther made a big difference to the trained eye of a professional. Jon-Keith now knew that the lion was facing left. He motioned to Lou with his off-hand to get ready to shoot. He then crawled on top of Lou's legs to assist Lou in pointing his rifle to the right place. Then he slid back to below Lou's feet to watch the action. While holding his right hand on the trigger of his stout .458, Jon-Keith put a one-inch stick into his mouth and began to bend it. At the crack of the stick, the lion jumped to its feet. At the same time, Lou couldn't help but fire. The lion was hit right in the guts, the absolute biggest part of the target, just as Jon-Keith had predicted from the way the lion was positioned compared to where Lou was when the shot was fired. Percentages are not always correct in predicting the actual action, and in this case, the lion ran from the noise that preceded the burning sensation that he had so suddenly felt in his abdomen.

Lou's eyes begged for a target, but the lion was gone. When Lou looked back, he was visibly upset to find his professional hunter hiding behind a tree. Lou didn't know what to do. Jon-Keith motioned him to turn around and follow him out. When they were able to stand upright, Jon-Keith told Lou that he was covering him when the stick broke, but moved sideways behind the tree to get a better look at the lion's retreat. Also, if the lion had charged, Jon-Keith said that he did not want to be so close to the client that he would be restricted in his movement with the rifle. He said that too many professionals get their aim knocked off by the client in tough situations. By standing a little bit away, he was ensured an open shot. Lou bought the story. The tree-perched tracker on their left signaled a *cooh cooh*. It was obvious to head in his direction.

Both natives and the two hunters met under the tree where the one tracker had last seen the lion. The cat had gone into the kopje some twenty yards ahead. The tracker thought that it might be heading for its own lair. All sat down to make a plan. The first priority for Jon-Keith was to make sure that they always knew where the wounded lion was. "Sooner or later we will get the bastard. We have to. There are too many people in the vicinity to have a wounded cat on the loose. I want the tracker and gun bearer to again watch the periphery." He then sent the two natives out to either side of the area where the lion was expected to be in waiting.

After Jon-Keith was sure that his two scouts were in place, he and Lou began a slow walk around the kopje rock castle. Blood spoor was picked up just where Jon-Keith expected. "We have to follow the spoor in this time. Have you reloaded the spent shell from back there?" he said as he pointed to the scene of the first shot.

"Yes," Lou answered.

"I'll be backing you up. Remember that a lion comes low, be prepared to drop to your knees to shoot if you have time. For god's sake, don't shoot to your left under any circumstances because I will be there backing you up. Stay as close as you can to my right shoulder without interfering with either of our abilities to make a clean shot. Let's try it again."

Jon-Keith knew that his plan was still workable, but he needed some good fortune to finish the task. Slowly, the two moved along the blood spoor. The brush wasn't half as thick as where they were when they first encountered their quarry, but they still exerted extreme caution. The lion was lying flat on his belly, waiting for the right moment to extract its vengeance. That was no secret to either of the two pursuers; that's exactly how they expected the lion to react. Ever so slowly they pushed forward. The blood spoor was thicker; a sure sign that the lion was slowing down. The spoor wiggled; it was no longer in a straight line. The lion must be close because his sign looked as if he was looking for a place to lie down and hide.

Searching with the utmost due diligence for any clue as to the wounded lion's whereabouts, Jon-Keith saw a black tuft of hair move in front and to the right, about fifteen yards away. He brought up Lou to just in front of him on his right and then he held Lou back by the shoulder to stop all movement. Jon-Keith was putting pressure on the hidden lion. He knew that the lion had already seen his targets; he was just waiting to make sure of his charge. Soon the lion could not wait any longer; the pressure tactic worked. With his outstretched front paws purchased in the dried red earth and his back paws dug in from his rear end crouched position, he propelled himself at near top speed in his first three bounds. The lion's eyes were fixed rigidly on his nearest target, Lou Maxie. With his mouth showing a crimson red, broken only by the glare of his protruding teeth, with his head vibrating from his terrible roar, with his flowing mane held back by the glue of the wind from his swift charge, this multiple-muscled mass of charging fury closed the gap between himself and Lou in less than three seconds. Lou managed a shot but no one would ever determine where it went. The big feline hit Lou around the thighs, breaking both legs just above the knees. The pain was short-lived, however, because even as Lou was falling the lion had managed to elude Lou's flailing arms and dropped rifle and had gone directly for Lou's forward-pitched head. He was so over-matched that it was no contest – like a prize fighter going against a baby. In slightly more than a nanosecond, the lion had Lou's entire head in its mouth. The lion pierced Lou's skull and brain with its powerful jaws and killer canines. Lou's body went limp. But the lion was not through with just killing his tormentor. He began tearing him apart. The lion released Lou's mangled head and grabbed his arm, shaking Lou's whole body as if it were a rag doll. He nearly bit the arm in two between the shoulder and the elbow. During all of this unabated slaughter, Jon-Keith stood motionless behind a small tree. He knew that if he moved, the lion would immediately pounce on him. When the lion turned over the body to tug at Lou's arm once again, Jon-Keith slowly brought his rifle to bear. He placed his shot right behind the lion's left ear. This time, it was the rifle that roared and the lion fell without another breath. The ordeal was over and the contracted accident was fulfilled.

Jon-Keith staggered out of the semithicket brush in the direction of his tracker. Both the tracker and the gun bearer had witnessed intermittent glimpses of the accident from their respective trees, and although they were not privy to the whole scene that included prior conversations, they would certainly vouch for the fact that it had indeed been an accident. When both of the natives saw that all danger had passed, they slithered down from their respective perches and slowly approached the open area where Jon-Keith had sought solace. After several moments of strict silence together, Jon-Keith issued orders. He had one of them go back into the bush by the lion and Lou to wait for help while the other helped him gather the Land Rover. It took almost an hour to get the Rover close enough to load the dead twosome. The natives and Jon-Keith had plenty of experience in loading animals, but this was a first for them to load a dead white man into a safari vehicle. They wanted to attend to the client first, but then the lion would have to be placed on the client if they loaded the client first. So they wrapped the client in a tarp that was always carried to lounge on at lunch and loaded the lion first.

The thing that Jon-Keith dreaded most was the radio call that he would now have to make. The camp headset was donned by the manager in charge as soon as Jon-Keith's urgent message for help came through. "Jon-Keith, is that you? Come in Jon-Keith, come in."

"We've had a tragic accident next to the big kopje in the north quarter of the ranch. We were following up a wounded lion and Mr. Maxie was mauled. Better get here as quickly as you can."

"Be right there. Are you off the main road or next to the river bed that runs on the other side of the kopje?"

"We are on the other side by the river."

"We'll be right there."

Lunch was quickly put aside at the main building in camp and everyone that heard the distress message grabbed a vehicle and started out for the accident area.

Jon-Keith's borrowed Land Rover had an open top and both of the front doors had been removed. It was common for every driver to ride along with their right knee jutting out from the side of the car. Being a right-hand-drive vehicle, it was quite natural to rest in this manner and it allowed the wind from the motion of the car to blow up the pants leg to cool that clothed portion of a man's anatomy that traditionally got hot first. The weather was hot, so all of the professional hunters and clients wore shorts and no socks.

There was a little-used dirt road that wound around the kopje that would take Jon-Keith and his gun bearer closer to the main road. Half-dazed, Jon-Keith started this short-distance drive like a road-racer. After going less than a half mile, the gun bearer noticed a long crooked stick lying across the road just after Jon-Keith had made a rather sharp turn to the right. It looked like a stick but it wasn't. As the Rover passed over it, the make-believe stick struck back at the big oxlike creature that had just inflicted so much pain in running over it. Instead of striking the metal body of the car, the snake's heat-seeking directional system directed its potent fangs on the calf of Jon-Keith's right leg.

The bite was fierce and the fangs buried themselves deep into the muscle and flesh. The snake hung on to its victim until Jon-Keith had to pull it off. Temporarily, Jon-Keith lost control of the Rover as it slid broadside across the narrow road; at the same time, Jon-Keith grabbed the thrashing snake just behind its head and jerked the submerged fangs out of his calf. He flung the ten-foot-long nemesis clear and grabbed his now-bleeding leg. The dilemma was apparent – both Jon-Keith and the native rider knew it had been a dreaded Black Mamba.

The Black Mamba is the largest of the deadly snakes in all of Africa. It has been known to strike a man on horseback, and it is rumored to be able to travel short distances at near twenty miles an hour. Its venom is neurotoxic as well as having other fatal properties, and it is so rapidly absorbed by the human body as to bring about paralysis of the nervous system within a few minutes. Two drops of venom is considered a fatal dose for a human being. Keeping in mind that a full-grown Black Mamba has a capacity of over twenty drops of this deadly venom, the future of Jon-Keith was literally in the hands of speed – speed to get an injection of antivenin. The antivenin is 50 percent fatal in itself, but that is an option that anyone would take if they knew that they had been struck by a Black Mamba. As soon as Jon-Keith had extracted the fangs of this deadly serpent from his calf and instinctively flung it away, he knew he had only a few minutes to live. The Land Rover was still rocking from its sliding broadside stop that almost turned it over when he yelled at his bearer for the medicine kit. "There is none on this vehicle; it will be coming with the others that are on the way." Jon-Keith then grabbed a rifle cleaning cloth from behind the seat and wrapped it around his leg above the fang marks but below the knee. He wound it as tight as possible to restrict his own blood flow. He was quick, but not quick enough. Within thirty seconds, convulsions began and Jon-Keith passed out.

The middle-aged native was a veteran to adversity and jumped into the front passenger seat. He grabbed hold of the tourniquet with his right hand and wound it as tight as he could. With his off hand, he fumbled for the radio. The ignition was still on and the radio buzzed when he hit the mike talk button. In his best but very excited native tongue, he called for more help. He never waited for a reply. "Jon-Keith been bit by a Black Mamba . . . bring antivenin . . . bring antivenin." He then began to blow the horn; in fact, he held the horn cover down to continue its sound. When the sound of the horn seemed useless, he maneuvered himself around back of his friend and slid him down in both front seats. He lowered the bitten leg to slow the flow of blood up to the vitals. He never let go of the tourniquet and he never stopped praying his native prayers.

In ten minutes, the dust from the approaching conglomerate of cars showed over the near hillside. "Hold on for five more minutes, Mr. Keith," the native begged. It was prayerful and it was natural to assume "Keith" was his new friend's last name. Sweat from the day's heat, the loading of bodies, and from the tenseness of the situation, had soaked the native's clothes. He found it hard to grip the tourniquet because of the sweat dripping down his arm. He began to sing and he began to sing loudly. He was relying on his old-time native custom of music and chants so often used in stressful situations. He was gradually working himself into a frenzy.

The first cars that were in the patrol headed straight for Jon-Keith's Rover. The two behind them were motioned to keep going to where the lion accident occurred to pick up the other native. The manager of the game operations at Kudu Hills was the first to reach Jon-Keith. Peter Smit already had the antivenin in his hand and he was ready to inject. He paused to think whether he should inject it in the stricken leg or in the arm. The arm would get to the upper vitals faster, but the wound was in a lower extremity and that is where the help was needed most. He chose the leg. He plunged the vial's contents hard into Jon-Keith's thigh and then he loosened the tourniquet. "His heart has stopped; help me get him on the ground!" Peter yelled. As soon as Jon-Keith was lying flat, Peter was on him doing cardiopulmonary resuscitation. It was no use. Peter could never get a pulse – no heartbeat and not a breath.

Peter shouted at the accompanying native to quickly find the snake. "It went in here," he said as he pointed to its track as it dragged its partially paralyzed body into the grass. "We have got to get it!" Peter ordered louder for more help. But the task was useless. No one wanted to face a wounded Black Mamba for its second chance to bite.

"The snake will die; no snake can live long after being run over," came the well-thought-out words from one of the native bushmen in one of the other vehicles.

"I know, but we must have it to make sure that it was a mamba," Peter shot back. "Beat the grass down with limbs until you find it." No one moved. Peter knew it was hopeless, but he had tried. Peter then ordered the second vehicle to go and tell the others at the lion site that he was taking Jon-Keith back to the main camp in his Rover and that he hoped the doctor that was hurriedly called would be there soon. With drooped shoulders and corrugated brows, the rest of the party headed for the site where they were instructed to go. Though he knew it was useless, Peter sped to the main camp in record time. A veterinarian from across the main highway had been summoned at the same time that the doctor had been called when Peter had radioed back to camp about the snakebite. He was waiting at the entrance gate for Peter to arrive.

The vet examined the body thoroughly. He inquired as to the circumstances of the accident and the antivenin. "Was it fresh antivenin?"

"Well within the expiration period, sir."

"It is the worst bite that I have ever seen, even counting those that I've seen on domestic cattle. The snake was obviously just coming out of a long sleep and he had a full store of venom to work with. Such a pity. The depth of the punctures are the deepest that I've ever seen. The force of the car going in the opposite direction to the snake's bite would account for that, I suppose. I doubt if any amount of antivenin would have helped if it were not given within a minute or two from this. It just couldn't have been worse." The vet then offered to carry the body into town for deposit at the morgue.

"Hold on, we have another body coming as well," Peter said.

"What on earth do you mean? There were two snake victims?"

"No, the other is a lion mauling. I am afraid that it will look much worse. I see the dust from the other vehicles approaching now."

Sure enough, the second corpse and the dead lion arrived through the main gate, escorted by two other cars. The vet went over to have a look. Lou's body was unloaded and the tarp was unrolled. The vet almost threw up. By now, all types of matter were oozing out of the tooth holes in Lou's skull from the viselike bite from such a big male lion. His arm was nearly detached and blood covered the body from head to toe. Peter ordered the two bodies wrapped in blankets for the vet to take them into town. He then turned to the driver of Jon-Keith's vehicle and said, "Please take the lion to the back of camp."

"The game department will need to see the lion to reconstruct the tragedy. Put the rifles up and unload the lion for skinning. Make sure that there are no knife slips on the hide; we have to show all of the wounds and we must not confuse the issue with a cut hide from skinning."

Peter Smit made the call to the Houston office of Hunters, Ltd. to inform them that they had just lost another client and a professional. The office was closed and Frank Black was not in when the call was placed, so Peter elected to leave an urgent message with his answering service for him to return the call as soon as possible. He did not leave any details. Next, he called the proper authorities in his country's capital, Harare, that would oversee such catastrophes. The game department had already been notified of the client's accident and they were on the way to the ranch as he spoke.

Never in their six-year history of game management and hunting had Kudu Hills been involved in a human death on their own property. It was a shock to all that were there. Not expecting any other visitors that day, Peter knew it was the game department officials when the next car pulled into the parking lot. He greeted them with a somber face and serious eyes. "I don't quite know what to do. The company that the professional works for has had awfully tragic luck the past few months. There have been two other clients and another professional that have been killed in similar accidents. I think that we must look closely at this one to make sure that everything points to its being an accident. The fact that previous accidents have occurred will make the investigation more tedious. I knew Jon-Keith very well and I certainly don't want to soil his wonderful reputation." Peter was forceful in his conclusion. He then joined the two scouts in returning to the scene of the lion mauling.

After viewing the site and after talking to the two natives that were there, the investigators and Peter couldn't help but come to the same conclusion as before – Lou died as a result of a terrible accident. They pieced everything together and it still came out as an accident. Certainly, Jon-Keith's tragic ending was an accident. There was no way that a snake-bite in that manner could have been planned.

When the three returned to camp for a spot of tea, a message from Frank Black awaited Peter on his desk. He returned the call immediately. Peter could feel Frank's apprehension on the other end of the line. He almost knew what was coming. When Peter finished giving him the gory details, he could hear Frank's heart pounding through the connection. "What could possibly happen next?" was Frank's reply. "I cannot stand another accident; these things just can't keep happening. I will notify the next of kin."

Peter then butted in, "Frank, you know that we did all that anyone could've done. As to your client, Mr. Maxie, it looks as if he just walked right into the charging lion. Maybe he was trying to get a better look when the thing charged. At any rate, his footsteps show that he left his cover and walked right into the charge. He shot at it, but there's no evidence of a hit. Mr. Maxie and Jon-Keith were several steps apart. That's unusual, but I would vouch for Jon-Keith's ability as a professional to anybody. It was just a crazy happening.

"As to Jon-Keith's snakebite; he was using the Land Rover he usually drives when he comes here. I guess he forgot to check it for a medical kit before he went out. There was no antivenin in the car. Let me know if we can be of any other assistance. It will take a few days to prepare the paperwork and get the bodies cleared for shipment; until then, you can reach me here at almost any time of day." Frank thanked him for his usual professionalism and then hung up.

Nothing could describe Frank's feelings. It was as if there was a curse on his company and it extended to his friends. It was awful. Frank was grasping at anything to take his mind away from its current terrible thoughts. Frank fell back on his numbers, the same numbers that he had fallen back on in each of the prior accidents that occurred during the year. Hunters, Ltd. averaged ninety-two safari bookings a year. They sent an average of eighty-nine separate people or groups on safari each year. They accommodated an average of 227 separate individuals each year in their camps in Africa, all of these on some type of hunting safari. To this, one should add an additional 250 clients or so for just photographic tours. Extrapolating these figures over the last five years meant that the company had entertained well over two thousand clients at their camps for five years without a serious accident. Sure, there was the time when a client died of a heart attack while in the bush, but he had been eighty-two years old. There was another client who received some bad news from the home-front, and he committed suicide on his last day of safari. But other than those two incidents, Hunters, Ltd. had a clear and precise record of no accidents that resulted in a serious injury, much less a death. As of today, they would have to carve five new notches on their corporate gun barrel to signify five deaths, all this year. Frank kept telling himself that unexplainable things seem to come in clusters, but when would this nonsense stop?

The people that usually booked hunts for next year at this time of this year seemed undaunted by these current events. In fact, they all asked about the adverse publicity and they seemed to enjoy the added excitement. "Our new bookings are *up* for Christ's sake! People are crazy. I guess the safari business really does rely on the danger syndrome for its popularity." Frank thought that he had figured it out. But when does a particular event break the camel's back and make all of his business dry up and go away? He had to make sure that day was kept far away from his door.

Sally was preparing to go out for the evening with some of her neighborhood friends when Frank's call came in. Every time she heard a telephone ring, she jumped. When she picked up the receiver, she gasped at the voice on the other end. She didn't know or recognize Frank's voice, but her intuition told her it was the call she had been anticipating. Even though the call was expected, she hadn't known when she would receive it, so it was natural that she was somewhat startled. Frank spared her the details, but he had to be accurate as to what had just happened.

After hearing an abbreviated final outcome, she had a hard time replying. She was so unfamiliar with the world of hunting, especially in Africa, she didn't know what questions to ask. All she could do was stick to simple words and say "thank you." She then asked Frank to call her immediately when there was more news and when there were things that she had to take care of. Before hanging up, she did have the presence of mind to ask Frank to hold on for a minute so she could jot down his telephone number. Frank gave her his home number, his business number, and his cell phone. She closed the conversation by expressing disbelief at her own husband's death, but sincere sorrow for the family of the man that had just worked for her husband. She wanted to know whom she could call to offer condolences on behalf of Jon-Keith Haley.

She is a terrific woman, Frank thought.

The morning newspapers in Dallas had a full story on the accidents. They were gruesome in detail, but for all Sally knew, they appeared accurate. Unfortunately for Sally and her inherited business interests, they focused more on Lou's playboy image than on the facts of his accident. They even referred to Lou's latest run-ins with IRS. *Nothing is sacred to the media*, Sally thought. *Couldn't they let a human being die without introducing scandalous activity to sell more papers?* She failed to put herself into the picture as the proximate cause for this scenario. She rationalized that the whole thing could have happened even without her involvement.

She had spent many hours in thought as to how she should and would react when the news finally came. She was well prepared; and because she was inundated with sympathizers both at her door and on the telephone, she managed to cope much better than she thought she would. Still, she hated that the media had to bring up current gossip. Every time she met one of her sympathizers, she wondered just what they were thinking – sincere sympathy or was he or she trying to figure out what would happen next? The news media had already started that speculation.

All of her church friends came to join her; they came by to give her strength. And all of the gun and camera club membership in town either called or came by to express their sorrow. After the last guest had departed, Sally telephoned Martin Smith at his home in South Africa. The house seemed eerily prepared for such an occasion. Sally had called her trusty maid that had been with her for years to come quick. She was a steadying force in all of the commotion. Almost everyone brought food and a few brought drinks, so the maid was just busy keeping the coffee cups and tea glasses filled. Three distinct clicks of friends bunched together, her true friends which included her church buddies, the hunting fraternity, and her Cancer Society associates. It was hard for her not to associate primarily with her friends, but she was congenial enough to give herself to all. Few sought details of the accident; they either already knew the details from news sources or they thought there would be time for that later.

Martin got Sally's number from Frank. He felt a sense of accomplishment when he dialed Sally's number. He had put Jon-Keith's death behind him for the moment. He had to. Carefully, he offered Sally his condolences and told her that he would contact her later from Europe. The call was intended to be short, but when Martin heard all of the people in the background, he shortened it even more.

Martin was really distressed about losing Jon-Keith. Rob had been his closest friend, but Jon-Keith was a close second. They had been close since their early days in Kenya. They had liked the same schoolgirls and they had grown to like the same vocations. Like the previous professional accident, no one could have foreseen a professional being killed by any means. Martin knew that he would have to live forever with the blood of Rob and Jon-Keith on his hands. It would be tough sleeping at nights, especially when Martin would have to spend some of those nights in a safari tent with the sounds of the very animals that had killed his friends actually ringing in his ears. He had no choice but to cope, and he knew he had the intestinal fortitude to do that.

With the help of her insurance agent and his referred attorney, Sally made all of the local arrangements for the funeral. Only the date was left up in the air. Lou's body was scheduled to arrive in two days, but Sally was warned that complications in scheduling were sure to arise. She got in touch with Lou's lawyer and his accountant and scheduled meetings for the following day with her new attorney. She hesitated from calling Artie; she would rather the lawyer handle everything with him. That was good planning, but it didn't quite work out that way. At just before midnight, Sally's phone began to ring. Naturally, she thought it was Martin – she was not so lucky. It was Artie. "Hello, ol' girl; I never thought you could pull it off! You really did it! How does it feel to be a rich widow?"

Sally was scared to death, but somehow calmly cleared her throat and answered, "I'm sure that I feel about the same as you, with one gigantic exception. I've been instructed by the man that you met in the parking lot to never talk to you again. That means that you must never talk to me again either. My lawyer will be in touch with you in the morning. He will have all of your contracts drawn up as soon as possible, and after they are executed, we will have no more need for communication between us. If you try to talk to me again without my attorney present, I am to tell you that you will be saying hello to that parking-lot government man again. He is a tough gentleman, and I know you want your hundred-thousand-dollar investment to prosper. I intend to live up to every clause in our agreement, and I expect you to do the same. I wish you good fortune. Good-bye." Sally was proud of her forcefulness and she was extremely glad that the ordeal was over.

Except for the unfortunate accident with the professional hunter, everything was following the prescribed script.

After meeting with her new lawyer and accountant at separate offices for over four hours the next morning, she pulled into the parking lot of a big travel agency at the shopping center near her house. She perused all of the material that they had on England. Life after Lou was going to be a real change and she was determined to make it wonderful. She wasn't going to let anything that she ever wanted or hoped for pass her by. But at the same time, she wasn't going to shirk her duties to mankind. She planned a well-rounded life with social and religious activities as equal. She was unimaginably sorry for John-Keith's death, but she wasn't going to let the unplanned circumstances ruin the rest of her life. She was owed a new life because she had endured a past one that was horrific. Besides, she had convinced herself that at this time she couldn't change any of the facts that now existed.

Lou's body arrived at the DFW International Airport the following afternoon, ahead of schedule. Sally was accompanied to the custom's office at the airport by one of her friends from the country club to claim the corpse and to fill out the necessary papers. The waiting hearse, previously arranged for, took the body to the assigned funeral home.

Funeral notices were released to all of the news media as soon as the body was released to the funeral home. The funeral was held on the second day after the body arrived back in Dallas. The weather cooperated in fine fashion, and the array of flowers and greenery that were sent by well-wishers were utterly fantastic. There was even a big bouquet from Artie. After the funeral and burial rites were over, a reception was held for

Sally in her own home by her closest friends. During that event, one of her friends asked her, "Did you see that 'flaunty' looking girl from Atlanta at the funeral? Who was she? Everyone was asking."

Sally sat puzzled for a moment, and then replied, "She was wearing that emerald green taffeta dress, wasn't she?"

"Yeah, do you know who she is?"

"No, but let's look through the guest ledger and see if we can spot her name. I would imagine that she was with one of Lou's hunting friends, but she might have been someone from the business." Sure enough, on the tenth page was a name of Jennifer Miller, and beside it, Atlanta, Georgia. That had to be the one. "Sally, if I were you, I'd call information in Atlanta and see if they have a listing for her."

Sally could now sense the subject getting nasty instead of fun. "I imagine that she was just one of Lou's flings, and stirring up that big cesspool with inquiries isn't going to make anybody or anything else any better." Sally had closed that bit of conversation with pure sound reasoning. Sally figured that she could endure the Dallas climate for a few more days until she was satisfied that all of her insurance and legal matters were in good hands, and until she heard from Martin Smith. Then, she would high-tail it for England for an extended vacation of flat-shopping. She was jealous of the time that she was missing in her soon to be new homeland. She was eager to get her new life started.

One of the last duties that Martin had to do before he left Jo'burg for London was to handle the burial rites for Jon-Keith. Like Rob Manson, neither of them had any close family ties that were still standing, so the emotional strain was lessened. It did, however, make handling the affairs more difficult. There was no family member around to hand off various arrangements to. To make things a little easier, Martin managed to get in touch with Jon-Keith's stepmother and advised her that he had found out from one of Jon-Keith's girlfriends that Jon-Keith and Rob Manson had thought about the possibility of death in their line of work and that if that should occur, they had both wanted to be buried under the baobab tree outside of the main Hunters, Ltd. camp in the Okavango. Martin told the old woman that Rob had already been placed there. Not wanting any more irregularities than absolutely necessary to concern her, she agreed to the plan without any objections. She also declined an invitation to attend a memorial. Martin wondered about her caring, but he finally decided that she was just too old to get involved and she knew it. Besides, Martin had never heard Jon-Keith even mention her name more than once or twice. Thinking back, Martin realized that he had never even met her while he was a playmate of Jon-Keith's in Kenya. "What a pity," Martin lamented.

With an excuse to handle Jon-Keith's remains in a fashion that saved time and energy for Martin, he turned over the task of getting everything else done to Anna Marie at the Lanseria office. He did say that he would attend and conduct the services at the main camp. Because Jon-Keith was so popular around the circle of professional hunters that gathered at the lounge there, Anna Marie arranged to have the actual funeral take place in those surroundings, after which the pallbearers would place Jon-Keith's body on the chartered plane for a final flight into the bush-land that he loved so much. It was an extraordinary undertaking with an unbelievable emotional charm attached to it when it came off. Many of Jon-Keith's fellow professionals flew their own planes to the burial site in formation with the hearse plane. It was indeed a splendid and moving scenario for a good friend.

It was five days before Martin Smith finally gave Sally Maxie a call. She understood the complications that Martin had to solve. Plus, she knew he had to have some time to get over his tragic loss of Jon-Keith. Martin's call came from London and he invited Sally to join him there at her earliest convenience. He explained that he had just taken an extended leave of absence from his job and he had plenty of time on his hands to entertain her. Although she was quite fond of Martin and although she had entertained in her own mind the thoughts of going to bed with him, all of that seemed to change now. She did say that she would be going to London in the next few days and that if he would like to help her get acquainted with the lay of the land there she would be grateful. She left no doubt in her voice that she wanted this relationship to continue but only in a platonic manner.

"I have not yet made arrangements for my tickets so I will have to try to get in touch with you when I get there. I still have a few loose ends to tie up here before I go, so I will probably see you in a couple of days. Where are you staying so I can get in touch with you?"

"For short visits I always seem to end up at the Hyde Park Hilton. I expect this visit to be short, so you can reach me there. I'll have the concierge put on notice that you will be arriving. May I reserve a room for you there?"

"Thanks, Martin, but I have already talked to my friend that owns one of the Marriotts here in Dallas and he has made some generous arrangements for me at the Grosvenor Square London Marriott. I plan to meet some of my friends in my charity work there after I arrive, and I'm sure they too will insist that I stay with them, but I prefer my own place if possible. I would like to call on you for your expertise and I do look forward to seeing some sites with you. I will call you as soon as I get there. Martin, I planned to express my feelings to you in person when I got to London, but I just can't wait. I am so dreadfully sorry that you lost your dear friend Jon-Keith in this accident. You know I feel guilty."

"Nonsense, Sally. Things like that happen. In the old days, professionals were killed or injured almost daily. It was the world's most hazardous occupation. There is even a separate cemetery in Nairobi that holds hundreds of professional hunters that met their maker in this occupation. We have made it safer today, but the same old risks are there. John-Keith and all professionals know the risks. The quirk of fate that happened to Jon-Keith was unbelievable, and for it to happen the way it did was just fate. Never has anyone known a snake to bite back at a moving vehicle, much less the driver inside it. And then it got lucky in finding Jon-Keith's warm leg. It was Jon-Keith's time to go. As strange a death as that was, if it wasn't the snake, it would have probably been a meteor."

The infatuations that came from the common-gains meetings of the past were now obviously in the past for Sally and Martin. Both enjoyed each other's company, but it was apparent that too much water had passed under the bridge to allow for any type of courtship at present. And there were too many complicated issues still left to be sorted out for there to be commitments. Of course, right now, a relationship that involved any type of romance should be put on hold, and both of them knew it.

12

Relocations and Disbursements

Mary Kyle's most difficult problem of late was breaking away from her close friend for many years, Helen Beasley. Helen shared so much interest with Mary – they were both members, via their past husbands, of Pine Creek Country Club, and they were both active in the local Cancer Society. Helen had lost her husband several years back in an automobile accident in Raleigh, North Carolina, and as of yet, she had not actively sought a replacement. Her two children by the only marriage that she ever knew were both married, and both were in the process of raising their own families. Consequently, Helen was always at Mary's beck and call. Of the two, Mary was clearly the leader, but that in no way diminished the wonderful undertakings of Helen. Both moved quietly in their socialite circles, but both accomplished a hell of a lot for others. For either, there was never a question as to whether their interests had ulterior motives.

Mary knew that Martin Smith had thought out her problems well when he insisted that she had to move to Europe after the alleged accident. She had been deluged with well-wishers since Dennis's death, and if she was ever going to have a life of her very own again, she had to move somewhere inaccessible. Europe was ideal and she had always loved London.

It was now June and her husband had died in March. All of the insurance proceeds from the life insurance policies had been paid without so much as a hint of a claim of impropriety. Even the accidental-death benefits that were applicable were paid without questions. Her lawyer handled their collection as deftly as he had handled her other financial dealings.

He sold the house. He leased the spas, with an option to buy, to a national manufacturing organization that actually made some of the equipment that was in them. He converted Mary's Pine Creek membership to an "out of town / social" membership, and he arranged all of her banking interests so that she could call on any of her funds in the U.S. or from her future home in Europe whenever she wished. For the time being, except for her casual spending money, she had all of her insurance proceeds invested in U. S. government securities that could be converted by her bank at a moment's notice.

The yield was nothing to brag about, but right now, she needed the flexibility to be able to move her funds where she wanted rather than to make great returns off of them.

Her accountant had been advised as to all of her remaining holdings and her receipts from the insurance companies. He had already prepared an estimated tax return for her to sign before she left for Europe.

Her insurance agent had upped her liability coverage commensurate with her newfound wealth, and he was put on notice by her lawyer to furnish him any information that needed attention when Mary was unattainable. Thanks to her efficient professionals, everything that had to do with money or business interests was taken care of. There were no professionals available, however, to help her suspend her longstanding friendships, and she dreaded what she knew she had to do. Considering each of her closest friends as special in their own way, she met with each separately, usually at a location that the two of them felt was unique to their friendship. It was always tearful, but it was the best way, and Mary tried to always do things the best way, even if it hurt.

She had taken two weeks off after Dennis's death to go to London to apprise herself of some of her living options there, and now it was time to make her newly acquired knowledge from that trip useful. It had been almost three months since her last London visit, and she was eager to get her future on the right track.

She had talked to Martin Smith only twice since the funeral, and he never mentioned money. That seemed to put even more pressure on Mary to make her agreed payment to his Swiss account. She had to do that and she had to find a place to live. While she was last in London, she hired a realtor to begin a search for her fantasy home. She wanted seclusion, but not too much of it. She wanted neighbors, but not too close; she wanted convenient shopping for necessities, and she wanted enough land for a garden. She needed at least three thousand feet of entertainment area, and she needed a locating service where help could be found to handle the kitchen and daily chores; she dreaded the interviews associated with picking help and the dismissals that usually accompanied such tasks. When the realtor hinted at a price tag of a half-million pounds, she got out her conversion calculator and refigured the price in U.S. dollars. She never blinked an eye. Privately, she was now going to have to get serious, but she didn't want to show the realtor too much excitement. The realtor had notified her that he had at least four places that might meet her demands and he was ready to show her all of them.

The London office of the International Cancer Society was pleased to have been notified by their affiliated Atlanta chapter that Mary was coming over to be a serious part of their program. She had a short meeting with the London director back in April, and he indicated to her that he would be readily available to put her anywhere she liked in their organization when she became a permanent resident of the area. Vicariously, she tried to decide just where she thought she might be the most helpful, and after considering some ten different positions, she narrowed her choices down to two: assistant fundraiser and/or assistant social chairperson.

June was going to be a delightful time to be in England for Mary and she knew it. The flowers would still be in full plumage, and the temperature would be neither too hot nor too cold. The nights would be perfect for her light furs, and the daytime would be perfect for her spring sweaters. She couldn't wait to visit the numerous public flower gardens. For the first time in her life, she was going to spend as much time as she liked going to the world-famous Chelsea Flower Extravaganza.

For being in her forties, she had a most attractive figure. She didn't like to flaunt her well-kept body, but she didn't like to hide it either. Never did she go out anywhere where she was not in full makeup, and never was her hair not well groomed. A new man was the last thing on her mind right now, but she was human enough to know that if and when a real "keeper" – like Martin – did come along, she was going to be ready. Her lawyer had cautioned her about the "fakes" that were sure to try their "stuff" on her when they found out about her wealth and circumstances, but she assured him that she could damn well take care of herself, and she would never make her past mistake again.

She left her hotel telephone number in London with Helen, her lawyer, and with Martin Smith's secretary Gloria in Houston. After her tearful good-bye meetings with Helen and the rest of her close friends in Atlanta, she boarded a Delta direct flight to Heathrow from Hartsfield International. Upon her arrival, she claimed her own bags, got her own taxi, and chose her own room at the Baker Hotel on Baker Street in downtown London.

The hotel was only a couple of blocks from Madame Tussaud's famous wax museum; actually, just within walking distance. Mary loved the place. She could literally spend hours moseying through the uncommonly staged wax life-size figures looking at all of the physical idiocincracies that she somehow missed the last time she was there. She could never be sure which she enjoyed more – the unbelievable figurines of wax art or the unruly crowds. As to the wax impersonations, there was always something new, but she enjoyed the old just as much as the new. If she ever got bored with wax sculptures, she would take in the London Planetarium that was located right next door to the wax museum, or she could choose from a thousand other sites that begged her attention in and around the London area. Temporarily, she was in her own little bit of heaven.

She contacted her realtor on her second day there. He personally picked her up at her hotel the morning after, and they toured his researched sites until there was no more light in the sky. After being politely deposited at her hotel, she dressed for dinner, and had a lovely meal in the main hotel dining room, alone with her thoughts. Prior to retiring for the evening, she inquired of the concierge as to directions and times available to see the coveted Chelsea Flower exhibit. Her interest in gardening made such an adventure an absolute must, and she couldn't wait for the opportunity to wander those hallowed grounds.

Two of the properties that her realtor showed her fit her new-world to a *T*. She scheduled reappointments a week later to revisit them. The economy was in her favor for house hunting, but again, she didn't want to show too much enthusiasm which might drive the price up. Besides, she had one other duty to perform before she could give her new home all of her undivided attention. She had to make a quick trip to Switzerland to make a promised deposit.

British Airways was her choice to Zurich and Swissair fit her timetable the best for her return. Mary called Martin's bank, Switzerland International, and spoke to Martin's personal banker by telephone before making her airline arrangements. She then notified her Atlanta bank about an impending money transfer to an account in Zurich and then set up a meeting with the Swiss bank officer to coincide with the office hours of the Atlanta bank – a seven-hour time difference.

The bank had a courier meet her plane and bring her to the bank. Martin's cordial officer showed her every courtesy imaginable, and took it upon himself to escort her back to her departing flight. While in the bank, she made a wire transfer from her Atlanta bank to Swiss International. The transfer was for $2,000,000. After the money had been successfully transferred, she instructed the polite officer to deposit $1,000,000 into Martin Smith's secret numbered account, and the remainder to a newly opened interest-bearing account of her own. She was quoted an interest rate of 7 percent per annum on her funds and it was explained in detail to her the advantages of having part of her finances placed there.

Her new account was a ten-digit numbered account with her mother's birthday as her chosen pin number. To have access to it, one would have to know the exact numbers in sequence, plus a pin number. The pin number could be any word of less than ten letters or a number sequence such as a birthday or the like. The officer suggested that she pick a name or word that had an early childhood memory so that it did not ever have to be written down. She chose her mother's birthday. She was given a deposit receipt for her new account, but the officer refused to give her any written documentation on Martin's account and her deposit into it other than a receipt of a transfer form her account to a confidential numbered account. He explained the confidentiality provision that attached to all of their accounts and convinced her that it was for her protection as well. The ever so polite officer said that his bank had never had an unhappy customer in this regard and that the bank was proud that it had never divulged any depositor's account or its holdings even to a threatening foreign government. He showed her the computer entry of her deposit into what he said was Martin's account, but the number and the password were blacked out. She left, thoroughly convinced that she had made a proper deposit and the officer told her that Martin would call her soon to verify the monies entered into his account.

Jennifer Miller was having a tough time. Her helping finances were literally cut off when Dennis died, and she had no reserves. Dennis left her nothing except three months' prepaid rent on her apartment and a relatively new car, a Buick convertible. Dennis had taken care of the insurance on the car, and her proof of insurance card in the glove box indicated that the insurance was paid for another four months. She quit her job a year ago to be with Dennis whenever he called so she had no income of her own, and that was her number-one problem. She did have a key to Dennis's unknown apartment and she had managed to loot it of all of its belongings before the on-site apartment manager knew Dennis was gone. Needing cash in the worst sort of way, Jennifer pawned Dennis's TV, stereo, and VCR, and she sold several other accessory-type items to her friends. The furniture was all leased, but the lamps, pictures, etc., were converted to cash by selling them to a company that answered a newspaper ad for buying used furniture and fixtures. The way she figured it, she then had enough cash to last her for four months. She didn't have any time to waste in getting a job or in finding out some answers to Dennis's accident that constantly boggled her mind. If she was right in her hunches concerning Dennis's death, could such knowledge be turned into money? She was determined to find out. Under the guise that she was just trying to do the right thing, to create justice, she was going to explore every avenue wherever it might lead.She had applied for work at a dozen places, but the outlook for immediate employment looked hopeless. She even went on an interview to the new management company that ran Dennis's old spas, but they told her up front, when they tied two and two together, they could not hire her under any circumstance. She thought of the positive side of her predicament: she was going to lose some weight. She made a pledge to herself that she was not going to buy any food; she would date every night, or she wouldn't eat.

Dating was easy. Jennifer was quite popular in the gun and camera club circles as well as the nightclub scene. It didn't take long for her friends to spread the word of Dennis's death and she was inundated with bachelor calls. Although these bachelors were constant meal tickets, they were not her preference – she liked dating married men. They were not nearly so demanding and they left her plenty of time alone to think and have her own life. Soon, she had narrowed her field down to three married men and she saw one of the three every night. Without a faucet of money to turn on, she liked the idea of resorting to married men feeding her.

Her thinking about Dennis's death and the two other deaths that occurred in similar fashion gave her nightmares. She constantly tried to piece together these three happenings as a plan. There was too much coincidence in all of them – the same safari company, the short time span that encompassed all of them, all of the victims were rich, all of the exes left their homes for parts unknown, all were gun and camera club members, and all had no dependent children. Every time she went out with a gun and camera club member, she would inquire as to what they thought or knew about any of the alleged accidents. None read any conspiracy into any of the deaths. They all just thought that three accidents really did occur. Jennifer wasn't so convinced.

Her father had retired to a golfing bungalow life on a resort just outside of Austin, Texas, Horseshoe Bay. Jennifer invited herself down there for a visit, provided her father would pay for her airline ticket. He did. Her father was a retired undercover officer for the U.S. Coast Guard. He had been in an intelligence field and his thoughts about all of these "accidents" were bound to be helpful. Helpful to the extent that Jennifer was barking up the wrong tree or that there are simply too many coincidences to ignore an investigation of some sort. Her first task with him was to run her conspiracy angle by him for his thoughts. After all, his specialty in the service was investigation, and he had been born with an inquiring mind, doubting anything that looked too good on its surface. She had talked to him several times about all of the coincidences of the accidents by telephone, but she felt she needed to talk to him face to face. During her visit, she was amazing with her recall of all the facts, the names, and the coincidences of all the "accidents," not just Dennis's. Every time she went over all of the facts, she became more convinced that more facts were being hidden. Her father could not deny her beliefs when he put everything together. When her visit was over, he had given her ten thousand dollars to further her cause into her theory. Of course, Jennifer promised to pay him back with interest when she collected on that theory.

She rescheduled her flight back to Atlanta via Houston. Unannounced, she called on Frank Black at his Hunters, Ltd. offices near the George H. Bush Houston Intercontinental Airport for a personal meeting. Frank remembered her immediately, and his curiosity of why she was asking to meet with him personally would have put off anything but the most urgent of business. Frank also had nightmares about all of the accidents, but they were mostly business related. Nevertheless, he often thought something was amiss with three tragedies stacked up so closely together. But he certainly didn't want to further those thoughts. Every time he had them, he tried to quickly dismiss them, but they would never go completely away. Now came this girl Jennifer that could only be here for one reason – to question the accidents.

Frank couldn't be positive on why she was there, and he didn't want to take any chances of a sour meeting being overheard in his office, so he suggested that they go out for lunch. Frank called the Doubletree Hotel for lunch reservations, and since Jennifer had come from the airport via a taxi, they departed the office in his Mercedes.

Jennifer never let on about her desperate monetary situation; in fact, she was so cool that Frank thought she was either a banker or a detective. She wore a tight but conservative skirt and a fully buttoned blouse for the meeting. Her ensemble included high heels and a casual handbag. Her hair was conservatively set and her makeup was strictly ordinary. She wanted to display a conservative image to gain Frank's confidence. For a supposedly "dumb blonde," she had real street smarts.

She asked many questions about all of the accidents, but she always seemed to know the answers before Frank would give his retorts. At the end of the lunch, Jennifer began to make some demands. First, she asked for all three of the widows addresses and their current telephone numbers. Frank took offense at her gall and explained his reluctance. "Jennifer, these ladies have suffered enough. I or my company can't give out such information. You wouldn't want someone to give out that information on you after such a tragedy, would you? Besides, don't you really think you're imaginations are getting the best of you? There have been huge insurance settlements on the deceased in every instance, yet none of these companies that stood to lose millions ever introduced an idea that anything was wrong. All three of the deceased had heirs, and even counting all of the wives as well as the heirs, no one has raised a flag of any concern. And finally, the local governments conducted mandatory investigations on each accident, and after the initial inquiries, there was no evidence that suggested any of them go further. So, I understand that you were actually present, within a few hundred yards, of Dennis's accident, yet no one has heard you raise any doubts about all of the published facts concerning this accident. And you were nowhere near the other two accidents, so where do you found your preposterous conclusions?"

"Mr. Black, I believe that these poor little innocent-looking old ladies that were the wives of these less-than-perfect husbands actually had something to do with their husbands' deaths, and I am prepared to put things together to prove it."

"Again I use the same word I just used, that's preposterous, Jennifer. How could they do such a thing without me knowing about it? And if not me, certainly Martin Smith."

"I don't know, but I am going to find out! If you won't give me the information, then I'll get it somewhere. And if I do get it, it'll look awfully fishy for you not wanting to help me. It seems to me that an open book about all of these cases can't hurt you, but if you are seen not wanting to help me, and if I find some – how do you say it? – impor . . . impropriety, then you might have to answer other questions under a different light. I believe you when you say that you knew nothing about any of these being anything other than accidents, but if I find out otherwise, I know you don't want to be implicated by not being of help to me. Do you?"

"Jennifer, let's be sensible. I had nothing to do with any of these unfortunate accidents. And quite frankly, I don't believe anyone had anything to do with these accidents. Although it has been a long time since tragedies like these have happened, you know they used to be an almost regular occurrence. If they did happen as you suggest, that would mean there was a plot to murder, and I can't conceive of that from anybody that was even remotely close to any of the three situations, much less all three! I've been miserable dealing with their aftermath since they happened. I understand your bitterness and I don't blame you for being mad at your loss, but my company had absolutely nothing to do with any of this. We are innocent, yet we have suffered just like you, maybe more so because we have gone through three of these horror stories. Our business is bound to be affected, and affected by something we had no control over. You see, there is plenty of injustice to go around."

"Mr. Black, I'm going to give you one more chance. If you want me out of your hair, then I want two things from you. If you don't give them to me, then you'll hear from my lawyer and maybe the district attorney." Frank started to interrupt, but Jennifer put her hand up and said, "Let me finish. Dennis and I paid for a three-week safari and we only got five days. You owe me at least a two-week safari, in the same place, with the same hunter, Martin Smith. If I can stand him again, then he can damn well stand me. I want to take my father with me. He'll pay his own airfare, but you must pay mine. Then, I want those telephone numbers and those addresses. I will never tell anybody how I got them, but I want them. I am not being outrageous, I have been hurt and your company owes me."

"Jennifer, I am sorry that you feel that we are responsible for your situation. We are not. But I do see your point on the safari part since we have not refunded any payments for the unused portion to anyone. I'll commit to your safari plan, but I will not divulge any of our confidential information about our clients. When do you want to go back to Africa?"

"I'll let you know, probably in October or maybe the first of next year."

"Either of those times will be fine with us," Frank said. "If Martin is available, then I'll see to it that you have him. If he is not available, then we'll have to get you someone else."

Jennifer jumped in. "That won't do. I want to go back with Martin Smith. If I have to, I'll adjust my times to fit his, but it has to be with Martin."

"Okay, okay!"

Jennifer sat silently for a moment; obviously pondering an important thought. "Mr. Black, I imagine that you are worried about me knowing Mary Kyle's new address more than the other two, considering my role with her husband, etc. Let me make you a new proposition. I think that I can get her new address and phone number, but I will have a tougher time with the other two. If you will give me the other two ladies' whereabouts and do my safari that you just committed to, then I will never let anyone know that you helped me. I'll fill you in on all that I find out, even though you think that I'm barking up the wrong tree, and I will forever hold you and your company harmless for any eventuality."

"Jennifer, you drive a hard bargain, and you're very persistent. I give you credit for both of these endearing qualities and your beautiful imagination. To be honest, I would love to help you because you could verify my beliefs that nothing criminally happened, and your findings wouldn't cost me a dime. If I could be sure that no one would know where you got their addresses – "

Jennifer saw her opening and burst in, "Mr. Black, you name any assurance that you want and I'll agree. How about my upcoming safari? Suppose I must finish my research before I get my safari. We'll set a maximum date of April of next year. If you have been accused of helping me in any way, then you are off the hook to give me my safari, but if I keep you totally out of the picture and only inform you of my findings, then you owe me my safari with Martin Smith."

"Okay. You have a deal. You can call me tomorrow at my office and I will have the addresses and telephone numbers of Sally Maxie and Barbara Jones. I'll tell you in advance, coincidently, they both now live in England. And you can save your investigation on one part – neither of them know that the other one lives in London."

The rest of lunch became more at ease and certainly more pleasant, and after a couple of drinks following the meal, Frank took Jennifer to the airport for Delta's next flight back to Atlanta.

The day after Jennifer returned home, she made two important calls – one to Frank Black to get her promised addresses and phone numbers and the other to Jerry Wright Taxidermy that was located just outside the Atlanta metropolitan area. One of Mr. Wright's assistants answered the telephone and informed Jennifer that Mr. Wright was out of town, but he was expected back that night. Jennifer left a message for him to call her at her apartment.

At approximately ten thirty that evening, Jennifer's telephone rang and it was Jerry Wright. "Jennifer, I know that I speak for a lot of our members; we sure do miss your pleasant smile at our meetings nowadays. How have you been?"

"Jerry, I miss all of you guys too. It's been pretty sad for me to suddenly be pushed out of that group that I enjoyed so much, but that's life, and I have to play the cards that are dealt me."

"That's a good philosophy, but I'm sure it's a painful one. What can I do for you?"

Jennifer took a deep breath, and then answered, "For starters, you could take me to dinner. I have a couple of things to talk to you about."

"Well, I'd like that, but ah . . . ah . . . you haven't met my wife, have you?"

"Sure, but we could keep it quiet. I really need your help."

There was an elongated pause. "Jennifer, let me look at my schedule for tomorrow afternoon. Hold on." Jerry was at his office. "Jennifer, I have to deliver a couple of trophy mounts into town late tomorrow. I could meet you somewhere after that if I wouldn't be too late. Are you still living in Buckhead?"

"Yes. Where are your deliveries going?"

"To East Paces Ferry, right near the governor's mansion."

"How about JR's Log House on Peachtree Industrial, where we had the October Gun and Camera Club meeting?"

"Sounds fine. It's a little out of the way for both of us, but then again, that might be better than somewhere else. I'll meet you there as close to seven as I can."

"Jerry, I really appreciate your meeting me."

If Jennifer was going to investigate her hypothesis of a conspiracy, then she needed to be able to contact all of the participants. There was no use in getting in touch with the two ladies that Frank had helped with unless she could reach Mary Kyle as well, and Dennis's taxidermist was her best logical shot at that. During the next day, she tried to put together a plan to uncover the details that she needed, but she knew it all depended upon the night's meeting with Jerry Wright. Seven o'clock that evening seemed like it would never come.

Jennifer had a hard time finding something to wear. She always dressed rather provocatively, but tonight she knew that she had to tone it down a bit, similarly to what she wore in her meeting with Frank Black. She didn't want to cause a stir if someone recognized either of them. She safely pinned her blouse up a little closer to her neck to cover her attractive cleavage, and she chose the loosest pair of blue jeans that her closet offered. She was thankful for the little weight that she had lost. Just in case Jerry was as anxious as she for this rendezvous, she arrived a full thirty minutes ahead of the agreed meeting time to secure a secluded table.

Jerry was only five minutes late and he quickly recognized Jennifer sitting alone in a rear booth. Jennifer rose to give him a prolonged hug and a kiss on the cheek when he was table-side. Jennifer thought that Jerry would rather face the back wall, so she took the booth seat closest to that wall. Despite his smelly occupation and his marital status, Jerry was a polite and good-looking gentleman that all the girls seemed to notice. He was only five years older than Jennifer, and he had obviously married too young. Jennifer had caught his stares in the past on more than one occasion. He was a bit uncomfortable and afraid of being spotted this night, but he wouldn't trade his place for anything in the world.

Jerry ordered steak and Jennifer opted for grilled chicken; each had a glass of the house's white wine. Jerry was always the hit of a party; he always knew the newest jokes and he had a real sense of humor in telling them. "I've thought about this meeting all day, and I finally figured out why you called me, you want my body!"

Both laughed and Jennifer was glad that he had broken the ice. "You know, you're right. Every girl wants a Mr. R-I-G-H-T," and she spelled the last name for emphases. "Actually, I need some information and I think you can give it to me." Jerry sat silently, trying to anticipate her wishes. "I know that all of Dennis's African trophies from his ill-fated safari were sent to you for mounting. I understand that Mary Kyle has arranged to donate them to the City of Atlanta Museum. That's commendable, but I want to tell you something that's not so commendable. It's very private, and I have to have you swear that you'll never tell a soul. I think that I can trust you. And if I'm right in my assumptions then I will pay you well for your information, but I don't have any money now to bargain with." Jennifer had planned the conversation well and she knew that she was making a bed for the answers she needed.

Jerry sipped his wine, and said, "Go ahead, you know that you can trust me. At this time, I have a lot more to lose than you."

"I gather that that's a swear?"

"It is." Jerry nodded his head in the affirmative.

"I know that you make your money on trophies, but I'm going to pay you much more if I'm right. I believe that Dennis was murdered, and I believe that the other two hunters that were killed in almost the same way were likewise murdered. I have narrowed it down to any one of two people who could have planned them: Martin Smith – you know him from being a guest speaker at the gun and camera club – and his boss in Houston, Frank Black. Of course, they had to benefit some way or they wouldn't have taken the chances in pulling off the jobs. I don't yet know how they benefited, but I do know some curious information that seems fishy to me.

"I was there when Dennis died. I mean, I was within two hundred yards of him when he was killed. Martin Smith was his guide and they left the trackers behind when they went into that thick stuff. You're a hunter. That is not supposed to happen, is it?"

Jerry answered, "No, it isn't, but there could have been extenuating circumstances."

Jennifer decried, "I don't think that there were any. Martin sold us the hunt, picked the place, and selected the animals for Dennis to hunt. Dennis wanted no part of any more dangerous game. He told Martin this, but Martin connived and made him hunt that buffalo anyway. You know that they were supposedly after a kudu, but they wandered into a buffalo path. Guys at the club tell me that it would be extremely unusual to corner a buffalo where you could not retreat and get out of its way. In this case, it looks like they thought it was going to charge, at least Martin thought it was about to charge, and Martin elected to shoot it before it had a chance to get them. The shot was messed up somehow, and then they were left with no choice but to follow up the damn thing before it made a problem for someone else. I guess you know the rest of what happened. Martin got into a position where he couldn't shoot at the buffalo, and Dennis was so surprised by the whole situation that he, for some reason, couldn't kill the thing. There are too many coincidences that should not have happened; at least that is what everyone at the club says. What do you think?"

"Well, I know the bush can get pretty thick over there in places, and that's where kudu and buffalo like to hang out. I also know that there are plenty of documented cases where the Cape buffalo has charged without provocation. They just don't like anyone intruding into their space, so they just have a go at them. In my limited experience over there, I would say that if the bull that charged was by itself or with only one or two other bulls, I would not doubt it a bit that it decided it was going to charge. In fact, sometimes, the crafty old bulls sort of side step a direct line to their intruder to build up momentum before they turn to charge. The bull that got Dennis might have been doing that exact thing, and maybe Martin picked up on that and thought that he better give him some lead just to protect Dennis. At least a shot of some sort would discourage a clean charge and give them both more time to assess the situation. I'm not trying to throw a wrinkle into your imagination, but strange things happen out there in the bush. I'm surprised that there are not more deaths and injuries on safaris."

"I can see that you're defending Martin and Hunters, Ltd. Is that because they send you a lot of business? I know their clients do. Anyway, I want you to really think about all of the back-to-back coincidences that did occur. I can't get them out of my mind, and therefore, I believe they may have some merit. I probably don't have enough time to convince you of my theories right now, so for the time being, please play along with me on my hunch. I need some information, and if I'm wrong, nobody is the worse for wear." Jennifer paused and both had a sip of wine.

"Here are some more coincidences. After the funeral, Mary Kyle moved to Europe. That in itself is not so strange, but the wives of the other two hunters that were killed also moved to Europe after their accidents. That company has not had a fatal accident in their twenty-odd-year history; suddenly they have five!

"I have the other two wives' addresses and telephone numbers in Europe, but I cannot come up with Mrs. Kyle's. I want to do some personal investigations of them; not here, not in this country, but over there, in Europe. If you could give me Mrs. Kyle's address, I will have all of the necessary starting points. I will keep your name out of everything, and I assure you that no one will know where I got my information. Jerry, will you please help me?"

Jerry was feeling the womanly heart tugs of a gal that was desperate, but he kept his cool. "Jennifer, you bring up some strange ideas. I feel like I am on 'Unsolved Mysteries' or something. I would like to help you, but I don't have any idea where Mrs. Kyle is, and I don't know how to find out. Her attorney called me and told me to contact him when the trophies came in. I think they were air-freighted, but I don't know when to expect them."

"I'm sure they were air-freighted, I know Dennis's were. How else would they get here, by ship?" Jennifer said sarcastically.

Both sat silently dejected for a minute. Jennifer was about to lose her one contact number that she must have to research her puzzle. Jerry was about to lose a possible good piece of ass. Finally, Jerry perked up and said, "I have an idea. I could call her attorney, and tell him that I needed Mary's signature to import the trophies through customs."

"Good idea. Jerry. My father was a customs official part-time with the coast guard and I know that he had to require certain people to sign things."

Jerry had another sudden thought. "Bad idea, I know that her attorney would have a proper power-of-attorney filed if she is truly out of the country, and he could easily sign for her. *Hmmm*. But what if I had to talk to her by telephone to find out how she wanted the mounts – whether they were to be rugs, shoulder mounts, head mounts, life-sized mounts, etc. Even which way she wanted the heads turned if they were to be wall mounts. I think I could get her attorney to give me her telephone number. I doubt if he'd give me her address, but would the phone number do?"

"Sure, I'd rather have both, but I'm sure I could hire someone to find out her address if I knew her telephone number. Will you try to get it for me tomorrow?"

"Of course, all of this will hinge on her deciding which way she wants certain animals mounted; she might have left those details to the museum or the attorney might try to refer me directly to the museum instead of cooperating with Mary's phone number. However, usually, the donor sets the specifics on mounts. I'll give it a try, and I'll call you after I get it – if I can get it. So, let's see if we could meet again tomorrow night."

Jennifer was delighted with the plan and she couldn't help but show her gratitude. "Tomorrow night, at my place. I'll fix dinner, nothing fancy, but another steak or something."

"Why don't you let me pick up some Chinese food to go and I'll be there around seven. Give me your address and leave the rest to me." After the second glass of wine was consumed, Jennifer planted a rather sloppy kiss on Jerry's lips and thanked him with, "See you tomorrow night."

The following day went as slowly as the day before for Jennifer. She felt that her whole life depended on Jerry coming up with Mary's telephone number. All of Jennifer's clocks were set ten minutes ahead to facilitate her natural tardiness. And at exactly ten minutes past seven, Jerry rang the apartment doorbell. "Here, I hope you like roses. Give me a hand with the paper bag. It's full of Chinese stuff, so be careful. I'll set the vase on the bar."

"Jerry, you are so sweet. I hope you had some luck."

"Do you want the number typed or will handwriting do?" With that, Jennifer grabbed him, and tore out his tonsils with a full half-minute French kiss. The evening was off to a solid start for both.

Barbara Jones had departed Houston two weeks before and she rented a lovely suite at the Piccadilly Hotel across from Piccadilly Circus. She loved the place; it transformed the meeting forum of the old fashion worlds into the new hustle and bustle of today's London aristocracy. Her favorite pastime was visiting the Royal Academy of the Arts which was located just a little southwest from the famous Burlington House, an easy jaunt from Piccadilly Circus. Until she settled on a permanent location, this was by far the best place for her to be. Her three months' lease was expensive, but she felt deserving. She rationalized that she actually owed it to herself for all of her miserable time she had had to spend with the creep, Cliff.

Barbara used the same transferring mode for the funds going to Martin Smith this time as she had used when the contract was initiated. She wired a hefty sum of money, more than was needed to fulfill Martin's demands, to her travel concern in London, and then got them to wire her a lesser stated amount to a stated account number at the Switzerland International Bank in Zurich. That numbered account was of course under the name of Martin Smith. This was all done from Houston the day after she received her first insurance check. Her obligations to Martin Smith were now things of the past.

Barbara's lawyer back in Houston had met successfully with the beer-maker's top brass in Colorado. The meeting had gone well, and they were in the process of working out a deal that would transfer management and eventual ownership of Barbara's interests to the company's headquarters back in Colorado. Barbara would draw a monthly stipend of $20,000 until the deal was closed and then she would receive four million in cash over the next four years. Being the smart businesswoman that she was, she contracted her lawyer to work on her behalf in this deal for one and a half his hourly fee, plus travel expenses. That beat the hell out of a lawyer's usual percentage commissions.

Her lawyer had finished all of the insurance collecting, and he only had Barbara's travel business and her house to sell to wind up all of her and Clifford's estate settlement. Her only lost asset in the whole ordeal was Clifford's country club membership. She knew the value of a dollar from working in her own business, and she didn't relish losing a $50,000 investment, but she took comfort in knowing that her other funds would help her get over it. Per Martin Smith's instructions, Barbara had ordered the lawyer not to divulge her whereabouts.

Everyday, Barbara was out early to see the many museums and other historic sites of London. On occasion, she would lease a cab for the whole day to take in some countryside as well. She had put off buying a car just yet so that she could learn to navigate the narrow streets from her hired cabbies and to get used to driving on the "wrong" side of the road. She was just plain having fun, but she was running out of different clothes to wear. She had brought only three suitcases of garments, and each day she urged the hotel concierge to check for her wardrobe arrival via Emory Airfreight from Houston. That seemed to be her only worry.

Sally Maxie had checked into the London Marriott Hotel near Piccadilly Square for her initial London stay. She secured a partial suite that included a bath, a nice-sized bedroom – at least nice-sized by London standards – and a lovely parlor that made a cozy seating place for three. She had made the arrangements through a friend in Dallas, and she was assured this suite for as long as she desired, up to a year. Her plans were to relocate into a medium-sized flat sometime within the next four to six months. She was in no hurry; the hotel offered her security, help in directions, and no worry about cleanup and laundry service. She missed her washing machine and drier, but she knew that those would be back in her life soon enough.

Sally was concerned over money matters. She had inherited far more than she ever envisioned, but she still remembered the difficult times that Lou used to tell her that they were in. Somehow, she thought that those times might reappear.

As soon as she settled into her lovely suite at her hotel, she called Martin Smith over at the Hilton International by Hyde Park. As expected, he was out, so she left her telephone number for him with the concierge.

Sally was still sleeping off her jet lag when her phone rang. Although she was dead tired, she was thankful to hear Martin's voice. "Sally, welcome to Europe's most fascinating city. Whenever you're ready, I'm ready to give you the 'cook's tour.'"

"Martin, it's so good to hear from you. I'm afraid that I might be a constant bother to you. I already miss my friends back home."

"You're not homesick already, are you?"

"Well, maybe I'm just tired. I need to rest a few more hours before I can even think of going out. I have to get my head on straight to talk to you anyway. How about eight o'clock down in my lobby? Nothing fancy, just casual."

"Sounds fine to me. I have a lovely French restaurant that I am dying to take you to. You won't believe the food. It is quaint, only six tables, but it's absolutely the best and the atmosphere is relaxed. I'll see you at eight."

Sally didn't need a room call; she was waiting in the lobby when Martin arrived. She offered him a drink before they departed, but Martin said that they had reservations at precisely eight thirty, and they would have to hustle to make them. Martin's rent-a-car was a Jaguar, a right-hand drive. Sally scooted in on her side and Martin sped away like he was an old veteran of London traffic. "Martin, before we go any farther, I have to tell you that I have not sent you your money yet. I have my checkbook with me and it would save both of us a hassle if you could somehow accept my check."

"That might be difficult. We don't want a paper trail. What if you make the check out to my Swiss bank in excess of whatever you owe me and let me deposit it into my account, and then tell them to transfer out of my account to a new account of yours the excess, or vice versa. In fact, it would be better if you opened your account first and then transferred to mine what you owed me. Unfortunately, you have to go there in person. They don't have any branches in London that I'm aware of. I think there is some legal difficulties in branch banking the Swiss way."

"Martin, you don't understand. I'm trying to get out of going to Switzerland right now. I'm tired of traveling, and I just want to leisurely explore London."

"Let's talk about it after dinner. Maybe tomorrow you'll feel much better."

The dinner was as grand as Martin said it would be. The wine was a bit much for Sally, but she regained enough of her senses to feel safe riding back to the hotel with her handsome foreign escort. Kindly, for Sally's sake, Martin didn't offer her a drink in the lounge bar when they got back to the hotel. Instead, they lightly kissed good night, and Martin left for his own hotel.

Martin let Sally sleep until nine thirty the next morning before trying to reach her. She was already back in her suite from a downstairs breakfast when Martin called. "Sally, I've thought it over. I have two more days in London for sure, and then I'll probably have to go to Rome for a few days. There are Italian clients that Frank Black wants me to book. I think we both have to go to Switzerland either today or tomorrow. I hate to ask you to do it so soon, but I really see no other choice."

Sally replied with a sigh, "All right, Martin, you choose which day."

"Let's go this morning and get it over with, then we'll have the late afternoon free. I'll pick you up in one hour."

"Gosh, I guess I'll be ready. Do I need my passport?"

"I don't think you need it for travel within Europe, but you would be safe to bring it for the bank, and don't forget to bring your checkbook and maybe some IDs."

The walk-on flight at Heathrow to Zurich was standard operating procedure. Martin had telephoned his banker prior to picking up Sally from her hotel to let him know that they would be arriving just after lunch. After touchdown, Martin ordered a cab and instructed the driver to take them to the Switzerland International Bank. Sally felt like she was back in London, her purse was thoroughly searched before being allowed to enter the bank, and both had to go through metal detectors as well. Martin's banking officer was on the third floor; it was a beautiful office, and the receptionist had already prepared them fresh coffee when Martin's officer arrived.

The transactions were quickly explained, and the young officer called his secretary on his intercom to bring in the necessary blank documents. Martin was politely escorted out of the office by the secretary while Sally opened her account. After the proper papers were filled out, Sally was given a card with her account number on it, but without her selected pin number/word "lion," an apropos word that had made all this possible. She made an initial deposit of $1,100,000, with instructions to transfer immediately $1,000,000 to Martin Smith's account. She watched all of the entries go into the computer and her interest peaked when the officer pulled up Martin's account. The TV monitor was situated on the officer's back credenza, so he had to turn his big chair around to access it. Sally was seated directly in front of his desk, so she had a clear view of the monitor. She was surprised at the large print the officer was using, and then she noticed the thick glasses he was wearing. It was no trouble for her to read whatever she liked. She particularly noticed the big balance at the bottom of the screen,

$2,750,775.00. She was sure about the commas, and she was sure about the two and the seven that led off the big figure. She also noticed the name beside the passport entry. It looked like it was either "hunter" or "hunting," but her eyes were tearing from the strain and she couldn't be sure. She silently scolded herself for being so nosey.

The officer turned off the screen when he was through, and buzzed the intercom for his secretary to bring Mr. Smith back in. The three of them chatted for another ten minutes, and then Martin said that he had to get Mrs. Maxie back to London for a very important dinner date with her Cancer Society friends.

The walk-on flight back was as easy as the one going, and they landed at Heathrow just after five o'clock. Traffic was already at a standstill when they observed the roads while in the landing pattern. So, Martin suggested that they have a couple of drinks at the airport lounge before they went to dinner and eventually headed back to their respective hotels. "I thought I had some important date to make; that's what you told your bank officer."

"Well, we needed an excuse to get out of there or we'd have been there all day and half the night if I hadn't said something. I think those bankers over there get paid by how long they can converse with their clients."

Dinner wasn't ordered at Alonso's Queenstown Road Restaurant until just before nine o'clock, and the two didn't leave the restaurant until well after midnight. Martin persuaded Sally to try the new club that had just opened in her hotel, and the two danced and drank until well past two the next morning. This time, Martin walked Sally to her room, but Sally was quite tired and again did not invite him in. The kiss goodnight for both of them lasted a bit longer than the one of the night before, and the embrace was certainly tighter and stronger than that of the night before, but nothing else materialized.

Martin Smith left London on schedule for Rome. There, he had prearranged meetings with two groups of potential clients. He spent three days and two nights there wooing them to come to his posh Botswana camps. In the end, Martin had corralled three hunters for the next season. From Rome, Martin had two more stops to make before returning to his southern home in South Africa.

In Paris, he met with several past clients who wanted new statistics on game available and hunter success on the same. He was introduced to one new potential client that he was unable to convert, but he did make good headway with his past clients. He booked three safaris for a total of ninety days in camp. For pleasure, Martin always loved touring the classic gun shops that frequently adorned the nicest shopping areas of Paris. Most of their hunting garments were for winter sojourns, but occasionally, he found some clever leather works that could be used in all seasons. To these sometime finds, he always examined all of the new rifles in stock. Rarely did Martin ever go into these shops for a particular item, but rarer still did he ever leave a shop without buying something.

After Paris, Martin spent three more nights in Frankfurt to wind up his European sales tour. There, he managed to book two more hunts for the next year. Both hunts were for the same time period, but each was a one-on-one client and professional arranged in separate camps. Although Frankfurt was a beautiful, clean, and efficient city, it was not Martin's favorite European metropolis. It was just not as friendly as the other big cities, or else he was always in a bad frame of mind himself when he came there to visit. Maybe he simply felt ill at ease because he didn't speak German very well. Nevertheless, he was glad to leave there for his home in Johannesburg.

All the while that he was making these smallish "pit stops" in Rome and Frankfurt and the like, he always tried to reach Sally for a chat. Only twice in over a dozen times was he successful, but her voice was always reassuring of a potential relationship. He was on-again and off-again with that thought. He constantly reminded himself of being "too close to the forest to see the trees." Everything had worked out quite well in his profit for a hired-accident campaign, and he certainly didn't want to mess it up just now because he wanted to notch another lady in his bedroom.

Martin still had three more weeks of free time given him by Frank Black to recuperate from all of his accident ordeals. He wanted to be left alone for a while and he gave explicit instructions to the Houston office and his Jo'burg office to hang out the Do Not Disturb sign for him. Unless something was a dire emergency, he was not to be found by anybody. There would be a few exceptions, but not many.

In the meantime, Sally perfected her stay in London, and every night she wondered just how Martin Smith had so much money in his Swiss bank account.

13

Investigating – Getting Even

Jennifer Miller was streetwise and college educated – at least three years of college at Georgia Tech in Atlanta. She possessed magnificent thought processes, and she used them daily in analyzing anything that she had a hankering to analyze. She didn't finish college because she didn't have to. She became an exotic dancer at one of the well-known strip joints in Atlanta during her third year at college and she continued on in that profession for two years thereafter. It was easy for her to understand that she could never make the kind of money with a bachelor's degree in business or education that she could make dancing erotically. She realized early that her good looks and body firmness would not last forever and if she was going to start off in life like some of her rich friends, then she was going to have to build her initial nest egg herself. She tried dancing and going to school at the same time, but her analytical brain and the tiring hours soon convinced her that her college degree could wait. She never made less than two hundred and fifty dollars a night, and it wasn't infrequent when she made over five hundred dollars in a single night.

With her tremendous income, she succumbed to living quite high. She lived in a Buckhead highrise, shopped at Neiman Marcus, and drove a new Mercedes-Benz 300SL. She bought her own furniture and she always spent more than she should on gifts for her family and friends. Before she met Dennis Kyle, she palled around with another married man who owned one of the town's famous sports teams. As with any successful animal that has ever inhabited the earth, she rationalized to frequently take the path of least resistance. When free meals were there for the taking, she would take them. Soon, even her profitable dance work was too much of a chore to continue. Her boyfriend didn't like her dancing and she knew that someday he would leave her if she continued, so she left her less-than-noble but most profitable profession. Her lifestyle didn't suffer, however, because her flamboyant friend kept her up. Jennifer had always been a philosopher, even when she was young; she never criticized anyone working on something or doing something that they liked or had a future to it, no matter how it looked. Conversely, she never minded anyone saying anything about her if she was doing likewise. "Everything that one does is everyone's own business that does it," she used to say, and snide comments about her and her life were never taken by her as an insult. She just blamed the messenger for not being very smart.

She had her own separate life when she was dating her sports magnate, but she knew she must be available when he called. As this relationship was winding down, she began to frequent more and more clubs every night she was free, and she was becoming freer every week.

She figured that there was someone else in the wings for her paramour, so she thought it smart to begin looking for another mate as well. It was on one of these free occasions that she was introduced to Dennis Kyle. They hit it off rather spectacularly from the start, and Jennifer's preceding interlude was quickly over. To the credit of Mr. Sportsman, he didn't give Jennifer any hassle at all. She kept her new mink coat and her new diamond watch, but she gave back her latest diamond dinner ring. With the ring, she boxed up all of Mr. Sportsman's clothes that were left in her apartment and sent them Federal Express to Mr. Sportsman's office – she did mark the box "confidential."

After Dennis's death, she dismissed the thought entirely of going back to erotic dancing or rekindling the relationship with Mr. Sportsman. Although she was still in fine shape and extraordinarily beautiful, she simply thought she had graduated from that type of life. She narrowed her new lifestyle to three directions: One, to hook up with another married man. Two, to find a well-paying job that would allow her to do most of the things that she enjoyed. Or three, to pursue her quest for answers regarding Dennis's death. Analyzing each very carefully, she decided that the first two could wait, but if she was ever going to delve into Dennis's alleged accident, she must do it now while the trail was still warm.

So far, she was hitting on all cylinders in regards to her investigation. She had a supporting father helping with her money problems, and his background made him an intelligent ear to talk into when she ran into a roadblock. She had confronted Frank Black to gain access to two of her necessary interviewees, and she had secured the other one's telephone number via her womanly charms. She had done all of this without hiring a private investigator or involving too many people. In fact, only her father, Frank Black, and Jerry Wright were aware of her activities. Of these, only Frank Black was considered by her a risk to the furtherance of her investigation. The way she figured it, Frank Black could not have acted alone to carry out the killings, but he could have cooperated with Martin Smith.

If Frank was involved and if she did go on that safari that she demanded, then her life would certainly be in danger when she went. Instead of her carrying out revenge, she might be eliminating herself. The more she thought, however, she couldn't seem to put Frank in the puzzle. He had a going company that was in no financial crisis, and in fact, it was generating more money every year. "How could he have been helped by any of this?" she wondered. He seemed truly upset at the accidents and his demeanor held no signs of being fake. On the contrary, he did try to suppress Jennifer's thoughts of finding the new widows. Adding all of this up, she finally concluded that Frank had much more to lose if he had been involved than to gain. "Martin Smith," she summarized, "has to be a single orchestrator!"

Jennifer made list after list of the answers that she thought were important to obtain. She had to find out if there were other people involved besides Martin, Sally

Maxie, Barbara Jones, and Mary Kyle. She assumed that the two professional hunters also killed had to have had a part, but they were dead now; and they didn't appear to have any families who stood to gain from their involvement. Nevertheless, she had to find out if their involvement meant anything at this juncture. She had to find out just how Martin Smith benefited – money, a business deal, sex, or just what? She had to find out how the three widows paid for their new lives and why they were all in England. And finally she had to determine the best way for her to benefit from her findings when all of the answers came in. "Now, follow the money and/or the sex, and you'll get your answers," she repeatedly told herself.

It was obvious: to start the ball rolling, she needed to get to London and have some type of meeting with the widows. Her next question was, do I meet with each individually or all in a group? If all of them were in on the deal together, she might have a fruitful meeting with the first one individually, but the next two would be warned and the other two meetings might never take place. She needed to meet with them all at the same time without either of them being aware that the meeting was to include them all. She had to figure out an excuse to pretend to meet with each separately, but in fact meet with them altogether. She decided to use Martin Smith as her ruse.

She would have to travel to London. There was no other way! She figured to call each widow when she arrived in London and leave a message with each at her respective hotel that something had come up and they needed to meet with Martin Smith at a prescribed place in London the following day – no excuses, drop what they were doing, they must be there, and they were not to try to verify anything for fear of being traced. While discussing Martin Smith over lunch with Frank Black a few days back in Houston, Jennifer remembered that Frank said that Martin had a voice-mail answering service in London. She would call it to find out if it would be useful in soliciting the meeting. Frank also said that Martin was now in seclusion in Johannesburg until the hunting season resumed. Jennifer convinced herself that she now had a valid plan and that she knew all of the components and their whereabouts. She knew who to worry about and who not to worry about. She was ready to assimilate into action.

Her first task was to actually try to get in touch with Martin Smith to confirm his whereabouts. She must make sure that he did not accidentally call one of the widows between the time that they were contacted by Jennifer to be at the meeting and the time of the actual meeting. If Martin got wind of Jennifer's planned meeting in London using Martin as an excuse, then all of the widows would surely be contacted and proper defenses would be set up by the group to fend off any future questions or inquires. Jennifer knew that she must plan for all eventualities and she must operate with the knowledge that all of those eventualities had been taken care of.

Jennifer's flight to London deplaned at Gatwick. She caught a train to Victoria Station after gathering her luggage and then transferred to a taxi for a short ride to her hotel, the Intercontinental on Hamilton Place near Hyde Park. Her travel book on London had already proved invaluable as she made her connections perfectly to get to her hotel. However, her jet lag was nagging her at every juncture and she wasted no time in getting to her room for a nap.

When she awoke, she called Martin Smith's voice-mail number that she had gotten from information. She confirmed it as the same number that she was given by Hunters, Ltd. just after Dennis's death. It was still listed under the name of Hunters, Ltd. instead of his personal name. She had brought along two recording devices that she had purchased back in Atlanta. One of them had an attached device that would allow her to plug into a telephone conversation and record it. She adeptly recorded Martin's full message. "Hello, this is Martin Smith representing Hunters, Ltd., we are not presently in our offices today, but we will be checking our messages regularly. If we do not return your call within five days or if you need information immediately, then please call our Houston office at area code number 713 and then the telephone number 621-2929. A message may be recorded at the sound of the tone. Thank you for calling." Jennifer duplicated the recording on her other recorder and she reduced the entire message to writing. From her written notes, she played with the words to see if she could come up with a message in Martin's own voice that would suit her needs.

She played it over and over again to listen for any flaws. There were some, but certainly not noticeable to someone unsuspecting. "Hello, this is Martin Smith, will be checking messages regularly, a message may be recorded at the tone, thank you for calling." Using one recording instrument in conjunction with the other, Jennifer managed to record what she wanted and deleted what she didn't want. She silently thanked the neat chap at the radio store in Atlanta for all of his help and suggestions. She had been well trained. She smiled when she thought if just another female that was not as good-looking could have managed the same help from the radio man. She next checked with her hotel concierge to see if the hotel offered an answering service for its guests – they did. That was also predicted by the radio man. She then asked for the room-availability clerk. Jennifer explained to the reservation clerk that she needed to reserve a room for her soon-to-be-arriving friend, Martin Smith. She also told the clerk that he had instructed her to set up a telephone answering message with the recording that he had given her to use in case one of his clients called before he arrived or when he was out. The accommodating employee was particularly glad to help another woman who was already a registered guest.

Jennifer was instructed to go to the registration desk and ask for Mr. Mobley and he would be waiting to assist her. She gave the reservationists a few minutes to contact Mr. Mobley and then she caught the elevator down to the registration desk. The supervisor of the telephone-switchboard operator had received instructions from Mr. Mobley and was waiting to help. She inserted Jennifer's taped message of Martin's voice into her automatic answering machine that was connected to Mr. Smith's room telephone, and after a few moments, all was set for incoming calls and recorded messages to Martin Smith's room.

Jennifer now wondered why she was so worried earlier about her contacts' addresses; all she really needed was their telephone numbers. If she played her cards right, they would come to her when she wanted to see them. She ate dinner alone in the hotel informal dining room that night and went over her next day's plan. If all of the widows were in their hotels, like nice little girls, then she was confident that her plan would work. After dinner, she went for a short walk in the brisk night air, and then returned to her room for a good night's rest. Before she went to bed, she called the main hotel operator to ask for a wakeup call at 6:00 a.m. It was imperative that she reach all of the ladies before they left their respective hotels for their already-planned day. Otherwise, she would have to start over and make a new plan.

Due to her jet lag, she was wide awake at four o'clock. Just about the time that she finally got back to sleep, the wakeup call came. She stumbled into the bathroom, washed her face to wake up, and then gathered her telephone numbers for her widows. She first called each hotel to ask to be connected to each of the widow's rooms. There was not a Do Not Disturb notice on any of the room telephone numbers. The first hurdle was over. As each widow sleepily answered, Jennifer would ask, "Sherry, is this you?" When each widow would explain that whoever was calling obviously had the wrong number, Jennifer would then gasp, offer the most convincing apology, and then hang up. After the three calls were made to verify that the widows were all in their rooms, Jennifer said a prayerful "thanks" and began to make the message calls. She was prepared to tell each hotel operator that she was the secretary of Martin Smith if they inquired why she was making the call.

The first call was to Barbara Jones at the Piccadilly Hotel. As she dialed the number, she made a mental note to find out just what Piccadilly Circus was all about. The hotel operator answered on the second ring and offered to transfer her call. "Ma'am, I have an early flight to catch and I do not want to wake Barbara. Could I just leave a message in her box? I must be sure that she receives it, though." The operator was most obliging and offered her own name as a guarantee that the message would be delivered.

Jennifer read the message that she had earlier prepared. "Barbara, a slight problem has come up concerning the accident and I need to see you this afternoon at 3:00 p.m. at the lobby of my hotel. Call my room and leave a message if there is a problem. My room number is 505 at the Intercontinental Hotel at number one Hamilton Place at Hyde Park. Please keep everything confidential, M. Smith." Jennifer asked the operator to read back the message and it was perfect. She also asked whether she would be able to tell if the message had been picked up if she called back later in the morning. The operator assured her that there would be a record. "I hate to be so picky, but I have a very picky boss; thank you very much for your help."

"Wow, one down and two to go." Jennifer clapped as she thought out loud.

The next contact was Mary Kyle at the Baker Hotel on Baker Street. The switchboard operator there was less cooperative. Evidently, she was on her last hour of an all-night shift and she wasn't much in the mood to help anyone. Jennifer explained how important the message was, however, and the young lady finally assured Jennifer that the message would be delivered and that Jennifer could call back later to confirm its deliverance. The message was identical to the one for Barbara Jones, but the meeting time was changed to 2:45 p.m. Jennifer didn't want more than one widow approaching the information desk at the same time, just in case one of the widows overheard another ask the clerk similar questions.

Jennifer's final call was to Sally Maxie at the London Marriott. There were two hotels listed in the Yellow Pages at Grosvenor Square, and she was a little confused by their listings but she finally managed to match the numbers. The hotel telephone operator was as nice as the first one that she had called. The same message was conveyed again, but with the meeting time changed to 3:15 p.m. Like her other two calls, she was assured the delivery and her ability to check that the message was received.

Jennifer doubted that all of the widows would call Martin's hotel, but she was covered if any or all of them did. She had already checked her manipulated recording of Martin's voice and it sounded as authentic as the real one. She again counted her blessings that all three were in town and that they all had chosen London as their obvious escape city. She imagined how much more difficult her task would have been if the three had been scattered all over the world. Unless by some slip any of the widows had just spoken to Martin Smith in Johannesburg, her meeting was going to come off as planned. Considering the comments of Frank Black that Martin was in "hiding," and her personal verifications, she felt confident of her plans.

Not one of the widows called Martin's registered hotel; all three did. Barbara Jones was a little shaken at Martin's message, but nowhere near as much as the other two. Barbara checked on Martin once at his hotel and was satisfied that the meeting was on the up and up when she heard his voice on the machine. She was a cool lady and she had learned a long time ago not to overreact at the first sign of potential bad news. She calmly reassessed her situation and came to the conclusion that nothing very bad could be forthcoming. She rather expected Martin to either be in trouble with his job or in need of companionship. She would honor the meeting but she wasn't going to look shook up.

Sally Maxie was devastated at her message and she could not imagine what had possibly gone wrong. Her imagination was running wild. She thought about calling her attorney back in Dallas, but cooler thoughts ultimately prevailed and she decided to wait until after the meeting when she had more information to judge the situation. During her day, she was a nervous wreck. She canceled her only appointment to get her hair fixed and she stayed next to her hotel telephone for any further news from Martin. She called Martin's hotel three times without finding him in, and that made her all the more nervous. After each call, she declined to leave a message on his recorder. There was never a question about her attending the suddenly called meeting – she would be there and probably be early.

Mary Kyle was closer to Sally in her reaction to Martin's message. She tracked down the hotel operator that took the message, and at first, she was skeptical because the hotel operator told her that she thought the message was left by a female. She then called the hotel again and asked for Martin Smith's room. He was registered. That expelled her skeptical theory somewhat, but she wanted more verification. Despite being told that Mr. Smith was not in, she asked the operator to ring his room anyway. Martin's recording erased any doubts that the meeting was genuine. Somehow, she even felt better at hearing Martin's own voice on the recording. She concluded that Martin's secretary in Houston or in Johannesburg had called station to station to leave the desired communication. Her day was free, so the meeting time scheduled was no problem.

Jennifer spent all of the day rehearsing and re-rehearsing the meeting. When the time came, she dressed for the meeting in simple slipshod fashion. She wore the most inconspicuous getup that she could muster from her travel wardrobe. She remembered meeting each of the widows at their husband's funerals, and she remembered her hairdo on each occasion. This day, she would put her hair up; a diversionary tactic in case any of her widows might be suspicious should they meet in the lobby prior to the scheduled meeting.

In less than two short days, Jennifer and the hotel's concierge had become close friends. Shortly after lunch, Jennifer approached her newfound friend for some favors. As she began the conversation, she slipped him a new fifty-dollar American bill. "My employer, Martin Smith, is in room 505. He is expecting three middle-aged women to meet him on business at around three this afternoon. They are supposed to meet him in the lobby, but his plane has been delayed and he asked me to meet with them in his room. I expect that the ladies will ask for Mr. Smith at the front desk when they get tired of waiting. These three are like cats and dogs with each other, so it is important that they be escorted separately to his room when they do inquire. I have scheduled their arrivals at 2:45, 3:00, and at 3:15 p.m. because of their minimum dislikes for one another. I will be in Martin's room to handle them if you will bring them up. If you get too busy with other things, just send them up in the elevator and tell them to go to room 505. If it gets too rough and rowdy for me up there, I'll call you for reinforcements," she chuckled. The concierge wrote down all of the information he thought he would need to carry out his assignment and then assured Jennifer that everything would be well taken care of. After Jennifer spelled each of the names for him, she grabbed his hand, gave him a kiss on the cheek, and thanked him for his help. With her looks, little did she know that the "fifty" she had slipped him was not at all necessary.

The lobby was scarce with people coming in off the street. Because of that, it was easy for the concierge to notice the first ritzy-looking lady that came through the revolving door alone. He had also noticed that she exited from a taxi. She stopped in the foyer of the lobby and observed all of the seated residents. When there was no one that she knew, she seated herself next to another vacant chair. The time was 2:40 p.m. The concierge walked over to her and asked, "Would you be here to meet Mr. Martin Smith, madame?"

"Why, yes. Is he in?"

"His plane has been slightly delayed and I have instructions to take you to his room. He is in room number 505. I will be glad to escort you or you may find your own way using that elevator, if you like," he said as he pointed to the proper elevator bank. "Mr. Smith's door has been left ajar with a Do Not Disturb sign hanging on the door knob. He expects you to enter and make yourself at home. There are fresh ice cubes and the minibar has been left open for your enjoyment." The concierge was proud of his coolness, even if he embellished the circumstances.

"Thank you very much. I think that I can find my way. I appreciate your help." With that, Mary Kyle rose and walked toward the prescribed elevator.

Jennifer now wished that she had put Mary at the end of the list instead of at the first because of her inquisitive nature, but she would try to adjust and hope for the best.

The door to room 505 was open, but there was no one in. Mary politely knocked and whispered, "Martin, are you decent?" There was no answer. Mary assumed that she was supposed to enter and wait for Martin to show his handsome face in a few moments. She did enter and seated herself at one of the four straight chairs that huddled around a small table in the far corner of the room. *Odd*, she thought, that four chairs instead of two were in a single hotel room, and she fought her imagination from running away with her. She picked up the hotel information folder and began to read. She declined the minibar.

As scheduled, the second well-dressed lady that exited a taxi came through the revolving doors. It was 2:55 p.m. Again, the concierge approached the obviously confused woman. "May I help you, madame?"

"Thank you very much. I am supposed to meet a gentleman here at three o'clock and I am a little early."

"Madame, by chance are you here to meet Mr. Martin Smith?"

"Yes. Has he been delayed?"

"Only for a few minutes, my lady. In fact, he asked me to escort you to his room. He is in room number 505. I will be glad to accompany you or you may find your own way, if you choose, by using those elevators over there. Mr. Smith left instructions for the door to be left ajar for you to go in. He will be there presently." He pointed to the same block of lifts that he had pointed to previously.

"You are so kind. I believe that I can go it alone. I have had a lot of practice lately in hotels. I've been traveling extensively." The concierge walked her over to the elevators and pushed the Up button for her.

Mary sat quietly when she heard the elevator doors open down the hall. An area of about twenty feet was tiled coming out of the elevator, and she listened intently to the type of walk of the person that approached. She could hear the distinctive walk of a female coming her way and not that of Martin.

Just as she had done, the attractive lady that now graced the doorway called for Martin. "Are you in, Martin?" The two women noticed each other at the same moment that Barbara opened the door to enter. Barbara backed into the hallway and looked up at the room number again and said, "Do I have the right room?"

Mary rose to her feet and answered, "I'm not sure. I'm here to meet Martin Smith. And you?"

"So am I." As both looked at each other in a quizzical manner, in walked Jennifer. She had been standing in the concession area around the corner from room 505. Barbara looked around at Jennifer and inquired, "Are you here to meet Martin Smith as well?"

"I sure am," was Jennifer's reply. "I understand that we are to have one more guest, but she is not scheduled to arrive until 3:15. May I order some coffee or other drinks for you?" Mary couldn't say a word; she was dumbfounded and she was trying to place the face of the last intruder. She knew that face from somewhere.

Barbara was not nearly so shocked. "Before I order anything, I would like to know what is going on. I understood that I was to meet Mr. Smith, but I assumed that I was to be alone. Do either of you have an answer?" Mary sat down again and remained quiet.

Jennifer slowly answered, "To be truthful, I'm not sure that Martin will be here, but I have some information for the three of you and some questions to ask you pertaining to that information. So that I will not have to repeat the story and the questions, I would like to wait for the other lady. You must be Mary Kyle from Atlanta, Georgia, over in the States," she addressed the seated woman.

"That's right, but who are you?"

"In just a moment, I will tell you all about me. But first, you must be Barbara Jones from Houston, Texas, right?"

"Right," shot back Barbara in as sarcastic a way as possible.

"Let me say that you two and the other lady who has not yet arrived are now my guests. We do have some mutual interests to talk about, but neither of you has anything to worry about. In fact, you are perfectly free to leave, but I think that I have some interesting information that you will all want to hear. It's about Martin Smith and Hunters, Ltd. I prefer not to get into it twice, so again, if we can wait another few minutes, I believe that the other person will be present any minute. Let me try again. May I order any drinks?"

Mary smiled for the fist time and said, "I hope nothing has happened to Martin. Is he all right?"

"Of course," Jennifer replied. "Drinks?"

Mary continued, "A double Scotch and soda for me."

Barbara also ordered. "A Scotch sour for me, thank you." Jennifer dialed room service and placed the order while the two women stared at the ceiling.

The door was purposefully left open for the fourth arrival. At shortly before 3:15, the concierge knocked on the open door and presented, "Mrs. Maxie to see Mr. Smith, I believe."

Jennifer politely thanked him, ushered in Sally, and then shut the door.

Now Sally Maxie joined the disbelieving. "Why am I here with the three of you? I am supposed to meet Mr. Martin Smith."

Almost in unison, the other two answered, "We are supposed to meet him also."

Jennifer then took complete control. "Mrs. Maxie, this is Mrs. Barbara Jones from Houston and this is Mrs. Mary Kyle from Atlanta. I'm Jennifer Miller from Atlanta."

"My god, I knew I recognized you. Just what do you think you are doing imposing on our time like this?"

"Mrs. Kyle, I understand your anger, and as I said before, any of you are free to go, but I do have some interesting information for you. Mrs. Maxie's first name is Sally; I would hope that we can call each other by our first names. Everyone has ordered a drink, Sally, may I catch room service before they come up and get them to bring you a drink as well?"

After a pause, Sally said, "Thank you. I'll have a vodka gimlet, please."

"Before I start this meeting, I have a sincere apology to make – actually, two apologies. First, I owe special sympathies to Mary. The reason that I do is that I dated her husband for almost three years before he was killed." Jennifer turned to look directly into Mary Kyle's eyes, and said, "I know that I cannot convince you of my sincerity so quickly, but I really mean it. If it had not been me that he was running around with, it would have been somebody else. But I am certainly sorry that it was me."

Jennifer now stood and turned away from Mary to address the other ladies as well. "By now, you all have probably figured out what we all have in common. Just in case you haven't, we all lost our husbands, and in my case a boyfriend, to an enraged animal in the bush of Africa. I have interviewed Hunters, Ltd., Frank Black, Martin Smith, and many of Hunters, Ltd.'s other clients. Add to that; I was unfortunately present when Dennis Kyle was killed. Coincidences don't just happen. All three of your basic stories match almost perfectly, including your new lives in London. Circumstantial evidence is the most powerful evidence that can be submitted in a courtroom. Direct evidence is always doubted by jury members. It confronts them as a challenge. But circumstantial evidence is an accumulation of overwhelming facts that paint a picture or a finished puzzle in each of the juror's minds. They individually reach a conclusion that cannot be dissuaded with future arguments. My daddy says so, and he is a former investigator for the U.S. Coast Guard. In each accident, all of the native personnel were held back and out of sight as to what was planned and what actually took place. Most unusual. None of the accidents happened on the same safari grounds or in the same country. That holds down the potential of investigations. One accident can get by, but two or more should raise questions. All of you were married to genuine bastards and these accidents were your way out. I can go on, but I will spare you the details if you will just listen to a plan that will keep you hidden and keep you well-off with all of your money."

All stared at Jennifer in stunned silence. "Martin Smith had nothing to do with this meeting. He is in quiet seclusion in Johannesburg, taking a leave of absence from his job at Hunters, Ltd. I called this meeting and Martin Smith knows nothing about it."

With perfect timing, a knock on the door signaled the arrival of room service. Jennifer signed the ticket and distributed the drinks as the attendant left. "I guess you now realize that I am presently living at this hotel, just like the three of you at yours. The only difference is I cannot afford to stay very long. You see, each of you was left a pot full of money when your husbands were killed, while I lost everything. I realize that I am partly to blame for putting myself into this predicament, but I am also innocent of what happened. I want each of you to understand one thing very clearly, I do not want any of your money, not a dime, but I do want your cooperation. As far as I am concerned, each one of you deserves everything you have. Although I dated a married man, and I knew it, I have no respect for his disloyalty to his wife, Mary. I tried for a very long time to get him divorced, but he was too greedy. From what information I've been told by some of your husbands' safari friends, you were all crapped on and you all deserve whatever you can get to make amends for your tortuous years. I really mean what I have just said.

"One more thing, no one gave me my information about the accidents, not Martin, not Frank Black, not anybody. "My purpose in finding each of you, and then calling this meeting, is to secure your cooperation with my investigation. I know each of your husbands was killed intentionally and I know each of you had something to do with it, but again I say, I do not begrudge your actions. In fact, I would have done exactly what each of you has done. Everyone in this complicated series of killings has gotten everything they deserve, except two people. One is me. I lost everything without any just compensation. The other is Martin Smith, and he profited handsomely from his arranged killings. He not only has the blood money for the designed killings, he also has blood on his hands from his two cohort-professionals that got killed carrying out his orders. I am not sure that I know all of the facts, so if I am wrong, please help me with some true answers."

No one said a word.

Jennifer took a drink of her vodka and resumed her narration of how all of these things happened. "I don't believe that Frank Black had anything to do with any of this. Am I wrong?"

All shrugged their shoulders without a hint of an answer, but none said a word. "I think all of the players that are alive in all three, quote, 'accidents' are in this room, save and except one, Martin Smith.

"I have no idea as to how or how much Martin Smith was paid, but I know that he didn't do these things for nothing. My plan is to take what money he got from the three of you to offset my hurt and my losses. If I have to kill him for it, I will."

All the listeners began to squirm.

"Again, I say, I have no problems with any of you, but I do need your cooperation to carry out my vendetta against Martin Smith."

Barbara was the first widow to conjure up enough nerve to speak. "Would you be honest enough to tell us if any part of this conversation is being transcribed or recorded?"

"Of course. I need all of your cooperation. As tough as I sound, I would never do anything to hurt any of you if you will just cooperate with me. You are welcome to look around if you suspect something, or we can move to another room if you like. I guarantee there is no recording going on, and I'll guarantee one other thing – I'll never lie to you. You've had enough lies told to you by your past husbands."

Barbara arose. "I believe I'll have a look."

Jennifer succeeded that comment with her cooperation. "I'll certainly be glad to help you look."

When Barbara came back from inspecting the bathroom and the bedroom, she continued, "And if we choose not to admit your outlandish assertions and we refuse to cooperate?"

"I wouldn't think that's wise. I know too much. I have put my hypothesis in writing and I've left it in my safety-deposit box back in the States. I've informed my family to open it and read it to the press if anything happens to me. As I see it, you have two choices – either help me get my share of money from Martin Smith, or tell him about me and probably help him get rid of me. I cannot be bought off by the three of you. My mind is made up. This is poetic justice. Mr. Martin Smith needs to pay for his terrible plots. He did everything just for money and that sets him in a completely different world from the three of you. He is a money-hungry villain, whereas you three just escaped torture and were just seeking a way out so that you could have some semblance of a normal life in the future."

"If you choose to cooperate with me, then I'm sure you will continue your new lifestyles and nothing will ever be connected to you. And in all probability, you'll never see me or Martin Smith again. If you choose to help Martin Smith, then you all will be exposed one way or the other when my safety-deposit box is opened. It looks simple to me.

"I know you do not like me jumping in here and spoiling your party, but I had to. I want my share of hurt paid back to me too; just like you. Now let me be quiet for a while and let me hear from the three of you."

It now became obvious that Barbara was going to be the leader of the three newly joined widows. "Just what kind of information are you asking us to provide? And, before you answer that, what makes you think that we can trust you any more than Martin Smith?" The other two widows nodded in agreement to the two questions.

Jennifer sensed that she had better answer these two questions before others popped up. "You have to trust me or kill me, and if you don't trust me, then the killings are going to be exposed. I have no vendetta against you. I want Martin Smith to pay for what he did to me; it is no different from what your lousy husbands did to you. As to the information that I want; it's quite simple. I want to know if there are any other people involved. I want to know how Martin profited and by how much. I want to know if he got cash or something else of value, and I want to know where it is. And finally, I want the three of you to help me get whatever you paid him or what is left. If there is any dirty work to do, I expect to be the one to do it. I'm not asking anything impossible or anything that will expose any of you by cooperating with my efforts."

It was Barbara's turn again. "First of all. I can't speak for Mary and Sally, but I swear that I had no idea that there were other wives in the same boat as me. Maybe it's the wrong time to ask, but I need some things made clear before I hear any more from you. Someone has got to get this thing started. Martin Smith came to me and said that he knew of my marital problems and he had a way out for me. I paid him something like a consulting fee and he arranged for an accident to happen while my husband was on safari. Did something similar happen to the two of you?"

This time, Sally was the first to respond. "That is exactly what Martin did for me. I don't know if the circumstances were the same, but that is essentially what happened in my case."

Mary didn't hesitate with her answer as well. "Same with me. I would think it would be interesting to hear how much you two paid him. I can tell you that I paid him a little more than a million dollars."

Almost in unison came Barbara's and Sally's answer, "Me too, me too."

Barbara then put her hands up to request the floor. "For lack of better words, I guess that the three of us have become unwilling partners. I cannot speak for my other two new partners, but I think that the three of us widows should be given a little time together to see how we want to respond."

Both Mary and Sally voiced a hardy, "I agree."

"That is perfectly fine with me," came back Jennifer. "I see no reason to rush this thing. I have enough money for a few more nights in this luxurious place. But I do want you all to know your options, and just what I expect of you. I don't consider this blackmail because I'm not asking any of you for a dime. I just want you to help me make things right!"

Mary now entered the conversation. "Obviously, you know how to reach each of us, and we all know where you're living, so I think the three new partners need to exchange our addresses." At almost the same time, Barbara said that she was at the Piccadilly and Sally said that she was at the Hyde Park Marriott. Mary then informed the others that she was staying at the Baker Hotel on Baker Street.

Jennifer decided to make it easy on the others. "I suggest that the three of you have dinner tonight at one of your hotels and discuss the whole matter then get back with me in the morning. I'll come to one of your places, or we can meet here again. How about ten o'clock in the morning?"

All agreed to both ideas and each took one more sip of her respective drink, grabbed her purse, and rose to leave.

Jennifer thanked them for coming, but she did not get a reply. As the three departed, Jennifer said good-bye with, "I'm in room 515 if you need me. I hope you have a pleasant dinner and I'll see you in the lobby of my hotel in the morning at ten. That'll give everybody a leisurely morning-get-up time."

There was absolute silence between the three ladies until the elevator door opened. Naturally, each widow had gone to bed night after night over the last few months wondering when, if ever, someone would seek her out to burst her bubble. In every daydream, it was always an officer of the law that would appear. This was a surprisingly different twist. All had invented prescribed answers to the inevitable questions. Jennifer had thought this would be a surprise of a lifetime for each widow, but it really wasn't. Meeting others that were in the same predicament was a surprise, but the inevitable had finally come true. In a curious way, all were slightly relieved that each had company in her plight, but no one could have predicted a blackmailer was on the prowl.

On the way down the elevator, Sally grabbed each of her new found cohorts by the arm, and said, "I have two things that immediately come to mind. First, I don't know what each of you was told to get you here, but I was scared that something major had gone wrong with my deal with Martin. My imagination was going wild. In a way, I'm relieved that whatever I perceive is about to happen, it doesn't appear to be uncontrollable. And secondly, it certainly makes things a bit easier to have others available to help me; in the same boat, so to speak. For better or for worse, I'm anxious to get to know you both better. And for now, I think we are all fortunate to have each other to lean on if something ever does go wrong."

Mary smiled back at Sally and said, "I think your feelings are mutual. I too am glad to know that I have company other than Martin to look to in case a problem arises."

Both women then turned to Barbara for a response. "I am likewise anxious to get to know both of you, but I think we better be careful with this Jennifer. I'm afraid she could cause more than a stir for her own interests. She is so dead-set to get Martin, I think she would rather kill him than make him pay money. I feel a certain gratitude concerning Martin Smith, and I think the two of you should feel the same way – that is, if he solved a similar problem for you that he solved for me. On the other hand, I know he would take care of himself first if something like this were to come up on his end. So like he would do, we must think of ourselves first and then worry about Martin. We all have some thinking to do before we meet for dinner. As I told you, I'm staying at the Piccadilly Hotel, right across from Piccadilly Circus; there's a quaint little restaurant just outside the lobby that would be perfect for us to meet. The food is good and I don't think we would be intruded upon. Unless either of you has a better idea, let's meet there at six thirty." Sally and Mary agreed, and each took a separate taxi to go on their separate ways.

All three ladies appeared at the lobby restaurant at exactly the same time, six thirty. Barbara was the first to speak. "Good evening, ladies. I'm glad everyone is so prompt. Whenever we meet, I want to say right off how much I appreciate others being on time. None of us will ever want to worry about a late arrival, that leads to a heavy dose of indigestion." Sally looked at Mary and Mary looked at Sally and both could read each other's thoughts – *Picky, picky*. The maitre d' already had the perfect table set and ready for the lovely threesome.

Barbara felt obliged to open the conversation because the three were at her hotel. "Whether we all go through with Jennifer's demands or not, we've all admitted by one way or the other to being involved in similar situations. We are destined to be friends of sorts regardless. So, we need to get to know each other. I can think of no better way to get to know each other than to let each one of us tell our own little life stories. Who would like to be first?"

Sally and Mary looked at each other to see which one would take the first challenge; it was Mary. "Why don't I burst the ice? I was born and raised in Atlanta, Georgia. I went to precollege school at a private church institution called Marist. After that, I won an academic scholarship at Emory University, also in Atlanta. I graduated with a minor in premed, but of course, I never continued in that direction. My major was biology. I went to work after graduation in one of my father's businesses, an insurance agency. That is where I met my only husband, Dennis Kyle. At first, he was so energetic and suave. He was destined to be a success. He was interested in general business, and he was particularly interested in my father helping him get started. I was so naive. We tried several insurance-related businesses without success. And finally, Dennis decided on a 'get – rich scheme' that involved the then current rage, health spas. Ideally, people would join these spas like clubs to stay in shape or get in better health. Well, he thought the way you make money is to take everyone else's money and then bankrupt the business. Over and over he did this. His personal reputation was lousy, and I rode that awful reputation as well. He couldn't get a bank loan if he tried. My family kept him afloat, and every time I saw them, I felt like I had to hide my face. "Business was not our only trouble. Dennis and two of our employees were indicted on prostitution charges on three different occasions. Each time, a well-paid lawyer got Dennis off. The employees were not so lucky. For the last four years, Dennis has had a string of girlfriends and live-ins – not at our house, thank goodness, but at his private apartment. Jennifer Miller was one of them. I don't know how they met, but she is right. As bad as I hate to admit it, if it wasn't her, it would have been someone else. I tried filing for divorce on several occasions, but each time Dennis would bankrupt everything and my lawyer would leave me. I led a very nice life financially, but I was miserable in every other aspect of our marriage. For the last few years, I have immersed myself in charitable and social work. I was chairperson for the North Fulton County Cancer Society for the last two years, and I've been offered a similar position with the London office here.

"I first met Martin Smith when he called me as he was passing through Atlanta on his way to Europe. He said that he was with the National Cancer Society and he had some material that he wanted me to see. Instead, he had photographs of my husband and Jennifer Miller in compromising positions that were just taken at the last Las Vegas Gun and Camera Convention. He showed me the documentation that he had booked a safari for the two of them in April. He showed me some press clippings, etc., about some past accidents on safari that were really staged and he offered to do the same for me regarding Dennis. As I know the two of you were, I was scared to death to even think of such a thing. Eventually, he asked for some up-front money, but I didn't have any so he told me to pay him $1,000,000 after Dennis's funeral. Martin was very understanding and helpful. There were some business complications that he helped me with in addition to being my new marriage adviser, but that's the gist of the situation. Finally, I reluctantly agreed to go along with his plan; everything went just as he had predicted, and I thought that I was home free before Jennifer Miller's call this morning. I have no children, and I guess I would be considered 'rich' by most standards, all because of Dennis's insurance policies." Nearly out of breath, Mary then looked to her other two companions for their turn.

Barbara looked over to Sally and Sally got the hint. "Well, I was born and raised in Ft. Worth, Texas. My family has been with Texas Christian University for as long as I can remember. My precollege was in Ft. Worth and then I opted for Baylor University in Waco, Texas, for my higher education. I majored in music. After Baylor, I came back to Ft. Worth to find a job. For three years, I worked for the Tarrant County Fat Stock Show. We put on the world-famous rodeo there and several other functions. At one of the rodeo parties one year, I met Louis Maxie. He was five years older than I and he was already a successful businessman. He held some very important high-profile city and county positions gratuitously. He just wanted to be in on the new developments.

"He was known as a diversified entrepreneur, but he never made any money except in quasi-illegal stuff. He owned several strip joints, but he hid behind leases to the real people that ran them. In other words, he owned the property and buildings but he leased the actual business to a 'front man.' He still controlled everything, though. For the last couple of years, he had been dodging the IRS for skimming profits on his main club. His manager turned him in, and in fact, he tried to have Lou killed! I was in a nasty situation. I had a good life financially – just like you, Mary – but everything else was horrible. I also tried to divorce him, but he threatened to kill me. I'm afraid I took the easy way around it all, and I just let things go as they wanted to go. I knew he was out every night with another woman, and sometimes he wouldn't come home for days. I had no idea where he was. We had no kids, so he really felt no obligation to anyone. My family never liked him, so I was always taking up for him to hide my past mistake in marrying him. I hate to admit it, but I was just a plain fool.

"I still don't know who it was, but someone in the Dallas Gun and Camera Club chapter recommended that Martin Smith talk to me. I don't think whoever it was knows the accident was not an accident, at least that's what Martin says. Martin met with me using bogus excuses many times before he actually offered me an out with the accident stuff. At first, I wouldn't consider it, but Martin hired a private detective that showed me documents and pictures of his illegal activities and his escapades with other women. According to Martin, I was in danger of prison if I didn't get out of my situation. This was a convenient answer, so I bit, and here I am."

All eyes then turned to Barbara. "I married an older gentleman, fifteen years my elder. He owned a beer distributorship in Houston and he was quite wealthy. Everything he did in the business world was strictly legit. I was in the travel business before I met him, and unfortunately for the both of us, that is how we met. I booked several trips for him. He was previously married, twice before. He had three kids by those prior marriages and he settled with both his first and second wives and his kids before we were married. They hated his guts, even his kids. They even refused to attend his funeral. After we started dating, occasionally at first, he was so proud of my success as an independent businesswoman, he wanted to do business with me – in what way, I don't know. All his bragging about me made me love him, I guess. I was the fool. No one I've met since we married would have anything to do with him. He was just a rich old goat that always got his way. After we were married for six months, I got a call from my best friend. She said that she had caught Cliff in the arms of some prostitute in the parking lot of a shopping center. From there, it got worse and worse. Like you, Sally, he threatened to kill me if I filed for divorce. He was so damned old and unhealthy, that I thought he would just die any day, but my misery kept on going and going, just like that damned little battery-operated rabbit that's on TV.

"I actually called Martin Smith myself with the idea of getting rid of Cliff the way I had read about an accident that had happened previously in Botswana. He seemed amenable to the idea and he came to Houston to meet me and talk about it. He asked me to hire a private investigator to find out some stuff on Cliff. And when I did, he returned to Houston and we made a deal for the same $1,000,000, but I had to pay him an additional $100,000 up front. That was no problem because I had it in my personal business, but I expect that amount of money would have been a problem for the two of you. Missing a hundred grand would cause a great concern in most households. Anyway, Martin and I set up a gift safari for Cliff and Martin arranged for one of his professionals to do the dirty work. That was the only part of the whole deal that I really found distasteful. I guess you know that the professional acting on behalf of Martin was also killed. I've been on several safaris myself, and I can't imagine how Martin could have been responsible for that man's death, but a lot of things in this deal don't add up. Hey, did I get gypped for paying an up-front fee of $100,000?"

Sally quickly blurted out; "I know that I was asked to pay an up-front fee in addition to the cost of the safari." And Mary joined her, "I too was asked to pay the same, but I couldn't get it. Just like Barbara said. So, Martin put a plan together with Lou's business partner to get it for me. It worked."

Sally again blurted out something that she had forgotten to say, "I forgot to mention that Lou's professional hunter was likewise killed. Maybe there is a little more greed on behalf of Martin Smith than meets the eye. Who was in charge of your husband's safari, Mary?"

"Dennis and Jennifer were chaperoned by none other than Martin Smith himself. There was no other professional involved as far as I know. We'll have to ask Jennifer when we meet her in the morning."

The rest of the meal's conversation dealt mainly with the future and not past misfortunes.

Due to Barbara's first controlling image when they met and now reinforced by her known business acumen, she was the logical chairperson for this and future meetings between the three. "We must address Jennifer's demands. And we must decide whether we are in this together or separately. I've been giving this thing a lot of thought, and I've come to several conclusions. First, I think we must stick together, but I think we must be careful not to be noticed with each other – at least for a year or so. I don't think we will ever be implicated, but I believe in playing it safe."

Both Mary and Sally nodded their agreement.

"We mustn't let anyone know we're aware of the other two in any way. Except for our own secret meetings, we must still be loners – no written messages, no traceable calls, etc. This sounds difficult and it's going to be hard for us to keep in touch, but we'll manage. My second most important observation is that we must keep our distance from Jennifer Miller, at all possible times! I think we have no choice but to cooperate with her as much as she absolutely needs, but we won't sacrifice ourselves for her to get rich, and we won't have anything to do with another death. The truth is, we all bought into a scenario where our husbands were put at risk, but they were not killed by us or anyone we hired. A provoked raging animal of one kind or another killed all of them. It might cost us a lot of money, but I think we would be proven innocent in a court at law. However, I'm not advocating either of us take the way of the court system. Our best way to continue our deserving lifestyles is to cooperate with Jennifer, unless she demands things that we just can't agree to. Have either of you got anything more to add?"

Mary spoke first. "I've also given heavy thought to every aspect of this mirage. I agree with every single thing Barbara has said. I do want to add that I also think we should cooperate as much as possible with Jennifer. I was too quick to judge her this morning. She's right; my husband tried to hop in bed with anything that walked. I would bet that she was lied to and mistreated just like I was. I would like for her to have an easier life, and I plan to tell her so. Still, we cannot sacrifice ourselves for her."

It was Sally's turn. "I don't have much to add. I believe in everything that's been said. I do want to make sure we are never out of touch, but how we stay in touch should be our private business. One thing bothers me that we've not discussed. What happens if we are nice little ladies, we cooperate with Jennifer, and then something strange happens to Jennifer? According to her, someone will open her safety-deposit box and find her accusations. We would not be deserving of that."

Barbara perked up. "Sally, you are brilliant. I never gave that scenario a bit of thought. You have come up with a real possibility and we better have an answer to it. It goes to show you we're all in this together and we can't rely on just any one of us to think of everything. We all must be on our toes. Sally, you make sure that you mention your point at tomorrow morning's meeting. What about Martin? We can't just ignore him in the future, even if we know that Jennifer is after him. For all we know now, we might have to play a part in getting some of his rat-holed money to Jennifer. Nevertheless, we have to act natural around him. We have to answer his calls and continue to show our thankfulness for him. Do you all agree?"

All answered in the affirmative by nodding their heads.

"How do you think our demeanor should be when we meet with Jennifer in the morning?" Mary had the next point.

Barbara again praised her other cohort. "Great question. I think we should be cooperative but stern. We'll tell her that we will help her all that we can, with all that we know, but we will never cross the line that would lead to another death or to our own misfortune."

"That says it all," chimed in Sally. "I think we've covered all of the known possibilities for in the morning. There's no need to speculate on a new agenda that might not come up. Let's finish dinner and enjoy our newfound friendship and let tomorrow take care of itself. I'm convinced we're all well prepared."

Meanwhile, Jennifer spent a rather sleepless night. She was confident that the newfound "rich bitches" would have to support her requests, but she would not be able to be sure of that until the morning. Her jealousy was showing. She visualized all kinds of problems that might be uncovered over the night, but finally, she settled into a light slumber, again more confident than not her plan would be approved.

Because of the diversity of hotel locations, the three widows arrived at Jennifer's hotel in separate taxis. Jennifer was on hand to meet each one as they entered the lobby. Barbara was predictably the first to arrive. "I've arranged a small meeting room next to the hair salon down the hall; after I meet the others, I'll join you. The concierge has already delivered fresh coffee and tea. Help yourself; we should get started in a few minutes."

Within the next ten minutes, everyone was in the room and everyone had poured her favorite morning drink. Jennifer opened the dialogue. "Well, I guess you would not be here if you were totally opposed to helping me."

Barbara clanged her coffee cup down on the saucer. "Don't ever take us for granted. We are not here by choice. We understand that you've been hurt, but in no way in the proportion that the three of us were hurt. Up to a point, we will help you because it does seem to be the right thing to do. But we'll only cooperate within certain guidelines. We will never be a part of a killing. We will not give of ourselves to any danger that might lead us to an admission of guilt. And we will insist that no other people become involved. One more thing, you mentioned when we first met that you had a manuscript concerning the accidents that would be uncovered if something happened to you prior to our full cooperation. To be honest, that got our attention as it was supposed to do. But maybe in a different way than you anticipated. Now, it's going to work against you. What if we were to cooperate as best we can and then something happened to you while we were carrying out our part of the bargain? We would suffer untold embarrassments without doing anything to deserve them. We all agree, you must cure that problem before we'll cooperate at all. If you have an answer for that, then we are ready to proceed. If you cannot assure us of anonymity under all circumstances, then we will wait for you to devise a plan that will."

Jennifer, for the first time, looked puzzled; she lost all coordination between her thought processes and her tongue. "I will always be completely honest with you, as I've said before, even if it hurts my position. I don't know what to say." It was evident that she was grasping for any thought that would extricate her from the stated problem. "If you are willing to cooperate with me, then I'll do anything you say to keep all of you out of any limelight. Obviously, you all have thought about this more than I. Have you got any ideas?"

Barbara paused to rethink and then she tried an answer. "I haven't passed this by my other two partners, but what if you gave Mary a letter that threatened her with extortion based on your letter about the accidents, something like you intended to expose the accidents as hired killings unless you received a certain amount of money from her. Of course, you wouldn't have any proof of any wrong-doings or such. Then, if something happened to you and the letter in your safety-deposit box accusing us was purposely leaked, then Mary and the rest of us could hide behind your threat as the cause of your tying our names to such participation. If we were later questioned about any of our actions, we wouldn't be admitting anything except that we wanted you and your accusations to go away as quickly as possible and leave us alone. We could plead ignorance and being just plain scared of someone even remotely thinking that we had a part in any of this, particularly someone that is demanding money for silence. That would give us a valid reason to deny your accusations and make your exposed letter look like a shot-in-the-dark blackmail scheme. Keep in mind we are not trying to hurt you either. We're just trying to protect ourselves in case something might happen to you and the letter were to be exposed. You can tell us you have destroyed it all you want, but there could be other copies, so we have to have an independent source tied to a believable story to exonerate us."

Everyone perked up with the idea, but not a soul was quite ready to endorse it. Jennifer saw through the plan first. "I cannot see where a letter like that would hurt me. I can think of no reason why any of you would expose my new letter to Mary unless you were already exposed. Otherwise, you would be exposing your own lives. I'll agree to write that letter if you think it will cure the problem."

Barbara quizzed the other two. "Do either of you have another idea?" Both women shook their heads in the negative. And then Mary spoke up, "What if you executed three promissory notes of a million each to each one of us with a letter attached that said if your story that was reduced to writing about us being involved in any way with our husbands' deaths were to be made public, you would instruct your estate to pay off these notes. Otherwise, if your written instrument was destroyed, so will the promissory notes. I can see that this idea doesn't cover copies of your story, and it might bring someone else out of the woodwork for blackmail purposes, so I really don't know what to do about your safety-deposit box."

Sally could sense Mary's uneasiness and brought forth her thoughts. "Well, in absence of better ideas at the present, I think we could accept your handwritten letter or notes as a solution if we can work out the details."

Mary then decided to utter a modification. "If any of us comes up with a better idea in the future, would you assure us now that you would perform on such a better idea if it surfaces?"

"Sure, you have my word! In fact, I've been thinking. We all need to trust each other. Why don't I make the first move by giving you my lock-box key and let one of Mary's friends in Atlanta go into it and retrieve my letter and either destroy it or send it over here to one of you? What I'm saying is, I now fully trust all of you to cooperate with me as best you can and I need no other backup."

Everyone smiled and nodded in agreement.

Barbara then turned to the widows' nemesis. "Jennifer, let me make one other thing very clear. We are ready to cooperate with you as you have asked, but we will only offer you the information that we know to be right. We will not speculate and we will not be a part of digging up new info. Now, we're ready for your questions."

"I'm sure all of you have better and more exciting things to do than be here with me. I understand that, and I will be as painless as possible. I will never seek your help if I can avoid it. There's no secret of roles here, everyone knows where everyone stands." Jennifer then paused to grab her notes. "My first question has to do with the number of players in all of your original deals. Aside from Martin Smith and the three of you, are there any other people that know the inside details of the alleged accidents?"

Mary Kyle answered first. "Absolutely no one that I know of."

Barbara studied the question a little longer, and then replied, "A private investigator helped me find out certain information about my husband, but I never led him to believe that Cliff was going on a safari that might cost him his life. He might put two and two together, but I doubt it. I haven't talked to him since way before the fateful safari."

Sally was thankful for Barbara's extensive answer because it gave her a moment to think. She decided to come clean. "Martin and I discussed the accident with my husband's partner."

Barbara grimaced and said, "Sally, I believe you hinted at something of that sort earlier. You could have opened a can of worms there for all of us, but of course you didn't know we would be in your same boat then."

"Before you all get to concerned, let me fill you in on what happened.

"Lou and his partner were being investigated by numerous government agencies, particularly the IRS. Martin hired an investigator to find out what really was going on. Martin and the private eye even got into my husband's office. They found that the two partners were skimming huge sums of money every night out of the night's proceeds. They also found out about my husband and his partner's extracurricular activities – ladies of the night, etc. They recorded a conversation with my husband's partner where he actually tried to hire a hit man to kill my husband. After all the dust had settled, Martin met with the jerk and negotiated a new lease for me on the property that housed the strip joint. Martin said that he and the investigator had enough on the guy to forever keep him from talking. In the end, my husband's partner actually thought that Martin was working for the U.S. government and he told me at the funeral that he knew the government had Lou killed. I left it at that. I sincerely don't think that there's anything to worry about. The guy has a most favorable lease, and he is making more than a million dollars a year on the business. If he hurt me, I would get my lawyer to somehow cancel his lease, and then he would lose his business. For sure he knows my lawyer and I have the upper hand."

Barbara inquired, "Does he have any idea about any of the other accidents?"

"Absolutely none. How could he? He knows nothing about hunting or the safari business. He just lives in his own little niche, and he hasn't got enough sense to come in out of the rain. Martin is convinced that he can cause nobody any trouble, and Martin has more to lose with him than any of us. Martin and the investigator still have all the recordings on the guy. Martin told me. And the investigator has no reason to believe that Cliff's accident was anything other than an accident." Sally wished that she hadn't mentioned the partner, but now that she had, she thought she had to convince everyone that there was no alarm.

Jennifer moved to the next question. "I'm satisfied with everyone's answer on my first question, so let's turn to the next one, a two-part question. How much did Martin benefit from each accident and how and when was the remuneration paid?"

All hesitated; it was apparent that no one wanted to divulge more than was necessary for reasons of incrimination and for it just not being anyone else's business. Yet all knew that if they didn't cooperate to some degree, each of them might be exposed by this ruthless-sounding lady. Finally, Sally decided to continue her oration. "Since I'm on a roll from the first question, I guess I'll go first while my other explanation is still in everyone's mind. My husband's partner paid Martin $100,000. Martin told him that it was for the negotiation of his lease with me. Then, after I got to London, I met Martin, only a couple of months ago, and we went to Switzerland together to make his deposit of the remaining $1,000,000 that he demanded in his private numbered account at the Switzerland International Bank in Zurich. Martin left for other parts of Europe the next day, and I think, on to Johannesburg."

Barbara expressed her reservations at someone else knowing about Sally's deal again. "This partner of your husband's keeps coming up over and over again. Are you sure you've told us everything and do you still believe he is safe?"

Mary tried to console Sally. "Barbara, I think you're being too hard on Sally, for Christ's sake. She's just told us her whole life history and she included in it a partner of her husband's that she really didn't have to tell us about. She could have just said that she paid Martin a total of $1,000,000. I think we are blessed to be dealing with a woman that has only our interests at heart and we need to be the same way." Mary turned to Sally. "I want to personally thank you for your detailed story. I know it was difficult to mention and we all appreciate it." Mary reached over and gently squeezed Sally's arm.

Barbara then sought to make amends. "Forgive me, Sally, I just want to be sure of things for all of our sakes. I believe the guy's no threat."

Barbara continued, "I also paid Martin Smith a total of $1,100,000. I paid him $100,000 from my travel business at the end of last year, and I sent him the balance after Cliff's funeral. I transferred both amounts to his personal Swiss account, at the same bank that Sally said, through another travel agency in London that was an associate of my travel business."

Everyone now looked at Mary. "After my jet lag wore off from my flight from Atlanta to here, I took a flight alone to Zurich and I met with Martin's banker. I arranged for my Atlanta bank to wire transfer $2,000,000 to a new account that I opened in my name at the same bank, Switzerland International. After the transfer was complete, I then did an in-house transfer of the full $1,000,000 to Martin's account. There were no problems at all as far as I could tell."

Sally begged to add to her story once again. "I forgot to say that I also opened an account in my name at the same bank. I did exactly as Mary did. I deposited $1,100,000 into my new account and then I took $1,000,000 out and put it into Martin's account – all within the hour that I was there."

Jennifer did a quick job of addition and stated, "That means that Martin Smith deposited, or had deposited, a total of $3,300,000 in his numbered account at Switzerland International."

Sally again jumped in. "I don't know whether it's important or not, but I happened to see Martin's balance when I was seated at his officer's desk while Martin was out of the room. It was just over $2,700,000. I could make out all of the big figures. I'm sure it was over the figure of $2,700,000."

Everyone could see Mary's mind churning. "Is that all that you saw, Sally? You know that we all had to makeup a password or pin number to use to enter our accounts. You didn't happen to see that word or number for Martin's account, did you?"

"In fact, I did. At least, I kinda did. It was either 'hunting' or 'hunter.' I can't be sure which. I was a good four or five feet away, but I have good eyes." She was telling the truth, if her appearance was an example. Sally was the only one of the four that did not wear glasses or evident contacts.

"Think hard, Sally," Mary implored. "If we knew how to get into that account, then Jennifer could extract what she wanted and none of us would have to go any further."

Sally corrugated her brow in deep thought. "I embarrassed myself at being so nosy when I looked at the screen behind that officer's desk, so I didn't study it. But I'm sure of the amount that I told you, and I'm quite sure that Martin's password at the time was either 'hunter' or 'hunting.' I don't remember whether the first letters were capitalized or not, and I don't remember if it was '-ing' or '-er' at the end. I just can't be that precise."

Barbara was due a word or two. "You know, we figured Martin was supposed to split all of the money with the two professional hunters that died. I don't know if it was an even split or not, but I'm reasonably sure that they planned to split all of the money that we paid him. It looks as if Martin has kept it all now. Maybe he's a greedy little bastard! He should at least share it with his buddies' relatives, if they had any. But, of course, that would bring new people into the game and that would mean more people to trust."

Jennifer's mind was now racing. "Somebody tell me about getting into a numbered account in Switzerland. How's it done?"

After each had looked at each other, Sally and Mary volunteered simultaneously to explain and Sally then yielded to Mary. "All the bank wants is your money. They have strict rules about using only an account number and a password or pin number for entry. I think you can make a deposit without the password, but you certainly can't make a withdrawal without both the account number and the password. I guess all three of us have Martin's account number. He gave it to me to get my money to him." Barbara and Sally nodded in agreement. "Since we know his account number, all Jennifer needs is the password."

Barbara said, "I don't have a Swiss account, but are you sure that it's that simple? Don't they have to have a clue of some sort as to who is asking for a withdrawal?"

Sally reaffirmed Mary's explanation. "That's what they told me as well. I was to guard the password with my life. They suggested that I use an old childhood memory, a friend, or relative in conjunction with my account number. They told me over and over that they took no responsibility for a withdrawal from anyone if he or she had a correct password. If you had the information that was on file, then you could get the money. They would even ship it to you, with no return address, even cash, if you wanted it that way."

Barbara smiled. "Sounds crazy to me, but I guess they've been successful at it for years."

Jennifer decided to ask a shocker. "Did any of you have to leave a will with them, a beneficiary or something?"

Mary remembered first. "Yes, I left one. I don't think that it was a prerequisite, but I chose to leave one, a beneficiary. I don't know how they would find out if I died, but I left one. I guess that's the only exception. If you die, you don't need a password, pin number, or an account number."

Barbara's logical mind went to work once more. "That doesn't make sense. The purpose of a Swiss numbered account is to never let a name come into play. I'll bet everything revolves around the account number and the password alone."

Jennifer began to pry a little harder. "Did you leave a telephone number or an address for them to contact you?"

Sally thought for a minute and then volunteered her answer. "I was given the bank's international toll-free telephone number, but I never gave them any of my home information. But, you know, I did see the name, Hunters, Ltd., on the screen for Martin's account. I wonder if he listed his company as his beneficiary?"

Jennifer asked another question. "Is there a personal officer that you have to use when you do something with your account?"

"No, you just call or go there and speak to whomever is handy."

Jennifer spoke, "There's no use quizzing everybody about other items, if I can access Martin's account for his money. Am I correct in assuming that you all will give me his account number to go with his password of 'hunter' or 'hunting' for me to try to enter his account?"

Sally and Mary acted like two tickled teenagers when they laughed and said, "Fine with me." Then both looked toward Barbara.

As Jennifer excused herself to go to the bathroom. Barbara spoke in a worried tone. "I think we've gotten ourselves into a pickle. If Martin's money turns up missing, he will surely blame us. We are the only ones that know anything about his damn money and his account. If we mess up his deal with any or all of us, I think he will either try to kill us or he will blackmail us the rest of our lives. We must decide whether we're going to be blackmailed by Jennifer into giving her money now, or be killed or blackmailed by Martin – I don't like the choices. We must think of another option. If we give her money, then I'm afraid that the end will never come. She'll keep coming back for more every year."

"Right now, Jennifer is the only clean one among us. I know that we don't think we did anything wrong because we've all been hurt so badly by our prior husbands and we really didn't hire a hit man, but the law might not look at it that way. We've discussed that before. Martin is guiltier than anyone; he had no motivation other than pure greed. Somehow, I think we've got to get Jennifer's hands dirty so that we can remove her future blackmail options."

"What do you mean?" asked pure, innocent Mary.

Barbara shook her head and answered, "I think we have to encourage Jennifer into terminating Martin."

"You mean . . . kill him . . . don't you?" Sally said.

"It's hard for me to use those words. For all of my life, I've been as sweet and innocent as the two of you. I would have given anything not to have had my accident happen, but it was the only way out for me. And I think it was the only way out for you two as well. Neither of us killed anyone, and neither of us is going to kill anyone in the future. I just think we have no choice but to tell Jennifer that she *cannot* access Martin's account or we will assuredly be held responsible. I think we must tell her that we need Martin *removed* before she can withdraw his money. To be honest, I think that's what she has been planning all along. As we mentioned before, if Martin's money turns up missing, he is certainly going to come after all of us. I hate to say it, but if Jennifer silences Martin, all of our troubles seem to be over."

All turned as Jennifer slipped back into the room. "Jennifer, I hope this room isn't bugged."

"Not by me, if it is. I don't think we have to worry about that. But I'm willing to search it if y'all want to."

Sally and Mary looked to Barbara. "Jennifer, if you withdraw any money from Martin's account while he is still alive, then we are afraid that he will do some tragic things to us. He might even kill us. We are surely the only ones who know his Swiss account number, and he would be a fool not to directly trace the security breach to one or all of us. You said that you weren't blackmailing us and you said that you could not be bought off by us, so we are taking you at your word. We'll continue to help you with information, but we are sincerely concerned about Martin tracing a security leak to us. We need some assurance that we will not suffer from giving out his account number."

Jennifer sat back in her seat and stretched her arms. "I suspected as much. I assumed that you would be in a heap of trouble if I took his money. I'm not angered by your decision. I respect it. I still stand by all of the promises that I've made to each of you. I'll carry out my own deal, but I do need your help in getting me enough information to allow me to get to his account. Keep in mind, he never told you his password, so merely having his account number could not hurt him in any way. It could only be used to fatten his account with deposits."

Barbara sighed. "We appreciate your understanding and we are ready to cooperate. When the time comes, when we are sure that we will be safe, then we will gladly give you Martin's account number. Let's just hope that there's still a lot of money left in there."

Barbara continued to monopolize the conversation on behalf of the three widows. "Jennifer, we've told you everyone that could possibly be in the know on any of the accidents. We've told you how we all became involved. We've told you how much we paid, and where we paid it. We've given you some idea of Martin Smith's password. Except for Martin's actual account number, I cannot think of any other information that you would want."

Jennifer thought a moment before answering. "I can think of two things. First, after I write Mary her letter or whatever we decide on – and I will do that before we adjourn – I will need Martin Smith's account number at the Swiss bank. I will assure you that I will not use it until either Martin agrees that I can, or that he is so out of the picture that he could never complain. And secondly, I will need to be able to get in touch with all of you someway after I leave London. I know that the contact will have to be secret, but I need that option."

Sally decided to share Barbara's chairpersonship. "If we have given you all of the information that you say you need, then why is there any need for further contact?"

"Sally, at the present time, if I get Martin's account number, then I don't visualize any further contact that would be needed. But you can never tell when some information that you all might have would be the key to my success. I deserve to be able to get in touch with you. I will never mean any of you any harm."

Sally remained in the conversation. "We know that your intentions are not to harm us, but what if unintentionally we got caught conferring with you? If you later were implicated in some crime, then we might be dragged into it."

Barbara was a little more sarcastic. "I resent the word 'deserve' that you used. You don't 'deserve' anything from us. You are asking information from us that might get us imprisoned for admitting something that we either did or did not do. And we are making a statement which might incriminate us. We are only cooperating with you because we don't want to defend ourselves in another forum right now."

Jennifer knew that she was intrusive, but she had to press on. "I feel some hostilities beginning to form, and I want to go on record as saying that I like and admire all of you. I do not want to inconvenience you or hurt you – ever! If either or all of you is ever connected in any way to my getting even with Martin Smith, then my plan has failed. I will give every move careful consideration on your behalf. I hope that I've not offended you; I just want to square the tables between Martin and myself and I need your honest help."

Mary finally spoke out. "Jennifer, I told the girls last night that I was too hard on you. I want to apologize. You are absolutely right about Dennis. If it were not you, it would have been someone else. I agree with you. I want you to get your due. We are all a little testy in this situation, even you! If you will give me the letter that we discussed and if you will promise that you will do everything in your power to keep us all out of your doings, then I will volunteer to be the go-between, between you and the three of us. I will give you my lawyer's telephone number in Atlanta, and I will instruct him to give you my contact number. By our agreement, Barbara and Sally will always be reached through me. This idea seems sensible because you and I have had a mutual interest, and we are from the same city."

Barbara and Sally thought that Mary's idea was a stroke of genius; it offered a buffer to the contacts, and it served Jennifer's needs as well. Mary didn't speak much, but when she did, it was always useful. Jennifer excused herself momentarily and then returned. "I have some plain white paper; I will write the extortion letter and fold it like you have just received it in the mail. You can say that you threw away the envelope or lost it. But we all know that the letter will never have to be used!" All sat silently while Jennifer finished the extortion demand and then gave it to all to read.

Jennifer pulled out a smaller piece of paper and asked, "Martin's account number, please." The three ladies each looked at each other. Mary and Barbara did not have anything on them to refer to that had the number on it. Sally came to the rescue. "I don't know why I still have Martin's scribbling with me, but here it is. The Switzerland International Bank account number is 3339750792; in the Zurich office, his officer is Hans Winston. We all understand that you will never say where you got the number and you will never use our names in any way to facilitate your plan. Agreed?"

Jennifer put her right hand in the air and said, "I swear!"

All of the widows now expressed an interest in leaving by collecting their respective purses in hand. Jennifer never moved. For the first time, she was overcome with emotion. As tears formed in her beautiful blue eyes, she sniffled and said, "I hate that we had to meet this way. I thank you all for your help. I admire you all so much, and I hope that I can be with you all once again someday – under happier circumstances."

14

Jennifer Prepares

Jennifer finally got a complete night's rest in London. Yet, no sooner had she gotten over her jet lag than she had to return home. She awoke full of dream-confirmed ideas and energy. She called her airline to see if she could exchange her ticket for that day's departure, and she accepted the rejection of her wish as if it were in the ordinary course of business. The lady attendant did, however, tell her that she could go out to Heathrow and try for a standby seat. The lady indicated that a very few were still available. She gathered her baggage, called for a bellman, and proceeded to the checkout counter. On the way out, she made a special trip to the concierge's desk to express her gratitude for helping her so much. She told the concierge that she would someday return to the hotel just because of him. Jennifer had a knack for making people feel good.

Standby reservations are no picnic for anyone, but on this day, Jennifer wasn't going to get upset at anything. She missed the first two planes to Atlanta, but she easily made the third. Her assigned seat put her right next to a new mother and a baby girl; it was obvious that this was not her lucky day, but she cheerfully made the best of it. Before the flight was over, she had made friends with everyone around her.

Atlanta never looked so good. The transatlantic flight of approximately nine hours plus was over, and home was indeed a blessing. She didn't bother calling anyone to meet her; she grabbed the first cab and had it whisk her straight to her apartment. There she went right to bed without even thinking of unpacking. She hoped that the next morning was going to be an extension of her day before, a royally fine day. When she awoke, her first task was to look up Frank Black's telephone number in Houston. Frank was an early riser and he was usually in the office by seven thirty. When Jennifer's call came through, it was still before normal working hours in Central Standard time and Frank himself answered.

"Frank, this is Jennifer Miller. I've just returned from London and everything went perfectly! I met all your lady friends, and they haven't a clue as to where or how I found them. I got all the information I wanted, and now I'm ready to go on safari. When can I go?"

Frank was dumbfounded and had to clear his head before he could say a thing. "Were any of the ladies you met suicidal when they found out someone had allegedly uncovered their sudden rise to happy independence?"

"Not really; I wouldn't say they were ecstatic, but they readily accepted my presence and my questions. What choice did they have? I told you I have thought this thing out from all angles. I still have some confirming of some facts to do, and when I tie everything down, then I'll give you my findings in full detail. But right now, I want to schedule my safari that you owe me."

Frank dreaded this call; he had hoped it would never come, but it did, and now he had to face the music that he had promised. "Well, the season is winding down; we are almost solidly booked for the rest of the year. How about the first of March next year?"

"That won't do; you said I could go before the end of this year. I was the one that suggested next year, but only if I hadn't finished my investigations. Now that I'm nearly finished, you aren't going to back out on me, are you?"

"No. You can go this year, but I will have to work you in. It'll be a lot easier if you don't have to have Martin Smith."

"No, Frank, I want to go with Martin. I think he's cute. My father may not be able to accompany me as I had first thought, so that will save you some money. But I have to have Martin. That's the deal, no other choices, period!"

"Okay. Give me some time to work out the logistics and I'll get back to you in a couple of days."

"Frank, I can't live in limbo for a couple of days, I have to make plans. I know you have a calendar; can't you give me a date right away?"

"You haven't lost any of your persistence; give me until later this afternoon. I'll give you a call by five o'clock your time this evening. Give me your number and I'll get back to you."

Jennifer made stops at the cleaners, the grocery store, and the public library before heading back to her house to receive Frank's call. She knew he would be a last-minute caller. If he wasn't, he would have certainly left a message on Jennifer's answering machine. When she got home, there was no call and Frank had less than two hours to honor his appointment.

Thanks to the kind young man at the library, Jennifer was quickly granted a library card. She didn't waste any time using it as she checked out three books on the African lion. She was going to be as prepared as possible for this safari, and she had no one to assist her like Lou had done on her last one. She tried to concentrate as she thumbed through the books, but she was really only a picture-looker. At least she managed to read the picture-tag remarks. After the first hour passed, she could feel herself regaining her fidgety nature in anticipation of Frank's call. Frank called at precisely five o'clock, just as Jennifer predicted. Jennifer picked up after the first ring.

"Jennifer, I have some good news for you. Can you be ready to go in two weeks?"

"Sure, Frank. Will I get to be with Martin Smith?"

'You will, but I can only arrange a one-week deal. Will your father be joining you?"

"No, I talked to him after I talked to you this morning. He can't break away this year, so I guess he's out. He's such a mess. I looked forward to taking him on a once-in-a-lifetime vacation with me, but now that he is retired, all he wants to do is do the same old things day after day – golf, golf, golf. So, I guess I'll have to endure it alone. You know I don't want to shoot things, just take pictures. I just want to be pampered like in *Out Of Africa*, and I want Martin to be Robert Redford."

"Well, that's awfully flattering for Martin. May I tell him you said that?"

"Sure, tell him that I love his body!"

"If that's the case, maybe I can substitute for him. I know a lot about the bush as well."

"Which bush, Frank?"

"Both, wouldn't you rather have me?"

"Someday, Frank, but not this time." Jennifer now became more serious. "I want to wipe out all of the memories of my first safari, and my doctor says I need Martin's help to do it."

Frank was just kidding along about earlier telling Jennifer that he had to substitute another professional hunter for Martin, and he was glad he didn't. He thought that Jennifer was more than slightly crazy. Frank then mentioned the cost and bookings for Jennifer's airfare. "I bet you haven't thought a thing about the cost of your airfare on such a short-notice trip, have you? I'm afraid it is going to cost you some pretty hefty dollars." This was Frank's last hope of totally discouraging Jennifer from going on safari at all.

"Frank, don't kid around with me like that. Your people caused my safari to get cancelled early, not me. And not Dennis. I'm not saying that you caused it, but your company damn sure did. I am the one that has been inconvenienced by having to fly over that big ocean twice each way to get the same safari that was booked to happen on only one trip abroad. Don't you even suggest that I pay for any of my transportation. My trip isn't going to cost me a red cent or I will start exposing everything I've found out right now! There is plenty of obvious truth in my findings to cause Hunters, Ltd. to have cancellations all over the place, not to mention immediate future bookings."

"All right, all right, Jennifer, I was just kidding. Can't you take a joke?" Jennifer made Frank promise that there would not be any future jokes of this nature. After that promise, the proper details to book the flights were exchanged and the conversation ended.

Frank had spent a lot of time thinking about just what problems lay a head with Jennifer, but he hadn't anticipated that Jennifer would want a romantic interlude with Martin. Maybe he was mistaken; he hoped so. His thoughts turned to the widows of the previous accidents. *God, I hope they don't associate me with Jennifer! She may have found them, even met with one or two, but I bet she really didn't get any details of a murder plot. They wouldn't have ever cooperated with her in the first place if in fact they were involved in such a scheme. I better go along with all of this nonsense just in case, but I'm sure Jennifer is pulling my leg,* he thought. Jennifer spent most of her time before going on safari chasing all of the knowledge she could find on the animals in the Okavango Delta in Botswana. She wished she had done the same research for her prior trip. When she sold most of Lou's possessions from their shared apartment, she saved Lou's binoculars and his 200mm-lens Nikon camera, and she still had her zoom digital camera. She had hoped they would soon come in handy, and now they were going to. Every day, she would go over her planned safari and the ramifications that went along with it. At night, she was her usual self, hitting all the Atlanta nightspots in Buckhead.

She made one call to Jerry Wright to tell him that her trip to London went off just as planned. He asked her out for dinner a night later and she went. Jennifer could feel the pressure that Jerry was putting on her to be more than a once-in-a-while companion, and she had to defuse it. Several months ago, she would have welcomed that idea but now she had to concentrate on the job that was before her. Jerry had helped her tremendously – she owed him and she couldn't forget that, but business was business and Jerry would have to wait. Besides, Jennifer knew Jerry's wife, and she knew they had a happy family, so she didn't want to be a part of something happy breaking up. Jennifer thought she had real scruples.

After their dinner, the two went back to her apartment. Drinks did lead to a roll in the sack, but only for immediate pleasure, after which they had a discussion of the future between them. Jennifer explained her fondness for Jerry, but she told him that she was afraid to let the association get serious. She reiterated to him that she was so involved in her investigation that she really didn't have time for anyone for a while. He bought the story reluctantly and asked that at least he be able to see her on special occasions. She agreed and Jerry went home to his wife. In the back of Jerry's mind, he had silently wished for just such an ending.

Jennifer was due for her regularly scheduled physical examination with her private gynecologist. Her examination went fine, and the doctor prescribed her usual birth-control pills, but he warned her about the new staggering dangers of promiscuity, particularly AIDS. Jennifer had asked the receptionist for a little extra time with the "good doctor" to discuss her upcoming trip.

"I understand that you are going back to Africa. I hope this trip ends better than your last."

"Doc, I am so excited about going back. It's so beautiful over there, so peaceful and serene. Don't you want to go with me?"

"God, I wish I could. This office stuff is getting to me, but my patients would never understand. Someday, I really do want to go over there."

"Well, Doc, I'll leave the place just as I found it when I come back so you can enjoy the same things that I do."

"I think I'm going to need some additional prescriptions, though. I talked to my druggist before I went to London a few weeks ago about some sleeping pills to get me through the flights over there and back. He gave me something off the shelf, but I tried it and it didn't work very well. I used it on a flight to Houston and I was still miserable. I'm afraid I'm just scared to fly. Can you give me something to knock me out? I mean, really knock me out?"

"I can. What did your druggist give you before?"

"Doc, I can't remember, but it sure wasn't very strong."

"I can think of a couple of drugs that might help you. You would probably be better off consulting your internist, but I'll try to help you if you want."

"Please."

"There's a new drug on the market that's called Halcion; it's made by Upjohn and it's getting great reviews in the medical publications. It's also getting some bad press from the traditionalists in the public press. But if you're careful not to overindulge in it, then I think it's your answer. You might have to have someone carry you off the plane, though." Doc always tried to add some laughter to every thing he had to say and he tried to suppress his giggle on his thought of someone actually carrying Jennifer off the plane.

"Sounds great to me. I'll do anything to be knocked out while I'm on that plane."

Again, Doc had a good inside laugh at that picture. "The pills come in 25 milligrams, and I suggest that you only take one pill at a time. It should last you for most of the flight. Make sure that you take it with your meal; we don't want any stomach trouble."

"Doc, what if I took four or five pills at a time?"

"Don't do it. This drug is powerful; if you took four pills at the same time, nobody would be able to wake you for twenty-four hours. You might go comatose. I don't think that dosage would kill you, but it certainly wouldn't be safe. You stick to one pill at a time. It'll do the job."

"Doc, one more question. Does it taste bad?"

"I don't know; as far as I know, it's tasteless."

"Can I dissolve it in a glass of water or Coke or maybe a glass of white wine?"

"I see nothing wrong with a glass of water or Coke, as long as you drink the whole glass. It is going to dissolve evenly throughout all of the liquid, so to get the whole pill into your system, you have to drink the whole glass. No wine with it, period. No telling what would happen if you mixed it with alcohol."

"Okay. Can I get it at my drugstore?"

"Sure, I'll have my nurse call it in before you leave and you can carry the prescription with you if you need more. You know you can call my 800-number on the bottle for verification if you have any trouble overseas."

"How many pills are you getting me?"

"How often do you intend to fly?"

"Better give me enough for two or three trips."

"Sounds like you are going to be a world traveler. Anything else?"

"Yea, I'm a little embarrassed to ask you, though." The doctor's eyebrows raised in anticipation of Jennifer's remarks. "I was once given a drug that is called a Mickey-Finn; it knocked me on my ass. I'm not even sure what happened next, know what I mean? I took it voluntarily, but I was out of it for about three or four hours. My friends couldn't even wake me. Would a Mickey-Finn be better than that drug you recommended?"

"Jennifer, I haven't heard of a Mickey-Finn since college. I doubt if a drugstore carries them. When I went to school, some of my classmates got them from Mexico and used them to get a gal laid. I don't think that I could recommend them for you. Not as a doctor."

"Okay, Doc, I'll use your new drug. Thanks a lot."

Jennifer picked up her prescription at her local Starlight Drugstore that was just around the corner from her apartment. While there, she asked her friend the druggist about a Mickey-Finn. He almost died laughing. "Mrs. Miller, I know you know about those things, but I've never heard a woman ask for them. Men, yes; but women, no. Are you trying to compare them to the Halcion your doctor just recommended?"

"I just need something to knock me out for at least seven hours on that long overseas flight."

"I suggest that you take the Halcion. That'll do the trick."

Jennifer had one more avenue to try before giving up on Mickey-Finns. She called her bird – hunting friend, Ed Evans. "Ed, I have a favor to ask of you."

"Sure, Jennifer, anything."

"Are you going to Mexico anytime soon to hunt those pretty little birds?"

"Now, Jennifer, have you become one of those animal environmentalists? You don't qualify to be one of that kind. You're too good-looking and they don't even wear makeup. They are pigs."

Jennifer laughed. "Hell, no, I'm not one of those animal-rightists. I love to kill things. In fact, I am going back to Africa next week to further my annihilations." Both laughed again. "Answer me. Are you going to Mexico anytime soon?"

"I'll go tomorrow if you'll go with me."

"Be serious, Ed, I want you to bring something back for me if you are going."

"Sorry, Jennifer, I just got back last week. What are you looking for? Maybe a leather whip or something?"

"No. Do you promise you won't laugh?"

"I promise."

"I'm looking for a drug called a Mickey-Finn."

Ed had to cover the phone to conceal his outburst. "You're crazy, Jennifer. Men only use those on women. What in the hell do you want a Mickey-Finn for?"

"I want them to knock me out while I'm on the airplane to Africa."

"They have better drugs than that by now. Why don't you call your doctor?"

"Ed, if I wanted your goddamn medical advice, I would've asked for it. I want you only to get me some Mickey-Finns from Mexico."

"I think I know someone that might have some. But he's got them for a different reason than you want to use them for. He's here in Atlanta. Do you want me to get you a few – if he still has 'em? And I might be wrong about their name – he just refers to them as 'Mickeys.'"

"Please, Ed, but don't let him know who wants them."

"You're crazy, Jennifer. If I don't tell him who wants them, then he will assume that I want them, and I don't. I sure as hell don't want to tell him my girlfriend wants them."

"You can think of something. Ed. Please get them for me."

"Okay. Give me your number and I'll call you back tomorrow – but no promises."

"Thank you so much, Ed. I owe you."

Ed did get Jennifer some Mickey-Finns. He telephoned the good news to her and then arranged to meet her for a drink that same afternoon to give them to her. Jennifer was most grateful and she offered to buy Ed his dinner. Unfortunately for Ed, he had other plans.

Jennifer had done her safari-clothes shopping the last time she went, so there was very little that she needed to buy for her upcoming trip. She needed more diskettes for her camera and film for Dennis's old one, but other than that, she was set. The days rolled by as slowly as molasses dripping from a can until there was only one more week to go.

Five days before she was to depart, Martin Smith got her on the telephone at her apartment. "Jennifer, this is Martin Smith. I understand I'm going to have the honor of escorting you around the bush. You can't be as excited as I am."

"I sure am. I want to get those bad dreams out of my head from the last time I was with you, and I think you can do it for me. I hope I was not too imposing on your schedule to demand from Frank that you take me. I told Frank that I just wouldn't go with anyone else."

"As I said, I'm honored. We'll have a good time. Is there anything in particular you want me to have in camp for you?"

"No, Martin, I just want to relax with you and have a good time. I look forward to seeing all the animals and I want to take some really good pictures. Will you help me get some that I can blow up?"

"Sure will. I'll meet your plane in Johannesburg, and if you aren't too tired, we can fly right out that afternoon into camp. I've reserved a little out-of-the-way camp that is seldom used. Most of our clientele are usually hunters and this camp is not particularly strong for any one of their usually desired species. We'll still see lots of animals, particularly buffalo, lechwe, and the like. It is good for lion, but for some reason, we seem never to be able to get on to a big male there. That's why most of our professionals don't want to go there. They want to go to the most recent proven territory. Their tips depend on results, you know. We'll see lots of bird life, and again I stress, we'll see plenty of animals. It's great for elephant, too. Since elephant has been on the protected list there in recent years, they have given the hunters there more trouble spooking other hunted game than it has been worth to just see them and capture them on film. You know how hunters are."

"Oh, that's wonderful. Tell me about the lions again. I always loved the lions."

"As a matter of fact, the lions are a cinch there. As I said, we've never been able to get any lion permits for hunting in that block because the males are obviously too clever to be seen. I think they must hunt at night more than at our other camps. We know they're there because of tracks, but the big males are seldom seen with the regular prides. The good news is that because the old males are gone, the rest of the pride is much easier to approach. You're in for a real treat. I'm sure we'll see some cubs as well. The timing couldn't be better for lion-cub watching."

"I can't wait, Martin. Can I bring you anything from the States?"

"Nope, just you. I'll see you at the airport. Sleep tight. Good-bye."

15

The Last Safari

Jennifer took a cab to Hartsfield Airport in Atlanta. She had a full complement of bags but not big ones. She had her regular suitcase, a hanging-clothes bag, and the largest carry-on that the airlines allowed as her makeup and overnight satchel. She checked-in a full two hours before her flight was scheduled to depart. She checked her two main bags all the way to Johannesburg via Cape Town. In her carry-on, she had her most precious commodities – her drugs (Halcion, Mickey-Finns, and birth-control pills), her cameras, and her diary. For the past two weeks, she had written in her diary every night. She mainly wrote about her anticipation of her safari and how she hoped it would cure her nightmares from her last safari with Dennis Kyle. But she also wrote about her Atlanta day and nightlife and her immediate family. Just in case her plan of revenge met with exposure by someone unsuspecting, Jennifer wanted her diary to read as natural as possible. Of course, included in it, she wanted her personal politics on the Dennis Kyle accident, but she wanted no hint of her upcoming plan.

Her nightlife was exposed in every detail. She included a short description of everyone that was materially involved with her, including how and when she had met that person and what the probabilities were that whatever the relationship was would continue – except Jerry Wright and Ed Evans, out of respect for their wives. The physical activities were highlighted, but she neatly wove into each relationship her innermost thoughts and concerns for the fella. If and when someone read her intimate secrets, he or she would see a completely unbiased person that respected each and everybody. As to her thoughts about her upcoming safari, she wanted to portray a sensible, excited young lady that was getting a wish of a lifetime to be able to go on her own safari. There was never any suggestion as to any type of plot or plan to do anything unacceptable on such an excursion. That meant that some things simply could not be mentioned in her literary work – drugs (how she got them) and of course her communications and meetings with Frank and the widows. Even her London trip was off limits. To excuse the time she was on her London trip, she merely wrote that she was sick.

Finally the day of departure came. She wasn't apprehensive about anything; she was just plain excited. Jennifer felt a high just thinking about circumstances that could take different twists, and she relished those highs. She knew the truth about the fact that she really had no control over everything that she wanted to happen on this trip. She would have to play it be ear, but her objectives were clearly thought out, and the likely scenarios played every night in her mind. Aside from making the monumental decision of quitting school to become an exotic dancer, this detective escapade was an even more important decision than quitting school. There was to be no turning back in this one. She recognized that fact, and she was set on go. The rest of her life would function as a result of her upcoming thoughts and actions.

Formulating her present decision to take this trip and go through with her carefully thought-out plan was a personal obligation that she knew she had to go through with. She actually radiated a sense of accomplishment in figuring out what she knew really happened on her last safari. And she was determined to make it right, one way or the other, for everyone involved.

The South African Airways check-in was subleased from Delta. For some reason, the South African Airways (SAA) name was nowhere to be located at any of the overhead check-in signs. After stopping one of the Delta Red Coats personnel to inquire as to where SAA boarded, she saw the temporary SAA sign propped up on the check-in counter. From that moment on, she had never been treated as courteously. The counter attendant processed her passport and her necessary entrance forms into South Africa, and then told her that she should try out the Delta Crown Room that was part of the extras from SAA. In the lounge, all passengers were offered free champagne or almost any other drink that was imaginable. She had heard about the "classiness" of South African Airways, and now she believed it. The boarding personnel were just as nice as the ticket agents. She was led to her seat by a most handsome young man that likewise noticed her good looks. As she sat down, Jennifer looked up to the tall steward and said, "I hope you are responsible for serving this section."

"It's my pleasure."

Jennifer then sat back in her window seat of the day and grinned from ear to ear.

Magazines and newspapers were handed out to everyone, and after a few safety announcements, the engines began to whine.

All South African Airways flights from the U.S. to their home country used a Boeing 747-B airplane. The configuration is designed for passengers and freight. The seating is a little roomier than most 747s, and the number of rows of seats is significantly less. The overall fuselage is shorter, and that characteristic enables the cruise speed to be increased from about 500 MPH to 550 MPH. For a fourteen-hour leg to Cape Town, that extra speed is a valued asset for all aboard.

Next to Jennifer's seat were two certified public accountants on their way to Cape Town to examine a major company being purchased by another competing U.S. company. The two gentlemen declined to give Jennifer much more information than that on their proposed acquisition, but they were extremely talkative about other matters. One of the accountants was from Texas, and the other was from Denver. Neither had ever been to Africa and neither had ever even thought about going on a safari. Jennifer had them drooling about safari life after the first two hours of flight. But they were on a business trip and the likes of a private safari were out of the question.

The movie was an English variety; and although the headsets were free, neither Jennifer nor her two seatmates elected to view the flick.

Dinner was unlike other airplane food, and afterward everyone had a clean plate. After-dinner drinks were the vogue, and Jennifer and her two friends had more than their share. At four hours into the first leg of their long journey, the three were asleep. At eleven hours, all were awakened by the flickering of cabin lights that the pilot turned on just prior to a wakeup service that included orange juice and steaming hot towels to wash their faces.

The flight was now continuing around the Atlantic border of the continent of Africa until the plane was abeam of Namibia. There, the plane headed inland over Windhoek and direct to Cape Town. The last leg of the flight offered another movie and a scrumptious breakfast. The flaps and landing gear extended just after sunup for the airplane's descent into gorgeous Cape Town. The captain pointed out Table Mountain and other significant air-to-ground sites. It was especially beautiful at sunrise.

All of the passengers deplaned with a frazzled look that would have scared Dracula. No one was allowed in the emigration area until everyone that was an off-passenger for Cape Town was inspected. All Johannesburg passengers were instructed to remain aboard the giant jumbo for refueling and new instructions for takeoff. The passengers remaining for the next hour-and-a-half flight represented about half of the plane's seats.

The descending view into Jo'burg was nowhere near as picturesque as Cape Town, but everyone on board didn't care. All they wanted was to get off that airplane. Clearing customs was a breeze compared to the USA. And in less than thirty minutes, Jennifer was claiming her baggage. As Jennifer pushed her free baggage buggy with all of her luggage through the double bumper doors to the outside world, Martin's smiling face was there to meet her. After an elongated hug of very close proportions, Martin was the first to speak, "Hope your fight was comfortable."

"Martin, it was fine, but my god, am I glad to be on the ground and to see you." Martin and Jennifer exchanged other menial comments while Martin toted her two bigger bags to his car.

After starting his vehicle, Martin turned to Jennifer and asked, "You have two options – we can check into a hotel for the night, or if you are up to it, we can get some lunch, have a short rest at Lanseria Airport, and then board one of our planes to go directly to camp. Which is your pleasure?"

Jennifer thought about how she felt and just how tired she thought she might be later on that day, but she really couldn't wait to get back in the bush. "I can stay in a hotel anytime; let's go to camp."

Jennifer knew that there was nothing to be gained by staying in town. She remembered the terrible time of jet lag adjustment from her last trip here, and she thought she might as well spend that time seeing things that were unusual. Besides, she didn't want to be guilty of enticing Martin into a hotel room with her, at least not yet. She could handle all of that better in a tented campsite, without public exposure.

On the way to Lanseria Airport, Hunters, Ltd's private-plane airport, Martin pointed out all of the historic and geographical sites that he had previously called attention to when Jennifer was with Dennis Kyle. Jennifer was courteous to relisten, even if she was dead dog tired and rather uninterested.

When they arrived at Lanseria, porters from the main office helped Martin load his and Jennifer's baggage into the waiting plane. Jennifer recognized Pat Herold as her and Dennis's previous pilot and gave him a hug and a kiss on the cheek. "Thank you for everything that you did to help us last time; this time will be different." Pat expected some type of teary meeting that did not occur; he was thankful for that. After Jennifer and Pat exchanged other short pleasantries, Martin showed Jennifer to the "freshen up" room just beside the lobby. After she returned with added makeup and rebrushed hair, the three boarded the sleek twin-engine Cessna and took off to their port of entry in Botswana.

Jennifer slept the whole two-and-a-half-hour flight. When they landed in Maun, Botswana, Martin almost needed a shoehorn to get her out of the plane. When Jennifer regained her senses, she thanked Pat for the delightful flight and then offered her excuse for having been so groggy. "I am so knocked out; I took a sleeping pill back at Lanseria and I was out. I promise to be more fun on our next leg."

Martin managed to have Jennifer clear customs without unloading her baggage. And after a quick Coca-Cola, they resumed their flight into camp. The final leg of Jennifer's exhausting flight schedule was one of low-level flight that allowed the typical passenger to see the beautiful Okavango Delta at its finest. The water is always crystal clear, the trees and grasslands are always green and lush, and the larger animals, particularly elephant, are always a novelty to observers from overhead. The short forty-five-minute flight is one of the highlights of any Okavango safari. Thanks to the ministop for a Coke at Maun, Jennifer was wide awake and enjoyed it all.

"Pat, I know you must have made this trip a thousand times. Do you ever get tired of seeing this beautiful scenery? And all of the animals?"

Pat was quick to reply. "Sometimes we are in more of a hurry than we are today, and believe it or not, I hate those times because I feel like I've been cheated from seeing all that you have described. My answer is hell no. I'd never get tired of looking at all of this. Without looking forward to a flight like this every day, I'd be back ferrying customers in America or somewhere in Europe. This is what makes me tick!"

The camp crew that met Pat Herold's charter was not the same crew that Jennifer and Dennis had on their previous safari. But they were just as pleasant and they hustled at every opportunity to please their new guest. It was a short ten-minute drive from the grass landing strip to the campsite, and already they were seeing animal and bird life. The remainder of the camp crew met Martin's vehicle as it entered the main grounds. Jennifer had an immediate comment. "Oh, what a beautiful view; the campfire is right next to the lake. I think it's even more beautiful than our last campsite."

Martin was pleased and he was all smiles as he showed Jennifer the rest of the camp structures. "This is your tent and behind is your shower tent. One of the boys will adjust your shower for you."

"Martin, aren't you and I going to share a tent?" Jennifer said with a smile that made the question either a serious one, or a joke. Jennifer's future plans would include at least a night's sleep with Martin. And by phrasing the question the way she had, she could better judge just how to pose such a future advance. She had her quick-thinking cap on.

Martin thought for a second or two before answering. "After you get over your jet lag, then we'll look at sharing some things. You're going to need some time for adjusting to all of the time zones you've just come through. You're not immune to jet lag because you've made two trips to Africa, are you?"

"No. You're right. I do need some serious sleep. I would be a very unpleasant tent companion right now."

The time was just after three o'clock in the afternoon and Martin suggested to Jennifer that she take an hour's nap, after which he would drive her around the concession area until sundown.

"The sunset at this campsite is by far the most beautiful in all of the Okavango. The sun seems to rest for several minutes right on the horizon, just over that baobab tree," Martin said as pointed to a strange tree that looked as if it were growing upside down. "I want you to be rested to see it. I'll call for you in an hour."

An hour later, Martin sent one of the cabin boys to Jennifer's tent to wake her. Fifteen minutes after that, Jennifer was sitting in the Land Cruiser, waiting to be chauffeured. Martin asked his assigned main tracker to ride in the back to assist him in spotting, and off they went. Elephant was certainly more numerous than the earlier camp that Jennifer shared with Dennis. Although they didn't see many on this ride, their sign was most evident, as pointed out by Martin – scraped trees, torn tree bark, piles of fresh dung, and numerous tracks that were really only evident to the on-board tracker. Gorgeous bird life was everywhere – fish eagles, bustards, lilac-breasted rollers, bee eaters, Martial eagles, Bateleur eagles, dove, Francolin, and guinea fowl. Non-meat-eating animals such as impala, lechwe, waterbuck, and Cape buffalo, dotted the landscape with the aforementioned odd elephant. Cats had to be there somewhere, but they were nowhere to be seen that evening. Martin stopped the vehicle at a prescribed spot to view the magnificent sunset that he had so beautifully described to Jennifer. The hues of orange, purple, and red literally took Jennifer's breath away. "It's the most beautiful sunset I have ever seen, bar none!"

"I'm glad you like it; I'll see to it that we enjoy a few more," Martin was pleased to answer.

On the way back to camp, the tracker-spotter pointed out a sly bushbuck and a grey duiker. Both were first-time spots for Jennifer, and Martin explained why – their habits were almost nocturnal.

Dinner was mashed potatoes and meatballs spiced with safari-grown onions. The hot soup and cold salad made the meal a dinner delight. Jennifer declined desert and so did Martin. Instead, Martin moved their two director's chairs to the open campfire. The camp crew had built a fire almost ten feet in diameter but short in height. This gave its guests a better warm front, and it lessened the glare for night sky viewing. The stars were brighter than ever and Martin gave Jennifer a short lesson in astronomy. "I remember telling you the last time you were here about the Southern Cross, only visible in the southern hemisphere. It must be a special treat for you northern hemispherers!"

The sky was simply miraculous with all its stars. That made it especially tough for Jennifer to find any of her childhood clusters – the dippers, the North Star, Venus, etc. – there were just too many stars in the way.

The two exchanged their latest life happenings for nearly two hours before Martin suggested they retire. Martin walked Jennifer to her tent and was held there an extra minute with a thankful kiss on the lips by an obviously grateful client. "Good night, Martin. I look forward to tomorrow. I'll be refreshed and ready for all you can give me."

As she entered her tent and zipped up her tent flaps, Martin rightfully wondered just what Jennifer meant by her last statement. He was looking forward to tomorrow to see for himself.

The next morning, Jennifer was awakened by her cabin boy who brought her fresh coffee and cookies in bed. Before he left, he filled up her thermos with fresh water, and then filled her wash basin with hot water. Jennifer slipped on her safari-furnished robe and slippers and moved out on her tented veranda to enjoy the morning mist and sunrise with her fresh coffee. The birds were also awakening and their morning chirps lent a special meaning to the beautiful scenery. Jennifer took that special feeling as an omen that she was there for a special reason and one that was sanctioned by nature. To add to that omen, she could occasionally hear a morning lion roar, but she had no idea where he was.

Breakfast was at the main dining tent and the table that could seat eight was rather under-matched by the mere presence of just two. Jennifer commented, "I feel as if I am Queen Elizabeth eating with Prince Phillip – one at one end of a big table and the other at the other end. Can we get a smaller table that is a little quainter for breakfast in future mornings?"

"Anything you wish. Tomorrow, I'll have the server set up one of the dressing tables out under the veranda. I would like that much better myself."

Jennifer made Martin promise that they would do their best not to bring up the last safari or Dennis's demise. So both talked only of recent pasts and the future.

"What is on the agenda for today, my lord?"

"Well, I know that you want to see some lion, so let's try to find some. I've heard several this morning – sounds as if they're near the river. I can't be sure because their roars can be heard for such long distances, remember, about ten miles."

Again, the tracker joined them in the Land Cruiser for their morning game ride. More of the same birds and animals offered new settings for snapshots from her relatively new automatic zoom digital camera. Martin was adept at knowing just where to stop the vehicle for the best light. He had been raised during the picture-taking time when one had to manually set the aperture to focus on the best "depth of field" and the best shutter speed. Every time a client wanted to take a picture, he would use this old-school technology to set the stage. Not surprising, most of the pictures shot with his expertise came close to capturing the intended beauty that was desired, whereas the novice photographer would waste over half of their snapshots taking poorly setup pictures.

"Martin, I have a couple of requests. My favorite movie of all time was *Out of Africa*. As I told Frank Black, you are my Robert Redford and I want to be in some of the same scenes. Remember the one where the two of them had a picnic on a hill overlooking a pride of lions? I thought that was *fantastic*. I cannot imagine a more romantic and beautiful experience than that. Can you arrange a scene like that for me?"

"First of all, that scene was shot looking directly at the lions. It gave a false picture of just how close the subjects were to the lions. The lions were already feeding or had just fed. They were not in a hungry or hunting mood. They were also out of range to feel threatened. So, they didn't mind the intruders. We also don't know about the wind and other external circumstances that allowed the subjects to be unworried. That's movie making. With me, we are not going to take any chances, but we can still enjoy the close proximity of all of the wildlife here. There aren't too many hills around; everything is flat on the delta, but I'll do my damnedest to get as close as possible safely. Now, we have to find some lions to make your dream happen. If we can't get to them in the vehicle, how do you feel about walking up on them? I do have my rifle."

"If it is all the same with you, I'd rather watch them from afar, in the vehicle."

"I understand, but maybe you'll change your mind later on in the safari."

The first drive of the day was productive with almost every animal except lion. Jennifer saw two new creatures, a cheetah and a hyena, to add to her list viewed in Africa so far. The cheetah was lazily strolling by herself in search of a high-enough perch to view an intended meal. The hyena seemed lost. He or she was moving at a faster pace than the cheetah, probably trying to get back to his or her den to watch over the pups.

After a couple of hours of riding, Martin could tell when one of his clients was about to get a little hungry, and he could always tell when a bathroom stop was beckoning. Martin had that unique feeling that Jennifer needed both. So Martin chose to head back to camp for lunch when their scouting trip was closest to camp. The tracker/scout that accompanied them was also grateful for heading back to camp. He didn't have to set up the lunch table and all of the trimmings in the bush. So lunch was served in the main camp, and then Jennifer suggested a short nap before going out again.

Jennifer sought out Martin at his tent when she awoke from her nap. "Martin, I love the little native that always goes with us, but can't we go alone?" The comment surprised Martin, but it also flattered him.

"Sure, Jennifer. I'll let him know that I have a few chores for him to do around camp instead of going out with us this afternoon."

"For some reason, being with the animals is not as important this afternoon as I expect tomorrow and the next days will be. I'm still being affected by jet lag. I just want us to kind of be alone."

"If you'll promise me one thing, then I'll agree."

"What?"

"That you'll change the tire if we have a flat."

"Oh, I see, you carry him only for manual labor, huh?"

"He can spot pretty damn well, but you're more right than wrong. It's awfully handy to have him there if there is any trouble. But we'll try traveling alone for a while this afternoon." Jennifer grinned and gave Martin a big hug.

Just out of sight of their camp, Martin and Jennifer ran into a small group of lions under one of their typical shade trees. Luck was apparent. The pride was obviously awakening from their all-day siesta, and they had not yet noticed the now quiet Land Rover sitting just over a hundred yards downwind.

The two onlookers sat and watched the young cubs frolic and play with their elders' tails. They were cuffed a few times, but generally, the older kin ignored the little ones' playful behavior. The vehicle was originally stopped about a hundred and twenty yards from where the small pride was lazily resting, but Jennifer asked Martin to try to get a little closer. Martin obliged, but after a few minutes, the lion pride felt the uneasy pressure of being watched at such a close range and lazily moved off to a more comfortable position.

Soon the lions were back to the original one hundred plus yards away from their intruders.

Jennifer overcame her earlier stated caution and suggested, "Martin, can we get out of the car and watch them?"

"If you want to get eaten, you can. We've already pushed them away from their chosen spot, and one can never tell when a lion has had its fill of being pushed. It might be a little chancy. As long as we stay in the vehicle, they will treat the occupants as part of the car. But if we get out, they can see all of our features, they're liable to become quite aggressive. There are countless stories in the parks where just such as that has happened. Without warning, a lion could cover the distance of a hundred yards or so in less than four seconds. I doubt if you could jump back into the vehicle that fast. And even if you could, there is no top on this thing to protect us. I guess you've noticed that the doors are back on all of the vehicles since you were last here. They offer some additional protection, but I'm afraid they might give too much confidence to the young breed of professional hunters; and they might cause them to venture in too close to a dangerous situation. I'm a seasoned veteran and know better.

"Frank issued the order about the doors after all of our earlier problems this year. I must confess, we should have never had them off. It's no real advantage for a hunter, and it's certainly much safer for photographic safaris." With a camera full of feline pictures taken from the confines of the Land Rover, Martin decided to head back to camp a bit earlier than usual.

Although the afternoon didn't offer an opportunity to advance her plan, Jennifer was comfortable in returning to camp a bit early as well. After all, she had categorized Martin's behavior carefully, and she had learned a great deal more about her favorite African animal, the lion.

The two cruisers stripped off their slightly dusty khakis and called for their prewarmed showers. Then they dressed in cleaned and freshly ironed khaki short-sleeves and shorts that are safari standards. Taking off the tennis shoes worn without socks was a pleasure, and each put back on some thongs for comfortable campfire life. As the evening was starting to get a bit cool, each wore a light sweater for dinner. Dinner was again divine. After a postdinner drink of Grand Marnier, the professional and his client moved to the campfire. After a couple of more drinks there and after Jennifer had noticed that all of the camp crew had gone to bed, she invited Martin to her tent for a nightcap. The tent chairs normally inside the tent were out on the veranda, so there was nowhere else to sit inside except on the separated twin beds. Martin sat in the middle of one twin, and Jennifer sat in the middle of the other. After a short bit of soft conversation and after Jennifer had taken a couple more sips of her nightcap, she moved over to Martin's bed. She set her drink on the bedside table and began to unbutton Martin's khaki safari shirt.

Martin was in no mood to resist. To hell with camp rules; she wanted him, and he wanted her. After thirty minutes of learned exotic sexual behavior by Jennifer, the event was over. Jennifer stayed with him until she sensed that he was beginning to get uncomfortable. Then she moved up to rest her head on his sweating shoulder. Her first planned sexual task with Martin was over. The first part of her plan went as scheduled. She had to make Martin enjoy himself in this manner in order to entice him to do a similar thing while they were alone in the veldt. She knew her plan had a better chance of success if Martin's guard was down.

Jennifer didn't try to prolong the act for her own personal satisfaction; she merely waited for Martin to somehow suggest that he wanted more. She read no such thoughts, and she closed her eyes to go to sleep; her head still resting on his shoulder. After about an hour in this position, the chill night air and the narrow bed caused them both to seek more warmth, and she moved over to the other twin bed.

Martin awoke before dawn and kissed Jennifer lightly on her lips. "I'm going back to my tent now. You sleep a little while longer, we'll go out about nine. Thanks for a lovely night." And he kissed her again.

Breakfast was pushed back to 9:30, and the two enjoyed the bacon, eggs, and fresh fruits together under the mess-tent veranda. Martin had thoughts of entrapment concerning Jennifer's forwardness, but he soon dismissed the thought and considered her just lonely and out for a good time on the safari of her dreams. After all, he knew of her past from Lou's stories in Las Vegas. At present, he was more than glad to be accommodating.

Martin was sensitive about his own personal life, and up to now, he had kept it entirely quiet from Jennifer. But now, in conjunction with her sexual advances, she began to pry. She was not overbearing in her questions, but she did hit on sensitive areas now and then. Although Martin prided himself on being a ladies' man, he was more frequently without a lady than with one. Since the year the accidents started, he had steered clear of any involvement with anyone other than company employees. Despite her questions, he was beginning to find Jennifer and her passions quite pleasing and not just in a sexual sense.

After breakfast, Martin ordered the cook crew to make a picnic basket for their morning game drive and informed them that they would probably not be back to camp for lunch.

Just like the evening before, Martin and Jennifer were alone in the Land Cruiser when it left camp. As they started to drive off, Jennifer asked Martin to wait a minute. "Do you have a couple of bottles of that red wine we had last night? I'd love a few swigs during our picnic." Martin jumped out of the vehicle and ran to the kitchen area to fetch the two suggested bottles. Unlike a hunting safari, there was no timetable strictly for animal viewing; and Martin had no urgency to get a client a trophy, so the two meandered through the bush as slowly as the vehicle would go.

"Martin, I want to know more about you. You've told me about your childhood and growing up in Kenya, but what about from then to now?"

Martin didn't quite know where to start. "I told you about my education in Europe, and then I returned to Africa to seek the very job that I now hold. Before Hunters, Ltd., I held the same position, more or less, with another company in Tanzania and Kenya. I've been with Frank Black going on ten years, and I guess I wouldn't know what to do if I left him or he left me."

"Have you ever thought of marrying?"

"Sure, a time or two, but things always fizzled out. I really enjoy new blood. I enjoy talking to new women, just like you now. I've had a most pleasant time with our conversations, and I have my doubts that the pleasantness would continue if we were married."

Jennifer had gotten the conversation going in the right direction, and now she needed her information. "Martin, isn't it lonely not to have any family?"

"When I lost my mother a few years back, I reluctantly came to the conclusion that my company was my family. With no brothers or sisters and no parents, what else could I ask for? My work is my family, and I treat it that way."

"What do you mean, you treat it that way? Is your will made out to the company?"

"Funny you should ask. I really don't have a will. I don't know that I need one, but I do have some holdings that have to go to someone; and I've made arrangements for them to go to Frank Black if something were to happen to me."

"That's terrible, Martin. Surely you have someone more deserving."

"No, since I lost my most treasured boyhood companions last season, Frank and the company are my closest folks."

"When you say that you might leave something for Frank, do you mean him by name or the company, Hunters, Ltd.?"

"Jennifer, quit worrying about me and my will; it's all taken care of."

"Martin, I guess it's my motherly instincts, but I can't imagine you leaving your fortune – if that is the right word – to your company."

"First of all, I don't have a fortune, but what I do have will go to my company." Jennifer finally got it out of him. She had deduced that he was leaving his numbered Swiss account to his company but not in the name of Frank Black. Strange, but that is how it appeared. She needed more confirmation though.

"Martin, where is your office? Do you have an office at your apartment in Jo'burg?"

"No, I live out of my briefcase that I carry with me everywhere I go. I get kidded about it from time to time; but it's convenient, so that's how I handle it."

"I know this sounds crazy, but I get a lot out of a person by knowing some of their favorite words. What is your favorite word?"

"Damn, Jennifer. Are you crazy? People don't have favorite words." Martin looked over to frown at his guest. Martin was about to feel that all of this free sex was not enough payment for having to listen to Jennifer's inquisitiveness. However, Jennifer exhibited her feelings of being hurt, so Martin decided to play along. "Okay, my favorite word is *S-E-X*," and he spelled it out with capital letters.

"See, I knew you were human; and I knew you had a favorite word. If you had to describe yourself in a single word that you wanted someone to remember you by, what would it be?"

"Well, finally an easy one, 'professional hunter.' Not that I'm some special professional hunter, but I want everyone to know what the word implies."

"Martin, that's not one word, 'professional hunter' is two words. Now pick one of those two words for your epitaph."

"This is a bit silly, but okay. I'm a hunter. Not only do I guide another hunter, I watch out for him, I feed him, I transport him, I find him game, and I judge it, then I processes it, or cause it to be processed, and then I ship it to his hometown.

And all of what I just told you I do is in the strict name of conservation. Every professional hunter is a true conservationist, and every client should be as well. If a client leaves our premises without being a dyed-in-the-wool conservationist, then we have failed our job."

Jennifer smiled at Martin, maybe she had confirmed her other answer – it had to be "hunter."

Jennifer decided to stop her questions for a while and rethink Martin's complex answers. After a few minutes, she couldn't stand the silence. "Do you think we're going to see our lions again today?"

"I think I've a good idea where they might be. I haven't noticed any vultures flying in circles, so they probably haven't killed during the night. I noticed yesterday that some of them had almost full bellies. They probably ate day before yesterday. They'll need to eat again tonight or early morning. They don't like to go more than three days without fresh meat. If my hunch is right, they will not have moved off much from where we spotted them yesterday. I think we'll find them.

"Wow, I'm so lucky. I'm about to have an African picnic with a true professional hunter just like Robert Redford. You did bring the wine, didn't you?"

"Jennifer, you have asked some pretty stupid questions, but that one takes the cake. Sure I brought red wine, you saw me go get it. Am I not the ultimate in hospitality?"

"I think you are the ultimate in everything, except last night; and you went to sleep before you finished your job." They both looked at each other, and then they heartily laughed.

Martin was about to be more accommodating than he knew. He thought he had a 90 percent chance of finding the lion pride; and he remembered that Jennifer had told him that she had dreamed of picnicking beside them, preferably on a hill just above them, like in *Out of Africa*. If his plans materialized, then she would get her wish. In the meantime, Martin elected to scour the countryside some more for other game viewing. "See the elephants up ahead? It looks like they're out for their daily baths." Martin brought the car alongside the washed-out riverbank that overlooked their presence.

"The little ones are almost submerged. Look at their trunks above the water. Sometimes, especially in severe flooding, elephants cross rivers and lakes by swimming; and because of their bulk, their entire bodies are submerged for the whole trip, except their trunk. They look like submarines that are just underwater with their periscopes up.

"Are you getting hungry?"

"Not yet, we had such a late breakfast."

"Good. There's a spot where sometimes we can spot a Sitatunga, and I want to take you there. Do you remember seeing a picture of one in our brochure?"

"I'm not sure; tell me about them again. They have something queer about their feet."

"They spend their entire life in the water. They weigh about three hundred pounds when fully grown. They have very elongated hooves that enable them to purchase on the soft bottom plants when they feed, and the surface area of the bigger hooves makes getting away from predators an advantage. They are really quite unique. Only the male has horns, and they twist upward to around twenty-five to thirty inches. The horns are topped by an inch or so of what looks like pure ivory, but it's only the worn-out tip of the horn. I think that they're the prettiest antelope in the world. Maybe we'll get lucky. Do you have your zoom lens ready on your camera?"

"Yep, it's automatic! How close will we get?"

"One never knows about Sitatunga watching. Normally, the only way to spot one is to pole through the heavy bamboo and papyrus grass in a wooden dug-out canoe called a makuru. Sometimes, it takes days of poling to spot one. When hunting them, you leave your client in the hands of a poler; and that's all there is to it. The poler climbs a tree now and then to spot, but usually the client is just slowly poled through the thick stuff until a splashing sound is heard; and that usually means that a Sitatunga is trying to get away. It's a very boring hunt, but there's no other way to get at them. Occasionally, I've seen one or two of them upriver, over there, right in the middle of that tall papyrus grass."

Martin stopped the Land Cruiser about a half mile from where the two would climb a small hill to observe a special little swamp. Martin carried his rifle, his binoculars, and a blanket for the two to sit on. After about thirty minutes of concentrated glassing, Martin was ready to give up; and he stood to refold the blanket. At that time, he heard the familiar splash of a Sitatunga running for denser cover. "There he is; see him?"

"Yeah, I see him." Jennifer fumbled for her camera.

"Give me the camera; you just keep watching him," Martin whispered. *Click, click, click.* "I think I got some good ones. The light was superb, but I'm not sure of how steady I was holding the camera when the shutter went off. I hope the fast shutter speed quieted my shaking. I know I got his horns glistening in the sunlight. I wouldn't be surprised if you can even see the ivory tips of the horns. We were very lucky. I doubt if one out of fifty people we bring here will see a Sitatunga."

Martin continued his meandering drive for another thirty minutes before turning in the direction where he thought he might find lions. Jennifer's head was now occasionally bobbing from the lack of action, so Martin knew that she either needed some food or a light nap, maybe both.

While looking for a romantic napping place, Martin spotted the lazy lion pride, but didn't mention it to Jennifer until he had chosen the perfect vantage point. When he stopped the car, Jennifer had still not seen the lions; and she wondered what was up. "Is there anything wrong?"

"Shhhh, your lions are resting just over there, under that palm tree."

"Oh, Martin, you remembered. Aren't they gorgeous?"

"No different from any other pride of lions, but I guess that they are gorgeous if you don't see them very often."

"Can we have our picnic here?"

"No, we're a little too close. I wanted to let you take a picture or two before we move downwind a little more." Jennifer took her pictures, and then Martin backed the vehicle slowly backward up a slight incline for a safer view.

With one eye toward their viewing quarry, Martin glassed the area for a half-mile circle for other threats before he unloaded the picnic basket, the portable table and two chairs. The coast was clear. Jennifer helped with the linen tablecloth, the napkins, and the silverware while Martin prepared the snack. Cold meats, lettuce, tomatoes, fresh-baked sourdough bread, and various types of dressings were put on the table. Martin opened two bottles of South Africa's finest red wines to let them breathe before being consumed. The crystal goblets were wiped clean by Jennifer, and the two sat down for the most romantic picnic lunch ever!

Jennifer took the hint that two open bottles meant some serious drinking, and she asked for a full glass. Martin matched her wishes, and the meal began.

On the first day in camp, Jennifer had taken four of her Halcion pills out of their plastic bottle, and with two Mickey Finns, had ground them into powder and placed the powder in a small envelope. The envelope was only one inch by one and a half inches, so it was not conspicuous. When Martin's eyes were focused on the lions behind him, Jennifer sensed this was her chance; and she poured the powdered drugs into her own glass. She swirled it around to help dissolve all of the residue. When Martin had enough swallows of his wine to match her glass, both a little less than half full, she reached for the wine bottle to pour more. "That is traditionally the man's job, Jennifer."

"Not today, you have treated me to the picnic of all picnics; and I am at your service." After she poured both glasses to within an inch or so from the rims, she asked Martin another question about the lions. "Why are the females over to one side and the males are on the other side?"

When Martin turned to look, she pushed her glass over next to his plate and began to sip out of what was previously Martin's goblet. "Jennifer, they must have just had a poker game, and the lionesses lost. They appear to be still mad at the males for taking all of their money, so they moved away." Both laughed and then began drinking their wine. Jennifer took special notice to see if Martin discerned any noticeable difference in taste. *So far so good*, she thought.

"Martin, I'm so tired. I bet neither of us got much sleep last night. I'm about ready for a nap."

"Sounds fine to me. I'll clean up the table, and then we can have a little rest."

"No, I insist that I at least be the cleanup crew. You take our bottle of red over there," she said as she pointed to the base of the tree that they were under. "And I will join you in a few minutes."

Martin grabbed his rifle and obeyed while Jennifer set about cleaning up. She recorked the second bottle of red and then wrapped up all of the uneaten vegetables and meats. She put all of the dirty napkins and uneaten sandwich parts in the same bag and put everything back in the Land Cruiser.

She had trouble folding up the table, and she called for Martin to assist her. No use. Martin was out. Jennifer's actions now approached warp speed. She slammed the table together somehow, and she smashed the folding chairs together in the same hasty fashion. She loaded them in the back of the vehicle from whence they'd come, and she looked around for any other trash. Every part of the picnic site was clean as a whistle. Jennifer then went over to Martin and lay beside him. She kissed him, but there was no reaction. She fondled him, and still there was no reflex. Then as hard as she could, she pinched him on the forearm. She nearly brought blood, but there was still no reflex. She checked his heart to see if it was still beating, and then she put her nose next to his to see if he was exhaling. All vital signs were functioning, but they were slow; and there were no other movements. Jennifer checked all of his pockets for anything important, and then she dragged him over to the passenger side of the Land Cruiser.

She had a terrible time loading him into the passenger seat, but somehow her adrenaline got her through it. She was now soaking wet from her efforts. She went back to where he had been lying and roughed up the place with a small tree branch drag to make it unnoticeable, then she grabbed his gun and hurried back to the car. She gathered the blanket, folded it, and threw it in the back with the gun, the table, and chairs. She gave one more look at the miniature campsite to make sure all was clean, and then she slid into the driver's seat of the car.

The lions had evidently not even noticed the cleanup nor had they taken notice of the people's activities. The car was already pointing toward the sleeping lions, and she released the brake to start her move toward them. She pressed in the clutch and turned the key and started the motor. Two lionesses raised their head at the shrill sound of the starter motor, but they quickly resumed their lying posture. She gradually slipped the car in gear, low gear; and she carefully let out the clutch. She was so nervous that the vehicle lurched forward and conked out. Martin almost rolled out of the door; she frantically grabbed him and pulled him back into his seat, reached across his body, shut his door, and then restarted the motor again. This time, she got it right. There was no lion movement. Slowly, she headed for the lions that were two hundred yards distant. As she got to within fifty yards, they began to take notice of her; and they lifted their heads and perked up their ears. At twenty yards, all but the two big males were on their feet; and the cubs had been whisked away to the thick grass directly behind them, away from the approaching vehicle. Jennifer now turned the Land Cruiser to the right to expose Martin's passenger-side door for when the time came.

All of the lions picked up their pace and moved off some twenty or thirty yards into rather tall grass. Jennifer became more uneasy as she couldn't spot but two of the lions. But she had no choice now; she had to finish her plan. As she continued her slow moving, she reached over Martin's relaxed body and opened the door latch. She came to a stop less than five yards from where the lions had been lying. She moved the gearbox to neutral in order to allow her the freedom to bully Martin's body out of the vehicle. She then set the parking brake. She shoved the door open, and she pushed with all her might with her feet to get the body out and clear. Martin's lifeless body was deposited nearly exactly where the lions had just been resting. During this exercise of near futility, Martin's left foot temporarily hung on the inside foot guard that was located just below the bottom of the door, but she managed to loosen it and push him completely out. She thanked her lucky stars that she had stopped for this last maneuver because Martin's right arm and right leg would have been run over if she had continued in motion. After closing the passenger-side door from her driver's seat, she tossed her camera as close to Martin as she could throw it. She then had to drive back and forth to maneuver the car around Martin's fallen body and the close proximity of the tree under which the pride was previously lying. She didn't want to make too many tire tracks, and she didn't want them spread out too much; but she had no choice. She could only hope that they would never be noticed or that the lions would somehow cover them with their own tracks. She hurried because she was afraid the lions might actually choose her for their next meal instead of the drugged Martin.

All of the lions were now up and facing the body and the Land Cruiser, but they continued to occupy the area of tall grass. This eased Jennifer's mind a bit, but she still knew they were only a bound away from her. Finally she got the car turned away from the abstract scene, and she gunned it to get out of there. At a hundred yards, she stopped to look back. The lions had not moved an inch!

I thought lions couldn't resist a free meal. What are they waiting for? Jennifer thought. She then gave them some more distance by retreating another fifty yards or so. Still, there was no lion movement. She decided to drive the vehicle behind the nearest tree and hide from them, maybe that would do the trick. On second thought, she had to make her getaway look natural and sudden. The lions would surely feed, and she had to get out of there. She then stepped on the accelerator and sped as fast as she dared to higher ground another hundred or two hundred yards away. She stopped the car on a little knoll, reached back behind the seat and grabbed Martin's binoculars to look back. The lions had moved. They were suspicious, but they were now next to the body.

Jennifer remembered Martin's comments when she first met him that lions were very crafty, very clever, and very suspicious. Suddenly one of the females let out a big roar and swatted another female that was getting too close to the deposited body. That was all it took to incite a feeding frenzy. They began tearing at Martin's body, and she began to hear growls from all of them. One male was trying to pull Martin's body away from three other full-grown lionesses while all of the others were grabbing what they could to claim as their own. It was a horrible tug-of-war, and the anesthetized Martin had no clue. During the melee, one of the smaller males put Martin's entire head in his mouth and crunched his killer teeth into Martin's brain. Jennifer saw it and was horrified at what she had just made happen. But after a few moments, the reality of the situation that she could not change took over. She reached back and grabbed Martin's gun, but she realized she didn't know what to do with it. It was so heavy.

Than she remembered why she was there and why she was doing this dastardly act. Then she felt vindication for herself and the widows. Although Martin never even flinched during the lions' mauling, this last act by the young male lion was the final closure that Jennifer was seeking. Martin had finally paid an adequate price for orchestrating the demise of his own clients. Just like Martin hadn't thought that his planned accidents were murder, neither did Jennifer for what she had just done to Martin.

Jennifer now drove in semiplanned circles as if she was trying to find her way back to the main camp. She wanted to appear scared and confused. And with a present thought, that all of the tracks she was now making would further camouflage her earlier tracks. After she had pretended to search for the right trail, she decided to stop and use the radio. It was about two o'clock, and suddenly she had another thought. *I must wait another hour before radioing; that way, I can tell them that the accident happened after our nap. It will also give the lions more time to feed.* The new thought was gruesome, but Jennifer knew that the last thought was natural. Her best therapy was to supplant the view with the thoughts of Martin organizing and killing all of his other victims, just for money. When she thought of this, she even managed a smile at her accomplished revenge.

After carefully timing the longest hour in her life, she reached for the radio as she started up the car. She took several deep breaths while preparing her emotions and called out on the radio. "Help! Help! Help me! Somebody answer me! Help me! Help! Help! Please help me! Somebody come in! Come in! Please, somebody come in!" She was surprised; she thought that someone back at camp would be monitoring the radio. She rested for a few minutes and then began her frantic calls again. "Please, somebody help me! Come in! Come in! Please, somebody help me!"

As she started to say those same words over again, someone broke into her speech. "Martin, Mr. Smith, is that you? Mr. Smith, is that you?"

"Hello, hello, this is Jennifer Miller. This is Jennifer Miller; Martin has been attacked by lions. I repeat, I repeat, Martin has been attacked by a bunch of lions. Please help me! Please help!"

"This is the cook, back at camp. Hold on, hold on, I am going to get somebody." Jennifer held the mike in her trembling hands – trembling because she really couldn't be sure what was going to happen next. She was going to have to fly by the seat of her pants.

In a few moments, Martin's head tracker came on the air. "Ms. Jennifer, Ms. Jennifer, come in; where are you? Where are you?"

"Melvin, is that you?"

"Yes, Ms. Jennifer, where are you?"

"I don't know; we traveled all over before we found the lions, then we had lunch and a nap.

Martin tried to approach the lions to take a closer picture for me, but they attacked him as soon as he got out of the car. Please help. Come get me." She was screaming into the trembling mike.

"Ms. Jennifer, are you away from the lions?"

"Yes, I started the car and drove away as quickly as I could, but the lion dragged Martin off. He didn't have a gun; he didn't have a gun!"

"Ms. Jennifer, if you are safe, stay there. Try and find something to burn, make smoke. After you start a fire, put something wet on it – that will make bigger smoke. After you left camp, did you always travel the main track away from camp?"

"I can't remember, but I think we did."

"Can you give me any landmarks?"

"No, everything looks the same; it all looks the same! Oh, we stopped a little while ago to see a Sitatunga by the river, by the river."

"I know where you are. Sit still, and be calm. Get Mr. Martin's gun out and put a cartridge up the spout. But do not shoot it until you need to, or until you hear our vehicle coming. We are on the way."

Jennifer did as she was told. She looked over the area around her to see if it was safe and then got out to start a fire. There was no imminent danger that she could see, so she ventured away from the vehicle a short distance to gather wood. She was fortunate to find several small sticks and two larger dead limbs to burn. After she was ready to start the fire, she realized that she didn't have any matches. She checked the cigarette lighter in the Land Cruiser, but it was gone. She looked all over the place, but all she found was the medicine kit. "That's it. The medicine kit; there has to be a match in there." She was now yelling out loud. Sure enough, a book of safety matches was there. They were waterproof, and they were hard to strike; but she managed. She took some of the paper from the trash she had gathered just a short while ago and started the fire. Soon the flames were waist high and burning furiously. She grabbed the sack that was supposed to contain the after-lunch garbage and wetted it with the canteen of water that was in the backseat. When she threw the wet sack on the fire, smoke immediately grew as a pillar to the sky. She then climbed back into the vehicle to wait for Melvin to come to her aid.

After thirty minutes, she got out of the car and rebuilt the fire. She grabbed some old rags from under the seat, soaked them with water from the canteen, and put them on the newly stoked fire. Because some of the rags were oily, the new smoke rose a hundred feet high. Fifteen minutes later she heard a motor car. She got out of the car, got Martin's rifle out, and clicked off the safety. She aimed it up into the air, and holding it solidly in her left hand, pulled the trigger. The sound was deafening, and the jolt of the recoil knocked the gun from her hand. It fell harmlessly to the ground. She picked it up and wiped it clean with another rag she found behind the backseat.

The people in Melvin's car had spotted her and were heading in a beeline right for her.

Before the vehicle came to a complete stop, she ran to grab Melvin. "Hurry, we have to get to him. Right over there; right over there." Melvin saw where she was pointing, but he could see nothing because of the hilly terrain and tall grass. Instead, he opted to follow her vehicle tracks in his own Land Cruiser. He dispatched one of his trackers that had come with him to stay and comfort Ms. Jennifer. Trained and educated in following animals, he knew their feet never lied. He was intent on following her tracks. Wherever he could see the tracks far in front of him, he would disregard the closest current swerves and go to the farthest sign. He went about his business coolly and with great aplomb. His eyes missed nothing; and although he was the one driving with two other trackers in the back, he was the first to spot the lions.

"There," he said, and he raced the Land Cruiser toward the now-running lions. "Hand me the rifle! Hand me the rifle!" As the car slid to a stop, Melvin jumped from his seat and fired the rifle into the nearest clump of bush. It was obvious that he intended to scare everything away so that he could examine the carnage.

Melvin ordered one of the trackers to get out a blanket. Then he ordered Belfast, the other tracker, to bring the blanket and help him with Martin's body. He ordered the other tracker to keep the vehicle running. The lions had dragged the body into the thick bush that he had just fired into. He then ordered the tracker behind the wheel to drive in a circle around the body to further scare off the lions and to push down the tall grass. Melvin and Belfast searched the scene for all the body parts while the driver of the vehicle continued to circle their fallen comrade. The torso had been gutted by one of the lions, and its half-eaten remains was the only section of the body under the thornbush. All of Martin's legs and arms had been torn away, and each had been eaten almost beyond recognition. Martin's head had been pulled away from the torso by the viselike grip of the big male's teeth. Bites were all over it, but most of the flesh still remained. The small bites that Melvin noticed on the head were obviously from the cubs playing with their newfound ball.

Melvin kept the rifle at ready while Belfast tried to put the smaller body parts on the unfolded blanket. When he had done all he could do, Melvin helped him lift the mangled torso, or what was left of it, onto the center of the blanket. They then rolled the blanket up to encase everything but the still partially flowing blood and motioned to the vehicle driver to come and pick them up. All three of them loaded the remains into the back of the vehicle and covered it with a small tarp. Melvin made it clear to the other two natives that he was going back to camp alone. The other two trackers were dropped off to ride with Ms. Jennifer. The sight was too gruesome for any female to see, and Melvin was certainly aware of that.

Melvin and Belfast had seen animal slaughters like this before. They were raised in the bush, and they accepted its gruesomeness. Nevertheless, this was particularly hard. Melvin thought, *White people are just not supposed to die like this. They are too smart. They never take chances. They always stack the odds insurmountably in their favor, and they were always in control of their senses. They never lie around drunk, and they never take drugs. How could such a thing have happened?* Melvin didn't like the circumstances; they just didn't add up. But he couldn't figure it out. *White people never, never murder each other, it had to be an accident; or maybe a wounded lion charged from an unexpected distance!* He'd analyze his findings later.

When Melvin dropped off his two trackers to ride with Ms. Jennifer, Jennifer jumped out of her vehicle and ran to him and buried her head in his shoulder, weeping uncontrollably once again. Melvin comforted her for a few minutes and somehow expressed his sorrow in a way she understood. Then he told her she was to ride back to camp with the other natives, and he would follow them with Martin's body. Jennifer moved to the backseat of Martin's Rover and held her head in her hands.

Belfast took over the driving duties in Martin's vehicle and headed for camp. Melvin followed a few hundred yards behind to let the dust settle before having to drive through it.

"Cooky, Cooky, come in, Cooky," Melvin called for the cook on the radio to camp.

"Roger, Melvin, Roger, this is Cooky. What happened?"

"Mr. Martin is dead; he was attacked by lions. Call headquarters; have them send a plane and a game warden. Call me back when you get them. We are half an hour to an hour away. Over and out."

Cooky hated to do what he knew he must. "Couldn't the radio be broke?" he cried. "Calling main camp, calling main camp." The new frequency was monitored twenty-four hours a day.

"This is Maun; who is calling?"

"This is Cooky at the picture camp with Mr. Martin Smith. Mr. Martin has been killed by lions. Please send a plane and a game warden. Did you understand me?"

"Roger, are you sure? Is Martin Smith dead?"

"Yes. A few minutes ago. Melvin has gone to get him. He was attacked by lions."

"What about his client? Is his client all right?"

"Yes. She is okay. Please send a plane and a game warden."

"Roger, I will get things started right away. Please stand by the radio in case we need further instructions. Please stand by."

Cooky then changed the frequency back to local and called for Melvin. "I have given the message. They said to stand by the radio in case of other instructions."

"Do that, Cooky. I'll be there in few minutes."

As soon as Jennifer's vehicle roared into camp, Jennifer rushed to Martin's tent. She picked up his briefcase, wrapped it in a towel, and hurried back to her tent. She figured that she had less than an hour to open and search through it. The case was locked, and the lock was a combination. She thought about what number Martin might have used to set it, but she couldn't remember his birthday or any of the other numbers that she thought might be important. Carefully, she tried to pry it open without evidence that anyone had broken into it. It was a tough job. She set it down for a second to zip her front-door tent flaps closed. She wanted no surprises. Next, she examined the hinges on the back to see if they would be easier to remove than the lock. No such luck. She had to pop open the main lock. She didn't have the proper tools to work with, and she dared not ask anyone for them. She noticed the metal legs on the twin beds, and she tried to put part of the metal leg between the latch and the case itself. It was no use. She needed more room, so she got out her scissors from he makeup bag and used them to bend the latch enough to get a piece of metal where she needed it. Finally, she pried open enough room to get both blades of the scissors in between the latch and the case. It popped!

Jennifer opened it slowly to keep from dropping any of the contents that filled the case to near explosion. There were keys, notebooks, letters, a few folders, and some legal documents. At the very bottom of the case were Martin's two checkbooks – one from Houston and one from Johannesburg. She tried to distinguish what she needed from what she didn't, but she was too rattled.

She decided to put the whole case into her suitcase and hope for the best. She then began to pack her belongings as quickly as she could. From her past experience, she knew that she could have the option of going back to Maun with the body. Hunters, Ltd., had several pilots, and her final wish was that Pat Herold would not be the one to come to her rescue again. He was so nice, and she didn't want to face him again.

There was plenty of light left for a plane to land and takeoff again. All she had to do now was wait. Just as Jennifer locked her own suitcase, she heard the approaching plane from above.

The next sounds that she heard were the two Land Cruisers starting up to go meet the plane. She decided to wait for the mourning committee in her own tent. She went to the bar, fixed herself a stiff double scotch on the rocks, and returned to her cloth home.

Melvin was smart enough to take the body and its parts with him to meet the plane. Pat Herold was the pilot, and he thoughtfully had brought along an extra-large ice cooler just in case the worst possible scenario really happened. Pat had experienced this sort of traumatic tragedy before and managed to live through it, but this time it involved one of his best friends. He could hardly speak. Melvin managed to put what was left of Martin into the extra-large Igloo chest, and Pat then threw Melvin some duct tape and asked him to seal it so there would be no smell.

"I'll ride with you back to camp. Do you think that Jennifer will want to go back with us?" Melvin shrugged his shoulders in an "I don't know" fashion.

Cooky met the two vehicles when they stopped in front of the dining tent. He motioned Pat to where Jennifer was.

"She's in her tent?"

"Yes, baas."

"Thank you, Cooky. You were great on the radio; we all thank you very much." And Pat gave him a big hug.

Pat knocked on the front center pole of the tent. It was unzipped, and he showed himself in. "Jennifer, you must be shell shocked. None of us can believe it. Are you too shook-up to tell me how it happened?"

"Oh, Pat, I'm so glad it's you. I must be a jinx. Can I get out of here with you?"

"Are you packed? Can I help you?"

"I knew you would rescue me, so I went ahead and packed. I had to do something!"

"We've got a few minutes; I really need to know what happened so I can call in the proper authorities."

Jennifer wiped her eyes and slowly gathered her thoughts.

"We went out this morning on a typical game ride. We stopped a few times to take pictures, and then we went hunting for the same group of lions that we saw yesterday. Martin was going to give me a picnic lunch while we watched them, just like in *Out of Africa*. We finished eating, and then we took a nap – kind of romantic like. When we awoke, the lions were still resting. We cleaned up our campsite, and then he drove us closer to the lions."

Jennifer had to wipe her nose before she could continue. "I tried to take his picture in front of the lions, kinda in front of the vehicle. I could rest the camera just above the dashboard on the folded-down window. He was clowning around and got out of the car. He moved away a little bit so I could get him and the lions all in the picture. He was posing in a funny way in front of the lions, making gestures, acting like a clown. They were still pretty far off, but they sort of perked up when he got out; but they didn't charge or anything. I was looking at the camera's video screen, so I didn't see one lion coming so close. It was my fault. It was my fault! I guess he sensed security, and he backed even closer to them. I continued to try and focus in on him and the lions. I don't remember whether I actually took any pictures or not, because the next thing that I saw was that big lion charging at Martin. I don't think he made a sound. He surprised Martin. I was so stunned that I couldn't even get out a yell. Martin turned just in time to see him. The lion knocked him down and it looked like he was rolling Martin all over, but he was biting him all over at the same time. In less than a second, the other lions joined the first one. I was so scared; I never thought about the gun that was in the back. I jumped over to the driver's seat, and I started the car. I couldn't get it into reverse, so I just crammed it into some forward gear; and I got out of there. I tried running at the lions at first, but I got scared. I turned away and started honking the horn, but it didn't work. It must have been disconnected."

"Most professional hunters disconnect their horns to prevent them from honking accidentally and scaring the game away. It could mess up a client's shot quite easily. Did you try to run over the lions with the car?"

"No, I never even thought of it. There were so many, about ten of them. I was so scared. I wish I had. Do you think I could have saved him if I had?"

"Of course not, Jennifer. Things happen so quick with lions. The first one probably killed Martin with his first bite. They try to knock you down with enough force to knock the breath out of you or incapacitate you in some way so you can't fight back when they are trying to get to a vital spot. It's their way of killing; whether it's a wild animal or a human. They are so big and they are so powerful and they are so damned quick.

"What a stupid mistake. I cannot believe Martin would do such a thing. I am so sorry that you are the brunt of another accident. If you are ready, then we can go now."

Saying good-bye to another camp crew under similar circumstances that had occurred before was about as unpleasant as Jennifer had imagined it would be. But she managed to get through it; and after everything was loaded into the vehicles, she and Pat left for the landing strip with Martin's briefcase hidden in her luggage.

The plane ride back to Maun was so reminiscent of the one involving Dennis for both Jennifer and Pat. Hardly a word was said for almost an hour. Pat wanted to ask more questions, but his good manners dictated to him that enough was enough. Jennifer simply did not know of anything else to say. The whole Maun contingent of employees met the plane. Arrangements had been made for the body, or what was left of it, to be taken straight to the morgue. In this case, there was no need to ship the body to Johannesburg. Jennifer had bribed Pat Herold with her tears to get her to Johannesburg as quickly as possible, and no one at the Maun office blamed Jennifer a bit for wanting to get out of there. In anticipation of this, one of the secretaries had arranged for one of the game warden authorities to have a brief interview with her before her departure.

The interview was quick and as painless as possible. Pat was with her the whole time, and he helped her talk her way through it. Pat told the officer that Jennifer had discussed the accident with him when he went to pick her up, and the officer was pleased to have him think of questions that he would have probably ignored. At the end of the interview, the quasi-investigator asked Pat if the story that Jennifer had just told matched the one he had previously heard, and Pat was emphatic that all of the details were the same. As soon as the three were through, Pat hustled Jennifer off to the airplane to leave for Jo'burg.

The two-and-a-half-hour flight to Jo'burg made the landing a night one. Anna Marie, the Lanseria secretary, met the plane along with one of the usual porters. Pat had the porter put his and Jennifer's bags into his car that was in the parking lot and then he drove Jennifer to the Holiday Inn next to the Johannesburg International Airport – a very thoughtful measure, knowing that Jennifer would want to try and get the first flight out for the States.

Before she went to bed, Jennifer contacted South African Airways to try to change her return flight ticket to as early a flight back to New York or Atlanta as she could get. The attendant that fielded her call was very sympathetic to her situation, and she guaranteed her a seat on the next night's departure. The following day was spent hiding from people who wanted to reach her to pay their respects and quell their own curiosity.

She awoke rather early, and she instructed the hotel operator to please take messages from all of her callers. She would try to return them in the afternoon. The hotel was most cooperative in letting her have as late a checkout time as she desired, and they offered their private van to take her to the airport that evening.

Before she checked out, she returned the call to Anna Marie at the Lanseria office. Anna Marie wanted to know her telephone number and current address back in Atlanta should any of the authorities want to contact her. Anna Marie expressed her sincere sorrow for the happenings again and hoped that someday she might return under happier circumstances.

Jennifer lied about returning telephone calls. She preferred to answer them on familiar ground back in Atlanta. She was sitting in the lobby when the hotel van pulled up front to chauffeur her the short distance to the departure check-in gate.

Jennifer's flight to New York was uneventful, and she managed to get back all of the rest she missed over the past couple of days. She had saved a Halcion tablet for herself to get the sleep she knew she needed. Her transfer from the international terminal at JFK to the domestic one was a hassle, but her Delta flight back to Atlanta was perfect. She arrived in her apartment via another taxi at just after noon the same day. She dreaded some of her calls that she knew she had to return, but she was eager to get her calls underway to Frank and the widows. The other calls that were placed to her in Botswana and there at the Holiday Inn would have to wait until the next day when she had regained her composure – at least that was going to be her excuse. She was not one to postpone dirty duties, but she decided that waiting until the next day was a good move. She knew all of her story had to be impeccably convincing, and she wanted to go over all contingency questions that she could think of pertaining to the accident before making her secondary calls. Plus, she needed everyone to think she was in devout mourning.

16

Tying It All Together

Frank Black had been trying to reach Jennifer for the past two days, but because of Jennifer's running around, it was actually she who succeeded in finally getting the telephone connection made to Frank. "Frank, this is Jennifer."

"Jennifer, I have been trying to reach you for days. How are you?"

"I'm fine, and I've a lot to talk to you about."

"You most certainly do. Indeed a face-to-face explanation of exactly what happened. I'm extremely concerned about you, but I'm more concerned about this last safari death and the loss of one of the best friends I ever had. Martin always knew there were extraordinary risks that attached to his profession, as did I, but something different seems to be involved here. I can't explain it, but somehow I smell a rat. I want you to know, this time it's going to be me that will be in charge of the investigation, and I expect to initiate that investigation with you. Will you cooperate with me like I cooperated with you?"

Jennifer held her composure when she responded, "I too think we should talk in private. So, do you want to come to Atlanta, or do you want to pay me to come to Houston? I don't think you need to worry about smelling a rat. But if you aren't your old congenial self, then I won't even go to the trouble of meeting you at all."

"Jennifer, you can't blame me for some of my off-the-wall feelings I might have after what I've gone through over the past year. But this catastrophe goes way beyond the others. This wasn't a hunting safari, it was a photographic one. Either Martin did something stupid and way out of character for a professional hunter, or he was somehow put in harm's way without being aware of it. I am devastated by all of this, and I want some answers. I'm a grown man, and I can take almost anything; but I'm a loyal friend to my friends and my employees, and I owe myself and my friends and employees a thorough investigation. So why don't you come to Houston? Where do I send you a ticket? Or better yet, I can have an electronic ticket waiting for you at the Delta check-in, either curbside or inside the terminal, your choice."

"It's much better when you are nice. I'm a little low on cash right now, so you're going to have to advance me a little more than just a ticket. But I'm not going to meet you at all unless you promise me that you will be civil."

"Okay, I promise. I'll have my secretary get you on the latest afternoon flight today. Your ticket will be at curbside check-in at Hartsfield International in a couple of hours. You'll need to call Delta to see which flight you're booked on. Wait about two hours for all of the paperwork to get through and then call. I'll meet you at the Intercontinental Airport in Houston, and I'll have you a room near the airport. I'll also have some spending money for you, but you are going to have to pay me back."

"That's fine, Frank. I hope you are ready to wheel and deal. I have a proposition for you, and if you accept, you can take my spending money advance out of the proceeds."

"I don't know what you mean by that, but I'm always ready to make a deal. As long as it is legal and it is not something that involves a crime. See you this evening."

Jennifer found out quite a few things from Martin's briefcase. In his telephone directory notebook, she found the Swiss bank's telephone number and the name of the officer who assisted Martin, Hans. At the bottom of the same page, next to a name, Hunter, was a telephone number that had the exact same digits that made up the account number that the widows had given her. The number had hyphens to make someone think that it was an actual telephone number, but Jennifer easily recognized the digits and disregarded the hyphens. Martin's Houston bank account had a stated balance of a little more than three thousand, while his Jo'burg account had nearly five thousand South African rand in it. That computed to slightly more than twenty-five hundred American dollars. There were a lot of client numbers, including the new hotel numbers for Sally Maxie, Mary Kyle, and Barbara Jones. There was a great deal of other business data that Jennifer had no use for. There were checks for various employees, supply lists for each camp, and general office supplies that needed to be ordered. She intended to give all of that and the briefcase to Frank Black when she met with him. Jennifer knew she had enough tangible and circumstantial evidence to make her case to Frank. After that, she didn't care if anyone else ever knew the story. In fact, it would be in her best interest if no one else ever knew the story. Frank was welcome to have anything in the briefcase except Martin's little black telephone book. That was Jennifer's key to future happiness.

Because her predicted stay in Houston was planned to be short, she drove herself to the Atlanta airport and parked her car in the short-term lot. She retrieved her tickets from Delta's main ground-level curbside check-in counter, checked her overnight bag, and went straight to the gate to try and get some sort of preferential seating. She had her way with male counter personnel, and she was about to use her special charms. Predictably, she jumped ahead of all of the Medallion Flyers that were waiting for an upgrade, and she deposited herself in a window seat on the third row of first class.

Frank met her at the Houston Intercontinental Airport gate as she deplaned. "I thought you'd be at the baggage gate; it is so nice of you to meet me here." Frank kissed her on the cheek and took her small carry-on.

"Is this all you have?"

Jennifer laughed at the question. "Of course not, silly. I thought you were going to meet me at baggage claim so I went ahead and checked my overnight bag. See, you messed us up by meeting me on the concourse!"

"I've been blamed for a lot of things, but I've never been blamed for meeting someone early at their arrival concourse. I have dinner reservations at Harry's Kenya, my favorite restaurant in the world; and it happens to be in Houston. I hope you didn't stuff yourself too much on the plane."

"I did fly first class, Frank, no thanks to you, but I didn't overindulge. I met the nicest guy at the check-in counter, and he insisted that I fly first class on him. Wasn't that nice?"

"Jennifer, you have some sort of womanly way. I bet you could have gotten on that flight even without a ticket. Let's get moving; dinner is going to be superb."

"Okay, I'm ready for a good American meal."

Frank claimed Jennifer's only bag quickly, and they hurried through the tunnels that led to Frank's car. It was parked in the street just after exiting the tunnel courtesy of a big tip to the officer on the beat there, and they headed for downtown.

"There's no better place to talk confidentially than in the car, so for God's sake, tell me what is going on."

"Frank, I love you, I really do. And I admire your business sense – is that cents or sense? Anyway, I don't trust you. I'm not going to discuss anything with you in your car, and I'll only talk to you at the restaurant if you let me frisk you. I or we could be in serious trouble, and I don't want any funny recordings that I'll have to defend. When you hear about my findings, then you'll understand."

"Okay. I have reserved a very special corner table at Harry's, and I've been assured that there'll be no snoops around us. They'll only seat someone close if they're sold out. So I guess you're going to have to frisk me. Shall we stop at the next motel and let me take my clothes off?"

"Only if I can take mine off as well."

Frank laughed and said, "I didn't feel like eating anyway; I'll pull in at the next hotel vacancy sign."

"We can leave that until later if we're both in the mood. I have a proposition for you, and I need your answer tonight! I'll frisk you in the dark corner of the parking lot."

Although there was light conversation about the weather and other mundane and nonmundane issues during the forty-five-minute drive to the restaurant, the tension about the upcoming conversation over food and drink was building for both of them every mile.

Harry's Kenya Restaurant was located on the corner of Smith and Dallas, right smack in the middle of downtown Houston. Frank parked in the covered garage that adjoined the restaurant. He purposely parked next to an end wall to facilitate Jennifer's wishes of frisking him, if that was really going to happen. "This is going to be fun, but I'm afraid you're going to be embarrassed when you don't find anything hard but my privates."

"I'll take my chances."

The two weirdos got out of the car, hid in the shadows away from the light, and tended to their frisking business next to the dark wall beside the right front corner panel of Frank's car. The search was less than professional, and by the time it was over, both parties, the frisker and the friskee, were rolling with laughter. "I'm so glad you're clean; I have special plans for us someday, and they would have all been ruined if you were wired."

"Wired? When did you start using that private detective language?"

"When you have nothing to do all day except watch soaps, you learn a lot of new things."

The maitre d', Kenny Dean, had Frank's table waiting. "We're so glad to have you here this evening, Mr. Black. Please let us know if there is anything special we can do for you."

"Bob, this is Jennifer Miller from Atlanta. I've told her so much about your restaurant, and she's glad to now be able to experience it firsthand."

"Welcome, Ms. Miller. It will be a pleasure to serve you." The headwaiter then took over and escorted Jennifer and Frank to their table. Drink orders were placed, and then Mr. Dean brought a special arrangement of fresh flowers to the table. "In honor of your guest, Mr. Black."

Jennifer appreciated the pampering touch. "Well, if the rest of the evening goes as well as this dinner seems to be going, then we may need the flowers to celebrate." Drinks were served while the long-awaited conversation began.

Both parties had up to now been surprisingly congenial. They had both been careful to not offend the other, and both wanted to keep the conversation as light as possible. But both also knew that a serious conversation was in order, and time was running out in postponing it.

"Martin orchestrated the three accidents. He was paid $1,000,000 plus for each. I can't confirm the first death, B. F. Clark – that seems to be legit. But I have all of the evidence that anyone could want to confirm the others. The son of a bitch killed my boyfriend; and he killed Cliff, Lou, and maybe his two professionals as well. Of course the two professionals were in on the deal with him from the beginning, but he was the ringleader. It stands to reason that if those two were eliminated after they did their dirty work, then he would prosper even more. Like B. F. Clark's, your professional hunters' deaths really do look accidental. But Martin was very clever, he just might have done them in just like the ones I have proof of."

"Stop it, Jennifer. I thought you were just kidding before; then Martin's accident – if it was an accident – and I began to think. If you had something to do with Martin meeting his untimely demise and if Martin had anything to do with those three client tragedies, do you think you're any better than he if what you say is so?"

"That's for you and the three widows to judge. I didn't kill him, I just dared him to get close to those lions so that I could take a picture of him with them, unarmed. I must confess, I would have probably driven off and left him if he hadn't been attacked."

"This whole thing is preposterous. I can't fathom such sequences. Those three ladies that are now widows were the salt of the earth. They were leaders in their communities. They were virtual saints!"

"Life is life, Frank. What has happened has happened. Left are three widows much better off than before – monetarily and companion wise. Then there is me. I would rather have Dennis back than what money I'm about to receive – and we'll get to that part later – but I'm left with only one choice to right that terrible wrong against me. You are the only one left on this earth that may have to suffer from all of this, and I feel a certain responsibility to try to make things right with you, because you really did nothing wrong except own the stupid company that Martin worked for."

Frank shook his head and answered, "Jennifer, I've been hurt – no, tortured, mentally and physically. I can't even sleep at night, but my business is up. It is UP! Clients like the thrill of danger, and it's obvious that my safari company is the most dangerous. Martin's death may fuel the fire even more! But then again, enough may be enough, and then all my clients might go away.

The fact that Martin was a professional should make clients think one of two things – either he died defending a client or he got too close to a dangerous situation by accident. In either case, the potential clients should love it. I am owed nothing. I just want this stupidity to end. And end it must!"

"Frank, it has ended. There are no more players in the game. All that are left are benefactors. Just benefactors. No inquiries, no questions, and no more greed; it has ended. I give you my word."

"How can you say that? And how do you know?"

"Frank, I told you that I was doing my homework, and I did it meticulously. I thought and thought. I met with other clients of your company and other companies. I went over all my data with my father. I traveled to Houston to see you. I traveled to London to see the three widows. And then I confirmed everything with Martin on safari. Trust me, I know everything there is to know about all three of the staged accidents."

"It's still hard for me to believe you in spite of all the work you've done to prove your case. You have no physical evidence. But I'm here to listen to you for whatever you are proposing. But I'll tell you the truth, all I want is for all of these things to stop happening. Now, if you are through giving me all of the details that you plan to share with me, what kind of physical proof do you have and how does that introduce a proposition that you have for me?"

"First of all, I do have plenty of physical evidence, just listen. I know where Martin kept his money. I have his will, I know his beneficiary, and I'm willing to share the wealth.

"It's all in his briefcase, all hand-written by him. And I can confirm every bit of it with other independent evidence such as the widows' words, the Swiss bank that he was dealing with, his deposits, and his current balance. Does a two-million-seven-hundred-thousand-dollar balance look weird to you for a professional hunter?"

"My god, he couldn't have a bank balance of anything like that. If true, and I want to see your proof, just what do you propose?"

"I have two choices – I can claim the entire sum of his bank balance for me or I can share it with you. I have all of the information needed to clean the account out, legally and without questions. I simply don't deserve it all, and since you were hurt in all of these deals, I think you are deserving of some of the money. Aren't I a sweet girl?"

"I just told you that my business is up, so why should I profit further from this misery? Why do I have to participate?"

"To help and comfort me. Plus, you're certainly owed something for all the pain and suffering that you have personally experienced." After a small pause, Jennifer continued, "There's a Swiss bank that holds all of Martin's big money. I know his account number and his password. I can try to get it without involving you, but it would be much more fun to have a deserving partner share the experience. Your company is named as Martin's beneficiary on the account. Now before you think that you can claim it all, let me tell you another thing. That bank would never call you. They know that you or your company has to call them first, and you would have never known there was any money available if it had not been for me. And I haven't told you which bank it is or what bank officer you need to go through or what Martin's password is. You simply can't find the money that is really yours without me! And I'm not telling you any more until I have your pledge of allegiance to me, signed in blood if I have to have it that way. We need to be each other's partner. You helped me get to where I am now in this investigation, and I'm more than willing to return the favor."

Sally Maxie renewed her hotel room lease for the last month at the Marriott, and she purchased a new Jaguar convertible to reinforce her new English image. Her business matters in Dallas were running as smooth as silk, thanks to all of her professional lawyers and accountants, and she hadn't a care in the world that bothered her now that Martin was out of the picture and Jennifer appeared to be gone. She missed her Dallas friends, and on occasion she would call them, especially to wish them a happy birthday or something special to them.

Her efficient realtor had found her a new home in just the right place outside of London and with just the right configuration. He was also her best friend. He was not quite a confidant, but he was good company; and his intentions were sincere. Sally went out with him frequently, and she was making other new friends constantly with his and her contacts. He was not married, never had been; and he was the perfect age. But Sally wasn't serious as yet. Sally had heard about Martin's accident from reading the *Herald*. She read that it was an accident with few details, but she knew better. She knew it had been Jennifer's plan, and she knew that Jennifer had carried it out. She deplored what had to happen for Jennifer's sake, but she excused it as poetic justice. What was done was done, and she had the rest of her life to live.

Barbara Jones finally found the perfect flat for herself. It was right around the corner from her previous hotel. Although the new flat was immaculately furnished, it was not ostentatious. She kept a toned-down version of her wealth for others to see, but she didn't want for a thing. Her dresses were still only the best, and her jewelry fetish persisted from her past married life. She purchased a new car, a Saab, and it had everything that the manufacturer could put on it. Barbara's daily schedule always included a museum or a garden show of some sort every day it didn't rain.

She had met a few new friends who lived close to her, but she still relished her privacy. Life was finally being as kind to her as she had previously been to it. She was still striking in her beauty, and her new gentleman friends never ceased fighting for her evenings. Being a new-generation European was fitting her just fine. She too had read about Martin's accident in the *Herald*. She had gone further than Sally to confirm the circumstances with a friend back in the States. Her suspicions were confirmed by her friend. Jennifer Miller had been with Martin when he died. Like Jennifer's predictions of the earlier accidents, she knew her prediction that Jennifer killed Martin was as true as anything she had ever known. There was nothing that she could do about it however. She would forever bear her grief for all of the accidents that she helped cause, but she wasn't about to commit suicide. She was going to live a good life for as long as she was permitted to live.

Mary Kyle still had nightmares about Dennis's accident, and she could hardly ever get Jennifer Miller out of her mind for more than a day. But she was getting better. The time intervals were expanding between those thoughts, and she saw hope of dismissing unhappy remembrances. She longed for conversations with her other two partners in crime, but as of yet, she hadn't heard a word from any of them, and she had no idea what Jennifer was up to. Until she heard from her, it was understood that she was not to contact the other widows. The chief officer at the London Cancer Society was ever so pleased at her employment – and for only a pound a year by her own insistence.

She was the new liaison officer that coordinated most of the society functions but was premiere in putting together meetings between foreign donors and the society. She also handled most of the business affairs and correspondence between the English office and American ones. She was happier now than she had been in a long, long time; and she saw everything getting better.

She was tired of waiting, but somehow she knew that as soon as Jennifer cleaned up her own personal business, everything would be over. And Mary was sure that there would be no more evil thoughts. She had not heard the news of Martin's death, but her thoughts reminded her that something morbid was bound to happen courtesy of Jennifer Miller.

17

The Gift

The receptionist at the London Cancer Society office took the long-distance call. "Could you refer me to the person in charge of receiving donations from abroad? I believe in your worthy cause, and I would like to get the proper paperwork filled out to accomplish my task. I have a nice gift for your organization, and I would like to present it in person with a few of my old friends present. Do I make those arrangements with you or with someone else?"

"Let me put you through to our officer in charge. His name is Stephen Clinton, and he will be glad to help you."

Mr. Clinton answered the phone on his desk after the first ring. "This is Stephen Clinton, may I be of service to you?"

"I hope so. My name is Frank Black. I presently live in Houston, Texas, but I have purchased an old mansion just outside of London; and I'm having it renovated for a second home. I'm scheduled to move in two weeks from now. I have some very dear friends who live in London and thereabouts, and I would like them to share my experience in presenting your noble society a substantial gift – this, in hopes that they too might consider a similar gift or pledge. It will be an honor to have them present when I make my intended gift to your society. I would like to start a regular giving plan, but I want to donate $100,000 American now. Have I just made your day?"

"Mr. Black, we would be honored. What a wonderful gift! It is not often that we get such a pledge of that size, and almost never from abroad. Please give me the details that you wish, and I will get to work on our preparations. If you would like, I have a new American assistant whose duties are to handle such wonderful functions as this, so you will be in good hands, as they say on your side of the pond. That's a joke, but God, I hope your pledge is not a joke!"

"Mr. Clinton, I assure you that it is not a joke. As long as I am able to make the presentation the way I prefer. What is your assistant's name?"

"Mary Kyle."

"Ha! Isn't that a coincidence? She is a very good friend of mine, and she is at the top of my guest list. But if she has anything to do with this, it must be strictly confidential. I do not want my other friends to know the amount of my gift or my future plans of giving. My intentions for having my friends present at some sort of gift ceremony is to encourage their own philanthropy. And I know I can get them interested in your worthwhile cause if the setting is right."

"Mr. Black, if you have any worry, I will be glad to handle all of the arrangements personally. I assure you that it would be no problem, and I will guarantee that not even Mary will know about it until your affair is over."

"Thank you very much, Mr. Clinton. If you could do that without Mrs. Kyle knowing, and yet she could still be an honored guest, I would like that very much."

"Your assurances are a certainty." The details of Frank Black's wishes for this memorial moment were faxed to Mr. Clinton, and all of the arrangements were put in motion. Other necessary papers to allow Frank Black a tax deduction State-side were sent to him, and he immediately faxed those back to Mr. Clinton for documentation purposes.

At the bottom of Frank's fax was a special note. "Stephen, confidentiality for Mrs. Kyle, she must not know anything except to be present at the function; this is very important. She is one of the real reasons for the gift, and she will understand thoroughly after the gift is finalized."

Frank made copies of his donation request for his office records, and he sent the originals to his tax attorney for inclusion in next year's income tax filings.

Engraved invitations from the London England Cancer Society were sent out to about eighty of Frank's good friends and former clients. Included, of course, were Sally Maxie and Barbara Jones.

Mr. Clinton called Mary Kyle into his office to personally request that she attend a special donation function that she was partly responsible for. "Oddly, the requesting donor has requested that you not know the name of the donor or the amount until after the donating function. I can tell you that the amount is substantial, and you should be very proud. You are to be a special guest at the reception in the donor's honor, and because of that, I am going to handle all of the arrangements so that you can just enjoy the moment. The donor asks that we all keep this very quiet until the program commences; the donor insists that you in particular have a good time when the ceremony begins and the donor will budget more time to be with you later in the evening."

Although Mary was more than extremely curious about the whole affair, she and her imagination had little to be surprised about when she was furnished with a perusal of the guest list. She was flattered with her newfound notoriety, and she swore herself to secrecy. With that pledge, Stephen presented her with the rest of the details involving the whole regalia. "Wow," Mary thought, "Sally Maxie and Barbara Jones, we'll finally be at a social function together. Could it be that either or both of them were involved in the gift? I hope there is nothing more to this than what I've been told."

When Barbara and Sally received their respective invitations by a personal carrier, they were momentarily stunned. They knew Mary was connected somehow to the London Cancer Society, and both independently put two and two together. Both called Mary at her office to find out what was really going on, despite their pledge to one another that neither of them would contact the other unless there was trouble brewing.

Silently, they both prayed that there was no trouble brewing. Mary was unavailable when each called. She decided to return their calls simultaneously with a conference call. She couldn't wait to talk to them.

After everyone had said hello to each other, all that Mary could say was, "I don't know who the donor is, but I do know whoever it is, is moving to London, just outside of it, and whoever that is, is going to make a large donation to the cancer society. Crazy, but it is to be in my honor. I am flattered, but I'm in the dark as to who it actually is. Needless to say, if all three of us are invited, it narrows the identity a bunch. It has to be someone that the three of us know. I have no worry about anything subversive because it involves the cancer society and my boss, Stephen Clinton, says that it is an up-and-up gift with more to follow. I look forward to seeing both of you so much. I know all of us have heard about Martin's unfortunate accident, so I guess our mutual safari business is all a thing of the past."

Both simultaneously agreed. But both women then questioned Mary as to whether she thought that Jennifer was in on this deal. "Absolutely not; I have seen the guest list, and she is not on it, not even on the revised list. I haven't heard from her since we last met, so I presume that no news is good news."

The rest of the three-way conversation was filled with questions and answers about where each had located and just what each was doing. At the end, all three were very excited about getting together once again. Plus, they relished the thought of being able to see who was the person that invited all three of them to the party and who it was who was going to be so generous. The conversation ended with both Sally and Barbara gladly RSVP'ing to be present at the festivities.

Mr. Stephen Clinton didn't leave a stone unturned in his preparation for Mr. Black's gift ceremony. The guest list had now grown to just short of a hundred. Mr. Black's acquaintances read like a Who's Who in international hunting and conservation – the Meehans, the Smothermans, the Kopecs, the Archers, the Burchfields, the Nicholses, the Camps, the Tinsleys (three sets), the Hawkinses, the Wilsons, the Bryans, the Butlers, the Weikels, the Houks, the Hunters, the Begiatises, the Sansones, Ginny Mattox and John Haubenreich, the Tidwells, Dan Fobas, Jim Culbreth, the Heuers, the Doyles, the Franklins, the Moores, the Rankins, the Vivoris, the Pucketts, the Borgeses, the Kaminskis, the Letts, the Burks, the Lynns, the Peters, the Harts, the Potts, the Oslers, the Blisses, the Dickenses, the Roberts, the Clarks, the Dawsons, the Walzels, the Perrys, the Colemans, the Tsitorises, the Burgers, the Knights, John Mahoney, the Grosvenors, the Martins, the Vantines, the Gentrys, Mike Tate, the Fischers, the Tailors, the Towns, the Herolds, the Halls, the Sharps, Phil Maulding, the Hamricks, the Miesels, the Elliotts, the Hamiltons, the Walkers, the Williams, Tony Bielawski, the Waughs, the Cronjes, and Ramnath Rajesh and his lovely bride, and many more. The *London Times* would surely pick up on this festive occasion and honor all of the attendees with their illustrious names printed in the Sunday edition.

On the day of the big event, everyone invited donned their finest apparel. All of the men wore tuxes, black on black; and all of the women wore full-length gowns. The pomp and circumstance began at 7:30 on Sunday evening. A specially hired butler with a booming but highly English accent announced each invitee's name upon entering. After Mr. Black personally met each, they were then ushered into the music room where a small ensemble of violinists softly entertained. Mary Kyle and Mr. Clinton performed admirably in introducing each entrant to every one present. And by the time Mary was introduced to Mr. Black, she had narrowed her choices of the donor down to four, including Mr. Black, so she was pleasantly surprised at her prediction. Two of the last to arrive were Sally Maxie and Barbara Jones. They arrived separately but well timed to enter almost simultaneously. After greeting them with hugs and kisses, Frank Black immediately put them at ease and escorted them personally through most of their introductions to the other honored guests, including Mary Kyle.

At half past eight, the entire company was ushered into the huge foyer of the mansion for Frank Black's monetary presentation. "It is with great pleasure that I honor my family, my past business associates, my friends that are here, and such a worthy organization as the London England International Cancer Society, with a special gift. It is my hope that everyone present will likewise consider a gift or pledge to such a worthwhile organization in the future. All of us have our favorite charities, but I must give credit for my interest in this one to the London chapter's newest recruit, from America, Mrs. Mary Kyle." Light but sincere applause greeted Mary's name. "I appreciate you all coming here tonight to make this evening as special as it can get for me. There is one other introduction that I feel compelled and honored to make. Your eyes to the top of the spiral staircase, please. I give you the former Ms. Jennifer Miller, my new wife!"

BVG